Praise for Gini Hartzmark's previous Kate Millholland novel, *Bitter Business*

"A page-turner."
—*People*

"A fast-paced tale . . . Crisp prose, sharply drawn characters, and a nicely subordinated subplot . . . all help keep the reader involved until the climax."
—*Publishers Weekly*

"A wonderful read . . . Gini Hartzmark and her lawyer heroine, Kate Millholland, take us on another expertly guided tour through the world of the rich and the superrich. It's like *Dallas* except that Hartzmark's people aren't cartoons."
—JEROME DOOLITTLE
Author of *Half Nelson*

"A refreshing protagonist . . . Hartzmark brings into play a fascinating behind-the-scenes look [at] the inner w̶o̶r̶l̶ an unusual manufacturing
—M

By Gini Hartzmark
Published by The Ballantine Publishing Group:

PRINCIPAL DEFENSE
FINAL OPTION
BITTER BUSINESS
FATAL REACTION

Books published by The Ballantine Publishing Group
are available at quantity discounts on bulk purchases
for premium, educational, fund-raising, and special
sales use. For details, please call 1-800-733-3000.

FATAL REACTION

A Novel

Gini Hartzmark

The **BOOKWORM** NEW AND USED BOOKS
1132 N. Fourth Street
Coeur d' Alene, Idaho 83814
(208) 765-0335

IVY BOOKS • NEW YORK

Sale of this book without a front cover may be unauthorized. If this book is coverless, it may have been reported to the publisher as "unsold or destroyed" and neither the author nor the publisher may have received payment for it.

An Ivy Book
Published by The Ballantine Publishing Group
Copyright © 1998 by Gini Hartzmark

All rights reserved under International and Pan-American Copyright Conventions. Published in the United States by The Ballantine Publishing Group, a division of Random House, Inc., New York, and simultaneously in Canada by Random House of Canada Limited, Toronto.

http://www.randomhouse.com

Library of Congress Catalog Card Number: 97-95289

ISBN 0-8041-1743-8

Manufactured in the United States of America

First Edition: March 1998

10 9 8 7 6 5 4 3 2 1

To William F. Morgan, M.D. . . .
    whose ideas inspired this book and whose medical prowess
kept John healthy so that I could write it

Acknowledgments

I'd like to thank Heather Raaf, Wendy Seidel, William Morgan, and Rick Schooler for providing me insight into their areas of expertise, not to mention answering my dumb questions. Thanks also to Ann Rocco, Elizabeth Gardner, Teague Von Bohlen, Donald Maass, and my editor, Susan Randol. As ever, I am grateful to my husband, Michael, for his patience and editorial advice and Dee and Lee Hartzmark for stepping up as grandparents par excellence when the going got rough. I also owe a huge debt of gratitude to Barry Werth, the author of *Billion Dollar Molecule*, whose brilliant and beautifully written account of Vertex Pharmaceutical's search for a new drug helped me to understand the intricate drama of high-stakes research.

This book is a work of fiction. Names, characters, places, and incidents are products of the author's imagination or are used fictitiously. Any resemblance to actual people or events, living or dead, is entirely coincidental.

FATAL
REACTION

CHAPTER

1

I always knew that Stephen Azorini's bed was a dangerous place for me. After all, his company, Azor Pharmaceuticals, was my most important client—which is why everyone was willing to ignore what was going on between us. Still, all it would take was the smallest sign that Azor was slipping from my grasp and there was absolutely no question of who would be sacrificed. My partners would not hesitate for a second before showing me the door.

That's why I was nervous about being summoned to John Guttman's office. Guttman had been my predecessor as Azor's chief outside counsel and he was still deeply unhappy that Stephen had chosen to replace him. A complicated man, Guttman was rankled by my success even as he sought ways to take credit for it. I also knew him well enough to be certain that nothing good could come out of his wanting to see me.

I'd spent my first years at the firm as Guttman's apprentice, indentured to its most vituperative partner through a combination of default and design. At the time, my arrival at Callahan Ross had been viewed with suspicion. Everyone assumed that I had been hired because of who I am, either to add the Millholland name as ballast to the letterhead or because my family had pulled strings to get me there.

My widowhood, at age twenty-five, also formed a sort of barrier around me that many, no doubt, found difficult to breach. I'm sure my own attitude did little to help. Looking back, that entire period of my life seems to have been characterized by a kind of bewildered belligerence. That after having been raised in a world of almost story-book privilege I'd chosen to toil as an associate at Callahan Ross, a firm notorious for their sweatshoplike treatment of new lawyers, was held to be further evidence of my eccentricity.

It didn't take me long to learn that John Guttman just chewed up associates. Irascible, unreasonable, and given to inexplicable fits of rage, he was nonetheless considered to be one of the best lawyers of his generation. Even so, no one wanted to work for him and no one who did work for him lasted very long. In a firm peopled almost exclusively by difficult, demanding men, John Guttman had managed to earn a reputation for being impossible.

I don't know what they were thinking when they assigned me to him. Perhaps they hoped that I'd cave in after his first tirade and run home clutching my debutante picture to my breast. Who knows? But I stuck it out for almost five years, finally earning my release in the form of an early partnership.

It was a grueling apprenticeship, but one that I was grateful for. I'd cut my teeth with one of the most infamous tyrants of the law. After being on the receiving end of Guttman's shit, there was nothing any other lawyer could dish out that I hadn't tasted already. Nevertheless, walking down the corridor to his office I felt the old terror return.

Arriving at his office, I found him on the phone, as usual, conducting business a few decibels shy of a shout.

"Of course it's an ambiguous question," he bellowed, waving me into my old associate's chair, "and I say we give him an ambiguous answer." He made a face at me. It was either a grimace or a smile. "Yeah, we tell him to go fuck himself."

He was an unattractive man in his mid-fifties, beetle-browed with a thick brush of black hair going to gray. His desk was a long rosewood table turned sideways which he invariably kept bare except for the single file he was working on and a Baccarat vase, a gift from a client, that he kept filled with freshly sharpened yellow pencils. He hung up the phone and I reflexively jerked to attention.

"Do you want to tell me what the hell is going on with Danny Wohl?" demanded Guttman without pre-amble. Danny Wohl was Azor's in-house counsel and there were several possible answers to this, none of which I cared to share with Guttman. "I've been trying to get him on the phone all morning," he continued without waiting for an answer, "and nobody seems to know where he is."

"What do you need him for?" I asked with the caution born of experience. With Guttman everything was a crisis—closing a $400 million deal, making sure his dry cleaning got picked up—in his world it was all the same; there were no gradations of urgency.

"Jim Cassidy called me this morning, very upset. He has some rather major concerns about this deal with Taki-sawa." Jim Cassidy was one of my fellow Azor board members, a fried-chicken tycoon who owned a large block of Azor stock. If he had concerns about the deal he wasn't the only one. The company was in the midst of nerve-racking—and for Azor, pivotal—negotiations with the Takisawa Corporation, a pharmaceutical company whose aging founder had parlayed the bestselling hangover remedy in Japan into a global empire. At stake was a promising new drug molecule called ZK-501, and with it much more of Azor Pharmaceuticals' future than Stephen Azorini would care to admit.

Derived from an obscure Brazilian tree fungus, ZK-501 was a spectacular trigger of a molecule, a hundred times more powerful than cortisone, the world's most widely prescribed anti-inflammatory medication. Like cortisone, ZK-501 also produced side effects—unfortunately, some of ZK-501's were deadly. Azor scientists were frantically working to eliminate the molecule's undesirable properties. If they succeeded, the new drug would supplant cortisone and capture a market conservatively estimated at $15 billion a year—provided they got it to the market first.

But Stephen was running out of money and he was running out of time. The ZK-501 project employed as many scientists as a small university and was hemorrhaging money at a terrifying rate. Raising the stakes further was the fact that Mikos Pharmaceuticals, the drug industry giant, was also working on the molecule with a rumored two hundred scientists assigned full time to the project.

In order to help staunch the flow of dollars, Stephen and Danny had spent the better part of the fall trolling for a strategic partner, another company willing to make a much needed infusion of cash in exchange for a share of the profits from any eventual new drug. So far, the only nibble had come from Takisawa.

"If Cassidy has concerns about the deal he should bring them up at the next board meeting," I told Guttman. I hated these behind-the-scenes intrigues and resented Guttman's eagerness to take part in them.

"If Jim Cassidy brings this up with the board he's going to start by demanding Stephen's resignation," announced Guttman.

"Then he's a fool," I said flatly, hoping that Guttman wouldn't see how shaken I was by this news. It didn't matter that Azor Pharmaceuticals was now a publicly traded company; it was still Stephen's child, the product of his vision—and his will.

Most new scientific start-ups are biomedical companies—fledgling enterprises that compete with each other in small, untested markets. But Azor was a drug company and as such had been forced from day one to compete with the pharmaceutical superpowers and their well-established lines of billion-dollar drugs. That the company had survived its first year was impressive. That it had succeeded was nothing short of miraculous. Six years later, Azor may have outgrown its David role, but it still had a long way to go before becoming a Goliath.

Recently the company seemed to be experiencing the growing pains of an awkward adolescent. The patents on its two most profitable drugs were due to expire in the coming year and its recently introduced antischizophrenia drug, Serezine, had so far generated more controversy than profits. Compounding matters, the company's most promising new product, a blood substitute called Hemasyn, which Stephen had planned to introduce the previous spring, was still bogged down with the FDA. In ZK-501 Stephen believed lay the seeds of redemption.

"Don't try to tell me that the ZK-501 project hasn't been a huge drain on the bottom line," insisted Guttman. "You and I both know that the company can't handle those kinds of losses for much longer."

"That's why they're lining up a strategic partner," I reminded him.

"And if the Japanese don't bite?"

"Stephen seems confident that they will. He and Danny were just in Japan and things seem to be moving ahead."

"Says who? Whenever anybody tries to get in touch with Danny he's never there."

"He's been having some health problems recently," I ventured, hoping it would placate him.

"Health problems. Head problems. It makes no difference. Stephen's got too much on his plate and so far Danny, who's supposed to be handling the negotiations with the Japanese, hasn't done a damned thing except drop the ball."

"I will track Danny down to the ends of the earth as soon as you and I are finished, and I will have him return Cassidy's call," I assured him fervently.

"I can have my secretary do that," barked Guttman. "That's not why I called you down here. I shouldn't have to tell you how to do your job. But if you're as close to Stephen Azorini as people seem to think you are then you had better find some way to use your influence to make sure that he makes this goddamned deal."

"Stephen runs his company as he sees fit, John," I replied coldly. "The last thing he needs is me telling him what to do."

"Don't let the fact that you're sleeping with him cloud your judgment on this, Kate," he snapped back, unpleasantly.

"What exactly is your point, John?" I inquired, determined not to let myself be baited. "When you're subtle like this it's so hard to know what you're really thinking."

"Come on, Kate. You know that I think of you almost like a daughter." It occurred to me, not for the first time, that there was a reason Guttman's own daughter had chosen to make a life for herself in Australia. "I'm just giving you a little fatherly advice for your own good."

"And what's that?"

"It's not just Stephen's ass that's on the line this time, it's Azor. Believe me, Kate, if Stephen doesn't make this drug, if he doesn't make a deal with Takisawa, Cassidy and his buddies on the board will throw him out and sell Azor to one of the big drug houses just to get some kind of return on their investment. What do you think will happen to your position in the firm if that happens? Stephen isn't the only one who stands to get hurt if this deal doesn't get made. You are up on the high wire, Kate, and the spotlight is on you. There's a monkey on your shoulder and all the people sitting underneath you in the audience have paid their money hoping to see you fall."

CHAPTER

2

I was so unsettled by what John Guttman had said that I stormed out of his office, took a wrong turn, and ended up in the library before I realized where I was. It is one thing to know that you are an outsider in the world you have chosen for yourself. It is quite another to hear it put into words and spoken out loud by someone who is most definitely on the inside. I did not need John Guttman to tell me that under normal circumstances any lawyer would jump at the chance to come to the aid of such an important client. But these were not normal circumstances, and the fact that they were of my own making helped matters not one bit.

My roommate, Claudia, says the trouble with Stephen is that he has the brains of a rocket scientist trapped in the body of a movie star. She may be right. I have known Stephen Azorini since I was a teenager and have counted him as a client from my first days practicing law. Though most people never got beyond his genius and his charisma, I know better than anybody just how difficult he can be. Besides, even though I would never tell Guttman, it was the current state of our personal life that

8

was making me reluctant to get involved in the negotiations with Takisawa.

While there was no doubt that our relationship had recently moved forward—we had just bought an apartment and planned to move in together once renovations were completed—things between us didn't seem to be actually progressing. No matter what conclusions outsiders chose to draw, ours remained first and foremost a relationship of convenience.

Stephen did not love me. He loved his company. And I was still in love with my husband, Russell, who'd died of brain cancer during the first year of our marriage. The fact that it was Stephen, then a resident at the hospital where Russell was being treated, who stood by me during those last terrible months only added another strand of obligation to an already complicated relationship.

Growing impatient with my own self-pity, I buzzed Cheryl, my secretary, and asked her to bring me a cup of coffee and my messages. The first three were from my mother, all reminding me of the five o'clock appointment Stephen and I had with her and the decorator at the new apartment. It had already been rescheduled four times and as much as I would have liked to get out of it, I knew that I was well and truly on the hook this time.

I picked up the phone and dialed Stephen's number. This was his first day back in the office after ten days in Tokyo and I was pretty sure that my news about Cassidy and his incipient cabal was the last thing he wanted to hear. Nonetheless, I owed it to him to let him know the extent of the plotting that was going on against him.

Rachel, his personal assistant, answered the call. She was the latest in a series of bright young business school graduates who all seemed to work for Stephen for about a

year before moving on to positions of greater glamour
and less responsibility at one of the big pharmaceutical
companies.

"He's on the other line and he's late for a meeting, but
I'll see if he can talk to you,"—she said, crisply putting me
on hold. Despite my best efforts to be nice to her, Rachel
didn't like me. I suspected she had a crush on her boss
and didn't think I was good enough for him. Having seen
it before, I recognized the symptoms. I didn't let it bother
me. All it would take was one good loss of his temper
and she'd not only get over her infatuation, but she'd get
busy buffing up her résumé as well.

"Kate?" demanded Stephen, coming on the line a few
seconds later. "I've got people waiting for me."

"Then I'll keep it short. I just came from John
Guttman's office."

"That must have been fun."

"Jim Cassidy is on the warpath because he hasn't been
able to get hold of Danny."

"Danny isn't in today. He's at home getting over his jet
lag. I told you, this last trip to Japan was very high
impact. We were in meetings all day and went out with
our hosts drinking every night. I've decided that all the
books are wrong. Negotiating with the Japanese isn't
about subtle strategies; it's about surviving the nightlife.
I'll make sure Danny calls Cassidy as soon as he gets in
tomorrow."

"It would be better if it was today."

"Fine. I'll try to catch him at home. What's the big
rush?"

"According to Guttman, if you don't make this deal
with Takisawa, Cassidy already has the votes lined up on
the board to demand your resignation."

"Really? Then he should be happy to hear that I got a fax from Tokyo this morning. Takisawa is sending a delegation of their top scientists and business people here on the nineteenth. They want to hear about our results, see our labs, and talk dollars and cents."

"Is there any chance of finalizing the deal while they're here?" I asked eagerly. The board was scheduled to meet the Monday after Thanksgiving. If we could present them with a signed agreement with Takisawa, it would stop Cassidy and his buddies cold.

"Let's not get ahead of ourselves on this, Kate. I know what Cassidy wants. He wants to jack up the share price, sell his stock, and cash out of the company. He doesn't give a shit what happens to us after he's gone. I'm not going to let Cassidy or anyone else try to scare me into giving away the store just to come to terms with Takisawa. The way I see it, a bad deal can kill us just as fast as no deal at all. This negotiation with Takisawa is going to be very, very tricky."

"Do you think twelve days is enough time to get ready?" I asked. The Japanese are notorious for detailing Westerners to death. Before they wrote a check with that many zeros on it, Takisawa was going to want to know absolutely everything there was to know about Azor right down to the number of fillings in Stephen Azorini's teeth.

"It won't be easy," Stephen assured me, "but we'll do it."

"Tell Danny to call me if he wants a hand," I said, disgusted that I was letting Guttman get to me even this much. "I don't want him to think I'm trying to muscle in on him, but you know I'm available if he needs me."

"I'm sure Danny will be thrilled to have your help," replied Stephen, suddenly turning grim. "There's going to be more than enough agony to go around on this one."

* * *

When Stephen Azorini finished school, he had a medical degree and a Ph.D. in organic chemistry. He also had his pick of academic appointments, not to mention offers from all the big drug companies. None tempted him. He'd long before made up his mind to challenge the giant drug companies at their own game. His plan was to start a pharmaceutical company daring enough to ride the cutting edge of scientific discovery and nimble enough to capitalize on opportunities that the pharmaceutical behemoths with their massive bureaucracies were too slow and cumbersome to exploit.

Danny Wohl was Azor Pharmaceuticals' first employee. Danny and Stephen had known each other since college. Danny had gone to Harvard on scholarship, while Stephen had gone to prove he had the backbone to defy his father. While there is little doubt it was Stephen's good looks that prompted Danny to strike up a conversation that first day, it was quickly apparent to both of them that they had something very important in common. What both men shared, what they immediately recognized in each other, was the same fierce desire to prove they were better than where they'd come from.

Danny grew up in a grim, blue-collar pocket of Detroit, the only son of an intermittently employed welder and his embittered, alcoholic wife. Stephen's father, on the other hand, was a Chicago business tycoon with ties to organized crime. What had become of his mother was a question you learned not to ask twice.

Over the years I have tried to imagine how Stephen must have seemed to Danny back then. It is hard to believe he wasn't mesmerized. At eighteen Stephen had been an Adonis—accomplished, athletic, and rich. That

Danny reinvented himself using Stephen as a model I am certain. Years later there were still things about him, from his taste for Bushmills to his deep-seated love of jazz, that he'd picked up from Stephen the way a poor relation might acquire a suit of hand-me-down clothes.

But Danny was no weak shadow. After ten years he bore little resemblance to the child of poverty and longing who'd gotten off the bus in Cambridge. Although Stephen routinely received the credit for Azor's meteoric rise, those closest to the company quietly agreed that while it was the fire of Stephen's entrepreneurial genius that had fueled the rocket, it was Danny's firm hand on the throttle that had kept it on course.

And yet, despite all the exigencies of business, Danny was able to remain a man of wide-ranging interests. A passionate collector of modern art, he also served on the board of the Chicago Academy of Sciences and raised money for the Lyric Opera. That he was gay always seemed one of the least significant things about him.

I will never forget the day that Danny came to my office to tell me he'd tested positive for HIV. I'd assumed he was coming to discuss a possible stock offering for Azor. Instead, he asked if I would draw up the necessary documents granting Stephen power of attorney in the event he became incapacitated. Up until that moment AIDS for me had always been a word on paper, nothing more. Now I sat and looked across the desk at Danny, blond and sunburned from spending the weekend on a friend's boat, and all I could see was a dead man.

Eventually the horror receded, papered over by other problems, different crises. Ironically it was new drugs developed by the very pharmaceutical companies he and Stephen had long decried as dinosaurs that finally offered hope. For the past year Danny had been taking a "cock-tail" of anti-AIDS drugs. While they reduced the amount of virus in his blood to below measurable levels, the regimen left him struggling with a plethora of side effects. Tormented by deep muscle pain, blinding headaches, and a general sense of malaise, Danny had been forced to cut back on his schedule. Even so, one day in ten found him too weak to make it in to the office at all. While Guttman had been railing about Danny's unavailability, Danny had probably been in bed, shuddering through waves of nausea and despair, no doubt feeling less concerned about the company's prospects of survival than his own.

At five o'clock I waited on the corner of Adams and LaSalle with the darkness gathering around me. In winter, night comes early to Chicago; by the time December rolled around, it would practically fall in the middle of the afternoon. I pulled the heavy cashmere of my coat around me and stamped my feet against the cold.

Stephen pulled to the curb and I slid gratefully into the warm, dark car. He was talking on the phone, immersed in a conversation I could not understand—something about chemical sequences and protein folding. As we glided through traffic I listened with half an ear, vaguely comforted by the thought of atoms and molecules binding and releasing like dancers in a quadrille.

We drove east on Adams then turned north onto Michigan Avenue through the thickening rush-hour traffic. It was a clear night and everything seemed crisp from the cold. Thanksgiving was still weeks away, but the trees were already hung with tiny white Christmas lights that glittered like diamonds strung against the dark velvet of the night.

As we turned onto East Lake Shore Drive it seemed as if someone had lowered the volume of the city. The cacophony of Michigan Avenue evaporated, buffered by an open expanse of park and the much larger silence of Lake Michigan. Our new apartment was in an elegant building nestled in the elbow of Lake Shore Drive just where it reaches out to embrace the shore. Built at the turn of the century, the apartment itself had been designed by David Adler, an architect whose sense of scale was so legendary that he supposedly could look at an eighteen-foot ceiling and tell instantly if the cornice was even a fraction off.

By any measure it was a grand apartment. My mother always said it was the best in the city. She should know—it had once been hers, a wedding present from my grandparents who'd made their home in the one directly above it. Later, after my grandfather died and my grandmother moved to Palm Springs, Mother combined the two apartments, adding a graceful curved staircase and creating arguably the most stunning duplex in the city.

They sold it when I was six and we went to live in the big house in Lake Forest where I grew up. In the intervening years the apartment changed hands a number of times. It had most recently been purchased by Victor Sanderson, who'd died six weeks later after choking on a piece of roast beef at the Saddle & Cycle Club. His widow, Phyllis, continued to live there but grew more eccentric with each passing year. Over time she closed off progressively more of the apartment until she was living in the smallest of its twenty-one rooms, eating cold soup by candlelight in order to save on the electricity. According to the attorney who handled the estate, she left behind a fortune totaling over $120 million.

Stephen pulled the car under the arched portico of the building and the liveried doorman touched the bill of his cap. We waited for a moment while he released the wrought-iron security gate. As the gate parted noiselessly, Stephen eased the car down the steep ramp into the underground garage. Beneath the luxury apartments of Chicago's Gold Coast lies a subterranean world. Cars are washed and filled with gas, dry cleaning makes its way in and out of closets, meals are cooked, and groceries are delivered. I wondered what my new neighbors would think of my battered Volvo. No doubt they'd assume it belonged to the maid.

Mother and her decorator, Mimi Sheraton, were already upstairs waiting for us. We found them in the living room which, without furniture, seemed roughly the size of the cargo hold of an ocean freighter. Despite the fact that the walls had been painted the color of Pepto-Bismol, the intricately carved egg-and-dart moldings made my heart turn over in their symmetry.

Dutifully kissing the air beside my mother's perfumed cheek, I immediately wished I had thought to put something else on that morning. Mother, in a scarlet Valentino cocktail dress, reduced the severe uniform of my navy suit and pearls to rags with one withering glance. If Mussolini had put one-tenth the effort into his quest for world domination that my mother spends on looking beautiful, we would all be speaking Italian right now.

Mother, who was due at an important party (one of her more irritating oxymorons), had come to advise us on the architect's latest sketches for the kitchen and the master suite. Mimi, drawings in hand, led the way while two assistants of dubious sexuality hovered in the background with clipboards and tape measures. Mimi Sheraton was the quintessential society decorator. At least two face-lifts older than my mother, she favored St. John's knits and was unabashedly condescending to everyone who crossed her path, carpenters and contessas alike. Much of her career had been spent endlessly redecorating my mother's houses, and as such she counted as more of a fixture of my childhood than many of my actual relatives.

I had grown up in a house that was in a constant state of redecoration. By the time I was ten I'd already had my fill of window treatments and floor coverings. Deciding where to move the file cabinet in my office was more than enough to satisfy whatever occasional urges I might feel to alter my surroundings. I was more than happy to entrust matters both large and small to my mother and Mimi. As far as I was concerned, the extent of my role in the proceedings was to write checks and feign interest.

Stephen, on the other hand, could usually be counted on to summon enthusiasm for the process. Once we bought the apartment I was surprised to discover in him an orphan's delight in all things domestic. While there is no doubt he enjoyed the idea of calling such an elegant residence his own, what he really seemed to relish was the prospect of—after a decade of sterile bachelor apartments—finally settling into a real home.

But tonight was different. From the very first he seemed preoccupied, too distracted to participate in the discussions about plastering and the problem of what to do about the hideous wood-grain Formica paneling that had been installed by some previous criminal against architecture. As we talked he slipped away entirely. When I was sent to fetch him, I found him pacing the entrance hall, cell phone in hand, punching in Danny's number for the fourteenth time that day only to be rewarded yet again by an endless ringing at the other end.

"Maybe we should stop over at his apartment when we're done here and make sure he's all right," I suggested.

"He's probably asleep," replied Stephen. "I did tell him he could take the day off. I'd feel like an ass showing up on his doorstep just because Jim Cassidy has decided he wants to swing his dick around."

Stephen was right, of course. That was the worst part about people like Cassidy and Guttman. They generated artificial crises and it didn't matter that their crises had no substance—they still managed to suck you in.

Eventually Mimi turned to Stephen's pet project—the exercise room that was planned as part of the master suite—and he was able to set his other concerns aside. After having spent the last half hour listening to Mother and Mimi debate where to hang the copper pots we did not own and would surely never use to prepare meals neither Stephen nor I would ever be home to eat, it was my turn to escape. I wandered down the hall to look at the small bedroom I planned on turning into my study. To my dismay, Mother came and found me almost immediately.

"I know you like to pretend that it's not, but how you live is very important," she said in her gospel-according-to-Astrid-Millholland voice. "You may not be interested in entertaining any of your old friends, but I am sure Stephen would like to have a nice home in which to receive guests."

"I would like to have a nice home, too, Mother," I assured her peevishly.

"Well, you would never know it from how you live now," she sniffed. "Honestly, I don't see how you're going to manage this renovation if you aren't willing to take an interest in the details."

"We've hired Mimi to handle the details."

"Mimi is not the one who is going to be living here. Don't you think you've taken this lawyer business far enough? Why don't you just give it a rest for a while and concentrate on what's really important in your life?"

"Important to whom?" I inquired.

From the end of the hall we could hear Stephen's approaching baritone. "So you really think we'd have room for a steam room next to the gym if we moved that one wall?"

"I wish you could see yourself," Mother hissed, unable to resist getting in one last shot. "That stubborn look you get is so very unattractive. It's a wonder Stephen puts up with it."

"I like being stubborn, Mother," I replied coolly. "That's why I became a lawyer."

CHAPTER
3

Stephen and I were already in bed when the police arrived. The doorman's buzzer caught us in midembrace, and his announcement that there were two uniformed officers in the lobby asking to see Stephen left us searching frantically for our clothes and filled with silent alarm.

We managed to be presentable by the time the elevator delivered the officers upstairs. His face ashen in alarm, Stephen opened the door to two middle-aged beat cops. One was white, the other black, but they both had guts that hung on them like saddlebags and strained against the black leather of their jackets.

All business, Stephen quickly identified himself and ushered them inside. They seemed oblivious to the size of Stephen's apartment and the view it commanded. I knew this was a bad sign. These men were professionals, they had a lot of years between them, and they still didn't want to be here—they didn't want to do what they had come to do.

The words of the formal notification may have been memorized, but their sympathy seemed real. They regretted to inform us that Danny Wohl had been found dead in his apartment earlier in the day. The detectives who'd been summoned searched his apartment and found a copy of the power of attorney I'd drawn up more than a year ago. However, it had taken some time to process the information and locate Stephen's home address.

We pressed for details, but there were only a few forthcoming. Apparently a building engineer had let himself in to the apartment to check a faulty thermostat and discovered the body. Immediately recognizing that Danny was dead he'd called 911. When we asked the officers how Danny had died they could give us only the official answer. In cases of an unattended death it was up to the medical examiner to determine the cause of death. An autopsy would have to be performed.

While they were obviously reluctant to offer us anything more, they did manage to leave us with the distinct impression that Danny had died peacefully—his life claimed by something from the doctor's lexicon of sudden death—an aneurysm or an embolism, perhaps. Later, after they had gone and the initial shock had worn off, we consoled ourselves with that.

As an intern, Stephen had had a chance to see firsthand the prolonged agony of a death from AIDS. Patients in excruciating pain, robbed of their sight, their strength, their dignity . . . At least, we told each other, at least, whatever malady had claimed him, he'd been spared that.

The next morning we were woken by the telephone. It was the woman from the management company shrilly demanding that Stephen come and see Danny's apartment for himself. He was perplexed by her insistence, her refusal to discuss over the telephone something as simple as having an apartment cleaned. Compared to the enormity of Danny's death, her concerns about getting the carpets cleaned seemed petty and ridiculous.

Of course, now that we were actually in the apartment, it all made sense. Her anger as we first spoke in her office. The way she'd bitten off her syllables as she told us how they'd found his body. The almost savage way she'd twisted her passkey in the lock and pushed open the door to let us in, careful not to cross over the threshold herself.

The last time I had been in Danny Wohl's apartment it was an elegant place, festive with fresh flowers and lit with candles for a dinner party. Today it looked like a slaughterhouse. The living room was in shambles. The glass top of the coffee table had been tumbled off its props. Cushions, covered with ominous dark stains, had been torn from the couch and lay scattered across the floor. Blood was everywhere. The walls were covered with it, splashed in arcing, elliptical stains, or worse, smeared with frantic, sliding hand marks.

I glanced over at Stephen to see how he was taking it. His leonine head was bent, his smoky eyes hooded, his face registering no emotion other than objective interest. It was all an act, of course. A trick he'd picked up in medical school. But I am a lawyer, not a doctor, and I was completely unequipped to deal with what I was seeing in Danny's apartment. I tried closing my eyes, but it did not help. Even the smell of blood was overwhelming—cloying and feral. What on earth had happened here?

Danny would have hated to see his place like this. He had loved his new apartment with its high ceilings and glorious views. An avid art collector, he'd recently been forced to move when his taste had turned to works larger than the Mapplethorpe photographs with which he'd begun his collection.

Had the woman from the management company known that Danny had AIDS? I doubted it. So far Danny had done his best to keep his illness secret. All that blood and all of it HIV positive. I wondered who Stephen was going to find to clean it up.

I tried to look away, but there were no safe vistas. Even the carpet, sticky under my feet, bore testimony to the violent drama that had been played out here. Mottled footprints started near the sofa and turned to drag marks where Danny must have fallen and then crawled through his own blood, trying desperately to reach the phone. He had died just a few feet short of his goal. A lake of blood marked the spot, so big that it still hadn't had time to dry.

A dark soot covered everything. At first I thought it was just the urban grit that drifts through every open window in the city, but the windows were shut tight. Then I realized it was the powder that the police had used to look for fingerprints. The dust scratched at my lungs while everything my eyes rested on tore at my heart.

"Haven't you seen enough?" I asked Stephen.

"I just want to have a quick look at the bedroom," he replied in a flat voice.

I followed, not wanting to be left alone. I had been ready to leave thirty seconds after we'd arrived. I could not imagine what could possibly make him want to stay.

Along the exposed brick of the hallway hung a series of monochromatic blue panels by a Dutch painter whose work Danny admired. I couldn't remember his name, only that the piece was called *A Moment After Sinking* and that there was something special about the brushwork.

The bedroom had apparently escaped the bloodletting. The room's decor was considerably less restrained than the rest of the apartment. In the center was a wrought-iron bed draped in enough mosquito netting to protect a small expedition down the Nile. There were Mapplethorpes on the walls here, too, but they were the photographer's graphically sexual work—not the sort you'd want your business associates to see. I turned my back on them.

Danny's desk, a large contemporary unit designed especially for a computer, with a pullout keyboard shelf, was near the window. Stephen came to a stop behind the ergonomically correct desk chair and stared forlornly at the black briefcase at his feet.

"You might as well take it," I advised him gently. "The police have already been through everything and I guarantee you won't feel like coming back."

Reluctantly Stephen picked up the case and set it on top of the desk. With practiced hands he flipped open the latches and popped the lid. The inside was crammed with file folders and legal pads, all swarming with Danny's tidy script. Satisfied, Stephen laid his large hands on top of the case and slammed it shut. In the silence of the apartment it sounded like a shot.

I trailed Stephen into the large bathroom, which was decorated in Danny's typical eye-catching style. A pedestal sink of white porcelain was set against a wall of exposed brick. The floor was a deep blue hand-glazed tile. A single white towel lay across the lip of the tub, and the toilet seat was up. Stephen reached up and pulled open the mirrored doors of the medicine cabinet above the sink. It was crammed with prescription vials of every description and a veritable arsenal of grooming supplies— bronzers, mousses, gels, and spritzes—even an eyelash curler. No wonder Danny had always looked better than I did.

"What are you looking for?" I asked.

"I don't know. I'm just looking." He paused and shook his head. "There's something very wrong with all of this."

"What do you mean?" I demanded, feeling the dull ache of apprehension growing in the pit of my stomach.

Stephen did not answer but instead began to make his way back into the living room. As I followed, I almost tripped over the telephone cord which lay across the entrance to the hall. The table on which the phone usually rested had been overturned in the struggle, scattering squares of notepaper like leaves across the bloodstained carpet.

"What do you mean there's something wrong?" I demanded again, and was immediately struck by the idiocy of my own question. There was blood on the ceiling. Of course there was something wrong.

Stephen, who was making his way toward the kitchen, did not appear to have heard me. I went after him, trying hard to avoid the frieze of dried blood that marked the wall near the door. The kitchen was large and fitted out for the serious cook. A set of Calphalon pots hung from an oval rack above the Viking range. The counters were made of gray-black soapstone, silky to the touch, but porous and prone to scratches. The glass-fronted cabinets matched the bleached oak of the floors. Two bar stools were tucked beneath a narrow counter that served as a kind of kitchen desk. There were no signs of blood anywhere that I could see.

Stephen lifted the linen shade that covered the window and was rewarded by a depressing view of the fire escape. Beside the sink were dishes from a hand-painted set that Danny had brought back from a vacation he'd taken in Tuscany. Brightly colored, they were stacked in a sleek chrome dish rack, waiting to be put away. On the counter off to one side stood a half-full glass of water. For some reason these domestic details unnerved me more than all the blood.

"Can we please go now?" I found myself asking in a small, desperate voice.

Stephen wheeled around almost as if he were surprised to find me still there. Then, without a word, he took my hand and led me out of the apartment.

As we drove back to my office I tried to focus on the touchstones of the city like a blind man fumbling for familiar objects in the dark. After the grisly scene in Danny's apartment I needed to reassure myself that the world had not somehow slipped off its axis. I sought comfort in the rumble of the city buses, the enduring twin corncobs of Marina Towers, the hulking permanence of the Merchandise Mart, squat and solid beside the opaque waters of the Chicago River.

"What happened up there?" I asked finally.

"I don't know," replied Stephen helplessly as we made our way through morning traffic.

"Do you think he could have surprised a burglar?"

"I don't know what to think," he answered, "but it didn't look like anything was taken."

We drove south on Dearborn in the deep shadow of the el tracks. We were almost to my office before I found the voice to speak again.

"When are you going to tell Takisawa?" I ventured.

"Not until it's too late for them to change their minds about coming," replied Stephen. "Losing Danny is going to be devastating for us. The Japanese hate it when the players change in the middle of negotiations. Not only that, but you may remember that our original entrée to the company was through Danny. He and Takisawa's son-in-law were friends in law school. To the Japanese, those kinds of relationships are critical. Who knows whether we'll be able to keep their interest in the project now that Danny isn't part of the equation."

"Maybe you should think about postponing the visit?"

"Science is a winner-take-all sport, Kate. There are no silver medals in this. Every time I have to wait to hire someone or hold off buying a piece of equipment because I don't have the money it puts Mikos that much closer to beating us."

"I understand that. But even ignoring for the moment the fact that Danny has been the lead man on this from day one, I don't see how you can possibly be ready without him."

"Obviously I'm going to have to find someone to take his place," said Stephen, pulling into the loading zone in front of my building.

"Like who?" I demanded, thinking how difficult it would be to find someone willing to plunge into this kind of fast-moving, highly technical negotiation in midstream.

"Like you."

"You can't be serious!" I exclaimed in a decidedly unlawyerly display of candor.

Stephen turned slowly in the driver's seat and took both my hands in his. He is a big man, handsome the way that Hercules was strong and with the kind of charismatic personality that in the closed confines of the car seemed to radiate heat like a bomb site after a blast.

"It has to be you, Kate. As outside counsel, Danny

always kept you up to speed on our dealings with Taki-sawa. You also know our business inside and out. I can't think of anyone who is in a better position to evaluate the impact that the different ways we might structure this deal will have on the company."

"I have other clients, Stephen," I protested. "What you're asking is absolutely impossible."

"You could take a leave of absence from the firm," he countered, "a temporary leave of absence. Lawyers do it all the time to have babies or work political cam-paigns. . . ." A delivery truck pulled up behind us and the driver pummeled his horn angrily.

"You'd be better off with almost anyone but me when you're dealing with the Japanese," I countered. "Everyone knows that women give them the heebie-jeebies." Nor-mally I would never have dreamed of using my being a woman as an excuse, but I was desperate. The thought of leaving the firm, even temporarily, to go to work for Stephen every day was enough to give me the bends.

"My head is on the block, Kate. My jugular is exposed, and from what you've been telling me Jim Cassidy is busy sharpening his knife. . . ."

"Which is why you need someone who knows how to deal with the Japanese, someone with a lot of experience with this kind of deal."

"No. What I need is someone who knows me. Someone whose judgment I trust." Behind us the truck driver leaned on his horn. Startled, I snatched my hands away. "I have never asked you to do anything for me before," Stephen continued, gravely.

I stared at him for a few seconds, but in the end there was no reply to this but motion. I opened the door of the car, scrambled out onto the sidewalk, and pulled my briefcase out behind me. Then, startled by what I'd done, I tried to stammer out some kind of explanation. But by the time I turned around Stephen had already pulled away.

CHAPTER

4

I pushed through the revolving doors of my building and crossed the gray marble of the lobby, which that morning seemed as sterile and oppressive as a tomb. Stopping at the newsstand, I bought a king-size bag of M&M's for my breakfast. Then I took the elevator to the forty-second floor.

Passing through the imposing double mahogany doors of Callahan, Ross, Peterman & Seidel, I produced a distracted wave for Lillian, the receptionist. On becoming a partner I had been surprised to learn that, in addition to picking up her weekly hairdressing tab, the firm paid her more than they paid a first-year lawyer. Lillian acknowledged my arrival with a regal nod of her head and then went back to the serious business of answering the phone, murmuring the firm's multiple names into her headset with the reverence of a prayer.

Callahan Ross is the third largest law firm in the city, one of the dozen or so biggest in the world. It is also an old firm—old moneyed, old-line, and old-fashioned—the kind of WASP institution forged long ago by men who assumed that theirs was an association of gentlemen and

would always be so. Things do change at a place like
this—I wouldn't be there if they didn't—but usually
someone has to die first.

Turning the corner into my office I made a face at my
secretary, Cheryl, who was busy on the phone. She took
one look at the bag of M&M's in my hand and rolled her
eyes. I shrugged off my coat and hung it up in the closet,
frowning at myself in the dim mirror that hung inside the
door. I tucked a stray wisp of my dark hair back into its
usual French twist and gave a couple of hairpins a shove
for good measure. I thought about putting on some lipstick but decided it wouldn't do any good.

When I kicked the closet door shut I found Cheryl
waiting for me, a cup of coffee in one hand and a stack of
pink message slips in the other. She looked very well put
together in a deep blue suit. I was on the verge of compli-
menting her on it when I remembered that it was an old
one of mine that I'd given her at the end of last season.

"Which do you want first?" she asked, offering me
both. I took the coffee cup and we made for our usual
places—me to my desk and Cheryl to the wing chair I'd
rescued from one of my mother's many redecorations.

"What's been going on?" I asked.

"Maybe you'd better have your M&M's first," Cheryl
suggested. She was three years younger than I was, with
an intelligent, heart-shaped face and straw-colored hair.

"That bad?"

"Larry Hanlon at Dexter & Brock is screaming for the
registration documents on Nuland Petroleum and Bob
Preston says that Lydia Cavanaugh's investment bankers
are having heart attacks about the valuation figures that
you okayed as final. Oh, and Mrs. McCreary has already

called me twice this morning. She's threatening bodily harm if you don't turn in your time sheets."

Mrs. McCreary was the firm's billing administrator. All the lawyers were accountable to her for keeping track of their time, which was billed to the client in six-minute increments—tenths of an hour.

"She made me promise that you'd have them in by the end of the day. I also didn't know if you'd make it back in time, so I rescheduled your ten-thirty conference call for one o'clock. Also, Ted Nicholdson at First Chicago wants to set up a meeting today or tomorrow to go over the offering documents on McKenna. Oh, and John Guttman just called. He wants to see you right away."

"What did he want?" I asked, reaching for chocolate.

"Why don't you ask him yourself?" Cheryl whispered, suddenly catching sight of him coming down the hall. "Here he comes." She sprang to her feet and beat a hasty retreat.

I took a deep breath and mentally braced myself.

"What's this about you not being willing to help Stephen Azorini on this deal with Takisawa?" demanded Guttman, charging in without even bothering to knock. "Isn't this exactly what I warned you about yesterday?"

"Why don't you have a seat, John," I said quietly. Inside I was seething. The minute I'd gotten out of the car Stephen must have gotten on his mobile to Guttman, looking for another lever to get me to do what he wanted.

"Of all the times for Danny to pick to drop dead! I can't believe you would even consider deserting Stephen at a time like this!" He made no move to sit down, so I got out of my chair and walked around my desk to face him.

"I have other clients besides Azor, John. Don't you think I also have an obligation to them? What do you propose I do with them while I'm spending all my time haggling with the Japanese?"

"Farm them out for a while. Get a couple of associates to help carry the load. Delegate, for Christ's sake. What are we talking about? A month? Two months? If you want, I'll go to Skip Tillman for you and make sure you get the help you need."

Skip Tillman was the firm's managing partner. The thought of him and Guttman discussing the handling of my cases infuriated me.

"Perhaps you should be the one taking over for a month or two at Azor?" I suggested, knowing it would gall him.

"I'm not the one that Stephen seems to want," countered John, sounding bitter in spite of himself. "Let me ask you something. You're so worried about your relationship with your other clients, what do you think will happen to your relationship with Azor Pharmaceuticals if you refuse to get involved and the deal with Takisawa goes sour?"

"You know how difficult negotiations are with the Japanese. What makes you think it will be any different than what will happen if I do get involved and it goes sour anyway?"

"Allow me to refresh your memory, Miss Millholland. If I'm not mistaken, we serve our clients by representing them," thundered Guttman, "not by refusing to do so. Or has your judgment been so distorted by personal considerations that you've lost sight of that fact?"

By the time my feet hit the pavement all I could hear was the blood rushing through my ears and the sharp intake of my own breath. I hurried along the sidewalk, trying not to think too hard about what it was that was propelling me. I told myself I needed to get out of the office, to put some distance between me and Guttman. I told myself there was no other reason, absolutely none, for me to go talk to Elliott Abelman in person rather than from the relative safety of the telephone.

I also rationalized that I was putting first things first. After all, if I was really going to take a leave of absence from the firm in order to take over the work of Danny's life, that meant I needed someone else to follow through on the details of his death. No doubt the police were hard-nosed professionals who would do their job. However, I knew enough about how Chicago works to know that it also wouldn't hurt to have someone making sure they did it right.

I hadn't seen Elliott in nearly six months. A former prosecutor and an ex-marine, Elliott had parlayed his legal training and connections with the city into a thriving practice as a private investigator. He'd also managed to get under my skin in a way that Stephen, with his matinee-idol good looks, never had.

Elliott had done work for me on a number of cases; however, the most recent one had ended badly. The fault was mine, not Elliott's. In my zeal to find the truth I'd given no thought to its consequences, which had turned out to be devastating. Unfortunately, in the emotional aftershock of its discovery I'd also come perilously close to behaving foolishly with Elliott.

I took the stairs to the second floor of the Monadnock Building and gave my name to the receptionist. While I waited I pretended to examine the Art Institute prints that punctuated the walls, too nervous to sit down. I sensed him before I heard him call my name. So many things came back at the sight of him—the smell of his skin, the gentle pressure of his hand on the small of my back. . . .

Compared to Stephen, Elliott is nothing special to look at—indeed, there is an economy about him that is a direct contrast to Stephen's swarming intelligence and extravagant good looks. A shade over six feet tall with a tousle of soft brown hair and warm brown eyes, Elliott is compactly built—good-looking without being handsome. The only thing extraordinary about his appearance is his smile, which not only completely transforms his face, but seems to illuminate the room.

Ignoring any subtext, we shook hands and I followed him back to his office, which was large and furnished like the smoking room of a lesser men's club. In the corner was a large telescope, new since the last time I'd been there. As Elliott took my coat and hung it up he explained that the telescope had been a gift from a grateful client who thought that turning it on the reaches of the heavens would be a welcome relief from scrutinizing the follies of mortal men.

We settled into our places, Elliott behind his antique oak desk and I in an armchair of confessionally soft leather. Declining coffee and having serious second thoughts about the wisdom of having come in the first place, I immediately launched into an account of the little I knew about the circumstances of Danny's death. I also filled him in about the pending negotiation with Takisawa and explained that it would leave Stephen and me little time to track the police investigation of his death.

"The way things stand right now you'll be lucky if there even is an investigation," replied Elliott as soon as I'd finished.

"What do you mean?" I asked, surprised.

"I guess you must be too busy to read the papers," he replied with good-natured disbelief. "But the police have their hands pretty full with this Stanley Sarrek thing."

Of course. Richard Speck, John Wayne Gacy, Jeffrey Dahmer. Stanley Sarrek was the latest in a long and hideous line. How stupid of me not to have put it together. Ever since his arrest the newspapers, the media, the very air seemed filled with nothing else. It was amazing how the actions of one psychopath could cast a pall over an entire city.

That Sarrek had been apprehended at all, much less in Chicago, was the sheerest of accidents. He'd been pulled over in a routine traffic stop. When the officers asked for his driver's license they noticed what looked like blood-stains on the running board of Sarrek's truck. When they made him open up the refrigerated trailer of his double rig they found the mutilated corpses of sixty-three women stored like so many flash-frozen sides of beef. It was, the media breathlessly assured us, a new record for a single serial killer.

"Do you really think it will have that much impact?" I asked, knowing full well what the answer would be.

"Are you kidding? This creep Sarrek picked his victims at random from all over the country. The cops don't even have a place to start. There's no way to narrow it down. It's even worse for the medical examiner's office—worse than a plane crash even. At least when a jumbo jet goes down they have the passenger list to start from and some idea how everybody died. Not only that, but the bodies have been so mutilated that identification is going to be next to impossible—we're talking body parts—and the fact that they've been refrigerated will make it hard to pin down any time of death.

"Just the whole process of identifying the victims is going to take months. In the meantime, the family of every woman who's gone missing anywhere in America in the last ten years is on the phone frantically trying to find out whether their wife or daughter is one of the ones who've turned up in the back of the truck."

"I understand that," I replied, "but what happened to those women doesn't make finding out who killed Danny Wohl any less important."

"I'm just telling you how it is, Kate."

"But you didn't see his apartment," I practically sobbed. "There was blood everywhere. It was his home and he ended up fighting for his life in his own living room and dying in a puddle of blood. What happened to those women is terrible, but it's even worse if it keeps us from finding out what happened to Danny."

"So what exactly do you want me to do?"

"Find out who killed him."

"You realize what that kind of investigation involves? Are you sure you really want me to do this? You're not just acting on impulse?"

"Of course not," I replied. Suddenly it seemed very clear. "It's bad enough that Danny is dead. It will be worse if he ends up the victim of an indifferent bureaucracy just because he had the bad luck to die when some homicidal psychopath got pulled over in Chicago."

"Why don't we wait a little before we jump into this," urged Elliott. "Let's give the police a little bit of time to do their job."

"You said it yourself. They couldn't even if they wanted to. They don't have the manpower and the external pressures of the Sarrek investigation are too great."

"You can't be sure of that."

"Oh come on! Which do you think is going to get first priority from the cops—investigating the death of a gay lawyer who was going to die of AIDS anyway or gathering enough evidence to convict the serial killer of the century?"

Back at my office I asked Cheryl to bring us both a cup of coffee and shut the door behind her. There was no question about what I was going to do. Even if Guttman was wrong about what was at stake there was really no way I could say no to Stephen. Personal considerations aside, we are talking about a man who once recruited an entire twelve-man lab from NIH and moved them to Chicago over a three-day weekend. Any reservations I might have had about taking a leave of absence from Callahan Ross were sure to be quickly overridden.

Even so I had my misgivings. I was currently billing close to 260 hours a month, a crushing load even by this firm's macho standards, and unlike most of my partners who surrounded themselves with a cadre of ambitious associates, I preferred to work alone. It helped that I was blessed with a secretary who was smart enough to do much of the routine work I would normally shunt off to a first-year associate. For more complex legal legerdemain I relied on a brilliant lawyer named Sherman Whitehead who'd joined the firm the same year I did. Sherman was a nerd-savant whose complete lack of interpersonal skills guaranteed that he would never achieve partnership— much less meet a client. However, he was a nimble legal thinker and realistic enough about his fate to not spend all his time jockeying for my attention or approval. Until today Cheryl and Sherman had been enough.

But the real problem was even bigger than that. What I really needed was not more help but less work. In the years immediately following Russell's death I'd found a haven from my grief at the office. The work anesthetized me and in consequence I'd piled it on greedily. Besides, I'd had things to prove. Now I wanted something else. I wanted a life. I wanted to read novels and go to the movies. I wanted to stop giving dictation in my sleep and to carve out some small corner of the week that had nothing to do with the law, or business, or my obligations to the firm that had somehow managed to invade the very fabric of my life. Recently I'd made some efforts to cut back on my workload. I'd started playing squash again and was volunteering a couple of times a month at the free legal clinic in my neighborhood. Now this.

Not surprisingly, my secretary greeted the news of my new responsibilities with well-considered trepidation. If, as Guttman had suggested, I was indeed on the high wire, then it was Cheryl who was standing at ground zero holding the net. There was no getting around the symbiosis inherent in our situations. When I was overwhelmed, so was Cheryl—and at about a quarter of my salary at that. And even though we didn't talk about it, we both worried what effect the additional pressure would have on her at night while she was enrolled in law school at Loyola. Six courses shy of graduation, the day was rapidly approaching when I would lose her. I viewed the prospect roughly the same way I would the pending amputation of a limb.

Cheryl was smart. She was funny. Loyal as a soldier, she compensated for my shortcomings, lied to cover my ass, and put up with my mother. While I pretended to be above office politics, she resolutely kept her ear to the watercooler and watched my back for me.

For the remainder of the day, between meetings and telephone calls, Cheryl and I barricaded ourselves in my office going through my files like a pair of triage nurses at the scene of an accident. Those too volatile or complex to survive a change in counsel went onto the stack of files that I would attempt to juggle on top of my duties at Azor. Matters that could be routinely moved ahead by associates went into another. The rest would, with a wink and a prayer, be allowed to lie dormant until either the deal between Azor and Takisawa had been hammered out—or it blew up in my face.

CHAPTER
5

The telephone woke me from the darkness. Numbly I groped for the receiver as research abstracts and financial projections slid off the bed and onto the floor, scattering dust bunnies silently through the darkness. I struggled to focus on the glowing digits of the clock radio. It was five o'clock in the morning.

"Hello," I croaked. As a rule I try to avoid all human contact until after seven o'clock and at least two cups of coffee.

"It's me, Stephen." He was calling from atop his exercise bike. I could hear the babble of CNN over the whirring of the gears. "I was thinking it would be a good idea if you sat in on the ZK-501 project council meeting this morning."

"The what?"

"The weekly research meeting. I'm going to announce the Takisawa visit and I think you should be there."

"What time?"

"It starts at seven."

I groaned.

"I take it that's a yes?"

41

I groaned again. Usually I make it a practice to at least be civil to my clients, but then again my clients usually don't call me at home at five o'clock in the morning.

"I hope you had a chance to look over that material I sent you."

I muttered something under my breath and was relieved that Stephen chose to interpret it in the affirmative. I'd stayed at the office until nearly midnight and still hadn't had time to read through the box of materials that Stephen had messengered over to acquaint me with the ZK-501 project. I'd taken them home and tried to read them in bed, but I didn't have the heart to tell him that of the dozens of scientific abstracts I'd tackled, I'd hardly understood a single word.

I let my face fall back into my pillow, but the reality that Stephen Azorini was now my boss was enough to prevent me from going back to sleep. I rolled out of bed and padded down the long hall that ran down the center of the apartment I share with my roommate Claudia Stein.

I live in Hyde Park, which most people know as the home of the University of Chicago. For the last fifty years it has been a neighborhood poised on the brink of gentrification. Socially, racially, and economically diverse, it is exactly the kind of community that social progressives invariably call for and yet inevitably flee as soon as it gets dark. My partners at Callahan Ross assumed I lived there in order to be close to Stephen, whose apartment a few blocks away was one of his ways of keeping close ties to the university. My parents had no such illusions. They just thought I'd chosen the neighborhood to piss them off. The truth was actually much more straightforward. Claudia was a surgical resident at the University of Chicago and she got withdrawal symptoms whenever she was more than ten minutes away from the mayhem of the emergency room.

Claudia was in the kitchen when I got there, pouring herself a cup of coffee and looking out the window through the steel bars of the burglar grille. She is a tiny woman, barely five feet tall, who wears her dark hair in a single braid that falls down her back like a schoolgirl's. In spite of her size she manages to convey a brand of instantly recognizable toughness, the kind that surgeons get after a couple years of sewing up bullet holes. She was dressed for work in her usual green scrubs and running shoes, but in her hurry to get to the hospital she'd managed to put the top on backward so that the label was in front and the V neck revealed her vertebrae.

"What are you doing up so early?" she demanded ungraciously. "Are you sick or something?"

"I have an early meeting," I growled, helping myself to coffee. "Did you know your shirt's on backward?"

"Yes. I turned it around on purpose," she replied. "I caught one of the anesthesiologists looking down my shirt yesterday in pre-op." She shot me one of her you-couldn't-possibly-be-naive-enough-to-find-this-surprising looks.

"So what's happening on the fellowship front?" I asked. Claudia was due to complete her residency in June and was going through something of a career crisis. Having decided to specialize beyond general surgery, she had applied to fellowship programs in two wildly different areas: eye surgery and trauma. Since then, she could have learned a foreign language in the time she'd spent debating between the two.

"Stanford ophthalmology has invited me to come out

for a visit and I'm going to spend a day at Northwestern trauma next week."

"Are those your two top choices?"

"I think so."

"So which one do you think you'll pick?"

"They have to pick me first."

"Assuming they both do, which one will you choose?"

"I don't know. . . . After last night I'm thinking of switching to pediatrics and signing up for the Peace Corps. Diarrhea and ear infections are sounding pretty good to me today."

"Why? What happened?"

"The paramedics brought in a fifteen-year-old kid from one of the projects who'd had the bad judgment to disagree with someone who happened to be carrying an assault rifle. When they brought him in he had holes in his stomach, his liver, his lung, and his spleen. As we're wheeling him into the OR he looks up at me and asks 'Will I be okay?' Can you imagine, I looked that kid in the eye and told him I was going to take care of him. Then I watched him bleed to death on the operating table. And why? Because some brain-dead piece of shit had an advanced weapon capable of shooting someone eleven times in as many seconds. When I came home last night I had to throw my underwear away because it was so full of that kid's blood. Now what kind of person would choose to see that kind of thing every day?" She looked at me as if expecting some sort of answer, but there was none.

"You have to remember all the times they don't die," I said. "That and the fact that they don't die because you were there to take care of them."

"Yeah," she replied bitterly. "I patch them together and send them out onto the same shitty street."

"I'll grant you that the idea of getting rich removing cataracts from nice little old ladies is sounding good this morning," I ventured, "but I promise you you'd be bored out of your mind inside of six months."

"But would that be so bad?" sighed Claudia as her beeper went off. "Sometimes I think you and I have got it all wrong. Work is supposed to be boring. It's your life that's supposed to be interesting."

The drive from Hyde Park to Oak Brook takes forty-five minutes and is equally ugly in both directions. As I headed west on I-55, which peels off Lake Shore Drive at McCormick Place, I saw the city fall away only to be replaced by a series of depressing industrial vistas—necrotic rail yards and crumbling factories—all punctuated by garish billboards advertising the riverboat gambling that is legal on the other side of the county line.

Azor Pharmaceuticals had recently abandoned its tony corporate offices downtown in favor of more utilitarian digs in the suburbs. Not only did the move save Stephen a small fortune in municipal taxes, but it also allowed him to consolidate his far-flung research efforts under a single roof. The fact that the roof was in a soulless industrial park in the middle of a suburban wasteland did not seem to bother him at all.

Oak Brook is one of those sterile subdivision cities carved out of cheap farmland and made attractive by its proximity to O'Hare airport. Home of McDonald's Hamburger University and a mammoth shopping mall, it is popular with professional athletes, corporate transfers, and airline pilots—in short, nobody who is planning on sticking around for more than a couple of years. I couldn't believe that Stephen was going to make me go there every day.

Azor's new home was in an antiseptic office building that seemed to have sprung from the asphalt of its parking lot. The outside of the building was shiny, coated with the same material used to make mirrored sunglasses. There was a very simple reason for this—whatever is of use to a legitimate drugmaker is of much greater value to an illegitimate one. Stephen was happy to have a darkly reflective surface be all that Azor Pharmaceuticals presented to the world.

Inside the building the decor was generic and security tight. Besides the ZK-501 project, Azor Pharmaceuticals had several other experimental drugs under development and the threat of corporate espionage was very real. All visitors were carefully scrutinized by a uniformed security guard who checked their names against an approved list before they were allowed in. Employees had to run the magnetic strip on the back of their IDs through a card reader mounted beside the double doors that led into the interior of the building. All bags were searched whenever anyone left the building and every twelve seconds video cameras swept the lobby.

When I arrived I was surprised to find Paramilitary Bill, one of the guards who usually worked the night shift, manning the security desk. He was twenty-four years old with a buzz haircut and a blank expression. Stephen and Danny used to joke that he spent weekends drilling with his militia group—nothing else could account for the combination of his rippling physique and rabid fanaticism. But all joking aside, there was something definitely creepy about Paramilitary Bill and the disconcerting intensity with which he went about his duties. Whenever I really tried to imagine his life outside of work, I always conjured up the same image: a squalid, stripped-down room with an army cot against one wall and a gun collection along the other.

"You've been assigned to Mr. Wohl's office," Bill informed me as I signed the guest sheet. "Dr. Azorini's orders. Here's the key. Do you remember where that is or do you need me to escort you?"

"I know the way," I assured him quickly.

"My condolences about Mr. Wohl. He was a good man."

"Yes, he was," I agreed and quickly made my way across the lobby, glad to have my encounter with Paramilitary Bill behind me.

Compared to the plush clubbiness of Callahan Ross the utilitarian corridors of Azor Pharmaceuticals seemed stark and alien. My high heels clicked against the polished linoleum while the entire building seemed to throb with the pulse of unseen high-tech equipment. From behind closed doors I heard laughter and from the adjacent corridor that housed the ZK-501 labs I heard country music, sad and sweet.

I turned the key and opened the door to Danny's office, scrabbling in the dark until I found the light switch. In the two weeks since he'd left for Japan the place had taken on a desolate air. When the company made the move to the suburbs Danny's old secretary had balked at the additional commute and taken another job downtown. Danny, busy with Takisawa, had not yet had time to replace her. As a result, unopened mail was piled high on his desk, and incoming faxes overflowed the machine spilling out onto the floor. A chain of Post-it notes trailed forlornly from the bottom of his computer screen and everything was covered with a thin layer of dust.

I was just taking off my coat, wondering where to begin, when I heard a knock on the door. I looked up and saw Carl Woodruff leaning against the frame with a thin smile of welcome on his face. Carl, a high-strung Englishman, was the project manager for ZK-501. Originally trained as an organic chemist, he'd had his graduate studies derailed by a bout with Hodgkin's disease. While he'd beaten his cancer, his illness had left him with a commitment to the practical side of pharmaceutical research. Still, his years at the laboratory bench stood him in good stead with the scientists whose work it was his job to oversee and I knew from Stephen that Carl commanded a measure of respect usually not granted to an administrator.

"I've been sent to officially welcome you to the asylum," Carl announced good-naturedly. He was about five foot seven, with a slight build and thinning sandy-colored hair that straggled over his collar. He wore a wrinkled white shirt and a pair of dust-colored corduroys. His aviator glasses seemed to be the biggest thing about him.

"I wish I could say I was happy to be here," I said, extending my arms as if to encompass Danny's entire office.

"Yes, shocking news about Danny and all that," replied Carl. "What was it? Someone told me a ruptured appendix."

"I don't think it was his appendix," I said, pushing down the images of Danny's apartment that were crowding themselves into my brain. "They won't know until after they do the autopsy."

"Stephen tells me you will be joining us full time,"

continued Carl. From his tone of voice I couldn't tell how he felt about it.

"Only until we're done negotiating with the Japanese."

"So then under the circumstances I guess it would be fair to ask you how much you know about chemistry?"

"Enough to know that I didn't want to take a second semester of it in college," I replied.

The look on his face told me that all his worst fears about lawyers had just been realized.

"Would it at least be safe to assume that you know what a molecule is?" he inquired dryly.

"Yes, Carl, I may be a lawyer, but I'm not a moron. I know what a molecule is."

"Good. Then allow me to give you a ten-minute chemistry lesson. Since you understand what a molecule is then surely you realize that while all drugs are molecules, not all molecules are drugs. What makes drug molecules special is how they attach themselves—scientists, of course, use the word *bind*—to other molecules during the course of a disease. Right now ZK-501 is a very powerful drug, but it's too toxic to be used in humans. What we're trying to do is redesign the molecule, to actually alter its molecular structure in such a way as to eliminate those adverse side effects. Given that, what would you think is the first thing we'd need to know?"

"The molecular structure of ZK-501?" I ventured, feeling that it was much too early in the morning for a pop quiz.

"Good answer, but the molecular structure of ZK-501 has been known for several years. Right now, what we're concerned with is trying to figure out the structure of ZKBP."

"What is ZKBP?"

"It's short for ZK-501 binding protein—that's the receptor protein that ZK-501 attaches to in the body. I'm sure you've heard Stephen's standard speech about how designing new drugs is like making keys for locks—diseases are the locks and drugs are the keys. In this case, ZKBP is an exact replica of the relevant lock. Since we're trying to make a better key, knowing how the lock is put together is the critical first step. Ideally, a drug should fit its target perfectly, like two pieces of a jigsaw puzzle." He clasped his hands in a token marriage to demonstrate his point. "That way there are no side effects. From the way it works we now know that ZK-501 doesn't fit perfectly with its target because while it works, it's also practically poisonous. That's why knowing the exact configuration of the target is so important. Once we know it, we can change the structure of ZK-501 to improve the fit and eliminate the side effects. Once we solve the structure of the receptor, the rest of what we have to do will be all mapped out and we'll leapfrog ahead of the competition."

"So how close are you to solving it?"

"Unfortunately the protein has been something of a ball buster," replied Carl apologetically. With his plummy Oxford speech he managed to make even this sound like a refined observation. "So far we've been able to isolate only tiny amounts from human tissue, and crystallography's attempts to divine its structure have so far been, shall we say, inconclusive."

"What about Mikos? Do they have the structure yet?"

"Rumor has it that so far they have the receptor, nothing more."

"Will you beat them to it, do you think?"

"At the rate we're going we'll be lucky if we all emerge from this with our sanity intact."

"What's that supposed to mean?"

"Let's just say that so far everything that could go wrong has gone wrong. We've been plagued by failed experiments, power outages, scarce reagents, unduplicable results, and primary investigators who seem to spend more time at one another's throats than they actually do in their labs."

"It can't be as bad as all that," I protested.

"Let's just put it this way. If it's true that, in science, it is better to be lucky than to be good—this project has been doomed from the get-go."

"Why do you say that?" I asked, with a terrible sinking feeling in my stomach.

"Stephen handpicked the scientists on this project because of what they can do. But when you put them all together and make them work together, you keep on bumping up against who they are."

"And who are they?"

"Half of them are academic scientists. By that I mean researchers who until now have held university appointments and had their research funded by government grants. Most lay people think academic scientists are propelled by some kind of noble search for the truth."

"And are they?"

Carl gave a derisive snort. "No," he replied. "They are looking for something else entirely."

"And what is that?"

"Oh, academic scientists want quite a lot of things." Carl ticked them off on the fingers on his hand. "Important publications, more funding, bigger labs, travel, star power, tenure . . . But in the end it all boils down to the same thing—peer recognition. Believe me when I tell you we are talking about people who are willing to claw one another's eyes out over who gets listed as first author on a research paper that only two hundred people in the entire world are capable of understanding."

"What are the other half like?" I asked.

"The rest of the investigators on the project are all experienced industrial scientists," replied Carl. His respectful tone of voice indicated quite clearly with which group his allegiances lay. "For industry scientists, unlike their academic counterparts, success depends not on reckless self-promotion, but on keeping their best work secret. They are driven not to get their name in print, but to get the drug made."

"And get rich," I interjected.

"Definitely," agreed Carl with a sly smile. "The trouble comes when you mix the two sorts. To industrial scientists, academics are glory-mad prima donnas. On the other hand, academic scientists think industrial scientists are whores." Carl smiled at me serenely from across the mountains of papers that littered Danny's desk.

"Sounds like an interesting group," I said, and wondered what the hell I had gotten myself into.

The ZK-501 project council meeting was held in the first-floor lunchroom, which was the only place big enough to accommodate all the people working on the project. Carl walked me down the hall to show me the way. Then, as we helped ourselves to coffee from a heavy-duty industrial-size percolator at the back of the room, he discreetly pointed out the various investigators as they straggled in for the meeting.

Watching the room slowly fill up, I was immediately struck by how young they all were—not to mention how scruffy looking. Rumpled and unshaven, the ZK-501 scientists looked for all the world like a ragtag bunch of graduate students rousted from the library at closing time. The younger scientists, true to their generation, looked like grunge-band refugees with Walkmen strapped to their belts and headphones slung around their necks. The older ones wore baggy corduroy pants that sagged in the seat and hand-knit sweaters of dirt-colored wool.

The exception was a young woman with a cigarette dangling from one corner of her mouth, her hair dyed a purplish black, who was holding court in the front row. She wore ripped jeans, motorcycle boots, and a T-shirt with one of those ubiquitous yellow smiley faces on the front. The only thing different about hers was that it had a small round bullet hole drawn on its forehead.

"Who's the Hell's Angel?" I inquired.

"That's Lou Remminger," replied Carl.

"That is Lou Remminger?" I demanded incredulously. Remminger was the chemist from Yale who was the lead investigator of the ZK-501 project. According to Stephen, she was to organic chemistry what Michael Jordan is to basketball—the kind of natural talent that turns up only once a generation.

"They say that if she's able to turn ZK-501 into a usable drug they'll have to give her the Nobel prize," Carl whispered, his lips curling into a small smile.

"I wonder what she'll wear to the award ceremony," I replied faintly, envisioning an auditorium filled with scandalized Swedes.

Carl touched my arm. "You see that man with the

turtleneck sitting off by himself? That's Michael Childress, the X-ray crystallographer."

"I've met him. Stephen and I took him out to dinner while Azor was recruiting him from Baxter." I shuddered inwardly at the recollection of that night. With arrogance that bordered on boorishness, Childress had bullied the waiters, monopolized the conversation with tedious monologues about his many accomplishments, and pointedly addressed all his remarks to Stephen as if I'd been invited along to merely fill a seat.

"Michael Childress is a world-class pain in the ass," announced Carl with real venom. "He thinks he was put on earth for the express purpose of telling everyone else what they're doing wrong."

"That must make him very popular," I observed.

"You notice no one will even sit near him." Sure enough, there was a ring of empty seats around Childress like some kind of quarantine. "Do you see the woman sitting behind him with the headphones?" Carl continued.

My eyes settled on a large, raw-boned woman with a cap of dark curls and a very intense expression on her pale face. Her hands twitched nervously across her lap and there were dark circles under her eyes.

"That's Michelle Goodwin," the administrator explained. "She's the second crystallographer on the project."

"Why do you have two?" Crystallographers were a rare and much sought-after specialty. A proven one like Childress was the scientific equivalent of a franchise athlete.

"We have her on loan for a year from Purdue. She was originally hired to work on the integrase project, but after it folded Stephen moved her over here."

"So how do she and Childress get along?" I asked,

remembering what Carl had said back in Danny's office about the rift between academic and industrial scientists.

"She tries to stay out of his way. Actually it's not that hard because he's almost never here."

"Where is he then?" I demanded, remembering how much Stephen was paying him.

"Giving papers, going to site visits, getting interviewed on National Public Radio. It drives Remminger nuts."

"Who's that over there?" I asked, chucking my head in the direction of a man with a wild head of brindle-colored hair and a tobacco-stained mustache.

"That's Dave Borland, our lead protein chemist," replied Carl with a mysterious chuckle. "I'll take you down to see his lab later, but I promise we won't go before lunch."

"Why's that?"

"He's the one who isolates ZKBP, the receptor we were talking about back in Danny's office. It's a very complicated process that we fondly refer to as *grind and bind*. You start by taking human spleens and putting them into an industrial-size blender."

"Where do you get the spleens?" I asked, not sure I wanted to know.

"From a medical supply house."

"You mean you can just call an eight-hundred number and get body parts?"

"Yes. But they're expensive. A spleen from a healthy cadaver costs four hundred sixty dollars. Ones that are discarded during transplantation of other organs we get at a discount. Same-day delivery is extra. It takes about forty spleens to make one gram of binding protein."

"I can see how that would add up," I remarked faintly.

"Believe me, Kate, one thing you learn in this business is that there is no shortage of people who are worth more dead than they are alive."

CHAPTER

6

When Stephen walked into the room conversation evaporated and all eyes turned toward him with the fluid certainty of magnetism. Even Lou Remminger stubbed out her cigarette on the pink frosting of a half-eaten doughnut and offered up the full measure of her attention. I didn't care what Carl Woodruff had just said about the differences in their backgrounds and motivations, the truth was that the scientists in the room had one very important thing in common. They had all come to Azor because Stephen Azorini had promised them personally that it was here they would have a chance to do the best science of their lives.

"What's our status with respect to the receptor?" Stephen demanded without preamble, rolling up his sleeves and scanning the room with his pale blue eyes. His shirt was a small miracle of starch. The old Polish woman who did his ironing was in love with him and somehow she managed to channel all her ardor into his shirts.

"Well, for one thing," sniffed Childress unpleasantly, "there isn't enough of it."

57

Stephen turned to Dave Borland, the protein chemist. "I thought the new process was producing higher yields," he said, lifting one black brow to eloquently punctuate the question.

"There's nothing wrong with the supply of protein," Borland shot back defensively. "The problem is that crystallography is pissing it away. So far they've gotten nearly a gram of pure receptor—twice what everyone else has gotten put together—and they haven't produced a single viable crystal."

"That's not necessarily true," ventured Michelle Goodwin timidly. "I've actually had some success with very small crystals."

"Considering the importance of solving the structure I don't understand why chemistry and imaging should be getting any at all," Michael Childress said, talking right over her as if she'd never spoken.

"There's one more thing we need to factor into all this," interjected Carl, trying to be heard above the others. "We're still having problems with the power."

The ZK-501 labs were so crammed with high-tech equipment that, within three months of moving in, Azor Pharmaceuticals' power demands had outstripped the available supply. For months Commonwealth Edison had been promising to install additional transformers, but in spite of twice-daily calls from Carl Woodruff, no date had as yet been set for the upgrade.

"The electricity is not the problem," announced Lou Remminger, glaring contemptuously at Childress. Despite her punk persona her voice was straight from the Smoky Mountains. The effect was as incongruous as her fingernails. "The supply of receptor is not the problem either.

The problem is that Dr. Childress is doing every other goddamned thing in the world besides his job."

"How dare you!" sputtered Childress, obviously stung by such a direct attack.

"Well," drawled the chemist sweetly. "Would you mind telling me when was the last time you spent a weekend in the lab—or better yet, a full week? Let me see, last week it was a site visit at Johns Hopkins, the week before it was the small-molecules conference in Brussels. . . ."

"Enough," announced Stephen, evidently deciding he had let things go too far. "As the saying goes, as of today all shore leave is canceled. That goes for you, too, Michael. Our friends the Japanese are coming. Takisawa is sending a dozen of their people to visit our labs a week from Monday. That gives us nine days to prepare for a full-blown site visit."

The scientists of the ZK-501 project received this news in stunned silence. Dave Borland, the protein chemist, looked like he'd just been punched in the stomach and I saw a flicker of something very close to panic cross Michelle Goodwin's face. Only Michael Childress seemed unperturbed by the news. Sitting by himself, buffered by empty chairs, he stroked his chin with mandarin-like indifference.

"What I want to know is why, when we have Mikos breathing down our necks, are we wasting time on some damn dog and pony show for the Japanese?" demanded Remminger.

"Because before we make a drug we have to make a deal," replied Stephen impatiently. "Right now this project, which is at least two years away from having a drug to sell, is burning through money at the rate of sixty-five thousand dollars a day. There's no way that this company can continue to absorb those costs without some kind of outside revenue. If anyone here knows someone who has forty million dollars they'd like to gamble on this molecule, speak up now. If not, I suggest we think seriously about how we're going to impress our visitors from Tokyo." He looked hard around the room and waited for a reply before he continued.

"During the next several days each lab head will be meeting with Kate Millholland to go over the information and cost projections. Some of you may have already met Kate in her role as outside counsel and member of the company's board of directors. She has graciously agreed to help us through this negotiation, filling in for the unfortunate vacancy left by Danny Wohl." While Stephen's voice had faltered as he'd uttered his dead friend's name, the other scientists in the room seemed curiously unmoved.

I nodded to the room at large to acknowledge Stephen's introduction, but no one took any notice. Attorneys, I was forced to conclude, were definitely not part of the tribe. From the scientist's perspective, lawyers as a category were a necessary evil—and as such, interchangeable.

"That's all very well," piped a heavily accented German voice from the back, "but while we're busy showing off to our Oriental friends, aren't we in danger of giving ourselves away? I mean, what's to stop Takisawa from taking a peek at what we have so far and going back home and deciding to try their hand on making a new drug themselves?"

"They won't do it because the only people who can make this drug are sitting in this room," pronounced Stephen with more certainty than I knew he felt. From the beginning the negotiation with Takisawa had been one long calculated risk, an elaborate dance of veils with each side seeking to gain the upper hand while revealing tantalizing glimpses of what it wanted and what it was willing to give up to get it.

"Not meaning to sound like a nervous virgin embarking on a date with a drunken sailor," ventured Borland, from beneath his walruslike mustache, "but how far do you think it's safe to go with these guys? I mean, up until now we've been signing lab books every day and having our bags searched every time we leave the building. Are you telling us that now you expect us to just lie back and let them lift up our skirts?"

"Let's put it this way," replied Stephen. "We have to do whatever it takes to make them want us. That means clean white lab coats will be required for all personnel." He stuck his hands deep into his pockets and grinned. "Fishnet stockings will be optional."

I had hoped to catch a word with Stephen after the meeting, but the minute it was over he was immediately surrounded by scientists all jockeying for his attention. I decided to try to catch him later and headed back to Danny's office. It was still so disgustingly early that I figured I'd spend an hour or two getting my bearings. That way by the time I headed back into the city I would have missed the worst of the morning rush hour. My first day working in Oak Brook and already I was developing a commuter's obsession with traffic.

While Danny was in Japan and in the days following his death, a small tide of work had washed up on his desk. Besides the scores of phone messages from people I'd never heard of concerning matters that were completely unknown to me, there were dozens of faxes from Takisawa, some received as recently as that morning, all requesting information in preparation for their upcoming visit. Scanning them, I could see there was nothing Takisawa didn't want to know about the ZK-501 project in particular and Azor Pharmaceuticals in general. Even taking into account the well-known appetite of the Japanese for detail, their inquiries struck me as excessive. Budgets, both actual and projected, personnel records, and depreciated equipment costs were all respectfully requested as a prelude to further discussions.

Putting the faxes in my briefcase to take back to Callahan Ross with me, I turned my attention to the mail, which was stacked a foot high. Flipping through the junk mail and the routine correspondence I came upon a certified letter that had been received and signed for in Danny's absence. I scrabbled in the top drawer of the desk looking for a letter opener and, with a growing sense of dread, slit it open. One look at the contents confirmed my worst fears.

It was another lawsuit.

Azor Pharmaceuticals was currently defending itself against a suit involving its newest drug offering, a compound used in the treatment of schizophrenia. Serezine, tortuous to develop and expensive to produce, had been a controversial drug from the first. Azor had taken its hits in the press when it was announced that a year's treatment with Serezine would cost $10 thousand. Despite the fact that this was only a fraction of what it cost to institutionalize these patients, the media had fed on stories of greedy drug companies for weeks.

Six months after the drug was first made available, Azor was served with a lawsuit, filed in Texas by plaintiffs alleging that the drug had improved the condition of a previously institutionalized nineteen-year-old man to the point where he could be returned home to his family. Unfortunately, once there, he proceeded to murder both his parents and a furnace repairman who had the bad luck to be in the house at the time. Although it appeared that the patient had stopped taking the drug soon after his discharge from the hospital, Azor had nonetheless already racked up close to $100 thousand in legal fees defending itself.

As I read through the complaint in my hand my stomach churned. The family of an East Lansing woman was bringing suit alleging that she had become so despondent while taking Serezine that she killed her three-day-old infant, then took her own life. Feeling sick, I dialed Stephen's extension only to have Rachel tell me smugly that Stephen was in a meeting with the Hemasyn clinical trial group and had left explicit instructions not to be interrupted. Nothing I said was able to sway her, so I hung up the phone and called Callahan Ross to speak to Tom Galloway.

Tom was the litigator at the firm who was preparing the Texas suit for trial. While Tom and, more important, Azor's insurer were both convinced the first suit was baseless, the existence of a second suit could under no circumstances be construed as good news. When I got Tom's secretary on the line she explained that Tom was out of the office for a few days due to a death in the family.

"Just my luck," I thought to myself callously as I slammed the receiver into the cradle. Now I had another crisis that was mine to deal with because someone else had inconveniently dropped dead.

* * *

I arrived back downtown in a foul temper without
having managed to speak to Stephen and with the news
of the second Serezine lawsuit nagging at me like a sore
tooth. As soon as I got in I had to spend a couple of hours
putting out fires in the Nuland Petroleum deal. After that
I devoted the rest of the day to a series of thirty-minute
meetings with the various associates to whom I was dele-
gating my routine cases. It was nearly four o'clock
before I finally found myself with five free minutes for
the corned beef sandwich that my secretary had brought
me as either a very late lunch or an early dinner. I had
managed to wolf down half of it when Cheryl buzzed to
say that Elliott Abelman was in reception wanting to
know whether I had time to see him. I told her to go
ahead and bring him on back, while I quickly consulted
the mirror in my top drawer to make sure I didn't have
mustard on my chin.

"Sorry to just barge in," said Elliott a few minutes later
as he appeared, grinning, in my doorway. He was wearing
a blue blazer and khaki pants, radically casual attire for
the suit-and-tie environs of Callahan Ross. If it weren't
for the bulge from the Browning automatic he wore hol-
stered under his arm he could easily have been mistaken
for a trust-fund brat dropping by to pick up his check.
After six months of deliberate avoidance I found it disconcerting to find Elliott suddenly, even casually, appearing at my office.

When he stepped aside to let Cheryl usher in Joe
Blades, I sprang to my feet. Blades was a homicide cop
and a good friend of Elliott's from his days in the state's
attorneys office when they had worked the gang crimes
unit together.

"Detective Blades," I said, extending my hand in greeting, "this is a very pleasant surprise."

Blades was young for homicide and looked nothing like you'd expect for a man who spent most of his working life gazing down upon the newly deceased. Indeed, with his beard and gold-rimmed glasses he had a vaguely professorial air. In point of fact he'd come to the police department from Princeton, of all places, during that brief season when the idea of recruiting for law enforcement from the Ivy League had come briefly into vogue. Unlike most of his cohorts who'd quickly fled the grim realities of the street for the safe haven of law school, Joe Blades had remained. He had found his calling.

"Come on, make my day, Joe," I said, folding my hands together on top of my desk once we'd all settled comfortably into our respective chairs. "Please tell me that you've been assigned to investigate Danny Wohl's death."

"Right now no one's been assigned to the case," replied Blades. "But as it happens I was one of the detectives who took the unattended-death call, so I did work the scene. Elliott tells me your firm represents the company that Mr. Wohl worked for."

"Yes. I'm also one of the directors of the company."

"So you knew him quite well."

"Professionally, yes. We didn't socialize much outside of the office."

Blades shot me a look that said he knew I didn't have much of a life outside of the office. In the past Blades had tried his hand at playing Cupid between Elliott and me. For a brief flash of time I found myself wondering what Elliott had told him about what had almost happened between the two of us but immediately forced myself to focus on more pressing matters.

"And I take it from what Elliott tells me," he continued, "you and Dr. Azorini have questions about his death."

"Come on, Joe. You went to the scene. Of course we have questions. From the blood all over everything it seems pretty obvious that Danny didn't die quietly in his sleep."

"So far the medical examiner hasn't made any ruling as to cause of death."

"Has the autopsy been performed yet?"

"No."

"Has it at least been scheduled?"

"Not that I'm aware."

"So tell me, when are they going to get around to it? Once they find a name and a cause of death for Jane Doe Number Sixty-three?" I knew it didn't make any sense to get sarcastic with a homicide cop, but the thought of what had happened to Danny passing unnoticed galled me.

"I can't answer that Kate," he replied, not unkindly. "But I can tell you what we have so far."

Blades pulled a small spiral notebook from the inside pocket of his jacket. As he flipped it open I noticed that besides his scribbled notes there were several drawings of stick figures. It took me a second to realize these were representations of Danny's body.

"Mr. Wohl was discovered Monday morning at approximately ten-twenty by the building engineer, who'd let himself into the apartment to check that the heat was on. The weather had turned cold Sunday night and they were having trouble with the furnace in that part of the building. Dispatch took the call at ten thirty-four A.M., and a patrol unit responded immediately. They took one look inside the apartment and got on their radios requesting backups. It was called into homicide at ten thirty-six as a possible fatal stabbing. Art Wypiszinski and I were out interviewing family members of one of Sarrek's suspected victims and took the call, but we didn't get there until eleven fifty-one. As soon as we walked in the door we figured we were looking at some kind of dispute between homosexual lovers."

"Why is that?" I asked, curious about what would lead him to draw that conclusion so quickly.

"No motive besides sex produces that kind of overkill," replied Blades matter-of-factly, "and no woman is strong enough to do that kind of damage to a man. Besides, there was no sign of forced entry, so it seemed likely that the deceased knew his assailant and let him into the apartment. From the blood trail it looked as though Mr. Wohl was on his feet when the attack started and despite sustaining severe injuries, he managed to stay on his feet for several minutes and put up a fight. That would explain not just the blood splatter, but the overturned furniture and the overall condition of the apartment."

"Did anybody hear anything?" Elliott asked.

Blades shook his head. "A canvass of the neighbors turned up nothing. In that kind of building no one knows anybody else. Besides, the victim's apartment was a corner unit on the top floor of the building. The only wall he shared with another unit was the bedroom and the struggle appeared to have been limited to the front of the apartment."

"What about the apartment below?" I demanded.

"Out of town for the weekend. I'm not sure they would have been able to hear anything because the building is pretty solidly built." Joe Blades consulted his notes again before continuing. "From the dishes in the sink and the condoms in the wastebasket it looked as though the deceased had recently had company. The condoms had been used two-ply, by the way."

"Why is that significant?" I asked, not meaning to sound naive.

"The condoms had been used two at a time, doubled. It usually indicates that one of the partners had AIDS or was afraid of contracting the disease."

"Danny was HIV positive," I said. "Whether he technically had AIDS is something you'd have to get from his doctor."

"Other than that, was he sick?"

"No. But the anti-AIDS drugs he was taking were giving him a bad time with side effects."

"What kind of side effects?"

"Nausea, weakness, muscle pain. About once every two weeks he'd just feel so crummy he wouldn't be able to get out of bed and drag himself into the office. That's why nobody thought anything of it when he didn't show up to work on Monday morning. He'd just been on a grueling business trip to the Orient. Everyone at Azor just assumed that he wasn't feeling well."

"It's going to be up to the medical examiner to give us the time of death, but when we got there rigor was already starting to pass off in the upper extremities. By my guess he'd been dead at least twenty-four hours. He didn't have a history of hemophilia or some other blood-clotting disorders that you know of, did he?"

"No," I replied, puzzled. "Why do you keep asking?"

"When we arrived at the scene the body was lying facedown in the living room a few feet away from the telephone in a large pool of blood. From that position there were no visible wounds, but we figured that once the lab boys were finished and we rolled him over, we'd find the killer's handiwork all over the victim's face and chest."

"And did you?" I asked.

"No," replied Blades, removing his gold-rimmed glasses and slowly polishing them with the fat end of his tie. "When we turned him over there wasn't a mark on him."

CHAPTER

7

"How is that possible given the condition of the apartment?" I demanded. "There was blood all over the walls and the furniture was turned over. You said yourself you found him lying facedown in a pool of blood. What you're telling me now makes absolutely no sense."

Blades raised both his hands in the shrug universally understood to indicate that this was not his problem. "I'm not pretending it makes sense," he countered. "I'm only telling you what I saw. When we rolled him over he was covered in blood all right. It was smeared all over his face, his hair was stiff with it, and his clothes were completely soaked. But there were no wounds of any kind that I could see and no other signs of injury or trauma. Certainly nothing like what we were expecting to see given the condition of the apartment."

"What about under his clothes?" I asked, mentally scrambling to try and make what Blades was telling me fit in with what I imagined had taken place in Danny's apartment. "Could the killer have removed Danny's clothes and dressed him in something else to hide the wounds?"

"Yeah," replied Blades, "but why would he want to? Besides, if that had happened we'd have seen much less blood on his clothes. As it was they were so saturated you couldn't even begin to guess the color of the fabric."

"Okay then," I said, my frustration mounting. "You tell me. What happened to him?"

"He bled to death."

"I'd say that was pretty obvious," I snapped, losing patience. "What I want to know is how."

"The medical examiner is in charge of how. My job is to find out who."

"Come on, Joe," urged Elliott. "You've looked at a lot of dead guys. You're telling me you aren't even willing to make a guess?"

"I honestly don't know," replied Blades, shaking his head. "Vampires maybe? I'm serious, this is a strange one."

"Could his AIDS have had something to do with it, do you think?" I asked, unable to come up with anything else.

"You'd have to ask a doctor, but I've got to tell you, there's lots of ways that AIDS can kill you, but none of them is quick. I honestly wish I had something else to tell you, Kate. I'm not jerking your chain. But I'm afraid I came here to tell you that all we really can do now is wait for the autopsy results."

"But when will we get them?"

"Right now the medical examiner's office is being squeezed from every direction to identify Sarrek's victims and homicide is stretched to the limit. I've been pulled off regular duty and assigned to the task force investigating Sarrek. Everybody else is working double shifts trying to put together a case against this creep."

"And in the meantime what about Danny?" I demanded, suddenly feeling very angry.

"Sorry, Kate," said Blades. "Word from above is 'no unnecessary inquiries.' The medical examiner's got to say the death's suspicious before anyone can take the next step. The way things are now it could mean my shield if I stepped out of line on this one."

"Just tell me one thing," I said. "If the highway patrol had pulled Sarrek over in Texas as opposed to Illinois, how would you be working Danny Wohl's death?"

"As a probable homicide," replied Blades with a rueful shake of his head. "Definitely a probable homicide, at least until I heard otherwise from the ME's office."

"Then what about Elliott?" I asked, my gaze shifting from one man to the other. "Why couldn't he start looking into things?"

"Under the circumstances I'd be willing to give him access to any information we have," said Blades.

"Good," I declared.

Blades turned to Elliott. "I'd start by trying to find out who was with him in the apartment when he died. We lifted his address book and his bankbook. I'll get you copies."

"What makes you think there was someone with him?" I asked sharply.

"There were two sets of footprints," answered the detective, "and only one of them matched the victim. One set corresponded to the dress shoes that Wohl was wearing when we found him. The other looks to have been made by a slightly smaller, narrower athletic shoe."

"Any chance the athletic shoes belonged to one of the people who found the body?" asked Elliott.

Blades shook his head. "The building engineer never made it past the front door. He took one look at the blood, locked the door behind him, and hightailed it down to the management office on the first floor to call 911. He swears he didn't open it back up until the uniforms arrived. Besides, it's not only the footprints that point to someone else having been in the apartment at the time of Mr. Wohl's death."

"What else is there?" I asked.

"We found traces of dried blood in the cracks in the wood floor in the kitchen and blood in the trap in the sink. Also, the tape was missing from the answering machine. We turned the place upside down looking for it, but we never found it. Of course, there may be some other explanation for why it wasn't there, but I'm willing to bet that whoever was in the apartment when Mr. Wohl died took it with him when he left."

"Why would he do that?" I asked even though deep down I already knew the answer.

"For the same reason he stood in the kitchen after Mr. Wohl was dead and washed his blood down the sink. Because whoever it was didn't want anyone to know that he had ever been there."

As soon as Elliott and Blades left, I picked up the phone and tried to reach Stephen only to be told by the officious Rachel that he was in yet another meeting and she didn't dare disturb him. Aggravated, I left another urgent message and tried to get back to work, but I found it impossible to concentrate. Flashes of Danny's apartment kept running through my head like a disturbing movie whose images were impossible to forget. As unsettled as I'd been while I was in Danny's apartment, I'd at least felt sure of what it was I was seeing. Educated by the movies, inured by the news, I had been certain I was looking at the aftermath of a violent and bloody crime.

Now, like stepping in front of a fun-house mirror, Joe Blades's revelations had twisted those assumptions around to the point where I didn't feel certain about anything I'd seen.

The phone rang and I jumped. I looked at my watch. Cheryl must have gone while I was still meeting with the two detectives. On Thursdays she had class at five. I was hoping it was Stephen, but instead it was Mimi Sheraton, the decorator. She was calling on her cellular phone from the new apartment. In her own restrained and aristocratic way, she sounded terribly upset.

"Oh, Kate. I'm so glad I was able to reach you. I'm here with Dick Brimstead, the architect, and I'm afraid he's found something that you need to have a look at right away."

"What is it?" I asked with a sinking feeling in the pit of my stomach. I was really not sure I could handle any more bad news.

"It really would be better if you could come and see it for yourself. Is there any chance you could run over here now?"

"I'm right in the middle of something," I ventured, staring helplessly around my office at everything I needed to get done before I called it a day.

"It would take only a few minutes," she pressed.

I looked at the pile of faxes from Takisawa still sitting in front of me, unread. "I'll catch a cab and be right over," I sighed.

Arriving at the apartment, I found Mimi waiting for me in the foyer with Dick Brimstead, a distinguished man of sixty with close-cropped gray hair and watery blue eyes.

I took a deep breath, forced myself to smile, and made a determined effort to not seem brusque. "So," I said. "What seems to be the trouble?"

"Let's go upstairs, shall we?" announced Mimi brightly, leading the way up the graceful curve of the David Adler staircase. We trailed her along the upstairs gallery and through the French doors into the ballroom.

It was my favorite room in the apartment. It didn't matter to me that it was a complete waste, that Stephen and I would never have a party big enough to fill even half of it. Whenever Stephen asked me what I was going to do with it I always told him I planned on taking up roller skating. The truth is, the only thing I wanted to do with it was own it.

If it is possible for an architect to give expression to his genius in a single room, then this was David Adler's. A masterpiece of proportion, it was a completely gorgeous, lavishly perfect space, lit by a mammoth confection of a crystal chandelier and lined with gracefully arched windows which overlooked the lake. My grandmother had commissioned an artist to paint cherubs on the ceiling, and he'd used my brother Teddy, my sister Beth, and me as models. In subsequent years Teddy had grown into a troubled teenager. He'd committed suicide when he was fifteen, but when I looked up at the ceiling in this place I still saw him looking down on me from beneath his halo, an impish smile on his face.

"It will be easier to see it if we turn off the lights," said Brimstead. Mimi obliged and the room went dark. In the distance I could see the beacon of the lighthouse on the lake and, to the south, the glittering lights of the Ferris wheel at Navy Pier. Dick Brimstead produced a powerful flashlight from his pocket and shone it up at the ceiling.

"There, can you see those deep cracks right along the line of the light?" he asked. "And there?"

"Yes. I see."

"They follow the line of the structural beams that support the ceiling," added Mimi, switching on the light.

"So does this mean we're going to have to replaster the whole thing?" I inquired uncertainly. As much as I hated to admit it, I wished my mother was here.

"It's a little bit more complicated than that, I'm afraid," the architect informed me. "Let's go take a quick peek at the roof, shall we?"

We went out the upstairs door to the apartment and took the elevator as far up as it would go. When I was little I had always loved to go up onto the roof. On the Fourth of July we used to haul out lawn chairs and set them up on the tar-paper surface, sticky from the heat, to watch the fireworks over the lake. Dick Brimstead held open the service door for me. When I stepped outside, I was astonished by what I saw.

In the years since I'd lived there someone had transformed the roof of the building into a private park. Instead of the tar paper that I expected to find under my feet, there was dirt and grass. Along the western side, trees and bushes had been planted. In the center of this urban idyll there was an enormous wooden play structure that looked like a castle.

"How did this get here?" I asked in astonishment.

"When Paul Riskoff bought the Maxwells' old apartment he petitioned the co-op board to let him put in a play area for his children. They agreed, provided he paid for building and maintaining it himself."

Paul Riskoff, not yet forty, represented a new generation of robber baron, so the lavishness of his private playground did not really surprise me. I'd seen pictures that *Chicago Magazine* ran of his apartment after he and his third wife, Tiffany, had redecorated it. It was filled with tapestries, winged statuary, and overstuffed and gold-leaf-stamped everything else.

"I'll say one thing for him," I offered finally. "When he does a thing, he doesn't do it halfway. . . ."

"That may be so," replied Mimi tartly. "But after it rains the soil gets so heavy that it's making your ceiling cave in."

When I got back to the firm I found a message waiting for me that Stephen had called. He was on his way downtown and would be downstairs to pick me up in five minutes. As quickly as I could I stuffed my trial bag with the work that couldn't wait until morning and lugged it back downstairs. When I got there Stephen was already waiting at the curb.

"I talked to my father today," he said as soon as I'd gotten into the car. "He says he'll see what he can do about speeding up the autopsy."

Anthony Azorini's ties to organized crime gave him a piece of every politician who could be bought in this city. Needless to say, Stephen's relationship with his father was somewhat problematic. Ironically, Danny was one of the few people who would have appreciated what that one phone call must have cost him.

As we drove I told him about my visit from Joe Blades.

"So who do *you* think was in the apartment with him?" I asked by way of conclusion.

"I have no idea. There was a whole part of Danny's life that you and I knew nothing about."

"You mean his sex life."

"I mean his gay life. I have no idea what Danny did when he wasn't working, who he was with, what he was into. . . ."

"So what you're saying is it could have been almost anybody," I replied mournfully. "A friend, a lover, or just some guy he picked up at a bar."

"You know what really pisses me off about all of this?" declared Stephen bitterly. "Today is Thursday. Danny died sometime on Sunday. Almost five days have gone by and we still have no idea who or what killed him. And why? Because of this animal Sarrek. He may not have confessed, but they know he killed those women. They know he killed them and they have him in custody. All the evidence they're ever going to need to convict him is inside that truck. But while the entire police department and the FBI are all working overtime on Sarrek, whatever clues there are in Danny's case are just slipping away. What does it matter whether they put Sarrek away for one murder or for sixty?"

"It matters to the families of his victims," I observed quietly.

"I'd like to think it's concern for them that is the engine driving this whole thing, but I'm not that naive anymore. The truth is that these days no misfortune goes unmined. There is money in this. Promotions, book deals, and media exposure. Political careers are being made on the backs of these dead women. Believe me, there are people in this town who will be feeding on the grief of those families until the day the made-for-TV movie is aired."

* * *

Once we got upstairs to Stephen's apartment, we began to unpack the cartons of Thai food we'd picked up on the way. As he pulled plates from the cupboards and set the table I poured him a beer.

"Drink this," I said, handing it to him. "You're going to need it."

He took the glass and eyed me suspiciously. "Why?" he asked.

"Just drink."

Stephen raised his glass and drained it.

"Okay. Now tell me what's going on," he said.

"Mimi called me today," I said, refilling his glass.

"Oh, no. Did she send us a bill already?"

"When we get Mimi's bill you're not going to need a drink, you're going to need anesthesia. No, she brought the architect over to look at the back bedrooms this afternoon."

"And?" he prompted.

"And there's a small structural problem with the apartment."

"What is it?" asked Stephen, accepting the refill.

"The ceiling is caving in on the second floor."

"What?"

"It seems that Paul Riskoff got the co-op board to allow him to build a playground for his children on the top of the building. But you know Riskoff. He didn't run out to Toys 'R' Us and pick up a plastic sandbox and a blow-up wading pool. He put about a hundred tons of dirt on top of the roof. He planted trees—big trees. Unfortunately it looks like the roof isn't structurally strong enough to support it."

"This can't be happening. . . ." he moaned. My heart

went out to him. Little did he know that in the grand
scheme of things the problem with the roof was the relatively good news. I poured him another beer. He drained it.

"Anything else?" he asked.

"Azor's been named in another wrongful-death complaint involving Serezine."

"Oh, no!" he wailed, laying his head down on the table
in front of him. I couldn't tell whether he was angry or
just afraid.

I produced a copy of the complaint from my briefcase
and poured myself a beer while he read through it
quickly.

"This is bullshit," he announced, looking up from the
last page. "Serezine is contraindicated during pregnancy."

"Meaning even if she was taking it she shouldn't have
been?" I ventured, wondering whether that, in and of
itself, would help us in court or whether it just meant that
the doctor who'd prescribed it was another deep pocket
to be sued.

"That's right. It contains tribulytarin which has been
known to cause birth defects. No doctor in their right
mind would prescribe it for a pregnant woman."

"What if she was given it after she delivered the
baby?"

"Then she wouldn't have been on it long enough for
the drug to have reached a therapeutic dose. It takes at
least a six-week course of the drug before it begins to
work. This whole lawsuit is complete bullshit."

"Let's just hope it's not the kind of bullshit a jury will
believe."

"What do you mean by that? I mean, I'm very sorry
about this young woman and her baby. But it's not our

fault. You know her family is just looking for someone to blame and everyone wants to go after a drug company because they think we've got the most money."

"Even if you're right, you're still going to have to defend yourself against it," I told him.

"So what you're saying is that right or wrong, it's still going to cost us a fucking fortune," he continued, working up steam. "The goddamned lawyers are the only ones who are going to make out like bandits. What does Tom Galloway have to say about all of this? When he got the news I bet you he ran right out and put a down payment on a condo in Aspen." Considering that drugmakers are probably the only people more widely vilified than attorneys, he'd generally be more reluctant to slam somebody else's profession, but in these circumstances I had to admit he had a point.

"He doesn't know yet," I told him. "He's out of the office because of a death in the family. He'll be back tomorrow. I'm just relieved you think the drug didn't have anything to do with this young woman's death and that of her baby."

"Serezine is a drug of last resort, Kate. They don't give it to you unless they've tried everything else first and nothing has worked. It's a very expensive drug to produce and it's effective for only some patients. We knew we were going to take a lot of flack the minute we decided to put it on the market. But for some patients, people who have literally spent years in padded cells and straitjackets, it gives them their life back." He leaned across the table and his eyes drilled into mine. "We can't let the actions of ignorant people stop us from doing what we know is right, Kate. Not now. Not ever."

* * *

Leaving Stephen to clean up the dinner things, I took my beer into the solarium, a circular room at the front of the apartment whose wide windows faced north, embracing my favorite view of the city. During the day, the room was filled with light, but at night it seemed to hang out over the dark void of the lake, the glittering splendor of the downtown skyline beckoning from a distance. I sat on the window seat, hugging my knees and nursing my beer. I felt bone tired from getting up so early and all the shocks of the day. I thought about what Stephen had said about this most recent Serezine suit and felt discouraged. I thought about the garden on the roof of our new building and what I knew about Paul Riskoff and I knew we were in for an ugly fight. Paul Riskoff didn't get where he was by being a gentleman. Indeed, one of my partners who knew him well said that he wouldn't believe Paul Riskoff if his tongue were notarized.

But finally what I thought about, what I couldn't stop thinking about, was what it must have been like to stand at the kitchen sink and wash Danny's warm blood down the drain. What had it taken to close the door on his apartment, step out into the anonymous hallway, and take the elevator to the street?

Stephen came in quietly and sat down behind me. I leaned back into his broad chest and felt his arms circle around me. In every other area of our relationship I feel as though we tread on constantly shifting ground. Fifty nights a year we stand side by side in evening dress, sipping champagne and displaying our good manners. By day we are lawyer and client, sorting through an increasingly difficult and complex world. It is only in his arms that I feel certain.

It is more than that we are physically good together.

That Stephen would be good with anyone, I have no doubt. He is a wonderful lover—athletic, inventive, and generous. But there is something else that draws me. It is as if through each encounter I strain to glimpse more of him. I am seduced, time and time again, by the promise of finally knowing him, of moving beyond the fireworks of physical attraction and the thread of shared history that binds us together.

My roommate, Claudia, does not approve of my relationship with Stephen. She has been known to call him my disease and tells me I am settling for the safety of a limited relationship. When she's really feeling pissy, she accuses me of being shallow, of being seduced by Stephen's good looks, or she insists I'm a coward for not being willing to step into the unknown and give someone else a chance.

All I know is that when Stephen puts his arms around me and buries his face in my hair, I cannot hear any of her warnings. He pulls me toward him, and Claudia's arguments, the unspoken criticism of my partners, the reasoned voice of my own judgment are all drowned out by the rushing in my ears and the power of an attraction that is like a force that comes right up out of the ground.

CHAPTER
8

I had a hard time reconciling the five-page curriculum vitae that Stephen had left on my pillow for me to read with the black-clad rebel who stood before me. My plan for the day called for me to begin with a brief tour of Lou Remminger's lab in order to get an overview of the ZK-501 project. The trouble was that every time I looked at the world-famous chemist all I could think of was what she would look like given twenty minutes in a room with my mother and an ample supply of soap and water.

About Dr. Remminger this much I knew already. She'd arrived at Azor unannounced the preceding April and marched into Stephen's office. To his astonishment she set a glass vial on the desk without saying a word. In it was three grams of ZK-501—at that time it was the world's entire supply.

A graduate student in Remminger's lab, fishing around for a dissertation topic, had purified it as an exercise and then spent the next several months divining its structure. When he presented his preliminary results to Remminger she immediately recognized the molecule's potential and hastily began conducting tests in animals. The results confirmed what she'd suspected—ZK-501 dramatically reduced inflammation in tissue. That all the animals in question also died did nothing to dampen her enthusiasm.

Before the day she showed up at Azor, Stephen had known Lou Remminger by reputation only. Heretical, brilliant, and blessed with a killer instinct for doing the right experiment, at thirty-one Remminger was considered one of the world's preeminent organic chemists. Yale had granted her tenure on her twenty-eighth birthday and since then Harvard had tried three times unsuccessfully to woo her to Cambridge. He could hardly believe that now she was telling Stephen that she wanted to come to work for Azor.

Lou Remminger believed that ZK-501, like cortisone, was a spectacular trigger of a molecule—one of the body's master compounds for reengineering the behavior of immune cells. No doubt scenting the possibility of a Nobel prize, she had come to Stephen hoping for the chance to turn it into a drug.

In New Haven there had been nothing but obstacles. Funding was difficult, lab space scarce, and Remminger had already exhausted what little patience she had for the endless committees from which she had to seek approval. In Stephen she sensed a kindred spirit, or at least a fellow gambler.

Historically, new drugs have all been discovered through a process known as screening—legions of scientists in factory-like labs cooking up obscure dirt samples and testing them for reactivity. Like panning for gold, it is an inefficient system that relies primarily on luck. Indeed, it was Stephen's disdain for just this monkeys-with-typewriters approach that had led him to launch Azor Pharmaceuticals in the first place.

What Lou Remminger proposed was something completely different. Using a process called structure-based drug design, she wanted to build a new drug the way you would build a new house—not brick by brick, but atom by atom. With ZK-501 as a blueprint, Remminger meant to construct a better molecule, one with the side effect–causing structures removed.

As he listened to her Stephen realized that for Remminger to successfully synthesize something as complicated as the ZK-501 analog she would first have to find a chemical reaction for each step of the process, one that placed the right atom in exactly the right configuration. The steps would then have to be ordered so that the later ones would not undo the earlier ones. Most important of all, the new molecule would have to be unique enough to patent, economical to produce, capable of being put into a pill or capsule, and hardy enough to survive in the digestive system long enough to reach its target.

New drugs are expensive long shots with sickening odds. Only one in thirty-five thousand new compounds becomes a successful drug. But Stephen had not gotten where he was by being afraid to roll the bones. He recognized that in Remminger's unconventional genius stood his best chance of seeing whether structure-based design could be made to work.

"ZK-501 is such a big, sexy molecule," confided Lou Remminger as she led me along a row of black-topped lab benches. "If I were a man it would definitely give me a hard-on." She stopped beside a decrepit Mr. Coffee and poured us each a cup of dark, thick liquid from the pot wedged in between an autoclave and a centrifuge. I took a sniff and even though I usually drink it black I reached for the cream and sugar.

"You know that the quality of coffee in a lab is inversely related to the quality of its research," she continued in her ripe Appalachian drawl as I dumped in a hefty slug of powdered creamer to drown the taste.

We made our way back into her office, a cluttered cubicle that held a desk piled high with papers, scientific journals, and a hundred other kinds of junk—pliers, a deflated soccer ball—even a Talbots catalog. Remminger shifted some piles in order to make a place for me to sit down. Then she took a seat behind her desk, pulled out the bottom drawer, and propped her motorcycle-booted feet on top of it.

"So tell me what you want to know," she announced with a smile of challenge on her face. Her teeth, I noticed, were crooked, especially on the bottom. The *Lou* was short for Amylou and my guess was that there had been little enough money for necessities in the depressed mining town of her childhood that braces had never even been spoken of.

"I want to understand what you're trying to do."

"Get famous. Win the Nobel prize. Save the world. Beat Mikos to a new drug. . . ." There was no amusement in her voice, no self-mockery.

"It sounds like you're pretty sure you're going to be able to do it."

"Right now that depends on whether crystallography can get their act together and deliver the structure of ZKBP," she declared flatly. "Until then we're just sitting around with our thumbs up our asses."

I looked over my shoulder at her lab. There were five or

six benches, each under its own ventilation hood, with more than a dozen people that I could see, all hard at work.

"Looks like you're pretty busy," I said.

"Busy doin' busy work," she replied. "Right now what we're doin' is exactly the same kind of shit we're supposed to be trying to make obsolete."

"What's that?"

"Trial and error. We make a compound, then we test it. Then we change it slightly and test it again. Then we compare the two of them then make a third molecule that maximizes the best features of the first two. . . ." She made a loud snoring sound and let her head flop down on her chest like a marionette on a dropped string.

"So when do you think Childress will solve the structure?" I asked, not knowing what else to say.

"Who knows? So far they don't even have diffraction-grade crystals."

"I apologize if I sound hopelessly ignorant, but why do they have to grow crystals in the first place?"

Lou Remminger picked up my coffee cup and looked at the muddy liquid it contained. "Let's say we wanted to learn the molecular structure of the coffee in this cup," she began. "How would you go about doing that?"

"I have no idea. Look at it under the microscope?"

"Wouldn't work. Coffee molecules aren't big enough to see under a regular microscope. It would just look like dirty water. No, the first thing you'd want to do is separate out the coffee from everything else you've got in this cup. Right now there's coffee, but there's also water, sugar, and whatever it is they put in that Cremora shit. The first thing we'd want to do is filter out all that stuff so that all we have left is coffee. If you want to draw parallels to this project, filtering out the junk would be Dave Borland's job."

"So then what happens once all you have left is coffee?"

"Then we'd have to find a way to be able to see its molecular structure."

"Please don't make me guess how to do that," I pleaded.

"The easiest way would be to crystallize it."

"How do you know it will form a crystal?"

"In theory, given the right conditions, any substance can be made to crystallize."

"Anything?"

"Anything. Of course, some things are easier than others. Sugar and salt, for example, crystallize real easy. ZKBP, on the other hand, is an absolute bitch."

"But why crystals?"

"Because the shape of the crystal that any substance forms is unique to that substance. A sugar crystal looks different from a salt crystal. It's like snowflakes. Every kind of molecule is unique."

"So assuming you are able to make a crystal of pure coffee, then what?"

"Then we'd shoot special X rays into it and use a computer to map how the X rays diffract. That way we'll be able to put together a picture of what the molecule looks like. It's kind of like shining a laser beam at a crystal chandelier and then deducing what the chandelier looks like from the scattered dots of light."

"It sounds complicated."

"Actually, the hardest part is growing the crystals. Computers grind through the mountains of data generated by the diffraction. Once you get crystals you almost always get the structure. It's just a matter of time."

"So what you're saying is there's a chance Childress won't be able to grow crystals at all?" I asked with a sick feeling in the pit of my stomach. I couldn't help but think of the millions of dollars Azor had already sunk into the project. Millions of dollars that would be as good as flushed down the toilet if Childress couldn't come up with the crystals.

"Crystallography is just like voodoo," said Remminger. "Sometimes you just gotta believe."

"I can't say I find that terribly reassuring," I said, knowing that I sounded like a stereotypical lawyer.

"Like my grandma always says: honey, sometimes you just gotta have faith." I'm sure I didn't look exactly convinced. "Did Stephen ever tell you how I decided to become a chemist?" she asked.

"No."

"Well, I wasn't much of a student growing up," she began. "Not that that was any big deal. Most everyone where I grew up either went to work in the mines or in the poultry processing plant after they left school. When people where I come from talk about higher education they're usually talking about beauty college. High school wasn't for getting an education anyway, it was for getting drunk and partying, two things I was plenty good at. At some point during my senior year, one of the guidance counselors talked me into the taking the SATs. Hell, I wasn't even sure what they were for. But it turned out that I scored real high—high enough to get a free ride to the University of Virginia.

"What the hell, I thought. Can't be worse than staying here and plucking chickens, so I figured I might as well give ole U.Va. a try. Well, I'll tell you right now, I hated it. All the other kids treated me like trailer-park trash—probably because that's what I was. By the end of orientation I had pretty much decided I was going to flunk out. With that in mind I didn't pay much attention to signing up for classes. Hell, I figured I wasn't going to be around for much longer so I picked them by the alphabet. You know, like ordering from a Chinese menu, I took one from column A, one from column B. . . . I ended up registered for anthropology, ballroom dancing, chemistry, and data processing. I told myself I'd go to each class for a week just to see whether there were any guys worth sleeping with. The rest of the time I concentrated on getting drunk.

"I stuck to my schedule so I didn't get to chemistry until the third week. That Monday I went to class and took a seat in the back row and started scouting out the guys. It was pretty slim pickings, let me tell you—worse than ballroom dancing. I'd practically made up my mind to get up and leave then and there when the professor went up to the board and started drawing atomic orbitals. Of course, at the time I didn't know what they were, but that didn't matter—to me they were absolutely the most beautiful thing I'd ever seen in my life.

"From that moment on I forgot everything else, how geeky the guys were, how miserable I was at college. . . . The orbitals were a revelation. Not only were they gorgeous—those big ovals of colored chalk—but I understood them. I understood everything the professor said. It was amazing, like going to another country and discovering that somehow you already speak the language.

"When the lecture was over, all I could think of was

that if this was chemistry, then chemistry is what I wanted to do, what I had to do. I ran right over to the bookstore and bought the textbook. Oh no, I thought, this is where it's going to start getting hard. I lay down on the bed and every time I started a new chapter I'd say to myself, okay, now this is where I'm going to not understand it. But that never happened. I read that whole book from start to finish that night. I just couldn't get enough of it.

"In four years I took every undergraduate and graduate course offered by the chemistry department. I took most of the biology and physics courses, too. When I graduated, they couldn't figure out which degrees to give me since I'd fulfilled the requirements for about four of them. And yet, you know what happened when I got to graduate school? I had to fight with guys like Michael Childress to work in a halfway decent lab. In every class, I had to put up with pencil-necked dweebs not listening to what I had to say because I was a woman. Believe me, if I'd been a man they'd have treated me like the fucking messiah."

"You don't think they might have been a little put off by your rather unconventional style?" I ventured, no doubt sounding like a female version of a pencil-necked dweeb.

Lou Remminger tilted her head back and cackled. "You don't think I dressed like this when I was in graduate school, do you? Hell, it's taken me years to get pissed off enough to start dressing like this."

When I got back to Danny's office I was surprised to find Elliott Abelman sitting behind the desk systematically going through the drawers. I wanted to say something clever, but I couldn't think of anything, so instead I just stood in the doorway watching him. He was wearing a blue dress shirt, open at the neck, and the soft mop of his brown hair flopped across his forehead like a little boy's as he peered and rooted through the various compartments of the desk. At some point he must have sensed he was being watched because he looked up suddenly, grinning and unrepentant.

"Whatcha lookin' for?" I asked, folding my arms across my chest.

"Clues," he said with a big grin.

"So what have you found?"

"Packets of soy sauce, take-out menus, breath mints, rubber bands, and four bottles of Maalox. Looks like Stephen must be a rough boss to work for."

"That's not it. Lots of the drugs Danny was taking were hard on his stomach."

"What was he taking?"

"You'd have to ask his doctor," I said, sliding into the visitor's chair, "but as far as I know he was on the 'Crixivan cocktail.' That's a combination of Crixivan, AZT, and 3TC taken on a very rigid schedule—three times a day with no food for an hour before and two hours after. It works out to something like twenty-two pills a day."

"And this was to get rid of his AIDS?"

"The drugs can't get rid of the AIDS. They just keep it from making more virus."

Elliott reached beneath the desk and pulled out Danny's briefcase. "Your friend Stephen asked me to bring this down to you. He said Danny took it with him on the trip to Japan."

"Oh, good. It has all of Danny's notes in it. I've got to go through them."

"Notes about what?"

"The negotiations he and Stephen were having with the Takisawa Corporation."

"Was that part of Danny's job as in-house counsel?"

"They had to call him something so that was his title, but he really did just about everything. In addition to overseeing the company's legal affairs, he negotiated transactions, managed the financial side of the company, handled shareholder relations. . . ."

"So what's the impact of his death going to be on the company?"

"It's never good to lose key personnel for any reason."

"What about the deal he was working on? Could someone have been trying to sabotage the negotiations?"

I made a face. "You need to stop seeing so many movies," I replied. "Besides, if a competitor wanted to torpedo the ZK-501 project they'd go after one of the key scientists, Lou Remminger or Michael Childress. They wouldn't kill Danny."

"What about his personal life?"

"What about it?"

"Could he have been involved with anyone from the office?"

"I don't know," I replied, thinking about the homely assemblage at the ZK-501 meeting. "I don't think so."

"Do you know if he was seeing anyone regularly, somebody from outside the office?"

"Danny was always pretty vague when he talked about how he'd spent the weekend. I mean, he did a lot of great stuff—went to the theater, parties—but it was always with 'friends.' "

"And you never got the sense that he was part of a couple, that there was someone special."

I shook my head slowly.

"You're sure he never mentioned anyone?"

I thought for a moment.

"Oh god!" I exclaimed suddenly. "There was someone once, but it was hardly the love of his life. This was a few years ago when we were doing the IPO, taking the company public."

"I know what an IPO is."

"Well, then you know what an intensely miserable chunk of work it is, all the regulations, all the filings. We were on an all-night jag at the legal printers, punch-drunk from lack of sleep and waiting to go over the proofs. I said something about wanting to get home to my own bed and Danny said something about being perfectly happy right where he was because nobody could find him. When I asked him about it, he told me he'd just started dating someone, but it turned out he was a psycho killer."

"Literally?"

"No, I don't think he meant it literally," I replied, thinking that we all had a bit too much of Stanley Sarrek and his freezer on the brain. "But he told me some of the things the guy did."

"Like what?"

"Like leaving creepy messages on his answering machine. Following him. I guess right before Danny and I had had this conversation this guy talked the janitor of Danny's building into letting him into Danny's apartment. Danny came home late from work one night and found him sitting there in the living room with all these candles burning. When I asked Danny how he managed to get rid of him, he said he grabbed the guy's wallet, dropped it out the window, and then after the guy ran downstairs to get it, Danny says he locked the doors and called the police."

"And when did all this happen?"

"We finished the IPO three years ago last October, so it must have been somewhere around then. You know, come to think of it, Danny moved not too long after that. I wonder if there was some connection."

"Did Stephen and Danny travel together often?" asked Elliott, seemingly from out of the blue.

"Of course they did."

"So this trip to Japan was not the first time?"

"Not by a long shot and I know where you're going with this, Abelman, and that dog won't hunt." Law enforcement types were all the same; they always assumed the worst. "Danny was gay; Stephen was straight. They worked together, but they didn't sleep together."

"For now I guess I'll have to take your word for it," shrugged Elliott, his tone of voice suggesting that nothing would make him happier than discovering that Stephen was secretly gay. "I've got a gay operative assigned to work on Danny's other life."

"What do you mean, his 'other' life?" I demanded, resenting the sleaziness his tone implied.

"Don't be so naive, Kate. I guarantee you, there are things you don't know about Danny, things that may lead us to finding out who killed him."

"That's true of everyone," I protested.

"Yes, but it's more true because he was gay. But for now, why don't you just tell me what he was like to work with?"

"He was a good guy."

"In what way?"

"He was very smart, good at his job, easy to deal with the way that competent people always are. You knew that if he said he'd do it, it would get done."

"How long had he worked for Azor?"

"From the very beginning. He and Stephen used to joke that in the old days he actually worked for food."

"How's that?"

"Like all start-up companies Azor didn't have much money and what they had they certainly couldn't waste on legal advice. I think the first six months Danny worked for Azor he actually slept on Stephen's couch."

"Why would he do that?" asked Elliott with a look that said he didn't believe for a minute that Danny had confined his slumbers to the couch. "He was a Georgetown-educated lawyer. Stephen told me that before Danny came to work for Azor he was an associate at McKenzie Valentine in New York. Why would he give up such a prestigious job in order to work for Stephen Azorini for free?"

"For the same reason they still come to work for Stephen," I replied, thinking about the scientists on the ZK-501 project. "Because he gives them a chance to do work they wouldn't otherwise get a chance to do. Besides, Danny was no fool. He knew Stephen well enough to realize the odds were pretty good that Stephen would hit one out of the park with his new company. He had a chance to be in on the ground floor."

"Did he own stock in Azor?"

"Quite a bit. I can look up the exact number of shares for you."

"What would you guess the dollar value to be?"

"I don't know. Somewhere in the million-dollar range at the price the shares are trading today."

"Do you have any idea how he left his money?"

"As far as I know he left it all to AIDS-related charities. From what he told me, I gathered his family were all dead."

"I still don't quite buy his leaving McKenzie just because he thought Stephen might strike pay dirt. There had to be something more, something personal, that would make him take that risk."

"Sure, but it's not what you're thinking. You're the one who was talking about the straight world and the gay world a minute ago. Well, if he'd stayed at McKenzie it would have meant staying in the closet for the rest of his life."

"From what I've heard about him, Danny was not exactly open about his homosexuality. Just from the few people I've talked to out here I didn't get the sense that people realized he was gay."

"He was a lawyer. At Azor that means he didn't even really exist. Besides, not telling the world about what's going on in your bedroom is a lot different from being terrified that if someone finds out, it will destroy your career."

"So do you have any idea what his life was like out of the office?"

"He collected modern art," I replied dryly.

"You know that's not what I mean. Did he have a steady boyfriend, do you know? Did he do a lot of one-night stands? Did he cruise leather bars? Was he a drag queen?"

"I have absolutely no idea."

"That's okay, we'll find out all his secrets soon enough," declared Elliott matter-of-factly.

"Not everybody has secrets," I shot back.

"No, they don't," agreed Elliott. "Especially once they're dead."

CHAPTER

9

Elliott wanted to have a look at Danny's personnel file, so I walked him down to human resources. While I was there I had my picture taken and my employee ID made. It took only a few minutes, but to me it seemed like a momentous step, a laminated piece of plastic that identified me as an employee—a person under Stephen Azorini's control. Well, *identify* might have been too strong a word. The company used one of those cameras that spit out a computer-generated image and the quality of the likeness that appeared on the ID was so poor that it looked like a Xerox of a morgue shot taken in bad light.

That done, I left Elliott to make his own way through Danny's personnel file and find his own way out of the building. Now that I was officially employed by Azor it seemed like a good idea to do something about earning my keep. I had a long way to go before I felt comfortable taking the helm of the negotiations with Takisawa and it was time I did something about it.

Walking down the corridor that housed all the company administrative offices, I noticed that Stephen's door was open and saw him sitting behind his desk doing something on the computer. He saw me out of the corner of his eye and called out for me to come in.

"When are you and I going to have some time to sit down and talk about Takisawa?" I asked him, folding my arms across my chest.

"I was hoping to block out most of the afternoon on Saturday. That way we'll hopefully have fewer interruptions."

"Don't forget we have to go to the Benefactors' Dinner that night," I said, congratulating myself that I'd remembered. It was a dinner at the Museum of Contemporary Art honoring its biggest donors. Skip Tillman, the firm's managing partner, had recently been named president of the MCA's board of trustees. As a result, Callahan Ross partners were now expected to take an active role in the museum. Worse yet, Skip's wife Bitsy and my mother were friends, so I had gotten both arms twisted about going.

Stephen pulled a large, thick envelope from the top of a pile and tossed it toward me. "This just came this morning," he said, moving on to other things.

I opened it. Inside was a set of interrogatories at least an inch thick. These were the written questions posed to Azor by the plaintiff's attorneys in the most recently filed Serezine case. They represented round one in what would no doubt turn out to be a lengthy—and for Stephen, expensive—discovery process.

"I'm going back downtown to my office this afternoon. I'll deliver them to Tom Galloway myself. He'll want to set up a time to meet with you early next week to go over your answers."

"Can't this wait until after the Takisawa visit?"

"Unfortunately, interrogatories have to be answered

within ten days. Don't worry, Tom will make it as pain-less as possible."

"Sure. The only place it'll hurt will be my wallet." He looked down at my Azor ID, which I'd clipped to the lapel of my jacket, and smiled. "At least I get a break from paying you by the hour for a while." He picked up another piece of paper from his desk and handed it to me. "This fax came in from Takisawa overnight."

I read it through quickly. It was a letter, brief by Japa-nese standards, informing Stephen that the company's chairman, old man Takisawa himself, would be making the trip to Chicago.

"I take it this is good news?" I asked.

"Very good. But it certainly ups the ante on their visit, especially when it comes to planning the logistics."

"In what way?"

"The Japanese traditionally read a great deal of meaning into how they are treated, and believe me, senior execu-tives like Takisawa are used to being treated like royalty."

"So you book them into a suite at the Four Seasons and hire a limousine to take them back and forth," I said, fig-uring that's what Stephen was already planning.

"It's a little more complicated than that. You're thinking about this like a business meeting when it's really much more like a state visit for a foreign dignitary. For example, it is expected that we'll come up with someplace special for dinner on the first night they're in town."

"What did you have in mind?"

"Someplace unique and not generally available. Pref-erably someplace with a sense of ceremony."

"What about church?" I offered, only half joking.

"I was actually thinking about your parents' house.

You have to admit it would be perfect. Old man Takisawa would love the idea that he could go home and tell all his rich old friends he'd been entertained in Astrid Millholland's house."

"You know my mother," I replied dubiously. "She's perfectly capable of snubbing people she's known for years. I can't even begin to imagine how she'd feel about a bunch of strange Japanese businessmen in her house."

"She wouldn't even have to be there. We could have the whole thing catered."

"I don't know. . . ." I ventured uncertainly.

"It can't hurt to ask."

I thought to myself that it very well might.

"Well, what do you think?" pressed Stephen. "Do you think there's a chance she'll say yes?"

"Oh, I'm sure I can get her to say yes," I replied weakly. "It's the concessions she's going to wring out of me in exchange that have me worried."

I went back to Danny's office and started pulling out his file on Takisawa. While I was at it I grabbed the ones on Okuda, too. The previous year Azor had been involved in an aborted courtship with the Okuda Corporation. For months Danny had pursued the possibility of a joint venture with that Japanese drugmaker in the hopes of financing the development of an HIV integrase inhibitor that would block the ability of the HIV virus to take over healthy cells. Unfortunately, right before the deal was signed, Merck published findings putting them ahead in the race to develop the drug and Okuda hastily bowed out. But not before they'd come to pay a four-day visit to Chicago to tour Azor's labs.

I was hoping to free ride on Danny's experience with

Okuda and I was not disappointed. Orderly to a fault, Danny had saved everything, from his correspondence with the general manager of the Hotel Nikko, the city's premier Japanese-owned hotel, to a detailed itinerary setting out every aspect of Okuda's visit. Stephen was wrong about it being like planning a state visit; after I read through the file I realized it was more like organizing the invasion of a foreign country. Meals, gifts, the logistics for dozens of people, all planned to the minute . . . I had no time for this.

As soon as I got back to my office I asked Cheryl to get my mother on the phone so that I could set up a lunch date. Cheryl looked at me, stood up, calmly walked over to my side of the desk, and put her hand on my forehead.

"What's that supposed to mean?" I demanded.

"I'm just checking to see if you have a fever. It's the only logical explanation."

"Oh, come on, I can invite my own mother to lunch, can't I?"

"You can do anything you want," replied Cheryl with great deliberation, "but do you realize how many times in the years I have worked for you that you have made me lie to your mother so that you didn't have to even talk to her on the phone? Do you know how often I have had to beg you to return her calls? Let me remind you that last year you deliberately scheduled the Cranfield Tire deposition in L.A. for the week of her birthday so that you could get out of going to her party. So it seems only natural to assume that there's some physiological reason for this aberrant behavior."

"I need to ask her a favor," I said sheepishly.

"That's kind of what I figured," replied Cheryl, grinning as she returned to her desk.

If anything, Mother greeted my invitation with even more suspicion than Cheryl, but curiosity won out and she agreed to meet me for lunch at the Four Seasons the following day. I had just hung up the phone when Tom Galloway appeared at my door. His look of roughened grief made me feel ashamed of myself. Cheryl said that according to the secretarial grapevine it was his brother who had died. One look at his face and I found myself wondering whether it might have been his twin.

Tom was one of the firm's up-and-coming stars, a talented litigator who'd had the good sense to marry into a well-connected political family—his wife's father was a U.S. senator, her uncle an appeals court judge. It was widely rumored that Tom would seek his father-in-law's senate seat when he decided to step down.

"I'm so sorry for your loss," I said, shaking his hand. He was tall—enough so I looked him in the eye—and had jet black hair and the fair skin of an Irishman. The same good looks that made him a favorite with the secretaries would no doubt some day serve him well in public office, but today he just looked exhausted.

"Thank you," he murmured wearily. I found myself remembering how quickly those well-meaning offers of condolence began to grate.

"I assume you've heard about Danny . . ." I ventured, hoping that he had.

"What a terrible thing . . ."

"I don't know if you've also heard that I'm temporarily taking over for him as in-house counsel at Azor."

"Guttman told me you've taken a leave of absence."

"Just until they've concluded negotiations with Takisawa."

"The Japanese thing?"

"Yes. But that's not what I wanted to talk to you about. While you were out of the office Azor was served with another wrongful-death suit involving Serezine," I said, handing him the copies of the complaint and the interrogatories that I'd had Cheryl make for him.

"Ouch," he said, reaching for the file. "I bet Stephen was pissed."

"You can say that again. Once you've had a chance to read through the complaint you two should sit down and discuss it, but he seemed to indicate there's a good chance that—"

Cheryl appeared in the doorway looking so flustered that I stopped in midsentence. Her judgment was as formidable as her composure. She would never interrupt if it weren't important, and she wouldn't look this shaken unless it was something beyond the pale of normal crisis. "I'm sorry to interrupt you," she began.

"What is it, Cheryl?" I demanded, trying to suppress my alarm.

"Stephen just called," she reported uncertainly. "He wants you to meet him right away at this address on Division." She held out her hand. In it was the piece of notepaper on which she'd scribbled the address.

"When?"

"Right now. He said it was urgent."

"Right now?"

She nodded.

"Did he say where it was or what it was about?" I asked.

"He wouldn't tell me," she replied. This in itself seemed to be cause for alarm.

"Why didn't you let me speak to him?"

"He was on the car phone. He was really upset, yelling. Whenever I asked him a question, it was like he couldn't hear what I was saying. He just kept on shouting that you had to get there right away."

"And he didn't say anything about what it was about?"

"I don't know. It was so hard to understand him. But he might have said something about needing a witness."

The address turned out to belong to McNamara's Funeral Home and as the cabby pulled up in front of the building I saw that Stephen was already at the front door, banging on it with his fists. I gave the driver a twenty and, without waiting for the change, sprang from the cab and grabbed Stephen by the arm.

"What are you doing?" I demanded.

"They've released the body," shouted Stephen over the pounding of his own fists. Pedestrians crossed the street in order to keep their distance. It was only a matter of time before someone called the police.

Suddenly the door was opened by a gray-haired gentleman wearing a cardigan sweater and a pair of reading glasses on a chain.

"Is there something I can do for you?" he inquired tentatively. I'm sure that in his line of work he did not have much of a drop-in clientele.

"I need to see Danny Wohl," announced Stephen.

"Excuse me? Who?" asked the man, obviously bewildered.

"Danny Wohl," repeated Stephen in frustration. "Danny Wohl. Danny Wohl."

"He's a . . ." I fished helplessly for the right word. What was he? A customer? A client? "He's deceased," I blurted stupidly.

"I'm afraid that unscheduled viewings are not permitted," the man in the cardigan sweater informed us in a shocked voice. "Are you family?"

In response to that question Stephen shouldered his way past the man into the building.

"Wait a minute! You can't come in here!" shrieked the man in alarm, taking off after him. Not knowing what else to do, I followed both of them. Before I knew it Stephen had pelted through a set of double swing doors, down a long, dimly lit corridor, and up a half-flight of stairs, guided, no doubt, by the increasingly powerful smell of formaldehyde.

Passing through a door marked *private*, Stephen came up short and we found ourselves in a large room with green tiles on the walls and a drain in the middle of the floor. On a steel table in the middle of the room, illuminated by a hanging fluorescent fixture, was the naked body of an elderly woman. Her sagging breasts had slipped to either side of her wrinkled chest and her feet were twisted obscenely inward by arthritis. All around the room other bodies lay on gurneys covered with sheets.

"If you don't leave immediately I will have no choice but to call the police," the man in the cardigan announced, his voice quivering with fear.

"Wait! Please!" I implored him. But Stephen was already moving across the room ripping sheets from gurneys. The man from the funeral home was off like a shot for the phone.

"What the hell do you think you're doing?" I shouted at Stephen. "Are you out of your mind?"

Stephen ignored me, crossed the room, and yanked the sheet from the farthest gurney. Suddenly there before us lay the bloodless body of Danny Wohl. I shrank back for a moment, limbs paralyzed, words frozen in my mouth. Then, in spite of myself, I drew nearer to Stephen in order to take a closer look.

CHAPTER
10

Danny's face stared up at us with the vacant eyes of the dead. His lips were the same color as the rest of his skin, so white it made me shiver, completely drained of blood. Carved into his pale flesh was the pathologist's trademark, a ghastly Y-shaped incision that spanned his chest from shoulder to sternum and then to the other shoulder and ran the full length of his body from neck to groin. They had hastily stitched him back up when they were finished and the long, uneven black stitches seemed horrible against his dead skin.

"I need some gloves," said Stephen, his eyes darting around the room. I barely heard him. I was transfixed, unable to look at anything but Danny. What lay on the gurney was someone I had known. Someone I had liked. But now the familiar tumble of his blond hair was matted with dried blood, his lips set in the grim rigor of death.

Tearing through the contents of a set of metal drawers Stephen came upon a box of latex gloves. He pulled them on with a practiced snap and grabbed Danny's body by the shoulders. He quickly ran his hands over Danny's arms and legs looking for cuts or abrasions. Joe Blades had been right. There were no marks on Danny's body larger than a pinprick.

"Help me turn him over," urged Stephen handing me a pair of gloves. I stood aghast. "Oh come on!"

I did as I was told though my hands were shaking so badly it was hard to work on the gloves. Once they were on I stepped up to the gurney.

"We'll lift him on three," instructed Stephen.

As my hand touched Danny's cold flesh I felt all the oxygen leave the room.

"One, two, three."

We lifted. I staggered awkwardly as we flipped him, suddenly understanding why they call it deadweight.

"Hey! Hey! Hey!" shouted the man from the funeral home. "You can't do that!"

"I'm a doctor," announced Stephen, as if that somehow explained everything. Personally, I didn't see what that had to do with anything seeing as Danny was already dead and we were obviously in a shitload of trouble. On the other hand, at least he hadn't run to get his shotgun.

"What's this cut on the top of his head?" I asked, bending over for a closer look in spite of myself.

"The pathologist makes that incision so he can pull the scalp down over the face, lift off the top of the skull, and remove the brain."

This was a piece of information I could easily have done without.

Once more Stephen bent over the body of his dead friend looking for signs of injury. He found nothing: only a small Kaposi's sarcoma lesion on the inside of his thigh—one of the classic signposts of the AIDS virus—a tiny shaving cut just beneath his left ear, and the mark left over from a recent inoculation—absolutely nothing that would account for the bloodbath in the dead man's apartment.

"What is it that you are looking for?" the man from the funeral home asked warily from the shadows.

"I'm not sure," replied Stephen, replacing the arm of his dead friend on the cold metal of the gurney. The fury that had driven him to force his way in here had left him, that storm spent. "I just wanted to see if I could figure out how he died."

Picking up the sheet from the ground, he carefully covered up the body. There were tears in his eyes.

"Who *are* you?" demanded the man from the funeral home, finally stepping up to face him now that the threat of violence seemed to be past.

Stephen looked up from the gurney as if waking from a dream.

"I'm Dr. Stephen Azorini," he said, stripping off the gloves. "You must be Mr. McNamara. We spoke on the phone." Mr. McNamara, still looking somewhat uncertain, allowed his hand to be shaken. "This is my attorney, Kate Millholland. I'm sorry we just barged in on you like this. I was so frustrated by the runaround I've been getting from the medical examiner's office I had to see things for myself."

"We are so sorry for this intrusion," I chimed in. While they may not formally teach it in law school, groveling cannot be overrated in the attorney's arsenal of indispensable skills. "I can't imagine what you must have thought when we arrived. I assure you we meant no harm to you, your place of business, or the dignity of your clients. I'm just afraid that in his grief Dr. Azorini was swept away by his desire to be sure the medical examiner's office was handling matters correctly. . . ." In the distance I could hear the whine of approaching sirens. "Now that those concerns have been addressed, I'm sure he's ready to turn his attention to the matter of funeral arrangements for Mr. Wohl. Stephen was just telling me that he was hoping he would be able to plan a really memorable final tribute for his friend."

"Well, I suppose there's been no real harm done," ventured Mr. McNamara, no doubt calculating exactly how many dollars constituted a fitting final tribute. We heard the buzzer from the front of the mortuary.

"That will probably be the police," observed the funeral director as Stephen and I did our best to look harmless. "I'll just go out front and tell them it was all a false alarm."

As he disappeared through the swinging doors I felt myself go limp with relief.

"A memorable final tribute," muttered Stephen, under his breath. "Do you have any idea what that's going to end up costing?"

"No," I replied. "But I'll tell you one thing. Whatever it is, it's a hell of a lot cheaper than hiring a lawyer to defend yourself against criminal-trespass charges."

It seems only fitting that, after that macabre burlesque, we ended up in a corner tavern a few blocks from the funeral home that was filled with people who'd apparently just come from some kind of barbershop quartet convention. Over the strains of "Down by the Old Mill Stream" in four-part harmony, I tried to get some kind of explanation out of Stephen.

"Do you mind telling me what the hell got into you tonight?" I demanded once I'd gotten my hand around a double scotch.

"The medical examiner's office called this afternoon while I was in a meeting downtown. Rachel must have been away from her desk so they just left a message on her voice mail. All it said was that they were releasing Danny's body to the funeral home. Unfortunately by the time she got the message and gave it to me, and I called them back, whoever had left the original message had already left for the day. I finally managed to speak to the morgue attendant, but he couldn't tell me anything except that the body had just been picked up by the funeral home. I asked him if he knew if an autopsy had been performed before the body was released, but he had no idea. I asked him to check his paperwork, but he couldn't find any for that particular case."

"They wouldn't release the body without doing an autopsy," I protested.

"Not necessarily. You're forgetting that I asked my father to see if he could make a couple of calls to see if he could expedite things. The trouble with organized crime, though, is that they're not that organized. At that point I had no idea whether my father had succeeded in getting the medical examiner's office to perform the autopsy and release the body, or whether some over-ambitious gangster had just paid off somebody at the morgue to look the other way while he made off with the body. I had to be sure. That's why I took matters into my own hands."

"Is that what you'd call it?"

"Come on, Kate. I had to see him before the embalmer got his hands on him. I had to see him for myself."

"And now that you've seen him . . ." I said, staring into the amber depths of my scotch. I still couldn't get over how lucky we'd been. It was a miracle the two of us weren't sitting in the municipal lockup right now waiting to make our one phone call.

I contemplated which one of my partners I'd burden with arranging my release and shuddered at the thought of exposing that kind of vulnerability to any of them. "So now that you've seen him what do you think killed him?" I asked, shaking off the thought.

"I don't know. But he definitely wasn't stabbed to death. You saw him. There was no sign of any kind of injury."

"Could he have bled to death internally?" I asked.

"Of course, he could have," replied Stephen. "But that still wouldn't explain why there was blood splashed all over his apartment or why the couch was turned upside down."

Customers in the bar swung into "My Sweet Adeline," the bartender set us up with another round, and I steered the conversation to other matters, different levels of distress.

"What's Takisawa's son-in-law like?" I asked. I'd seen his name on the list of people Takisawa was sending over. I wondered how he was going to take the news about Danny.

"You'll like him, Kate. Not only is he very bright, but he's also outgoing and personable, especially for a Japanese."

"How well did he and Danny know each other?"

"They were very close, at least during the time they were both at Harvard. After that . . ."

"So you're saying he and Danny were more than just friends?"

"My guess would be yes."

"But now he's married."

"Like I said, he's a very bright guy. After he got his law degree, he picked up an M.B.A. at Wharton, then he went back to Japan and made what was probably his smartest career move—he married old man Takisawa's only daughter."

"Do they have kids?"

"They have one child, a boy."

"So I gather it's safe to assume he's never told his family about his relationship with Danny."

"Let's put it this way, Kate. Who knows what confidences are exchanged between a husband and his wife, but I think it's a safe bet a homosexual relationship in one's past is not exactly the kind of thing Hiroshi would be likely to advertise to his father-in-law."

I had Stephen drop me off at my office. It may have been Friday night, but we both still had work to do. Besides, with each day that passed it seemed that the stakes for the ZK-501 project grew higher. With the rumblings of unrest among the company's board of directors it was becoming increasingly urgent to strike a deal with Takisawa. With that in mind I settled down to read the thousand-plus pages that to date chronicled the history of Azor's negotiations with Takisawa.

I didn't finish until well after midnight. Then, instead of taking myself home, I made my way to the firm's library, not surprised to find the lights still on and a beleaguered first-year associate grimly wading through casebooks. He looked up, astonished through his fatigue to find that he was not alone. While my appearance no doubt reinforced the work-animal reputation I still possessed I felt a pang of gratitude that at least those days were behind me.

I offered up a small nod of compassion and went off in search of what I was looking for. As it turned out the firm possessed an ample collection of books concerned with doing business with the Japanese. That night I read them all.

It didn't take me long to conclude that in choosing me to take Danny's place, Stephen had made a terrible mistake. Not only was I as ignorant about Japanese business as I was about molecular chemistry, but that ignorance put Azor at a tremendous disadvantage. I'd always known that the Japanese conduct business very differently from Americans, but until that night I had not realized how deep the cultural roots of those differences went.

There was a lot more to it than bowing and eating sushi. Japanese culture placed a much higher value on physical etiquette and group harmony than on the personal expression and individual freedom celebrated by Americans. Over time the Japanese with their single language, homogeneous culture, and common life experiences had developed highly evolved systems of informal consensus building and formal decision making that were strikingly different from our own.

But what really frightened me was that Japanese businesses operate according to a completely different concept of time. While Jim Cassidy fixated on Azor's single year of soft performance, the Takisawa Corporation was probably being operated according to a twenty-year plan. The Japanese, I reflected, had the time to grind you down.

With their tradition of permanent employment, the Japanese were also highly averse to the transience of

American employees. For that reason, author after author counseled against making any changes on the negotiating team once discussions had begun. Great.

I was also depressed to learn that, if anything, Stephen had underestimated the importance of the physical arrangements for Takisawa's visit. Not only were esthetic minutiae in business transactions seen as tremendously important by the Japanese, but the entire Japanese concept of hospitality differed wildly from our own. By Japanese standards a good host tries to anticipate and fulfill every need of his or her guest. To that end, it was best if everything were arranged ahead of time down to the smallest detail.

The more I read the more my stomach hurt. Just the accommodations, transportation, meals, and scheduling would take a tremendous amount of time and effort to organize. Time that I, still unfamiliar with all but the most general terms of the proposed deal with Takisawa, did not have.

It was the small hours of the morning when I finally walked through the darkened corridor back to my office and pulled the Takisawa file out of my briefcase. It was late, but I was too frightened to be tired. I had promised Stephen that I would take Danny's role out of loyalty to him and to a company on whose board I served. Now I learned that my presence, even my gender, taken alone, might be enough to derail the negotiation. And I would be dealing with a culture so profoundly different from my own that I could only guess at what hidden pitfalls lay before me.

In my reading about the Japanese I had come across the same adage over and over again: The nail that stands up gets pounded down. The Japanese use it to illustrate their emphasis on group harmony and consensus building. But sitting alone in my office with the rest of the world asleep, with Danny dead and Stephen's hold on Azor on the line, I found myself interpreting it as a warning.

CHAPTER

11

I drove home in the dangerous single digits of the morning when the streets belong to somebody else. Shooting south toward Hyde Park on the empty ribbon of Lake Shore Drive, I saw parked cars clustered in the swath of green that buffers the lake. Inside people were getting high, getting laid, and committing crimes in the soft glow of the dashboard light. Suddenly I felt old and impossibly cut off from the rest of the world.

Danny Wohl was dead and I had spent the last seventy-two hours swept up by events that were beyond my control. I had seen the blood-splattered walls of Danny's once elegant apartment, the stick figure of his body in a homicide cop's notebook, and his blood-drained corpse on the metal gurney of the funeral home morgue. What made it worse was the fact that from the very first I was so consumed by the problems of taking Danny's place that there was no time to feel much of anything about his death. Now, suddenly, it was all catching up to me.

When I got home I was glad to see from the diminutive sneakers lying in the entrance hall that my roommate, Claudia, was home. I hadn't worn shoes that small since grade school, but Claudia was so tiny that she sometimes had to stand on a stool when assisting a tall surgeon. I poured myself a drink and sat down on the couch to take my shoes off.

I woke up four hours later to the sound of the front door buzzer. As I struggled to my feet I noticed that the room was just beginning to fill with light and that one of my arms was numb from being wedged between the cushions of the couch.

Shaking my arm in the hopes of restoring circulation I pushed the intercom and demanded, "Who is it?" in the hostile tone employed, under the same circumstances, by every woman living in the city.

"It's Elliott Abelman."

As I pushed the button to let him in I realized that I must look like hell. Unfortunately, I didn't have time to do anything about it.

"I'm sorry if I woke you," he apologized as I met him at the door. He had a steaming container of Starbucks coffee in each hand.

"You are forgiven," I replied, accepting one gratefully and ushering him into the apartment.

"I was just about to head over to Wohl's apartment," he explained, "and I was kind of hoping you'd come with me." If Elliott was casting about for ways for us to be alone together he'd certainly stumbled onto an interesting choice. Even assuming a lack of ulterior motives, it seemed like something worth avoiding. As if reading my thoughts, he continued. "It would really help to have someone who's been there before. Otherwise I have no way of knowing if anything's missing or out of place."

I tried to think of some excuse that wouldn't make me

seem like a complete wimp, but it was too early in the morning for that kind of invention. Instead I said no.

"I'm surprised you haven't been there already," I said.

"Someone must have tipped off the building management company that Danny had AIDS. They called the health department and they came out and put it under seal. It took Joe Blades most of the day yesterday to get them to agree to give me permission to go inside."

He put his arm across my shoulder and gave it a squeeze. "Come on. Ten minutes of your life and it will be over."

"Ah, the hooker's mantra," I replied, taking a sip of my coffee. "Is there time for me to take a shower?"

"Sure. Take your time," he said. "Say," inquired Elliott, casting a dubious eye over the dust balls under the radiators, "when are you guys going to get a cleaning lady?"

The apartment Claudia and I shared was the poor cousin of the one Stephen and I had just bought. Born in the same grand era, it was much smaller and the wood floors were scarred from years of neglect. Our furniture, which consisted of discards from my mother interspersed with sixties-era castoffs from Claudia's parents, comprised a decorating style best described as an assault to the eye.

"If it really bothers you I think there might be a broom in the closet in the kitchen," I informed him sweetly. "Make yourself at home."

I showered quickly, but mindful of my lunch with my mother, I chose my clothes with care, selecting a black cashmere turtleneck, a pair of gray wool trousers, and a black snakeskin belt with a heavy gold buckle. After I was dressed I brushed my hair a full hundred strokes, a habit left over from an otherwise forgotten nanny. Knowing that Mother loathed my usual style, I elected to wear my hair down, which involved spending ten minutes on my hands and knees emptying out the cabinet under the bathroom sink until I finally found an old tortoiseshell headband. As an afterthought I pulled a pair of gold earrings that had once belonged to my great-grandmother and a heavy gold bracelet from my jewelry box.

"You look very nice," said Elliott when I emerged from my bedroom. What I looked like was a brainless North Shore society princess with a lunch date, but being well brought up, I said thank you nonetheless. As I got my coat I took a quick peek under the radiators. I was relieved to see that the dust bunnies were still there.

If anything Danny's apartment was worse the second time. At least the morning I'd gone with Stephen I had no idea of what awaited me. Even before we got there, just watching the numbers in the elevator increase as we rose to Danny's floor had caused a hard knot of apprehension in my stomach. Now, as Elliott paused to remove the health department seal, I had to remind myself to breathe.

He turned the key in the lock and pushed open the door. The stale smell of old blood, like rotting meat, had gotten worse.

"Let's just take a quick walk through it together," said Elliott, putting his arm around my shoulder and steering me into the living room. I felt an adolescent shiver that had nothing to do with the blood-splashed walls. It was all exactly as Stephen and I had left it except that the stains had grown darker and the pool of blood near the phone was now dry.

Elliott whistled softly. "I don't know what he died of but whatever it was he sure didn't die quietly," he observed, so close to me I could feel the warmth of his breath.

Joe Blades once told me that every crime scene tells a story. Looking around Danny's living room I knew instinctively that the story I was seeing was one of violence. The overturned furniture, the pillows hurled to the floor, the telephone toppled from its table, all these things spoke of some sort of physical struggle. Even to my untrained eye it seemed obvious from the splatter patterns on the walls that they could have been made only if Danny had been moving as he bled.

"Look here," said Elliott, stooping near the edge of a long stain beside the slipper chair closest to the phone. "I'd swear this looks like two different sets of footprints." He studied them in silence for a few minutes, considering. "At least this lets your friend Stephen off the hook," he concluded, straightening to his full height.

"How's that?" I asked, having never really considered Stephen on the hook in the first place.

"I think we can rule him out just on the basis of size. How tall was Danny?"

"Average. I'd guess five foot ten or eleven, a hundred and seventy pounds."

"So that would put his shoes somewhere between a size eight and ten. We'll check his closet to be sure. But see here, the waffled print that looks like it was made by an athletic shoe? This one's definitely smaller and narrower than the others. Now, I don't know what size shoe your boyfriend Stephen wears, but how tall is he? Six two, six three?"

"He's six foot five," I replied, much amused. Elliott, who made his living on his faculty for observation, knew very well how tall Stephen was.

"Well, it's a good bet that his gunboats make a much bigger print than that," replied Stephen, indicating the clear tread of a pair of athletic shoes.

"How can you be sure that whoever made the second set of footprints was in the apartment at the same time as Danny? Isn't there a chance he came in after it was all over?" I demanded.

"Joe says he and Wypiszinski had the crime lab check and they found several places where Danny's footprints were superimposed on the running shoes'. I'll have an independent forensics lab send a team through here and I'll make sure they send a footprint expert."

"So what we have to do, à la Sherlock Holmes or Cinderella, is find the person who matches the footprint. Even if he didn't kill Danny, it's a sure bet he knows how he died."

"Yeah. He was there," replied Elliott. "When I talked to Joe yesterday he said that every bought politician in the state has been on the phone to the ME's office about getting the autopsy done. He expects to hear from the ME any day now."

"The autopsy's been done already," I replied. "I didn't call you because I assumed you'd have heard it from Blades."

"What do you mean it's already been done?" Elliott demanded. "When?"

"Sometime late yesterday afternoon."

"I talked to Joe this morning before I went to your place. He didn't say a word about it."

"Oh, there's more," I continued and proceeded to tell him about Stephen's and my unscheduled visitation of Danny's body.

"Now I know why you stick with the guy. It's not

that he's good-looking, or rich, or successful. No, it's because he really knows how to show a girl a good time," quipped Elliott humorlessly. "I can also assure you that Joe's going to be real pissed about the autopsy."

"Why is that?"

"The detectives assigned to the case are supposed to get three hours' notice from the medical examiner so that they can be present for the autopsy. This thing with Sarrek has got the whole system tied into knots. So what does the ME say killed him?"

"I don't think they know," I replied, shuddering inwardly at the thought of Danny. "Everything Joe said was true, though. There was no blood left in his body and there wasn't a mark on him."

"What does your friend Stephen think? After all, he's a doctor."

"Even when he was still seeing patients I think he knew a lot more about the living," I pointed out. "I don't think he knows what to think."

Elliott sighed and began walking slowly around the apartment as if trying to look at it again in light of this new information. He picked up a photograph in a brushed chrome frame from a side table.

"Is this him?" he asked. I came over and took a look. It was an arty black-and-white shot of Danny looking soulful. Droplets of blood had dried dark brown on the surface of the glass.

"Yes, that's him."

"Is it a good likeness?"

"Yes."

"Good," said Elliott. He carefully removed the picture from its frame and slipped it into his pocket. Then he turned to me and gestured at the paintings and photographs that hung on the walls. "These are what he collected?"

"Yes. I don't understand it, but supposedly Danny not only had a passion for contemporary art, but a good eye."

"Which don't you understand?" inquired Elliott, squinting at a canvas covered thickly with murky acrylics into which the artist had stuck pieces of broken glass and hair, apparently at random. "The paintings or the passion?"

"Neither," I replied.

"What would you say all of this was worth?"

"I have no idea," I replied.

"Joe says it's insured for a million bucks."

"You don't say."

"Anything missing?"

"I don't think so," I replied slowly. "As far as I can tell there's no big empty space on the wall that catches my eye, but it's so hard to tell. Danny liked to move things around, and besides, the stuff all looks the same to me."

Elliott put his hands in his pockets and rocked backward on his white sneakers, surveying the room. "That's at least twenty grand's worth of stereo equipment," he said with a note of jealousy in his voice. "Bang & Olafsen CD player with tape-to-tape dubbing. It doesn't look like whoever was here with him was interested in boosting anything. I guess we should have a look in the bedroom."

I led the way, relieved at the idea of a change of venue.

"These are some interesting pictures," observed Elliott after we arrived in the bedroom and he'd had a chance to look at the photographs.

"Mapplethorpe is considered by a lot of people to be a great artist," I replied, embarrassed nonetheless.

Elliott sniffed and pulled open the bifold doors of Danny's closet.

"Wow!" I exclaimed. It was the male version of my mother's closet. Danny had more shoes than Imelda Marcos, more ties than Countess Mara, not to mention sweaters in every shade, and shirts and jackets all arranged with Danny's fanatical tidiness by color and style in a system of racks and drawers from one of those closet-organizing companies. On one side, suits hung from wooden hangers with military precision, ranging from dark to light. On the other side, the hangers had been pushed to one end and several garments had fallen to the floor.

"It's weird that everything's shoved over to one side like this," said Elliott, carefully examining the inside of the closet door.

"Maybe that's why whoever was with him cleaned himself up afterward. Even if he didn't come to steal the stereo, he might have come looking for something else."

Elliott stepped into the closet and felt all along the back wall and then got down on his hands and knees, picking up racks of shoes to examine the carpeting underneath.

"What are you looking for?"

"A safe or some other kind of hiding place," he said, his voice muffled from kneeling.

While I waited for him to complete his search I sat on the edge of the bed and wondered what it would be like to go to bed looking at pictures of naked men in various S & M poses every night. Then again, I could never come home to some of the abstract paintings in the living room either.

"I can't find anything," reported Elliott, getting back up onto his feet with a small grunt. "Just clothes."

"Maybe that's what he was looking for," I replied slowly.

"What do you mean?"

"I mean maybe he was just looking for something to wear. Think about it. Do you think the only thing that got bloody was the person's shoes? I bet whoever was with him must have gotten blood all over himself. He couldn't just walk out the door and onto the street that way. I bet you he just took off what he was wearing and put on something of Danny's."

"So what happened to the clothes that he was wearing?"

"Thrown away, burned, dropped from the Wacker Street Bridge. . . ."

"I'll still have my people go through the garbage dumpster in the off chance that whoever was with him was stupid—or lazy," Elliott said. "Let's take a look at the kitchen."

As we walked through the living room I realized that familiarity was beginning to inure me to its horrors. The puzzle of it, the unanswered questions of what had happened, was taking over. The lawyer's instinctive response— head over heart.

The kitchen, like everything else in the apartment, was exactly as it had been when I was there with Stephen. But now that the shock of seeing it had subsided, I found myself seeing it in much sharper focus—thinking about it instead of just letting it assault me.

"I wonder why he used this sink to wash up," I said. "You'd think it would have just been easier to step into the shower."

"Maybe he was cleaning off something besides himself."

"Maybe, or maybe in the heat of the moment he didn't think of it."

From the front of the apartment I heard the chime of the doorbell. "That'll be my guys," explained Elliott.

While he went to let them in I stayed in the kitchen. From the other room I could hear Elliott as he instructed his operatives on their door-to-door canvass. I walked up to the sink and stood there for a long time trying to imagine what it must have been like. What was it that Mr. Running Shoes was trying to clean up in the kitchen? What was it that he was trying to conceal? How had he felt on that fateful day, standing where I stood? Panicked surely, or at the very least, afraid. Covered with blood, terrified of discovery . . . And what else? Frantic. Desperate. I stared again at the sink before me.

Off to the right on the counter by itself, about an arm's length from the sink, stood a drinking glass. A drinking glass. Off to the right. Exactly where I'd set it if I were standing doing dishes and stopped for a drink of water. I stared at it for a long time. Yes, he'd been frantic, desperate, and afraid. But there was also a good chance he was thirsty.

There was something very comforting about the dining room at the Four Seasons, very civilized. When I arrived, I found my mother comfortably settled at the very best table overlooking Michigan Avenue being fussed over like royalty by the head waiter and the maître d'. Her hair, always perfect, had just been done and she was wearing a blouse of butter-colored silk and a string of Mikimoto pearls. I dutifully kissed the air beside her cheek before sliding into my seat. I wondered whether it was normal to be so nervous having lunch with your own mother.

Of course, Mother wasn't your normal mother. Dubbed the first lady of Chicago by the gossip columnists, she was instantly recognizable to anyone with even a passing interest in the society page. In the blue book of Chicago's upper crust, Astrid Millholland was the one who decided whose name got included on the A list.

To say that she had not been the warmest or most nurturing of parents would be something of an understatement. Even from the time I was very young, it must have been clear to her that I lacked not just the physical beauty that had been her birthright, but also the star quality of her personality. I was awkward where she was graceful, intelligent where she was charming, and her disappointment in me suffused even my earliest memories.

And yet, as I grew older—or possibly just grew up—I had finally begun to see her from a different vantage point. I told myself that beneath the flawless exterior, the preternatural poise, my mother was just a woman. Driven to succeed in one of the few arenas available to her, indeed the only one she'd ever known, she was no better and not terribly much worse than many women of her generation and social stratum.

Strangely enough, I had hoped the new apartment might turn out to be a kind of bridge between us. While I had no illusions about developing the kind of closeness I suspected that other mothers and daughters enjoyed, I at least hoped in time for some kind of rapprochement—a pattern of civil relations and possibly even common ground. To a limited extent it seemed to be working. At least we now had something to talk about that didn't inevitably lead to one of us stalking away from the table—usually me.

And while I had been bloodied more than once in fierce business situations, sitting across the table from my mother in the alien environs of a ladies' lunch, I found myself paling at the prospect of what I intended to do. I let her rail about the "crime" Paul Riskoff had committed on the co-op roof and discuss her latest ideas for the new apartment, all of which seemed to involve moving walls at what I suspected would turn out to be shocking expense.

Finally, with a plate of crab cakes in front of me, I managed to get up the nerve. Without going into the details I explained to her about Danny Wohl's sudden death and how I had been drafted to take his place in the negotiations with Takisawa. But when I began explaining the difficulties I anticipated in dealing with the Japanese, she cut me off.

"Of course, the Japanese can be terribly difficult," interjected Mother. "It's an entirely different culture. Do you remember Lissy Magnuson? Her daughter, Sarah, was two classes ahead of you at Chelsea Hall. Lissy's husband, Herbert, served as ambassador to Japan under Reagan. They contributed so much money to his campaign that Lissy really thought they ought to have been sent to France. Well, compared to Paris you can understand how Tokyo was a tremendous shock. For one thing, the ambassador's residence was ever so much smaller than her house in Lake Forest. And besides being very foreign, the Japanese are very peculiar about things. Everything has to be done a certain way or they take terrible offense. After four years she said she finally began to appreciate what the country had to offer, but I think in the end she was relieved when Bert started having trouble with his angina and decided to return to the States."

"Then you can understand how important it is that everything go perfectly when they come and visit."

"You're in for quite an education, young lady. You may have been to your share of parties and dinners, but I don't think you have any idea of the amount of work that goes into planning one."

"I know, Mother," I said, with my heart in my throat. "That's why I need your help."

Try as I might, I could not remember ever having said those words to my mother before.

CHAPTER
12

From my perch on the stool beside his lab bench, I watched Dave Borland pick up a thin strip of human spleen and drop it into a steel cylinder filled with roiling liquid nitrogen. After lunch with my mother, I had driven like a mad woman, dodging little old ladies and construction barrels, in order to get out to Azor in time for my one o'clock meeting with Stephen, only to find that his pharmacology meeting was running long. Borland had come across me pacing outside Stephen's office and suggested roguishly that I come get into trouble with him.

Rubbing his hands together, Borland explained that he was just starting to isolate another batch of ZKBP. While I was eager to continue my ongoing education, I soon realized that Carl Woodruff had not been joking when he'd warned against visiting the protein lab before lunch. Indeed, it didn't take me long to realize that after lunch wasn't all that much better.

"What we're doing," Borland informed me as he continued to drop pieces of human tissue into the nitrogen with his gloved hand, "is a lot like looking for a needle in a haystack." Beside him at the bench his dour assistant cut the sallow spleen tissue into strips with a pair of surgical scissors before passing the strips to the protein chemist. "The problem is not just that we have to isolate one specific protein among the thousands of others in the crushed guts of the spleen cells, but we have to do it in such a way that doesn't unfold that protein from its biochemically active shape."

Even though it was a Saturday, the scientists of the ZK-501 project worked as if it were any other day. Borland explained that he had been on a twenty-hour-a-day, seven-day-a-week schedule for four months now—ever since the day he'd first set out to find a way to isolate the receptor protein.

Physically Borland was a wild man, an unrepentant hippie with a walrus mustache and a greasy ponytail. According to Stephen he'd worked his way through graduate school tending bar in Boston's notorious tenderloin district. Once you knew that about him, it was hard to picture him doing anything else.

Now Borland's hands were as raw as a boxer's, chapped and cracked from the solvents used in the isolation process. He wore clogs because they were easier on his legs and he moved with the limping gait of an exhausted marathoner from the endless hours spent standing at the bench.

The lab itself was as grisly as a butcher shop. The smell of raw meat mingled with acetone seemed to fill my lungs like a viscous fluid. Under the high-pitched whine of centrifuges I could pick out the pounding beat of Nine Inch Nails from the cassette player on Borland's desk. On the wall in front of us someone had hung a dog-eared poster that read: Life is Chemistry—Chemistry is Life. Beneath it someone had scrawled, "life sucks."

"When I was in graduate school, this friend of mine and I used to steal frogs from the biology lab and give 'em a bath in this," Borland said with a nod toward the container of liquid nitrogen. "After a quick dip they'd be frozen as brittle as glass. Then we'd tap them against something hard—"

"And try to make the girls scream," Lou Remminger interrupted in her Appalachian drawl as she came up behind us. She was dressed entirely in black except for a necklace that appeared to be made of safety pins.

"I don't know about that," chuckled Borland, "but I bet I would have gotten your attention."

"Pig," replied Remminger without malice. "Have you seen Michelle Goodwin anywhere? She borrowed some slides of mine that Stephen wants me to use for the Japanese inquisition."

"Oh stop whining about the Japanese," chided Borland. "Takisawa won't be any more painful than an NIH site visit and you've survived your share of those."

"Yeah, but the reason I took a leave of absence from Yale was so that I wouldn't have to suck up for money anymore."

"I have news for you, Dr. Remminger. It's the same in the real world as it is in the ivory tower. If you don't pay, you can't play."

"Yeah, but instead of playing with my chemistry set I'm running around chasing down slides and preparing presentations," she complained, "and now Michelle has disappeared with my slides."

"The last time I saw her she was in the modeling room."

"I just checked there. His royal pain in the highness was the only one in there, which is, of course, why Michelle is nowhere to be found."

"I take it Michelle and Childress don't get along," I remarked.

"It's only because Childress is such a complete dick," offered Remminger.

"You've got it all wrong," Borland chimed in. "It's not because he is a dick, it's because he has a dick."

"Oh would you cool it," Remminger shot back. "I know it makes you feel better to think so, but not every woman who won't hop into bed with you is a lesbian."

"You'd still better take a look in the animal labs," said Borland. "I heard that Lisa's dissecting beagles today. Michelle sometimes likes to go and watch."

"You dissect dogs?" I asked, horrified.

"What do you think we try out new drugs on, hairdressers?" replied Borland, clearly enjoying himself. "They start out with rodents, and if things look good, they work their way up—you know, guinea pigs, rabbits, dogs. . . . I'm an animal rights activist myself," confided Borland conspiratorially. "I think they should abolish animal testing altogether and instead just try the stuff out on crystallographers. Much more efficient."

"What is it with you guys and crystallographers?" I demanded.

"Crystallographers have the highest PITA quotient of any scientific subspecialty," said Remminger.

"What, pray tell, is that?" I asked.

"Pain in the ass."

"Shall I tell her the joke about crystallographers?" Borland asked Remminger.

"Sure," replied Remminger, pulling out the stool beside me and making herself comfortable.

"A very famous chemist dies and goes to heaven," began Borland, "and St. Peter is showing him around. The chemist is very happy. Not only is heaven a very beautiful place with rolling hills and big, fluffy clouds, but he's getting a chance to see his colleagues who've preceded him through the pearly gates. Finally, as they are finishing up the tour he tells St. Peter that there's something bothering him. St. Peter seems very concerned. 'Please,' he says, 'it's my job to make sure you are perfectly happy. Tell me what's on your mind.' The chemist explains that while he's seen any number of his old friends—chemists, physicists, biologists, even mathematicians—he hasn't seen a single crystallographer. At that, St. Peter leads him up to the top of a tall hill from which they can see another, identical heaven populated entirely by crystallographers. 'I don't understand,' says the chemist. 'You see,' explains St. Peter, 'our job in heaven is to make sure everyone is perfectly happy and the only way to make the crystallographers happy is to make them think they are the only ones who can get in.' "

We all laughed. I decided that if I had taken a job in Katmandu it would have been less foreign than coming to work at Azor. Compared to the earthy reality of grinding spleens and autopsying dogs, lawyering seemed like little more than spinning words in the air.

Dave Borland turned his attention back to the lab bench and Lou Remminger went off to search the animal labs for Michelle Goodwin. The protein chemist began decanting the frozen pieces of spleen into a large industrial-size blender. He pushed a button, and the blender sprang to life with a high, metallic shriek. Borland switched off the machine and added purified water from a graduated cylinder, then he poured the sickly, salmon-colored broth into a large beaker.

"This is where the fun really begins," he assured me with a piratical grin, and motioned me to follow him down the hall. We stopped in front of what looked like a large commercial meat locker. "We have two cold rooms," he explained, yanking the long, stainless-steel handle. "One that's kept at zero degrees Fahrenheit and one that's kept right at thirty-four degrees. We do most of our protein work at just above freezing."

I followed him inside. The cold room was as big as my office. Naked lightbulbs hung from the ceiling at three-foot intervals, casting harsh shadows. The walls were lined with metal racks. Against the far wall was another lab bench identical to the one we'd just left. Borland went up to it and made a notation in the lab notebook that lay open off to one side. In science, where priority, not possession, is nine-tenths of the law, the importance of documenting one's work was ingrained in everyone who worked at Azor.

"There's a parka over there on that hook if you want to put it on," the protein chemist offered over his shoulder. "It's Michelle's, but she won't mind if you borrow it."

I took his suggestion and slipped it on gratefully.

"What about you?" I asked. "Don't you get cold?"

"Sure I get cold, but this protein is so tricky to work with that I don't have time to get in and out of a coat— it'd just slow me down. Proteins, as a rule, are a bitch to work with, but this one must be the devil's favorite."

"Why's that?"

"Proteins are held together with the molecular equivalent of spit. That's what makes them so temperamental. Heat them up and they cook like eggs, rough 'em up too much and they fly apart. They'll only do what you want if you talk to them nicely and baby them every step of the way." Borland poured the contents of the beaker into a large centrifuge and touched the switch that sent it spinning.

"We know that ZKBP is a relatively short protein, so what we're doing here is first spinning out some of the larger, heavier proteins. After that we filter the liquid through cheesecloth and then centrifuge it again, this time at two hundred thousand times the force of gravity. Then the clump of membranes is washed through a set of solvents, filtered again, and then centrifuged. You get the picture."

"How many steps are there in total?"

"Twenty-seven," replied Borland, folding his hands across his broad chest. His eyes were dark in their deep sockets and glittered like a bird's. "I'd like to see Michael Childress freeze his pansy ass off in here."

"What do you guys have against Childress?" I asked.

"Oh, I've had my belly full of Childress for a long time. He and I were both at Baxter together," replied Borland, turning to switch off the centrifuge. "Everybody who's ever worked with him hates him."

"Why?"

"Because he's a self-serving, egomaniacal, preening bastard who'd stop at nothing—up to and including stabbing colleagues in the back—to get the credit. Michael's great gift isn't crystallography, it's using people." Borland spoke so bitterly that I was sure there was some personal history between the two men. "Childress has a talent for making himself look better than he really is. He's been using the same M.O. since graduate school. He surrounds himself with ambitious young scientists who are aching to prove themselves and gets them to do all the dirty work, to endure the heartbreaking dead ends and the frustrating trial and error you go through at the beginning of any project. Then, as soon as they get close, Childress shoves the young guy aside, takes it to the obvious next step, and gathers up all the glory. I'll guarantee you that's what he's got planned for Michelle Goodwin. You just wait and see. Childress has been working the same scam for years."

"So how does he get away with it?" I asked.

"Science is a blood sport, Miss Millholland. The only thing that matters is being first. Nobody gives a shit what you did to get there."

When I finished with Borland I went back to Stephen's office to see whether he was free of the pharmacologists yet. I found him sitting behind his desk, his back turned to the door, apparently staring out the window at the half-empty parking lot.

"Are you okay?" I asked from the doorway. Stephen was always doing seven things at once, talking on the phone, opening his mail, punching up something on the computer . . . there was something almost disturbing about seeing him idle.

He swiveled his chair around to face me, his face a mask of suppressed emotion. "I just got off the phone with Julia Gordon," he said.

Julia Gordon had been a classmate of Stephen's in medical school. Now a forensic pathologist with the medical examiner's office, she lived in Hyde Park with her husband, Hugh, who was a professor of hematology at U of C. Stephen had been trying to recruit him to Azor for years.

"She called to apologize about the mix-up in releasing Danny's body yesterday. She says it's chaos over there on account of this Sarrek thing. The pathologist who performed the autopsy on Danny isn't even on their regular staff; he's on loan from DuPage County."

"So what did she have to say about cause of death?"

"Danny died from a bleeding ulcer."

"What?"

"She says they found an ulcer that eroded into one of the major blood vessels in the stomach."

"You're kidding," I said, leaning back in my chair trying to absorb this information, trying to make it fit with the mental picture of Danny's apartment that I seemed destined to carry around with me forever. "I still don't get it. If he was bleeding into a hole in his stomach, then wouldn't he have died from internal bleeding? How would blood from a bleeding ulcer get all over the apartment?"

"Blood is an irritant, Kate."

"I'm sorry. I don't understand."

"Blood is an irritant. As soon as there was a significant amount in his stomach Danny would have started vomiting it up. He wouldn't have stopped until all the blood was gone."

"Oh," I said weakly, my hand involuntarily rising to cover my mouth in what no doubt looked like a cartoon of well-bred shock. I took a deep breath and tried to push down the horrific images crowding into my head. "It was almost easier to deal with the thought of him having been murdered—"

"Oh, he was murdered, all right," Stephen cut in coldly. "There is absolutely no doubt of that."

"What?"

"Oh, maybe it's not murder within the legal requirements, but he was murdered nonetheless."

"What do you mean?"

"Think about it, Kate. Bleeding to death is a process, not an instantaneous event. Even if the hole in the blood vessel were huge it would have probably taken between ten and fifteen minutes for him to have bled out completely. At that rate he would have still had five or six minutes on his feet before he'd start to get weak and lose motor coordination. After that he'd go into shock and lose consciousness."

Suddenly I understood how Danny's apartment had come to look the way it did. I saw the arcing bloodstains and felt almost physically sick.

"Danny was intelligent, physically capable, and in an apartment that contained a working telephone in a building full of people," continued Stephen relentlessly. "Why didn't he use the telephone to call for an ambulance? Why didn't he run out into the hallway to get help? If medical help had gotten to him quickly enough there was a good chance they could have saved him."

"It wasn't that he didn't try," I replied, thinking of the bloody wall by the kitchen door and the pool of blood by the fallen telephone. "Danny tried with everything he had. But whoever was with him in the apartment forcibly restrained him. That's how the apartment got torn apart.

It wasn't because someone was trying to kill him. It was because whoever was with him when he started to die physically held him down to keep him from going for help."

CHAPTER
13

For a long time we just kept going over it, laying out the few nuggets of hard fact we had, hoping there was some way of putting them together that told a different, less terrible story. But in the end it always came out the same way. While Danny was bleeding to death someone had wrestled him down to keep him from summoning help.

"But why?" I asked for the dozenth time. "Do you think maybe he just panicked at the sight of the blood?"

"If that were the case you'd expect him to stand back or even run away. The last thing you'd think he'd want to do is get any closer. No, whoever did this wanted Danny dead."

"If he'd gotten help right away do you think Danny would have lived?"

"If the paramedics were able to get there quickly, then yes, there's a good chance he would be alive right now."

"Maybe whoever was with him didn't know that. Did Danny have a living will? Maybe he'd told whoever was with him that he didn't want to be resuscitated if something happened to him."

"Danny wasn't ready to think about a living will. Even

145

though he was sick, he wasn't planning to die of AIDS—he said he was going to beat the virus."

"Then maybe he was with someone whose judgment was impaired. Maybe whoever it was was on drugs or something."

"Maybe. Or maybe he just didn't want it known that he was in a gay man's apartment."

"Oh, please," I protested, "in this day and age? I guarantee you, as we speak, gay couples are registering for wedding china at Marshall Field's and deciding who gets to wear the wedding dress."

"The world is not as liberal and forgiving as the media would have you think, Kate. How many attorneys are there at Callahan Ross?"

"Worldwide?"

"Just in the Chicago office."

"Five hundred and something."

"How many men?"

"Close to five hundred."

"Something like ten percent of the male population is homosexual. So how many of your colleagues would you expect to be gay?" He let that one sink in for a minute. "Now how many of them are open about it?"

"Okay, I get your point. But still, even if it was someone who wasn't public about his homosexuality, calling the paramedics is not the same thing as putting up a billboard with a picture of yourself in drag next to the Dan Ryan with the caption 'I am gay.' The only people who would know would be the paramedics and even then I guess you could give a phony name."

"Unless you were someone well known."

"You mean a celebrity?"

"Yes, but not necessarily in the way you're probably

thinking. It could be anybody the paramedics might recognize, anyone who could be hurt by that kind of whispering—a politician, a newscaster, a judge, someone prominent and recognizable—anybody who would have reason to be afraid that one of the paramedics would sell the story to the tabloids."

"That narrows it down some. . . ." I mused.

"Oh, I don't know about that," replied Stephen in frustration. "This is a big town and I don't think there's any shortage of people leading secret lives."

Eventually we had no choice but to turn the conversation to Takisawa.

"I spent a long time in the firm's library last night," I said as we began laying out various sections of the burgeoning Takisawa file on the long table Stephen used for meetings. "I was reading up on negotiating with the Japanese."

"Did you learn anything?"

"Just enough to understand the extent of my ignorance, which is frankly pretty vast. Enough to know that I am definitely the wrong person to be doing this. It's going to be bad enough that Takisawa is going to have to deal with a new face, but I'm exactly the kind of face you don't want sitting next to you at the negotiating table. I'm serious, Stephen. I want you to think seriously about bringing in someone else, someone with greater experience in dealing with the Japanese."

"You mean a man."

"As much as it hurts me to say it, yes. You need a man. A man with experience in negotiating with the Japanese. This is going to be hairy enough without my gender complicating things further."

"And I think it's already so complicated that you could be a green Martian and it wouldn't matter. Do you really think that after they've had a look at Lou Remminger they're going to give a damn about you?"

"That's the reason you need an experienced male negotiator, to help balance that out. You can't make a deal without Lou Remminger, though somebody has got to talk to her about her clothes. As unpalatable as she may be to the Japanese, she's the key to what you're trying to do with ZK-501. I'm the least important variable in this equation."

"I think you're wrong. It's true that it's going to make them nervous that we're changing people in midnegotiation. After all, most Japanese businessmen work for the same company for their entire lives. They find the kind of movement that takes place in American business completely incomprehensible. But Danny didn't leave to work for a competitor. Surely death is understandable in every culture. If you take Danny's place, then at least it's an orderly progression. As a member of the board and chief outside counsel, you rank above Danny in the hierarchy. It is logical that you would step in to take his place. I guarantee Takisawa will have done their homework. They will know that you and I have a relationship outside of the office and the fact that you have my ear both professionally and privately will give you greater credibility than any negotiator I could ever bring in from the outside."

"That may be, but I still don't have enough experience dealing with the Japanese. No matter what you say, I'll be flying blind."

"You're not just the toughest negotiator I know, Kate, but you're also the most intuitive. You'll figure out how to deal with Takisawa," Stephen reassured me. "Now, tell me, have you had a chance to speak to your mother about using her house for dinner on the first night?"

"I took her out to lunch today," I reported. I could tell by the look on Stephen's face that he was impressed. "Not only has she agreed to personally act as hostess for the dinner, but she has agreed to take charge of all the arrangements for the entire visit—hotel, meals, transportation, everything. It turns out that the husband of one of her good friends was ambassador to Japan under Reagan, so she's got the inside track on everything we're going to need to do. You've been to my mother's parties. Everything will be perfect."

"I can't believe you got her to agree to do all that. Are we going to have to pay her anything?"

"Not exactly."

"What does that mean?"

"She doesn't want any money from you—indeed, she'd be insulted if you offered. But if it comes down to a choice between putting up cheap wallpaper and the one my mother likes, we'll be putting up the one my mother likes."

"Fair enough," replied Stephen, thereby demonstrating his complete ignorance of what hand-painted French wallpaper could cost. "But I still can't believe she'd take on all of this. This is going to take a lot of time. No offense, but your mother has never struck me as someone who's itching to roll up her sleeves and work at something."

"You don't understand," I replied. "To mother, this isn't work. This is throwing an elaborate party for some people she doesn't particularly like. She does that all the time. Besides, that's not why she said yes."

"Then tell me. Why did she?"

."Because she knows there is no way I am ever going to compete with her in her world."

"So?"

"So this is Mother's chance to show me that while I can't play on her court, she can sure as hell beat me on mine."

Driving back into the city, I cursed the suburban hordes who were already clotting the expressway as they made their way into the city for Saturday night. It wouldn't have been so bad if the MCA dinner were only a law firm function. After all, my partners were used to my pared-down—my mother would call it frumpy—style. The trouble was that my parents were going to be there, too, and even though I had been in my mother's debt only since lunch, I already felt the pressure to pay her back.

As a result I found myself, twenty minutes before Stephen was supposed to pick me up, standing in front of my bedroom mirror in my underwear fumbling with a set of electric rollers that I hadn't used since college. The worst part was I kept getting their little spines tangled in my hair, and for the life of me I couldn't figure out how the weird metal clips were supposed to attach to my hair. Claudia wandered in in midepithet and took a seat on the corner of my bed, looking vastly amused.

"If I ever fall off a ladder or burn myself or get electrocuted while we're alone together in the apartment," she said, "please do me a favor and don't give me first aid."

"Why not?" I asked, wishing desperately that I either had longer arms or eyes in the back of my head.

"Because I would be terrified to have you touch me,"

replied my roommate, ever the surgeon. "It's remarkable what a klutz you are."

"Thank you very much."

"Do you want some help with that?"

"No thank you."

"Come on. I'm afraid you're going to hurt yourself."

"What do you know about electric curlers?" I shot back. Claudia's parents were sixties radicals who to this day lived from one protest march to the next. When I first met her she hadn't even seen a tube of mascara before.

"If I can sew two ends of a severed blood vessel together, I can put rollers in your hair. Now, come over here and sit down. What did they feed you growing up to get you this tall?"

"I'm only five eleven. Just think of how much taller I'd be if I'd actually received maternal love as a child."

"I take it your mother's going to be wherever you're going, otherwise you wouldn't be torturing yourself like this. What disease is it tonight? Muscular dystrophy? Cancer?"

"Modern art. It's the Benefactors' Dinner for the new Museum of Contemporary Art."

Claudia responded by making snoring noises.

"So what are you doing tonight?" I asked.

"Packing. I've got an interview at Stanford on Monday for their fellowship program."

"Eye surgery?"

"Surgery."

"I can't see you in California."

"I can't see you in an evening gown, but that doesn't mean you're not going to put one on." She eyed my dress that was hanging from the top of my closet door. "Is that what you're going to wear?" she asked, rolling up the last section of hair.

"Yeah."

"Can I see it?"

"Sure. How long am I supposed to keep these things in for? My head is starting to get hot," I complained.

"Just be quiet and put your makeup on," she said, climbing up on a chair to take down the dress. It was a deep copper color and the fabric had a dull metallic sheen to it, not enough to be shiny, but enough to catch the light when the fabric moved. It was off the shoulder with a set-in waist and a full skirt, much more dramatic than what I usually wear.

"It's gorgeous," sighed my roommate, "but you didn't buy this, did you?"

"No, Mother ordered it for me when she was in Paris for the couture shows."

"How much does something like this cost?"

"I don't know for sure," I said, concentrating on my mascara.

"Ballpark?"

"It's better if you don't know. I don't want you throwing up right before you leave for your trip."

"I know it won't fit me, but could I try it on?"

I turned and looked at my roommate in surprise. "Of course."

Claudia quickly stripped out of her scrubs and kicked off her running shoes.

"I don't think I've ever worn a long dress," she confided, slipping it off its hanger and holding it up to herself in front of the mirror. "That is, if you don't count the times I wrapped an old tablecloth around my waist to play princess when I was little. It used to make my mother furious." She undid the zipper and stepped into it.

"Here," I said, setting down my lipstick and turning to help her. "Let me zip you up."

The dress was so long it pooled around her ankles. I grabbed my evening pumps from the floor of my closet. "Put these on," I instructed. Claudia slipped her tiny feet into my shoes. They were so big, she looked like a little girl playing dress-up. I stepped behind her and pulled the extra material back so that the dress appeared to fit smoothly in front.

Claudia took her glasses off, revealing dark circles from hours spent in the OR, and squinted at her image in the mirror. "I feel just like Cinderella," she announced.

"Believe me," I informed her sagely from over her shoulder. "Four hours in those shoes and you'll feel like a tired old cleaning lady with arthritis waiting at the bus stop."

A city like Chicago erects a new museum perhaps only once a generation. As Stephen and I pulled up to the new Museum of Contemporary Art I felt fairly certain our grandchildren would someday stand on this very spot and wonder what on earth we must have been thinking. From the street it looked like something out of a scary Bauhaus dream. Everything about the building was hard and forbidding, from the mountain of knife-edged stairs leading up to the second-story entrance, to the cast-aluminum panels that covered the building like high-tech graham crackers.

Even though the building had been lit up for the evening's festivities and a red carpet laid down like a slash against the sharp limestone steps, I still felt like I was about to pay a visit to Dr. No. The building seemed as welcoming as a twenty-first-century jail—a feeling that was only reinforced by the phalanx of black-clad security guards with arms clasped behind their backs and black earpieces plugged into their ears. They looked like extras in a futuristic thriller.

It was, I noted as we passed through the doors, not your usual benefit crowd. Besides the smattering of the old guard who'd turned out for Skip's wife, and the lawyers from Callahan Ross and their sullen wives, it was definitely an arty group. There were lots of gray-haired men sporting ponytails, no doubt telling themselves that their black collarless shirts not only made them look younger but were slimming as well. Their wives wore hand-painted dresses and looked like they patronized the same hairdresser as Lou Remminger.

We waited for our names to be checked off from the list and then passed into a tall, narrow room, which looked like the interior of a very large, white shoe box. In the center of it stood an enormous golden sphere about twelve feet in diameter. The wall plaque announced that the piece was titled, *Monument to Language*.

I turned to Stephen. "I need a drink," I said.

I spotted my parents on the far side of the room, talking to the mayor, who I decided looked more like his father every day. Tribute having been paid, the mayor moved on. Most of the $46 million that it had cost to erect the new building had been donated by the people in this room. His honor had many more hands to shake before the night was through.

Stephen reappeared at my side with two glasses of white wine and thus armed we made our way through the black-clad crowd toward my parents, who were having their picture taken by the photographer for the society page. The *Sun-Times* society columnist hovered malevolently in the background waiting for him to finish.

As we made our way toward them we stopped every few feet to shake hands and say hello. I couldn't help but marvel at Stephen. With his most trusted business advisor dead, control of his company threatening to weaken, and the deal of his lifetime looming ever closer on the horizon, he amiably worked the cocktail crowd, effortlessly remembering names and lightheartedly flirting with my mother's friends and my partners' wives. I'd long ago concluded, albeit enviously, that it was a masculine talent, this ability to compartmentalize, to focus completely on what was at hand.

We finally reached my parents. Mother was radiant and in her element, stunning in a Halston gown of midnight blue. Even though she managed to convey the impression that somehow the party was being given in her honor, the truth is she wouldn't have entertained in a woodshed most of the people who were gathered here. But as an icon of arts philanthropy in this city, she felt it necessary to make an appearance at the event. She wasn't even staying for dinner. After cocktails she and my father were headed to the cystic fibrosis benefit at the Four Seasons. Catching sight of us, Mother greeted me with more warmth than I'd seen her muster of late, while Father, in his usual semi-inebriated state, was as sweet, and vague, as ever.

"That dress looks lovely on you," she said, congratulating herself on her choice.

"Thank you."

"Have you said hello to Skip and Bitsy yet?"

"Yes, Mother," I replied, wondering how it was that

she always managed to make me feel like I was exactly nine years old. "It was the very first thing we did."

"Very good," she said.

"Well then, let's have a look around this joint," suggested my father, adding under his breath, "it's not like we're ever going to be coming back."

Stephen chuckled and my father flagged down a waiter to bring him a fresh drink. Once my father had enough gin and tonic in hand to safely make the trip, we made our way into the closest of the museum's barrel-vaulted galleries.

A sign beside the entry explained that the gallery housed a show whose intention was to demonstrate how the concept of rapture transforms lives and is expressed through modern art. After looking at the first couple of paintings I was secretly grateful they hadn't chosen depression as a theme. Whoever thought that several large, black panels communicated anything about rapture was completely out of their mind.

I went to say something to Stephen, but he was reading the explanatory text beside one of the installations with such great concentration that I stepped back to look at it myself.

It was a large painting, eight feet by six feet, painted white and superimposed with a thinly lined grid of pale red squares. I didn't bother reading the description. They were all so pretentious and absurd that they only reinforced my deep-seated belief that much of modern art is to our century what the new clothes were to the emperor— nothing but a very elaborate fraud.

"What do you think?" demanded Stephen, appearing at my side. "Shall we buy it and hang it in our new living room?"

"Thank god they're not for sale," I replied. I studied his face and was alarmed to find no trace of a smile.

"It must have been hard to get all those thin lines perfectly straight using a brush."

"I wouldn't care if you told me it was painted by an armless Buddhist monk holding a toothpick in his teeth using his own blood. It still looks exactly like a big sheet of graph paper."

The lights flickered, signaling dinner. We took our leave of my parents, who would wait until the majority of the guests were seated before slipping out to their next function. Stephen and I made our way up the stairs to where tables had been set up in the galleries housing the museum's permanent collection. Ours was beneath a series of Calder mobiles from the thirties that I recognized from art history class. I wondered whether that made them too old to be classified as contemporary, but I was so grateful that they'd decorated the tables with flowers instead of something more avant-garde that I didn't feel inclined to quibble.

I took my seat beside a partner from corporate whom I barely knew. His wife, plump and pretty, seemed flustered to find herself seated beside Stephen, who immediately applied himself to the task of charming her. My other dinner companion had not yet arrived. I thought nothing of it until, turning my head to tell the waiter that I wanted wine, I chanced to glance at the place card, partially obscured by flowers. I must have said something, or at least drawn back in shock, because Stephen turned to me, a look of concern on his face.

Memory flooded back. A heated discussion about art over lunch at the Standard Club nearly three months ago. Danny raving about the work of Dorothea Lange, a famous realist photographer whose work was scheduled for an exhibition during the coming year. A note jotted down and cast from memory as soon as it was handed to Cheryl. Until that moment I had completely forgotten I'd invited Danny to join us at the benefit that evening.

CHAPTER
14

Sunday morning when I came home from Stephen's I was surprised to find my roommate sitting at the kitchen table companionably enjoying coffee and bagels with Elliott Abelman. For the first time in months Claudia wasn't wearing scrubs. Instead she was dressed in a brown turtleneck and corduroy pants. She'd put her hair into a French braid and she was smiling. She looked like a completely different person.

"Well, good morning, all," I announced. "What's the occasion?"

"I'm leaving for the airport in a couple minutes. I'm going to California for my Stanford interview."

"And I'm on a mission of mercy," chimed in Elliott with a grin. "I took a look in your refrigerator yesterday and realized you ladies are in danger of starving to death."

"Oh yes," replied Claudia, patting her stomach. "The dietitians are always stopping me in the halls to tell me how undernourished I look."

The front door buzzer sounded harshly. "That must be

my cab," she announced, rising to her feet and brushing crumbs from her lap.

"Good luck tomorrow," said Elliott, standing up. "Do you need any help with your bag?" Obviously they teach more than hand-to-hand combat in the marines.

"No thanks. I just have the one," replied Claudia.

"I'll walk you out," I said, itching with curiosity. From the looks of things Elliott had been there for quite a while. I was dying to hear what they'd been talking about.

"Okay, what were you saying about me?" I whispered as soon as we were out of earshot.

"You are out of your mind."

"What's that supposed to mean?"

"This guy is terrific. I don't know what you're doing with Stephen. You know, somebody just told me he was listed in the *Guiness Book of World Records* as the world's coldest human."

"You must be mistaken," I replied dryly. "I know for a fact that my mother still holds that title." All joking aside, I was less than happy with the direction this conversation was taking. "If you think Elliott is so marvelous maybe you should go out with him yourself."

"I would," replied Claudia as she opened the door to the cab, "except for one little problem."

"What's that?" I asked.

"He's completely in love with you."

"Bagel?" inquired Elliott innocently as I returned to the kitchen.

"Did Joe tell you about the autopsy results?" I asked, rooting in the bag for a pumpernickel.

"Yeah, the ME thinks he bled to death from a perforated ulcer. Nasty."

"So what does that mean from the point of view of the police?"

"Joe says he'll push for a continued investigation, but he thinks he won't get it."

"Meaning?"

"Meaning that barring new evidence they'll close the case."

"And if Sarrek had been pulled over in Gary instead of here?"

"They'd still probably close it."

"How can that be?"

"Face up to it, Kate. Even if they could find the guy who was with him, the chances they'd be able to gather enough evidence to charge him with a crime—much less convict—are practically zero."

"Don't you think you're being unduly pessimistic?" I asked, tearing the bagel in two.

"Well, according to what the ME told Joe, there was only something like a fifty-fifty chance that Wohl would have survived even if the paramedics had gotten there."

"Fifty-fifty is a hell of a lot better than the odds he ended up with," I replied. "You know as well as I do that the guy who was with Danny fought with him to keep him from getting help. And afterwards he tried to conceal the fact that he'd been there. You don't think that's guilty behavior?"

"I'm not denying that's probably how it happened, but that still doesn't make it murder."

"Stephen thinks whoever was with him was somebody well-known, someone who was afraid the paramedics or the police would recognize him."

"That would make sense. Remember I told you yesterday I was going to send my people through the building and recanvass the neighbors?"

"Did you turn up anything?"

"A witness."

"A witness to what?"

"Someone who claims they saw Danny leaving his apartment around four o'clock last Sunday afternoon."

"When did he die?"

"According to Joe the ME put the time of death between ten and two."

"Then I don't get it. Either your witness is wrong about the time or he's wrong about what he saw. I don't see how it gets us anywhere."

"He's positive about the time. The guy's name is Mark Freelig. He manages the Italian restaurant across the street from the Steppenwolf Theater, a place called Biscotti's. He says he got to work around quarter to five last Sunday. The restaurant is closed on Mondays, so he stayed over at his girlfriend's and slept in. That's why the police didn't interview him on Monday when the body was discovered."

"What does he say he saw?"

"Freelig lives in 12C, the apartment diagonally across the hall from Danny's. He says he was just getting ready to leave for work when he remembered he'd left some clothes in the dryer in the laundry room. You know how it is in an apartment building. You leave your laundry in the dryer and you come back to find half of it gone."

I nodded, though I had no practical experience in the matter. I dropped my dirty clothes at the Chinese laundry on Harper and 53rd Street and picked them up neatly folded the next day. Mrs. Chen had a son at Northwestern and I figured with what she charged I was making a nice dent in his tuition bill.

"So anyway, this guy Freelig decided he'd better run down to the basement and retrieve his stuff. He said he'd just opened the door of his apartment when he heard the elevator bell ring at the end of the hall and he saw Danny standing in front of it waiting for the doors to open."

"What made him think it was Danny?"

"He recognized his raincoat. A real expensive gray Armani number. I guess Freelig had seen him wear it before." I nodded. I'd seen him in it, too.

"What else was he wearing?" I asked.

"A Yankees baseball cap pulled down low. He was carrying a yellow and black athletic bag, the kind that's on a strap so that you can carry it on your shoulder."

"Did Freelig speak to him?"

"Freelig just called out to ask Danny to hold the elevator."

"And did he?"

"No. That's why this guy Freelig remembered it. According to him Danny was normally really friendly, so he was surprised when he didn't hold it. Freelig figured Danny must have been in a hurry—either that or he didn't hear him."

"You and I know why he must have been in a hurry."

"Oh, yeah. There was one more thing. According to Mr. Freelig it looked like the man's hair was wet under the baseball cap."

It took me a couple of seconds to grasp the significance of this. "So what you're saying is the guy we're looking for cleaned up as best as he could, put his bloody clothes in the sports bag, put on Danny's coat and hat, and hoped to make it out of the building unnoticed," I said.

"I bet it gave him a heart attack when Freelig asked him to hold the elevator," observed Elliott.

"True, but I'm still not sure where all of this gets us."

"For one thing it gives us a physical description of who we're looking for."

"How's that?"

"Now we know that whoever was with Danny was close enough in size and build to wear Danny's clothes and to be mistaken for him—at least at a distance. I'd say we're probably looking for a white man about five foot ten, one hundred sixty pounds, between twenty and fifty years old."

"That narrows it down to a couple million guys," I said dubiously.

"There's also a chance the security camera in the lobby might have picked up something. I've got someone tracking down the tape, but the company that has the security contract on that building isn't open on the weekend so we won't know until tomorrow at the earliest."

"Maybe we'll get lucky."

"I also had a pair of operatives showing Wohl's picture around last night. I sent them out to all the bars and restaurants that showed up on his American Express bill for the past two months."

"What did they turn up? Anything?"

"Couple places remember him, especially where there were gay waiters. Apparently he used to spend a lot of time at a Japanese place in his neighborhood called Kamehachi."

"Sure," I said, "it's a sushi bar on Wells, just down the street from his apartment."

"He ate there at least once a week."

"By himself?"

"Sometimes. Sometimes with another man."

"Always the same one?"

"It sounds that way."

"Description?"

"Six feet tall, dark hair, brown eyes, good-looking, but not in the same league as your friend Stephen."

"Age?"

"Between thirty and forty."

"That's not exactly pinning it down."

"There's more. According to what the waiters overheard they weren't sure that it was all romance."

"What do you mean?"

"The consensus was the two men must have worked together."

"Why's that?"

"Because all they talked about was work. The waiters said every time they overheard them they were talking about the problems the company was having with some new drug."

Elliott was supposed to meet Joe Blades at ten-thirty. Joe had promised to show him the medical examiner's autopsy notes and the items of evidence that had been taken from Danny's apartment. Elliott asked if I wanted to come along. With Claudia's words ringing in my ears I agreed to go along for the ride.

When we arrived at police headquarters a scuffed and acrid-smelling elevator carried us to the sixth floor where the special detail investigating the Sarrek murders had set up camp. We found Joe behind a government-issue metal desk, one of twenty in the open area in the middle of the room. Phones rang and keyboards clacked while the guys with rank went about their business in partitioned areas along the back wall.

Blades looked terrible. Since the last time I'd seen him his skin seemed to have become almost transparent from fatigue. At the sight of us he rose to his feet and offered up what was meant as a smile. On the wall behind him was an enormous ceiling-to-floor chart that was divided by black rules into lines. Each line was marked with the heading *Jane Doe #1, Jane Doe #2,* and on through the full complement of Stanley Sarrek's sixty-three victims. Some of the lines were filled with physical descriptions—hair color, height, and weight—as well as a shorthand of what, at even the briefest glance, seemed horrific injuries. There were places for other information to be filled in: real names, addresses, next of kin. These were also blank.

No wonder Blades seemed pleased to see us. Compared to the painstaking task of filling in the details of tragedy for each of the murder victims on that wall of grief, anything having to do with Danny's death must have seemed like a relief.

"So how's it going?" asked Elliott as Blades led us behind a partition that had been erected to form a kind of conference area. We took seats around a chipped rectangular table of wood-grain Formica. On the portable blackboard someone had drawn a diagram in chalk. Shaped like a spider, it looked to be some kind of organizational chart.

"This whole case is a jurisdictional nightmare. I swear, if we spent half as much time following leads as we did arguing about who's responsible for what and who's going to get the credit, we'd know a lot more about the women in the back of Sarrek's truck than we do now. It also doesn't help matters any that the fucking FBI has a procedure for everything and a twelve-page form to go with it," complained Blades. "I swear, they do twenty minutes' worth of paperwork every time they use the john."

"So when are you going to put this guy away already?" demanded Elliott.

"Oh, we'll put him away. But I've got to tell you, I'm starting to get nostalgic for the bad old days. We could save ourselves a ton of aggravation if we just took this piece of shit in the back room and beat a confession out of him."

"I take it he hasn't talked."

"Not except to ask for a lawyer. I'm telling you, this squirrel is one slick sociopath. They've got three separate interrogation teams going at him in shifts, including two from some crack FBI unit, and so far nothing. Nada. In the meantime we're going through his driving log, trying to piece together where he's been, and working with local law enforcement to see if we can't make some identifications. The trouble is there may be sixty-three lines on that chart out there, but a lot of the bodies were dismembered, so it's hard to know exactly how many victims there were. Just documenting what's being done so that it can be used at trial is going to take six months. We have a family coming in later today from Wisconsin to see if they can ID their daughter. It's a start, but even if we put a name up on that board we'll still have sixty-two more blanks to fill in."

"I can't tell you how much I appreciate you taking the time to help us out," I said.

"Like I was telling Elliott yesterday," replied Blades, "I'm not sure that what happened to your friend is ever going to add up to murder, but it sure stinks to high heaven." He opened the manila folder that lay on the table in front of him and turned to Elliott. "I made you copies of the preliminary police report and the crime-scene photos. There's also a fax of the medical examiner's notes and a copy of the list of items taken from the apartment and put into evidence."

As Elliott flipped through the photos I forced myself to concentrate on the evidence list.

"What's this about a plastic needle cover?" I asked Blades.

The detective stooped to produce a cardboard box from beneath the table. Inside were individual plastic bags containing items the police had removed and tagged as evidence. He fished out one of the smaller ones and laid it in the middle of the table. Inside was the plastic sheath for the needle of a hypodermic syringe.

"We found it under the living room couch," he explained. "It looked to me like it must have been lying on the floor and got covered up when the couch got turned over."

"Did you find a syringe anywhere?" I asked.

Blades shook his head.

"You'll see in the autopsy notes the pathologist indicates the deceased had a needle puncture on his arm," said Blades.

"Which one?" demanded Elliott.

"On the back of the left upper arm," replied the homicide detective.

"Which means that since the victim was right-handed, he could have conceivably given himself some kind of injection," offered Elliott.

"Yeah," replied Blades, "but why would he? You don't shoot up drugs in the back of your arm."

"Maybe it was something he was taking for his AIDS," countered Elliott. "Vitamins. Anything."

"I think all the AIDS medications he was taking were oral," I reported. "But it can't hurt to ask his doctor."

Elliott turned his attention to the contents of the box. Looking over his shoulder, I didn't see much of interest: Danny's address book, an accordion file filled with bills and receipts, all of which Elliott already had copies.

"The phone company just came through with a printout of Wohl's phone records," Blades said, pulling another piece of paper out of the folder. "We haven't had time to run a check on the numbers, but I made you a copy anyway."

I took a look at the sheet Blades slid across the table in my direction. Before Danny and Stephen left for their trip to Japan there were dozens of calls every day, but the number dwindled to a trickle while they were abroad. During the forty-eight hours preceding Danny's death there were three calls, all on the Saturday he and Stephen arrived back from Japan. There was an incoming call at four forty-six for seventeen minutes followed by a twenty-six-second call to Stephen's home number. Five minutes later Danny made an outgoing call that lasted just under two minutes. Besides the call to Stephen I recognized that the other numbers were all at Azor Pharmaceuticals.

As I drove to Azor Pharmaceuticals the business of the phone numbers nagged at me. While Elliott was confident that the identity of the mystery man who was in Danny's apartment when he died would emerge from the scores of numbers that appeared earlier in the month, somehow I kept coming back to the three calls that were made the Saturday Danny returned from Japan. I was convinced they were important.

I remembered that Blades had said there was no cassette tape among the evidence the police had gathered. Presumably whoever had been with Danny when he died had taken the trouble to remove it from the answering machine and take it with him. Granted, the evidence he was attempting to conceal may have come from any one of the half-dozen short incoming calls received at Danny's number during the ten days he was in Japan. However, I figured it was safe to assume that whoever was with Danny when he died knew him well enough to be aware of the trip to the Orient—and when he was scheduled to return. That put the focus squarely on the calls received the day immediately preceding his death.

Of course, there was also the chance of some other perfectly logical explanation for the cassette tape's absence—perhaps it had broken before Danny had left for Japan, and he hadn't had the chance to replace it before leaving for his trip—but then there would have been no record of calls received by his number. No, the cassette was important.

As soon as I arrived at Azor I pulled a copy of the company's internal phone book out of Danny's desk drawer and began looking for anything that matched the incoming calls received by Danny to the numbers I had copied from the sheet Detective Blades had shown us. It took me a while because I had only numbers and the book was arranged alphabetically according to department, lab, or employee, but eventually I found a match. The two-minute call had been made to Carl Woodruff's office. I couldn't find the other number, though it was clearly one of those assigned to Azor Pharmaceuticals. I checked the cover of the internal directory and noted that it had been more than six months since it had been last updated. Perhaps the number had only been recently assigned. For the hell of it I picked up the phone and dialed the number. It rang four times before the company's internal voice-mail system picked it up.

"Hello, this is Dr. Michael Childress. I am away from my office at the moment, but if you will leave a message, I will promptly call you back."

CHAPTER
15

What was Michael Childress to Danny Wohl? Why had the crystallographer called him at home on the day before he died? It had always struck me as odd how, with the exception of Stephen, no one at Azor seemed particularly affected by Danny's death. I'd assumed it was because science was a closed fraternity. Now I learned that Michael Childress and Danny had had seventeen minutes' worth of things to talk about in the last twenty-four hours of Wohl's life. What else did they have in common?

The phone rang, jarring me from my reverie. It was Stephen, wondering whether I had forgotten about our meeting and reminding me he had yet another meeting, this one with the virology group, scheduled to begin in an hour. I grabbed a legal pad and hurried to his office. However, no sooner had we begun than we were pelted with a steady stream of interruptions—a question from Carl Woodruff, a phone call from a German enzymologist whom Stephen had been trying to get in touch with for days and whom he had high hopes of recruiting, Dave Borland stopping by to lobby for money to hire another technician. Before I knew it the virologists were knocking on the door and I was forced to contemplate the fact that the only place I was able to command Stephen's complete attention was in bed.

I arrived back at Danny's office feeling frustrated and discontent. I sighed and forced myself to shake it off. I decided the time had come to get all of Danny's personal things out of the office. Not only did I need room to work, but all the reminders of Danny were too distracting. I found a couple of empty boxes in the little room beside the copy machine and used them to pack up the diplomas, photographs, coffee cups, and bottles of aspirin that those of us who are desk-bound inevitably amass. There were a couple of things I thought might conceivably hold interest for Elliott, such as a Laurie Anderson concert stagebill that was a couple of months old and a receipt from a trip to the doctor. I set those aside.

In the back of the bottom drawer of his desk I found a bottle of Bushmills, three-quarters full, lying on its side beneath the Yellow Pages. I left it in the drawer. Once we'd inked the deal with Takisawa I figured I'd drink a toast to Danny.

With my impromptu exorcism complete I felt better and was able to settle down to carefully read through the Takisawa file.

Companies have distinct personalities, just like people, and while I was trying to learn the nuts and bolts of the deal that was on the table, I was also trying to get a sense of Takisawa's personality. The more I read, the more apparent it became that any alliance between the two companies was not going to be a natural fit, but rather a Kissingeresque marriage of convenience. Azor desperately needed money to finance its efforts with ZK-501, but Stephen was every bit as desperate to give almost nothing away. The company had already gambled heavily to get this far and it could ill afford to concede too much to its new partner.

On the other hand, Takisawa was being asked to drop forty million dollars into the slot machine of the ZK-501 project and would almost certainly want to be sure that it not just understood the odds but would get a large enough share of any eventual jackpot to justify the risk in the unlikely event their investment paid off.

The entire discussion was complicated by the fact that what was being negotiated was the rights to something that did not yet exist and might never come to be. The oft-quoted rule of thumb was that only one of every six promising research projects ever yields a drug. Even so, most new drugs do not represent a breakthrough. Their action is not novel. They just do what an existing drug does a little differently and hopefully a little better. A new drug that does something new or works in a previously undiscovered way is very rare. When he was being honest about the odds Stephen would tell you that, at best, he was asking Takisawa to stake him to a hundred-to-one shot.

Stephen's position in all this was colored by his belief that forty million dollars constituted mere pocket change for a company of Takisawa's size. Nonetheless, judging from the correspondence we'd thus far received from Tokyo, Takisawa was nervous at the prospect of laying out that kind of money to back the scientific hunches of a cocky wunderkind like Stephen. In addition to all manner of reporting requirements, the Japanese proposed a payout schedule for the forty million that was based on performance benchmarks, while Stephen naturally preferred to receive a check for the full amount on the day the two parties shook hands on the deal.

There were other issues as well. Takisawa wanted a training component that provided for three of their scientists to be sent annually to the labs in Oak Brook to observe and study. Stephen had announced that he had no intention of running a vocational school for Japanese chemists, but despite his protests I sensed there might be room to maneuver. I imagined a trio of earnest, white-coated Japanese scientists taking notes as Borland demonstrated his frozen-frog trick.

There were some points on which I knew Stephen would not budge. Tops on this list of potential deal breakers was Takisawa's insistence on receiving in exchange for their investment enough shares in Azor Pharmaceuticals to justify a seat on the company's board of directors. Stephen believed he had too many enemies on his board and after my conversation with Guttman I was inclined to agree with him. I made another note and decided to give myself twenty-four hours to come up with a list of palatable compromises.

The rest of it I broke down: documents to be pulled from files, financials to be updated by the accountants, phone calls to be made, issues to be addressed with Stephen, and questions that might be able to be answered without him. When I was finished, my "to do" list filled eight pages of my legal pad.

I found myself wishing I could clone Cheryl. While I desperately needed her to hold down the fort at Callahan Ross, I could have used her unflappable intelligence here. I was also glad my mother had agreed to take over the planning of the actual visit. I didn't care how much it ended up costing me in draperies and antiques. Looking at the monumental size of the other tasks that lay ahead of me I didn't see how I could have possibly managed otherwise.

And still I wondered whether all the effort was for nothing. When I listened to it, there was a small voice in my head that rattled off the hundred ways the deal could go wrong. If Mikos announced that they'd solved the structure first, Takisawa could get cold feet and back out, just as Okuda had with the integrase inhibitor. The Japanese, who possessed a horror of litigation, might recoil when they learned of the Serezine suits which Azor was obliged to carry on its balance sheet as a liability. Or, as we'd feared all along, their interest could just dry up and blow away as soon as we revealed to them that Danny was gone.

I didn't know enough about the science to understand the full extent of the reversals that were possible, but what little I did know chilled me. Even if Azor's crystallographers were able to solve the structure of the receptor molecule before Mikos, there was no guarantee Remminger would be able to design the new drug or even that it would work. There was always a chance that the toxic side effect–causing structures of the molecule could not be separated from its anti-inflammatory action and could therefore not be eliminated. Or they could make it and then find out it made you crazy or caused cancer or birth defects.

The more I thought about it, the more anxious I got. I felt overwhelmed and defeated without having even begun. I had to remind myself that that always happened at the beginning of a new case and I'd been there enough before to know it would pass. I found myself thinking of that hoary business riddle, "Q: How do you eat an elephant? A: One bite at a time."

By the time Lou Remminger knocked on my door she found me at the center of a blizzard of paper, as immersed in the problem of capital dilution as she was in the search for a successor molecule to ZK-501.

"I didn't think high-priced downtown lawyers had to work on Sundays," she drawled as she came in and took a seat. She was dressed in a pair of low-rider black jeans and a T-shirt that was two sizes too small and best described as phlegm-colored. I'd heard that Remminger had been invited to a dinner at the Chicago Academy of Sciences honoring Stephen Hawkings, the world-famous mathematician, only to be turned away at the door when security refused to believe she was Dr. Lou Remminger, the famous chemist.

I wondered why she did it. Maybe she'd decided the attention she got was worth the occasional hassles. It was hard to believe there were many places she went professionally where she didn't turn heads.

"I thought I'd come by and see if you were interested in furthering your scientific education," she continued.

"Always."

"Michelle's got some crystals she's going to try to diffract in a little while. I thought you might want to come down and watch."

"Does this mean she's close to the structure?" I asked with transparent eagerness. I couldn't help but think how wonderful it would be if we had the structure in time for the Takisawa visit.

"I don't know about close, but we'd sure be closer."

"So, tell me, how do they grow the crystals?" I asked.

"Michelle starts out with the receptor that Borland

purifies and then she adds another drug for the protein to latch onto. After that she suspends a drop of the solution from a glass slide and very slowly changes the composition of the solution and the surrounding vapor over a number of days. I think there may also be a magical chant involved that they teach you as a postdoc, but don't quote me on that."

"So how big are these crystals when they're ready to be looked at?"

"A big one would be a sixteenth of an inch long."

I found myself marveling, not for the first time, at the certitude with which scientists like Borland and Remminger seemed to deal with the subatomic world. I found it nearly impossible to imagine what a piece of furniture would look like upholstered in a different fabric while to the scientists of the ZK-501 project atoms and molecules seemed as solid and tangible as a sack of apples.

"The trouble, as you have no doubt heard, is that proteins in general and ZKBP in particular are a pain to work with. The conditions have to be absolutely perfect to grow crystals and even if you grow them once there's still no guarantee you'll be able to grow them again."

"So it's largely a matter of luck, then?"

"I wouldn't say that, but crystallography is one of those things where it's better to be lucky than good."

"And is Michelle lucky?"

"We'll see in about ten minutes, though I've got to say that up until now *lucky* is not a word I'd have picked to describe Michelle."

"Why's that?"

"I guess you wouldn't know him, but Michelle did her dissertation under Max Guzak—literally. Max is the big crystallographer at Rutgers. He's a lot like Childress except that on top of having a big ego he has something of a dick control problem. Too bad nobody ever warned poor little Michelle. She just showed up all starstruck that she'd been chosen to work in the great man's lab, having never had a date in her life—and all of a sudden there's this good-looking, Nobel prizewinner stroking her cheek and telling her how devastatingly attractive he finds her. I'm sure he told her she was the love of his life and fed her some story about how they were destined for each other."

"So what happened?"

"He fucked her for a couple of weeks and then dumped her for some new techie in his lab with blond hair and big tits."

"How did Michelle take it?"

"Michelle is tougher than she looks. Instead of running home to mama, Michelle stuck it out and finished her dissertation. Not only that, but she told him that if he didn't recommend her for a postdoc at M.I.T., she'd tell his wife all about what had gone on between them."

"So did she end up getting the postdoc?"

"Yeah. When she was finished there she was offered a postdoc at Purdue. That's when she started her work on PGHS-1 and doing triathlons."

"What's that?"

"A race where you swim for two hours, bike fifty miles, and then run a marathon."

"I know what a triathlon is," I replied. "What's PGHS-1?"

"It's one of two enzymes that aspirin binds to in the body. When Michelle started working on it, it was considered a key enzyme for the development of a new generation of analgesic compounds."

"And was it?"

"Nope. It turns out that it's the other enzyme, PGHS-2, that represents the active site. Michelle spent three years demonstrating that she could solve the structure of a complex molecule; unfortunately it was the wrong molecule. That's why she jumped at the chance to come to Azor to work on the integrase inhibitor. She took a lot of flack from her department when she took a leave of absence from Purdue. I've even heard rumors that they might not take her back at the end of the year, that they're going to say she violated her contract by coming to Azor."

"So why did she come?"

"Because she thought she was getting another shot at stepping into the spotlight. It's like a tryout in the majors. How can you not step up to the plate and see if you're good enough?"

"But Mikos solved the structure of integrase first, and Azor had to abandon the project when Okuda pulled out."

"There are some people around here who think that if they didn't waste so much time putting on a dog and pony show for every company that Danny and Stephen brought through here in the hopes of striking up some kind of joint venture deal she might have gotten to it first." Lou looked down at her watch and hopped to her feet. "Come on, it's time to see whether Michelle's luck has changed."

I followed Lou Remminger into the basement. Crystallographers, she explained, are by necessity bottom dwellers. The computer equipment and X-ray generators necessary for their craft are much too heavy to be supported by an upper floor. At Azor they are relegated to the bowels of the building, somewhere between the loading dock and the animal labs.

The main crystallography lab was nicknamed the aquarium on account of the large plate-glass window that separated it from the hallway. Through it could be glimpsed all manner of bulky and unfamiliar equipment, which collectively seemed to emit an ominous, low hum.

Before I'd become involved with Azor I'd always thought of scientific research as a highly cerebral enterprise. But the reality had much more in common with carpentry than with philosophy. I had seen for myself that laboratories are frustrating, physical workshops, places where the gap between the concepts and successful experiments formed a cruel and difficult chasm.

By the time we arrived in the basement a half-dozen investigators were already gathered around the aquarium window, peering into the darkened crystallography lab where Michelle Goodwin labored alone. The room was so crammed with equipment that there was no room for spectators. Also, many of the scientists no doubt preferred to avoid exposure to the high levels of radiation that were the inevitable by-product of the X-ray equipment. Everyone who worked in the basement, not just the crystallographers, wore a small device on their ID card that measured the cumulative amount of radiation to which they were exposed. Because it was colored red it was naturally referred to as "the red badge of courage."

Perched on a library stool, Michelle sat hunched over the superstructure of the X-ray generator like a bicycle racer poised over the handlebars. Her short dark curls were disheveled and her face, never pretty, was pulled into a tight frown of concentration. Her hand trembled as she mounted a thin capillary tube into the generator's rotating top. The generator, which was shaped like an industrial freezer with computers mounted at either end, was so big that it took up most of the available space in the lab.

"That's the crystal," Remminger informed me in a whisper. "It's floating in the liquid inside the tube."

Michelle moved quickly to one of the monitors and punched commands into the computer console. I couldn't begin to understand what I was seeing, but the tension on Michelle's face spoke volumes about its importance.

"She's just sent the X rays through the crystal," said Remminger.

As the machines hummed into action Michelle stepped away from the monitor to give all the spectators an unobstructed view.

"It'll be a few seconds before the pattern emerges," whispered Carl Woodruff, coming up behind me. There was anxiety in his voice—and excitement.

"Is Stephen here?" asked Remminger, looking over her shoulder.

"No," whispered Carl. "He thought his presence would make it worse if she doesn't succeed."

We all waited, straining in anticipation. For a full minute I don't think any of the people gathered in that hallway even breathed. When the first spots appeared on the screen a murmur of excitement rippled through the assembly, and even though I didn't understand any of it, my heart soared. But just as suddenly as it had started a hush descended. I couldn't see Michelle's face, but her body stiffened in disappointment as if she'd been dealt a blow.

"Oh shit," whispered Remminger.

"Proteins have very large, complex structures," Carl

explained as Lou made her way into the crystallography lab to console Michelle. "They have hundreds of atoms, thousands of electrons, protons, and neutrons. Shoot an X ray through a protein and you should see a small galaxy of spots. But look at this, there are only a dozen. What she's got in there isn't ZKBP, it's something else. A salt maybe."

Through the window I saw Lou say something to Michelle, but when the crystallographer turned around, her face was pale and rigid as a mask. Wordlessly she stalked out of the X-ray lab, past the rapidly dispersing scientists, and made her way quickly down the hall and out through the animal labs.

"Poor Michelle," someone whispered.

"Poor Michelle is right," echoed Borland. "Somebody better go after her and take away her damn car keys."

CHAPTER
16

By Monday morning I felt I had slipped back into the grip of routine that had ruled my life as an associate. I had gotten up before it was light, exercised, showered, and begun my workday as soon as I got into the car, dictating letters into my little tape recorder as I avoided potholes on Lake Shore Drive. The fact that I would spend only a couple of hours at my desk at Callahan Ross before driving out to Oak Brook to begin my day all over again at Azor did little to improve my outlook.

When I arrived at Callahan Ross, I was surprised to experience a pang of something very much like homesickness. Clearly, it was all starting to get to me—Danny's death, the sterility of the suburbs, the foreignness of the labs—room after room filled with unfamiliar equipment and people who for all intents and purposes spoke a language I didn't understand. Fluent in the jargon of due diligence, stock splits, and black-lined drafts, I had been trapped in a place where the air was filled with talk of receptor assays, X-ray diffraction, binding sites, and autoreactivity. It was nice, for an hour or two at least, to be back on home ground.

As I made my way through the still-empty corridors I was surprised to see Tom Galloway pacing the floor in front of my door. My heart sank. No one, not even Stephen, knew I would be coming to the firm that morning. Only something truly disastrous would be enough to propel Galloway to wait for me on the off chance I'd show up. Even from the other end of the hall I could see that he was agitated. There must have been another Serezine death over the weekend. There was no other explanation.

Six-thirty in the morning is no time for small talk so I unlocked the door, switched on the light, and ushered Tom Galloway into my office.

"Have a seat, Tom," I said as I unwound the cashmere scarf from around my neck and slipped out of my coat.

"I heard you were looking for me," he said in a voice so charged with emotion that it was practically a snarl. Not knowing what else to do I retreated to the relative safety of my desk.

"I don't think so," I answered, genuinely bewildered.

"Don't insult my intelligence by denying it," snapped Galloway. His fair skin was flushed to the roots of his jet-black hair, and his blue eyes flashed. His emotions, displayed so close to the surface, made him seem very attractive. No wonder juries loved him.

"Tom," I insisted calmly, "please sit down and tell me what it is you're talking about." He sat, but only reluctantly. After all, there was no pretending that this was a conversation between equals. I was a partner and Tom was an associate. When I said sit, he sat. "Now, what's this all about?"

"It's about you sending private detectives to every restaurant in town trying to catch me."

I sat back in my chair and wondered whether Tom had

just told me what I thought he had. I took a deep breath and slowly clasped my hands together, making a steeple with my index fingers and pressing them to my lips. It was one of the lawyerly gestures I had learned from John Guttman. He used it to buy time when he was caught off guard and I put it to the same use now.

After all the talk of the "famous fuck" theory, as Blades had dubbed it, the mystery man in Danny's life was a fourth-year associate at my own firm with a politically prominent wife and dreams of partnership.

"So you and Danny were involved," I said, careful to make it a bald statement of fact—nothing more.

"What business is it of yours?"

"None," I replied, clasping my hands together in front of me on my desk and looking him in the eye. My brain exploded with questions competing to be asked, but all litigators are actors and anyone, like Tom, who made his living by thinking on his feet would soon have the upper hand in any exchange. Instead, I decided to turn my silence against him. Surely he would be smart enough to realize that if I didn't ask the questions then someone else would come along who would.

"Do you want to tell me why you hired a private detective to find me?" he asked, after several seconds of painful silence.

"There are questions about Danny's death," I replied, but offered no details.

"What kind of questions? I thought he died of a heart attack."

"Who told you that?"

"The girl who answered the phone at Azor when I called on Monday."

"Why did you call?"

"I'd just received a letter from the carrier of Azor's liability insurance and I needed to talk to Danny about it," he replied defensively. "When he didn't answer his line, it flipped over to the receptionist. She was the one who told me about the heart attack."

"That's not how he died," I replied. There must have been all kinds of stories floating around that day, I thought to myself. The girl at the desk must have just repeated something she'd heard.

"So then how did he die?"

"A complication from his ulcer."

"I didn't know he had an ulcer."

"As far as I know, no one did. Maybe not even Danny."

"So if he died from an ulcer, why the private eye?"

"When did you first learn he was dead? What time did you call?"

"Oh, I don't know. Some time in the afternoon."

"Had you seen him since he came back from Japan?"

"Yes."

"When?"

"Sunday morning."

"What time?"

"I left Danny's between ten and ten-thirty."

"You went to see him at his apartment?"

"I spent the night," he replied. I could tell the words cost him. With every grudging admission I'm sure he felt like he was committing career suicide. He may very well have been. Frankly, Galloway's career was the least of my concerns.

"And how did he seem when you left him?"

"Seem?" demanded Galloway, his temper flaring. "He seemed fine. What the hell are you trying to get at? You just told me Danny died of an ulcer. If you want to accuse me of something, why don't you just come out with it? You expect me to sit here and set fire to my career, but you won't even do me the courtesy of telling me why?"

"Assuming you cared about Danny, I'd think you'd want to help."

"Help whom?" countered Galloway bitterly. "No one can help Danny, not anymore."

"Listen Tom," I said, with more kindness in my voice than I actually felt. "If you want, anything you tell me will be protected by attorney-client privilege. I just need you to answer a couple of questions."

Tom fished his wallet out of his back pocket, extracted a single dollar bill, and handed it to me. "I want a receipt," he said.

I grabbed a scratch pad from beside the phone and scribbled one. As every first-year law student knows, there are two parts necessary for a binding contract—the oral or written agreement and some form of material consideration that changes hands from one party to the other. I had never been a dollar lawyer before.

"When did you two start seeing each other?" I asked. "Was it when I gave you the Serezine litigation?"

"Yes. I knew the minute I met him in your office. We both knew."

"What about your wife?" I asked.

"I don't expect you to understand."

"I'm your lawyer. Try me."

"Most people think that being gay means hopping into bed with someone of the same sex. But you know what it also means? It means you're a member of the last minority that it's okay to hate. It means the things that most people work so hard for—the kids, the station wagon, some kind of social standing in the community—all those things are closed off to you."

"Does your wife know you're gay?"

"No."

"So tell me this. I was there that day in my office and frankly, the only thing I remember going on was a discussion of Azor's exposure on Serezine. How did Danny know you weren't the happily married young lawyer the world thinks you are?"

"Gaydar. It's the sixth sense gay people have. When you're gay, you can always tell when someone else is."

I tried to listen with an open mind, but images of Tom Galloway's wife and children kept intruding themselves. The idea that he'd been cheating on his wife—with someone who was infected with AIDS no less—did more than offend me. It also made me wonder what Danny must have seen in him. Surely someone who was capable of such betrayal would be capable of anything—including keeping his hemorrhaging lover from using the telephone if he thought it would hurt his chances of partnership.

"So you've been seeing each other pretty regularly since then?" I asked.

"Whenever I could get away."

"And you had no idea he was dead until you called his office on Monday?"

"No idea. How do you think this makes me feel?" he cried. "When I left him he was fine and the next day I find out he's dead. You of all people should understand."

"What did you do when you heard he'd died?"

"I had to leave the office."

"Did you go to Danny's apartment?"

"No. Why would I go there?"

"Did you have a key?"

"No. Danny had once dated a real psycho. Since then he's never given anyone the key to his place."

"After you found out, did you call anybody to tell them the news? Any of his friends?"

"I didn't know any of Danny's friends."

"So where did you go? Home?"

"I went to the Ritz-Carlton and got myself a room. I needed to be alone."

"So is that where you were when your secretary told me there'd been a death in the family?"

"Yes."

"What did you tell your family?"

"I said I had to go to Philadelphia for a deposition," he said, his face darkening.

More so than when we talked about the details of his affair with Danny, whenever we talked about Galloway's family I knew I was treading on dangerous ground.

"After you said good-bye to Danny on Sunday where did you go?" From the corner of my eye I noticed that Cheryl must have arrived for the day because the light to her extension was illuminated.

"Home. It was my son's birthday."

"Which one?"

"Jeff's."

"I didn't mean which son, which birthday?"

"Four."

Cheryl knocked softly at the door and stuck her head in apologetically. Normally she didn't disturb me when the door was closed, but at this time of the day she knew that coffee was a priority.

"Would you like some coffee, Tom?" I inquired. He nodded and I stuck two fingers up as Cheryl retreated.

"What did you get him?" I asked.

"What?"

"For his birthday, what kind of present did you get him?"

Tom looked at me like I was mad.

"One of those toy electric cars that he can sit in and drive up and down the driveway. Nancy picked it out. She's usually in charge of all the stuff like that."

Nancy was his wife. The senator's daughter.

Cheryl knocked softly and came in with two cups of coffee and cream and sugar on a tray. Tom took his, had a sip, and set his cup on the coaster I had placed on the edge of my desk.

"So now that I've told you, what's going to happen?" asked Galloway, once Cheryl had retreated and we were alone again. "Will you call off the private detectives?"

"From trying to find you, yes," I replied quietly. "From investigating the circumstances of Danny's death, no."

Before I left for Oak Brook, I wrapped my hand in Kleenex and carefully picked up the coffee cup that Tom Galloway had drunk from. I poured the remaining liquid into the potted plant on Cheryl's desk and asked her to find me a brown paper bag. She produced one from her desk drawer, shook out the crumbs from yesterday's lunch, and held it open for me while I dropped the cup inside. I told her to hand-carry it over to Elliott's office with instructions to have the prints lifted and compared to the ones that had been found on the glass of water on Danny's kitchen sink. From the look on Cheryl's face it was obvious that she understood the implications of my wanting to check for Galloway's prints in Danny's apartment, but also knew me well enough to realize that this was not a good time to be discussing it. Cheryl was as patient as she was intelligent. She was willing to wait until I had more information—and time—before pressing me for the details.

As soon as I got into my car, I punched in Elliott's number, but it was still early and all I got was the answering service. I left him a message to call me if he had any questions about the coffee cup. I wasn't sure what I was going to tell Elliott about Tom Galloway. With Stephen, however, there was no question. Not only was Stephen in a position to hurt Tom professionally, but more important, after the episode at the funeral home I was afraid of what he might do.

Traffic was, as they say on the radio, "slow and go" on the Stephenson. As I slogged through it I also worked my way through the call list that Cheryl had prepared for me. I had to confess that, despite my general misgivings about technology, voice mail was a wonderful thing. By returning calls before people arrived at work for the day, I was able to create the illusion of eagerly trying to reach them without being in danger of actually speaking to anyone.

I had just hung up on one call and was getting ready to dial up another when my phone rang. It was Rachel, Stephen's assistant. She told me I was needed urgently at Azor, but when I pressed her for details she had none. I told her I was on my way and put the accelerator to the floor. This is how I'm going to die, I told myself, dodging construction barrels and bellowing into my car phone as I race from crisis to crisis.

I arrived at Azor with all the worst-case scenarios screaming through my imagination: Azor had been named in a class action lawsuit involving Serezine, Takisawa had unilaterally killed the deal, Mikos had announced that they'd solved the structure. . . . I swiped in and walked as quickly as I could through the lobby without actually running and went straight to Stephen's office without even stopping to take off my coat.

When I got there I found Stephen and Carl Woodruff waiting for me. Both men were on their feet, pacing around the room.

"The power company has decided that we're finally going to get the new transformers we've been begging for," Stephen said as soon as I stepped into the room.

"You've been pleading for them ever since you moved into the building," I ventured uncertainly. Normally I would have expected that the power company's coming through would be considered good news. Azor had been suffering through brownouts and starved for electricity for months, but everything about the two men's demeanor spelled catastrophe. "When are they going to do it?" I asked, uneasily.

"Commonwealth Edison has informed us they are shutting off our power this Friday at five P.M. and working on the installation over the weekend," reported Carl. He sounded sick.

"When will they turn it back on?"

"They say six A.M. Monday," said Stephen.

"But that's the day Takisawa is set to arrive here at Azor," I protested. "I assume you've already asked them to push the work ahead by a day or two. . . ."

Carl nodded miserably indicating that he had and to no avail.

"Then what about rescheduling Takisawa?" I asked, wondering how many things could go wrong before it could be safely concluded that the deal was jinxed.

"We're having cash-flow problems as it is," snapped Stephen. "We can't afford any more delays."

"How will the power shutdown affect the work in the labs?"

"Virology will be hardest hit, of course," responded Carl. "The air handlers on the sixth floor completely exchange the atmosphere every six minutes. It will take several days to get that system back up and running after it's been shut down. I'm also not sure how many of the experimental animals will have to be moved to other quarters." I wondered where you'd find someone willing to take on a couple hundred rodents for the weekend but didn't say anything.

"Hematology, of course, will just be happy for the day off."

"What about the ZK-501 project?" I asked, thinking about all of Dave Borland's work in the cold rooms and what Lou Remminger had said about crystals having to be grown under ideal conditions.

"I figure we'll shut down the computers and bring in a diesel-powered refrigeration unit. Our tissue and reagent inventories, which aren't quite so sensitive, will be fine if we just turn the temperature down in the cold rooms as far as it will go and tape the rooms shut. Theoretically they'll hold below freezing until the juice comes back up on Monday morning."

"And if they don't get the power back up in time?" I asked.

"In that case I suggest we all show up bright and early with mops and flashlights," replied Stephen, without the slightest trace of humor.

* * *

By the time I finally sat down at Danny's desk I felt as though I'd already lived through a year's worth of catastrophe and it wasn't even nine o'clock. With a heavy heart I turned around and checked the fax machine for the transmissions that had arrived from Takisawa overnight.

Instead of slowing things down, the time difference between Chicago and Tokyo had a weirdly accelerating effect. Fifteen hours ahead of us, the Japanese business day ended as mine began. This meant I'd spend the day crafting our response to their most recent fax which I'd transmit to them at the end of the day. With the time difference they'd receive it just as they were arriving for work. Thus the faxes shot back and forth, communications hurtling forward much faster than if Takisawa were across the street.

I read through the various communications intently. There were requests for details about their proposed itinerary and politely worded inquiries as to when they would be receiving the financial information they had thus far requested. All the faxes were still personally addressed to Danny. Stephen had yet to settle on a strategy for breaking the news of Danny's death to Takisawa.

The last fax in the pile was the shortest, but I still had to read it through twice. Its contents were so disturbing that they got me on my feet and propelled me down the hall to Stephen's office. The door was closed, but I didn't even bother to knock.

"We have to tell Takisawa about Danny," I said.

"I'll have to get back to you," Stephen said quickly to whomever he was talking to on the phone. Once he had hung up the receiver I handed him the fax.

"It's marked personal to Danny," I told him.

Stephen read it quickly. It was a short personal note

from Takisawa's son-in-law, Hiroshi, saying that he would be traveling to New York on business before coming to Chicago and asking whether Danny might be free to meet him for dinner in New York later in the week. He would be staying at the St. Regis and had an extra ticket for *Sunset Boulevard*.

"We have to tell them," I said. "But more important we have to tell Hiroshi."

"I don't know," said Stephen.

"What do you mean you don't know? What if Hiroshi calls him here? Do you want him to hear that Danny's dead from whoever happens to be covering the switchboard that day? Or maybe you'd prefer to instruct all the secretaries that if anyone with a Japanese accent happens to call to speak with Danny they're to lie and say he's in a meeting."

"You're right. I'll write them."

"I'll draft something formal for you to send to Takisawa," I said. "But I had something else in mind for Hiroshi."

"What?"

"I think I should go to New York and tell him in person. I'm sure he'll appreciate being told privately," I said, thinking of the regrettable way Tom Galloway was dealt the news. "It'll also give me the opportunity to ask for his continued support for the deal."

"You mean you're planning on blackmailing him," said Stephen, vastly amused.

"Absolutely not," I replied, genuinely shocked. "I am merely going to explain to him how much I admire the finely honed Japanese traditions of loyalty and honor."

* * *

I didn't speak to Elliott until the end of the day. He was being deposed in an insurance-fraud case and had spent the day being grilled by a phalanx of defense attorneys. I wanted to tell him about what I'd learned about Tom Galloway and Danny, but he had other news that he was eager to share and that he managed to get to first. It turned out that despite his being otherwise occupied, someone from his office had managed to track down the tape from the surveillance camera in Danny's building. He suggested that we get together to have a look at it.

We agreed to meet at my office downtown at seven. When I hung up the phone I called Cheryl and asked her to please make sure that she set up a TV and a VCR in my office before she left. Driving back to the city I felt guilty. There was a mountain of work sitting on my desk in Oak Brook and I was leaving it undone in order to spend time with Elliott Abelman.

Back at Callahan Ross I stopped in the ladies' room long enough to brush my hair and put on fresh lipstick. As I pulled the pins out of my French twist I looked at myself in the mirror. Never quite beautiful under even the best of circumstances, today the face that looked back at me was tired and preoccupied. I wondered what Elliott saw in it that attracted him.

I knew what my mother would have said; I could even imagine her tone of voice: It wasn't my face he was interested in—it was my money. Having the Millholland family name was like wearing a bankbook around your neck. No one could look at you without attempting to calculate your net worth. Growing up I'd endured endless sermons on the subject of what men were really after. Girls with my kind of background were taught to protect their inheritances as assiduously as maidens in other centuries safeguarded their virginity.

Elliott arrived right on time, the videotape tucked under his arm like a box of chocolates. It had started snowing and the dark wool of his topcoat was dotted with melted flakes. As we walked back toward my office I asked him how his testimony had gone and he just rolled his eyes. Back in my office I took his coat and waved him into the same seat Tom Galloway had occupied that morning. Not wanting to change my mind, I immediately plunged into an account of Galloway's relationship with Danny.

"I was wondering what the story was behind the cup you sent over," he replied. "You've got to admit he's got one hell of a motive. He's gunning for a partnership, he's married with little kids, and his father-in-law is up for reelection. If he was the one in the apartment he wouldn't want to be anywhere near Danny when the paramedics showed up."

"He says Danny was alive when he left him."

"You wouldn't happen to have a picture of this guy, would you?"

I rooted through my desk drawers until I found a copy of the firm directory, which was known around the office as the face book. In addition to names and phone numbers it also contained head shots of every attorney at the firm. Callahan Ross had gotten so big and had offices in so many cities that I'd had to use the face book more than once just to make sure I'd know who was on my side when I walked into a meeting.

"He's a good-looking son of a bitch, I'll give you that much," mused Elliott, studying the picture. "That's probably why she married him, don't you think? Women are always suckers for looks."

"And men aren't?" I countered, trying to pretend he wasn't talking about Stephen.

"He sure matches the description of the guy who was seen with Danny at Kamehachi. Do you mind if I borrow this long enough to have some copies made?"

"Keep it. I'll get another."

"We'll have to see if we can get Joe to find out if his footprints match."

"You can't tell Joe."

"Why not?"

"Because what Tom told me about his relationship with Danny is protected by attorney-client privilege. What I just told you is off the record."

"You've got to be kidding. This guy is lying to his wife, he's lying to his partners, and you're worried about giving your word?"

"Wouldn't you be?"

Elliott Abelman stared at the ceiling as if seeking divine guidance. It didn't matter. We both knew I was right.

"Let's take a look at the tape and see if it puts him in the building around the time of death," he suggested. "With any luck we'll spot our friend leaving the building. That way we can go to Joe without sullying your reputation."

Elliott handed me the tape and I slipped it into the machine. The film was taken by a fixed-location camera mounted on the ceiling of the lobby and aimed at the front door of the building. It captured almost the entire area of the lobby with the elevator doors in the extreme left of the picture. There was no furniture, only a mean-ingless abstraction in a frame hung above a pillar-style ashtray on the wall opposite the elevators and a large ficus tree on either side of the doors which I strongly suspected of being artificial. The images were grainy and in black and white. A digital readout of the time appeared in the lower right-hand corner of the picture.

Elliott adjusted the tracking and explained that the tapes were automatically changed every six hours. The one we were about to see conveniently spanned the hours between eight A.M. and two P.M. the Sunday that Danny died. We watched the tape at regular speed for a minute or two, but it was so tedious that Elliott reached for the fast-forward button. Even speeded up it was like watching paint dry. People went in. People went out. But mostly the lobby stayed empty. At six minutes after nine a man in spandex shorts and a tank top struggled to get his bicycle through the door. At nine forty-three a woman in jeans and a T-shirt dropped an apple out of her grocery bag without noticing, and it lay untouched until a man in coveralls who looked like a building engineer picked it up, rubbed it on his sleeve, and took a bite as he walked out of the picture.

Tom Galloway stepped out of the elevator at ten twenty-six, well within the window of time that the medical examiner had given during which death had occurred. I reached across Elliott's lap and pushed the button to slow down the tape. In the picture Tom was dressed in chinos and a denim shirt. He wore a sweatshirt draped over his shoulders with the sleeves tied loosely across his chest. His hair looked wet and freshly combed, but there was nothing in his demeanor that spoke of any urgency or agitation. Indeed, his body language had seemed much more tense this morning when I'd found him waiting for me in the hallway outside my office door.

Elliott pushed the rewind button and we watched Tom walk backward across the lobby and back into the elevator. Then we watched the section of the tape again in slow motion but noticed nothing new. I shook my head.

"Maybe Tom left by the front door and then came back later," I offered.

"Let's see who else comes to pay a call," said Elliott, pushing the fast-forward button. An elegantly dressed woman with a mane of blond hair walked into the lobby at ten thirty-six, consulted a piece of paper in her pocket and left again, presumably having come to the wrong address. Two men arrived a couple of minutes later, one carrying a box from Dunkin' Donuts and the other a copy of the Sunday paper. While they waited for the elevator I could read the banner headline announcing Sarrek's sixty-three victims.

At ten fifty-one a large bald-headed black man with arms like a stevedore came in followed immediately by a tall woman in a bandana and sunglasses. They were immediately followed by a family with two toddlers who had to practically wrestle their double stroller through the door. It looked like the husband and wife were yelling at each other and both children were crying. We fast-forwarded through another twenty minutes of vacant lobby. I found myself wondering why I was doing this.

Then suddenly Elliott hit the pause button. "There!" he exclaimed. "This must be who the neighbor saw."

He hit the slow-motion button and we watched a figure in a gray Armani raincoat with a baseball hat pulled low over his face walk quickly through the lobby. The time in the lower right-hand corner of our screen read eleven twenty-seven. On one shoulder was slung an athletic bag, which looked as though it was filled to near bursting.

The tape was black and white, but even so the bag was distinctive—two colors, one dark and one light, dappled in what looked like a zebra pattern. In the other hand, the person carried a Marshall Field's shopping bag, large but apparently not heavy. Whether by accident or design, he kept his head down and turned away from the camera as he walked quickly through the lobby and disappeared out the door and into the street.

CHAPTER
17

Elliott rewound the tape and we looked at it again. I wish I could say we saw something new. But every time we viewed the tape, which we did dozens of times—backward, forward, in slow motion, and in freeze-frame—every time it was exactly the same. The figure of a man wearing Danny's raincoat and a baseball cap, with an athletic bag slung over one arm, darted quickly through the lobby and out into the street. . . .

By the time we finally gave up I had a headache from squinting at the grainy images on the video screen. I was also starving. The dinner the firm brought in every night for people working late had long ago been served. From long experience I knew that by now only the picked-over dregs remained. There aren't many restaurants that stay open for dinner in the loop, so I suggested we grab something at the Union League Club.

Outside the temperature had dropped and the wind roared through the canyon of office buildings, gathering speed, and seemed to drive right through us. It was literally too cold to speak. I clutched my coat around me and leaned into the wind. LaSalle Street was completely deserted except for the man huddled over the newspaper machine across from the Board of Trade, filling it with the next day's edition. It was hard to miss the headline that announced in ten-point type that the body of Sarrek's first victim had been identified. They were running what looked like a high school graduation picture beside the now familiar head shot of Stanley Sarrek. I thought of Joe Blades. One down, sixty-two left to go.

We arrived at the Union League with the relief of refugees. Shedding our coats in the cloakroom we made our way up the club's graceful central staircase to the main dining room. At that hour there were only a half-dozen diners lingering over their brandy. Louis, the maître d', wished us a good evening and ushered us to a quiet table by the window.

The Union League Club is a bastion of emphatic political incorrectness. After all, it had once boasted General Philip Sheridan—he of "the only good Indian is a dead Indian" fame—as a member. Women were a very recent concession and our presence had in no way altered the deliberately staid gentleman's club atmosphere.

Tonight I didn't care. I just wanted food. A few seconds later a waiter appeared in response to my telepathic summons and deposited a basket of fresh rolls. I helped myself as Elliott watched me, grinning.

"What?" I demanded, greedily tearing one in half.

"Nothing."

"Oh, come on. What?"

"I just get a kick out of watching you eat."

"You can't possibly mean that."

"You don't understand. Most women are afraid to let anyone see that they're hungry. They tell the waiter to take the butter away and order their salad dressing on the side."

I was curious about these breadless women of his acquaintance but realized that by asking I would be opening myself up to questions I did not intend to answer.

"Well, tonight I'm so hungry that I'm thinking of ordering a glass of salad dressing as an aperitif," I announced.

"I've missed you, you know."

I shook my head in warning. "Don't," I said, meaning it. I looked at him across the table and wished I didn't want to sleep with him so badly. I was just being a spoiled little rich girl, I scolded myself, wanting what she knew she shouldn't have.

The waiter came and we ordered steaks for both of us and a very nice cabernet to wash it down with. Like many clubs, the wine cellar at the Union League was generally much more reliable than the kitchen.

"So," ventured Elliott. "Tell me about this guy Galloway. Do you think he's our bad guy?"

"How can he be?" I countered. "We both saw the tape. He left the apartment just like he said."

"He could have come back in another way, maybe from the garage."

"For that matter so could the guy we're looking for."

"Tell me about Galloway anyway."

"Well, up until this morning I'd have told you he was a star. You know the type—top of the class without breaking a sweat, good-looking, socially poised. The kind of charmed young lawyer who comes along every couple of years and makes it all look easy. He's popular with his peers, the partners are falling all over themselves to help his career, and the secretaries are all in love with him."

"Good lawyer?"

"Whatever else he may be Tom Galloway is a crack litigator. He's equally good in a courtroom or a settlement conference. He made a splash with a couple of big wins with very complicated cases in front of a jury. That's why I recommended him to Azor for the lawsuit involving Azor's new antischizophrenia drug."

"Is that how he and Danny met?"

"Apparently."

"Now that you know about the two of them what's your opinion of Galloway?"

"Beneath contempt pretty much sums it up."

"Because he's secretly gay?" Elliott inquired.

"No, because he's a liar," I replied. "I don't think I'd feel any differently if he'd been sleeping with his secretary. Come to think of it, as far as I know he could be sleeping with her, too. When a man is not who he says he is then he could be anybody. It opens up whole vistas of deception."

Elliott laughed.

"What is so funny?" I demanded.

"You know what you sound like?"

"No. What?"

"A partner in a large and prestigious corporate law firm."

"Your point?"

"You realize that your reaction is exactly what he's afraid of, especially since you say he's up for partnership soon. That kind of fear is a powerful motive."

"Motive for what?" I countered. "Danny died of natural causes. Joe's right, no matter what we find out about what happened in that apartment it's not going to turn out to be legally actionable."

"Then you tell me," replied Elliott, "why are we doing this?"

I thought for a minute. The answer I came up with surprised me.

"Because Stephen is a scientist," I said.

"Meaning?"

"Before I started working at Azor I don't think I could have told you what that meant. I had always assumed that being a scientist was just another kind of job, like being a teacher or an airline pilot. But on some level being a scientist means operating in the world in an entirely different way. A scientist is someone who embraces a much more rigorous and demanding view of the world. Scientists can't just accept that something happens. They spend their lives relentlessly asking why things happen. They are driven to know, to explain, to understand what makes things work." I thought about Michelle Goodwin's tearful flight from her lab when her crystals failed to diffract. "I never realized it before, but their obsession with finding out can be a terrible thing. With Stephen it's more than just wanting to know what happened to Danny. I don't think he has any choice. He won't be able to stop asking questions until he does know."

"What about you?" asked Elliott. "Do you care about what happened to Danny?"

"Of course, I care," I replied. "Of course, I'm curious. But I'm a lawyer. Intellectually I live in the gray spaces, somewhere where there are shades of meaning. I want to know what happened to Danny, but on some level I can accept that I might never know what happened in that apartment that day. Stephen can't."

The waiter appeared with salads and refilled our glasses.

"I found out who called Danny the day he died," I continued once the waiter had retreated out of earshot.

"Who?"

"Michael Childress. He's a crystallographer who works on the ZK-501 project at Azor."

"What's that?"

"They're trying to find the next generation of anti-inflammatory drug, one that's more effective than cortisone but with fewer side effects. Michael Childress is a senior investigator on the project."

"What can you tell me about him?"

"I should have pulled his curriculum vitae for you, but I didn't think of it. All I can really tell you about him so far is that he's famous and despised."

"Despised?"

"I really don't think that's too strong a term. Stephen and I took him out to dinner once. I found him extremely unpleasant—arrogant, self-centered, abrasive. I gather he has something of a reputation for expropriating other people's work."

"So what was his connection with Danny?"

"That's the big question. At the time he died, Danny was working almost full time on the ZK-501 project, trying to find a source of outside funding to keep the project afloat. I'm sure they must have had some dealings, but I can't tell you anything more than that."

"I'll have to check him out."

The waiter came and took away our salad plates, materializing a few seconds later with our entrées.

"You know," I said, cutting into my steak, "while we're on the subject, there's somebody else I think you should check out." As we ate I explained to him about Danny's friendship with Takisawa's son-in-law, Hiroshi Toyoda.

"The plot thickens," remarked Elliott, taking careful notes as I spoke.

"Not necessarily," I replied. "At this point I have no reason to assume Hiroshi was even in the country on the day Danny died."

"That shouldn't be too difficult to find out. But if he was the one with Danny when he died, we don't have to go looking too far for the reason he wouldn't want anyone to know he was there."

"Before you get too excited you'd better think about what's on the videotape," I said. "I don't know about you, but I think the guy in the raincoat looked too big to be Japanese."

As the doorman flagged down a cab Elliott helped me with my coat. Both of us had drunk enough cabernet to constitute an excuse for just about anything. Standing in the darkened cloakroom, his hands lingering on my shoulders, I would not be honest if I said I didn't consider the possibilities. But I was not drunk enough to guarantee that I wouldn't bolt as I had the last time, nor stupid enough not to foresee the burden of any indiscretion, like a piece of awkward baggage, that would then have to be carted around.

We parted as we had so many times before, with things unsaid or deliberately ignored. I must confess that the whole ride home I thought nothing of Danny or Takisawa or Azor Pharmaceuticals' predicament. Once inside the apartment I found Claudia's suitcase sitting in the entrance hall and a message waiting for me on the answering machine. Whoever called must have done so after Claudia had gone to bed. My roommate's sleep is much too precious to her to allow a phone in her bedroom. Instead she sleeps with her beeper on the pillow.

I pushed the button to rewind the tape and kicked off my shoes, willing the circulation to come back to my feet. The lights were off in the hallway that led to the back of the apartment and everything was quiet except for the whir of the machine. Finally the tape clicked and a female voice filled the room.

"Ms. Millholland? This is Dr. Julia Gordon with the Cook County medical examiner's office. I've been trying to reach Stephen Azorini, but I see your number is also in the file, so I thought I'd try you as well. I was hoping that one of you would be available to come and see me at my office tomorrow. Morning is best for me, but I'm sure I could accommodate you anytime that is convenient for you. I'll be in at eight and I think you'll have an easier time the earlier you arrive. I'm afraid the media has become a permanent fixture outside our building, but they're not generally out in full force until after ten o'clock. I'll leave your name at the front desk so that they'll know I'm expecting you. If there's a problem . . ."

I waited for the end of the message. Then I picked up the receiver and dialed Stephen's number. It was after eleven o'clock and I was afraid I might wake him, but the phone just rang until the answering machine picked up. I tried his office and got no answer. I tried his car phone with the same result. Walking back to my bedroom I was filled with curiosity. I couldn't help but wonder what had happened to Stephen. It wasn't like him to be unreachable. I also could not imagine what was so urgent that Dr. Gordon was trying to track Stephen down after hours. In my experience, doctors seldom came chasing after you except with bad news.

The next morning I tried Stephen again, to no avail. Instead I arrived at the Robert J. Stein Institute for Forensic Medicine a few minutes after eight o'clock. While a number of white news vans were parked haphazardly on the curb like so many beached whales, my arrival did not seem to stir their interest. A tall fence topped with cyclone wire had been erected around a portion of the parking lot where it abutted the loading dock. Beyond it could be glimpsed Stanley Sarrek's infamous refrigerated trailer.

I hadn't been to the ME's office since they'd moved into their new building. Once I was inside it struck me as a kind of Marriott for the dead. Even the dove-colored lab coats worn by the pathologists were of the same soothing shade of gray as the carpeting. In deference to the newly deceased, the temperature of the building was kept almost as low as that in Borland's meat locker. But one thing all the new carpet and boring lithographs could not disguise was the stale stench of death that no amount of air freshener could mask.

I consulted with the woman at the reception desk, a stately black woman whose hair had been swept up and arranged into a single coil, who directed me to Dr. Gordon's office on the third floor. On my way several people raced past me, their looks of focused determination speaking volumes about the current crisis.

Dr. Gordon's door was open and I found her behind her desk, eyes closed, dictating into a small handheld recorder, the twin of the one I use. I knocked softly on the door frame. Her eyes shot open and her sagging shoulders snapped to attention as I announced myself.

"Ms. Millholland," she said, rising to her feet. "I'm so glad you received my message. Please come in. I've been getting into the office so early on account of this Sarrek business, I've missed seeing you at Starbucks."

Hyde Park, where both of us lived, is essentially a small place. Surrounded by the ghetto, it is ruled by a kind of siege mentality that fosters a small-town friendliness you wouldn't normally expect in an inner-city neighborhood. For the last several months Julia Gordon and I had found ourselves on parallel schedules, running into each other as we stopped for coffee on the way to the office a couple of mornings a week. I was hoping this sense of neighborliness would help her to be forthcoming.

Julia Gordon was a small woman in her late thirties with a loose cap of blond curls and the wide blue eyes of a China doll. On the credenza behind her desk sat a framed photograph of her two daughters, smiling girls who looked to be about four and six years old. Behind the photo hung a poster showing the characteristics of wounds made by unusual bullets illustrated with color photos. I wondered whether she brought her daughters with her on Take Your Daughter to Work Day or whether they visited the hematology lab with her husband.

"I'm sure you're wondering why I called," she said, searching through the clutter on her desk for something. She shifted through the piles until her hand lit upon a file.

"I'm actually surprised you even have the time," I replied.

"We are a bit stretched, I'll give you that," she said, smiling weakly. "The Sarrek case presents a tremendous challenge. The work of identifying his victims is especially painstaking, because so far the inside of the truck is the only crime scene we have. Even though we're receiving a great deal of help from the FBI, it's offset by the amount of coordination that must be managed among the various law enforcement agencies. Since it looks as though there's a good chance the case will be tried in our jurisdiction, we're anxious not to give up too much control over the investigation. Of course, dealing with the media has been a nightmare in and of itself. The day Sarrek was arrested I actually found a reporter hiding in my garage."

"They're jackals," I said in a simple statement of fact.

"Unfortunately, cases like this have an appeal, an entertainment value if you will, that somehow manages to transcend the enormity of the taking of human life."

"I know by comparison Danny Wohl's death must seem terribly inconsequential," I said apologetically.

"No death is inconsequential," replied Dr. Gordon with sudden fierceness. "No matter what the media would like us to believe, the circumstances of a person's death in no way alters the meaning of their life." She took a deep breath. "I didn't mean to serve up a lecture, but I'm afraid that what I've seen from the media since Sarrek's arrest has sometimes made me wonder which of them is the bigger monster.

"Now, about Mr. Wohl. As you know I was not the pathologist who visited the death scene, nor the one who actually performed the autopsy. Under normal circumstances the way it works in our office is that whichever pathologist goes to the scene also performs the postmortem exam. Unfortunately, with our resources spread so thin on account of the Sarrek deaths, one pathologist went to the scene and another actually performed the autopsy. Complicating matters is the fact that neither of the forensic pathologists who examined Mr. Wohl is permanently assigned to this office. Dr. Barrows, who took the unattended-death call and went to Mr. Wohl's apartment, was on loan to us from the DuPage County coroner's office. Dr. Breuner, who actually performed the autopsy, is an assistant medical examiner from Lake County in Wisconsin. Both men have subsequently returned to their own jurisdictions, though I have talked to Dr. Breuner several times on the phone."

"So what killed Danny?" I asked. "How did he die?"

"I don't know if you realize it, but what you're asking is actually two separate questions. Before I answer let me explain some things. As a medical examiner I'm actually interested in three things: cause of death, mechanism of death, and manner of death. The cause of death is the event which sets into motion the mechanism of death."

"I don't understand."

"Let me give you an example. Yesterday I performed an autopsy on a thirty-one-year-old, Caucasian male who had been shot at close range in the chest and bled to death before the paramedics could get him to the hospital. The cause of death in this case was a gunshot wound to the chest. The mechanism of death was exsanguination—he bled to death."

"Like Danny."

"Yes. Even though the two deaths—your friend's and the man who was shot—were completely dissimilar in their cause, the mechanism was the same. While there are a huge number of possible causes of death, there are only a handful of mechanisms: respiratory arrest, cardiac arrhythmia, myocardial infarction."

"What's the manner of death, then?"

"The manner of death is a description of the circumstances of death. This is indicated on the death certificate by checking off a box at the bottom. The choices are: natural, homicide, suicide, accidental, and undetermined."

"So what was the manner of death in Danny's case?"

Instead of answering my question, Dr. Gordon reached for a file on her desk and began reading to me from it.

"Daniel Allen Wohlinski, age thirty-two, height one hundred eighty-six centimeters, weight seventy-six kilos. Found in his apartment by the building engineer. The victim had obviously been dead for some time; rigor was already beginning to pass off in the upper extremities so he was pronounced dead at the scene, which, if the photographs are any indication, was pretty grisly.

"Physical examination of the body revealed several indications consistent with AIDS. Kaposi's sarcoma lesions on the upper thighs, evidence of thrush in the victim's mouth, and some slight lymphatic abnormalities. Blood-alcohol levels were not taken because the technician was not able to draw an adequate sample. The same for toxicology." Dr. Gordon turned the page. "Stomach contents were essentially zero, which is not surprising considering he vomited up almost his entire blood supply. Dr. Breuner located evidence of severe arterial erosion caused by a gastric ulcer. In other words, he had a hole in his stomach big enough to stick your finger through. Unfortunately, it was in a place where the wall of an artery was compromised as well."

"Which is why he bled to death."

"Yes."

"So why aren't you ready to check the box at the bottom of the form that says 'natural' and be done with it?" I asked, knowing that if the circumstances of

Danny's death were as clear-cut as that we wouldn't be having this conversation.

"In reviewing the case I've come across some rather unusual findings."

"Unusual in what way?"

"Well, for one thing, some curious abnormalities have showed up in the microscopic slides of organ tissues."

"What kind of abnormalities?"

"There are pervasive thrombi in the glomeruli of the kidneys. In lay terms that means that there are lots and lots of blood clots in the filtering apparatus of the kidneys."

"Big clots?" I asked, without thinking. "I take that back. How big can they be if you have to use a microscope to see them?"

"It's not the size that's the issue, but rather their pervasiveness that makes me suspicious."

"Suspicious of what?"

"Well, for one thing, D.I.C."

"What's D.I.C.?"

"It's short for disseminated intravascular coagulation. It's a clotting syndrome that's usually associated with things like massive thrombosis, pulmonary embolism, cardiogenic shock, liver failure due to cirrhosis, snake bite, anaphylaxis. You also see it in some end-stage cancers."

"Could Danny have had one of those things?"

"Dr. Breuner found no evidence of them at autopsy and these are things that would be hard to miss. Dr. Breuner just assumed that D.I.C. had followed the erosion of a blood vessel by the gastric ulcer. Certainly that is possible, but it would have occurred over a much longer period of time than is consistent with the blood evidence at the scene. However, since Dr. Breuner was not the pathologist who examined the body in situ he had no way of knowing that."

"I don't understand."

"Judging from the condition of the apartment, D.I.C. must have occurred very rapidly—too rapidly to have been the result of an ulcer."

"And AIDS couldn't have caused it?" I asked.

"I'll grant you that AIDS poses some special issues for forensic pathologists. For example, lung cancer can kill in only so many different ways, all of which are recognizable. HIV, on the other hand, offers a seemingly endless range of scenarios depending on which organ system is set upon by the virus and which of a wide array of microbes breaches the immune system first. I think that's why Dr. Breuner initially discounted the abnormal tissue findings. He sees many fewer cases of AIDS in his jurisdiction than we see here and I think he just assumed that the virus was in some way involved."

"So what does all this mean?"

"Unfortunately, Ms. Millholland, there is no cookbook that tells us how to figure out how people die. Some things are clear-cut—gunshots, dismemberments, strangulation— but sometimes the footprints that death leaves behind can be very subtle. I don't usually take my work home with me, but in this case I took the liberty of showing Mr. Wohl's tissue slides to my husband, who as you probably know happens to be a hematologist."

"What did he say when he looked at the slides?" I asked.

"He took them back to his lab, where they have a setup that allows them to photograph microscope slides. He took these and suggested that Dr. Azorini have a look at them." She handed me a manila envelope.

"Why Stephen?"

"I understand that Azor Pharmaceuticals is currently trying to get a new artificial blood product approved by the FDA."

"So?"

"So Hugh seems to think there's a good chance that a substance being used at Azor in one of their labs might have been the cause of D.I.C. in Mr. Wohl."

CHAPTER
18

As soon as I arrived at Azor I went straight to Stephen's office. I didn't even bother to take off my coat. I wanted to show him the pictures that Julia Gordon's husband had made of Danny's tissue. I needed to know what explanation, if any, he could offer for its appearance.

Blessedly he was in. I found him deep in conversation with Michelle Goodwin. Anxiously I hovered in the doorway, hoping for a good opportunity to interrupt. I didn't understand a word of what they were saying. Whatever it was must have been important—to Michelle Goodwin, at least. Her entire body sang with intensity as she leaned forward to make a point with the keenness of a runner straining for the finish line. She had shed her customary shyness. Her manner was animated, her skin flushed with excitement. For a moment I thought I caught a glimpse of what the lecherous Nobel prizewinner had seen in her.

I also couldn't help wondering, once again, where the myth of the cool and unemotional scientist had come from. From my brief experience at Azor it was obvious that nothing could be further from the truth. I had come to see firsthand that a laboratory is a frustrating place from which to view the world. It took passion, obsession even, to see an investigator through the daily grind of making experiments work.

"I'm so sorry to interrupt," I said, having no choice but to just break in on them, "but I need a word in private with Stephen."

"We'll just be another couple of minutes," replied Stephen.

"I've just come from the medical examiner's office . . ." I ventured.

"I'm sorry, Michelle," said Stephen, turning to the crystallographer. "I'll stop down in the modeling room for that reprint. We can finish up then."

For a minute I thought she hadn't heard him, but finally she rose to her feet. She was a tall woman, with the blocky, squared-off gait of a triathlete. Michelle's physical assurance stood in strange contrast to her abrupt social mannerisms. Whenever I saw her outside of her lab I got the sense that she felt most at home in the computer-generated world of crystallography and she was eager to get back to it as soon as she could.

"What did the medical examiner want?" demanded Stephen, as soon as the door had closed behind Michelle.

"You, actually. Julia Gordon and I were both trying to reach you last night. Where were you?"

"I was going over our results on Hemasyn with Gus Sandstrom and a couple of the other senior investigators. We worked all night getting them ready to send to the FDA."

"I tried you at the office."

"We were upstairs in the hematology conference room. I must have forgotten to switch my line over. What did Julia Gordon want?"

"She wanted you to have a look at these." I took the photographs out of my briefcase and handed them to Stephen. While he studied them I sat down in the chair Michelle Goodwin had just vacated. It still felt warm.

"What am I looking at?"

"They're photographs of kidney tissue taken under the microscope."

"Why does Julia want me to look at photomicrographs?"

"It wasn't Julia Gordon who suggested that you look at them. It was her husband."

"Why?" he asked, looking closely at the photographs for the first time. "What could I possibly tell Hugh about kidney tissue? Why are there all these thrombi in the small blood vessels?"

"That's the question. Is there anything at Azor that could have caused that kind of clotting?"

He looked up and his eyes met mine. I saw the weariness in his face and my heart went out to him. As much as he hated to admit it, Danny's death, his high-wire act with the Japanese, the dissension on the board—they were all taking their toll.

"PAF would do this," he said, quietly.

"What's PAF?"

"Platelet activating factor. It's a powerful procoagulant. They use it upstairs in the Hemasyn labs as a control in clotting studies. But you didn't tell me where the tissue in this photograph came from."

"It was taken from Danny."

Stephen dropped the photograph onto the surface of

his desk and leaned back in his chair as if trying to get some distance.

"Is there some way to test for this PAF stuff?" I asked.

"I wouldn't think so. PAF is metabolized by the body almost instantaneously. It disappears without a trace."

"So how does it work? What does it do?"

"Just like the name says, it's a powerful enzyme that makes blood clot, especially in the very high concentrations we use in our labs. Even a tiny dose injected into a person would cause almost immediate D.I.C. The PAF causes the body's clotting mechanisms to spring into action, which is why you'd see all that microscopic evidence of clotting in the tissues."

"But then why would you bleed to death?" I demanded. "Wouldn't all your blood just clot?"

"No. The body's clotting mechanisms, the platelets and proteins that cause the blood to clot, aren't sufficient for the body's entire blood supply. Once they're exhausted—which would happen almost instantaneously with PAF—the remaining blood wouldn't clot at all."

"So tell me, if Danny hadn't had a perforated ulcer, would the PAF have killed him?"

"Most definitely, but in that case he would have bled to death internally. Compared to what went on in that apartment it would have been a relatively quiet, comfortable death. He might not even have known what was happening to him."

"Are there other substances that could do the same thing besides PAF?"

"Maybe some of the more conventional anticoagulant drugs at very high doses. . . ."

"How many people in the company have knowledge about this PAF stuff?"

"I should think just about everybody, especially after what happened in the animal labs this summer."

"What happened?"

"I can't believe I didn't tell you. You must have been out of town. One of our summer interns, a college kid from the University of Illinois who should have at least been able to read English, was supposed to mix twenty-five ccs of profluralkynase, an animal sedative commonly known as PFA, into the drinking water of the twenty-five rabbits about to be tested in the AZU-90 protocol. He was either dyslexic or in a hurry, because when he went into the supply room he grabbed the bottle of PAF off the shelf and mixed it with the water."

"What happened to the rabbits?" I asked.

"They all bled to death."

When I got back to Danny's office the phone was ringing. It was Cheryl, sounding uncharacteristically ruffled.

"Who told your mother she could buy a fax machine?" she demanded without so much as a hello. "She keeps sending me these memos about things she wants me to do."

"Like what?"

"This morning when I got in she faxed me a list of twenty-eight florists that she wants me to call. I'm not exaggerating. She wants to see if they can get some type of orchid whose name I can't even pronounce. She claims it's for these Japanese businessmen who are coming next week, but I'm beginning to think I'm in some kind of Martha Stewart nightmare and I just can't make myself wake up."

"What can I say except that you're going to go straight to heaven for this?" I replied. "What else is going on today?"

"So far nothing urgent. I'm just about to fax you your phone messages and I have a messenger on his way with some things for you to sign. Oh, and someone named Mimi Sheraton just called. She's got to be a friend of your mother's. How come they all talk like that?"

"I think they wire their jaws shut their last year of finishing school. Not only does it make them very thin, but it teaches them how to talk while clenching their teeth."

"Ms. Sheraton says to tell you she's arranged for the structural engineers to come and look at the apartment this afternoon and she thinks it would be good if either you or Stephen would be there."

"Call her back and tell her she can either handle it herself or reschedule for after the Takisawa visit. You might also tactfully suggest that in the future she check with you before she schedules anything."

"I hope you don't mind me asking, but why do you need a structural engineer?"

"Nothing really. It's just that the ceilings are all falling down."

"You don't think this is some kind of sign, do you?"

"No, I do not," I replied promptly. "Have I already asked you yet whether you want to work this weekend?"

"No. Do I?"

"I'm desperate."

"How desperate?"

"Time and a half and as many suits as you need when you start interviewing."

"I guess if you twist my arm . . ." replied my secretary, sounding pleased. Clothes gave her a kind of pleasure I could never understand. "But you have to promise me one thing."

"What's that."

"You're not going to make me call florists or make up seating charts."

I hung up the phone and tried to settle down to work, but I couldn't concentrate. All I could think about was PAF. Stephen had said it was kept out in the open in the hematology labs upstairs, but there was also a quantity stored in the reagent room in the basement, which was adjacent to the animal labs. According to Stephen the reagent room was in such constant use that it was kept unlocked during the day.

Too restless to settle down to the tasks before me I decided to pay a call on Carl Woodruff.

I found the project coordinator in his office, sitting behind his desk and methodically working the length of white cord that hung from his Venetian blinds into a professional-looking noose.

"Shall I call the local suicide prevention hot line?" I inquired.

"Just practicing," he replied brightly, and began unraveling it. "Besides, it's not for me."

"So tell me," I ventured, "who are you fitting for a noose?"

"Michael Childress, who else?"

"Who else, indeed. What has he done this time?"

"I went down to the modeling room this morning to talk about what he's going to have to do to get ready for the electrical shutdown over the weekend. Naturally, he handed me a long list of things to be done and immediately announced that of course he would not be available to do any of it himself. He's leaving for Boston on Friday for some conference so he expects Michelle and me to get the crystallography labs ready. I also had the nerve to mention that I needed the radiation logs for crystallography before he leaves."

"What are radiation logs?"

"Every employee who works in an area where they may be exposed to radiation wears one of these little red devices clipped to their ID card."

Carl pulled his card off his belt and handed it to me. The device was a red rectangle about two inches long and half an inch wide attached to his ID.

"It measures the amount of radiation you've been exposed to. Everybody in the crystallography lab is required by the EPA and OSHA to wear one. The radiation levels have to be recorded once a week and we have to submit the readings to the government or we're slapped with a fine.

"Naturally Childress considers himself above government regulation. How could he be expected to be bothered with something as trivial as keeping track of how much hazardous radiation people in his department are exposed to? At Baxter they had people who did that for you. Scientists were not expected to clutter their craniums with such trivia. Oh god, how I miss Danny."

"Why Danny?"

"While Danny was alive Childress complained to him."

"Why? Were they friends?"

"Are you kidding? Danny hated Childress's guts."

"Why?" I asked. This was hardly the answer I had expected.

"Because Childress is a complete tick. He was always sauntering into Danny's office with some grievance that he insisted was a breach of his employment contract."

"What kind of things did he complain about?"

"Important stuff—his office was too small, he insisted on flying first-class but accounting would only reimburse him for coach. The man is a first-class pain in the ass."

"Why didn't he come to you with these complaints? As the project administrator I'd think you'd be the natural one to go to."

"I think he just liked going over my head and Danny was gracious enough to put up with it."

"Speaking of Danny," I said, trying to sound casual, "did he try to get in touch with you at all when he got back from Tokyo? I found a note he'd made to call you, but I couldn't tell whether he ever managed to get in touch."

"He phoned me the day he got back," replied Woodruff easily. "He left a message on my voice mail that he wanted to have a look at the files I had on the integrase project. Normally I'm in all day on Saturday, but my wife's parents were visiting that weekend, so I didn't find out he'd called until Monday. It's strange to think that by the time I got the message he must have been dead."

"Was there anybody from the company who Danny was friends with outside of work?"

If Carl thought my question strange he didn't show it. Instead he thought for a minute. "It's hard to say, really.

Over the years the projects change, people come and go. Danny was always in a funny position. As you have no doubt noticed some of the labs can be quite close-knit. It always depends on which project was taking a lot of his time. A couple of years back, when the company was going flat out to develop a new antirejection drug for transplant patients, he got real friendly with a molecular chemist named Gregg Waskowitz. But Gregg's been back at M.I.T. for a couple years. . . ."

"What about recently?"

"These days Danny was working almost full time on finding funding sources for ZK-501 so those were the people he had the most interaction with. But really he didn't seem particularly close to anybody. He occasionally liked to go to Remminger's lab and give her a hard time, but I don't know whether they ever got together outside of the office. Every once in a while I'd see Michelle in his office, but I think they were just commiserating about Childress. I must say I'm beginning to acquire a renewed understanding of what that poor woman has to put up with working in the same lab as that man."

"Was there anybody besides Childress that Danny didn't get along with?"

"You knew Danny, he got along with everybody. But even though he never said much about it, I know he didn't really care for Dave Borland," replied Carl. "The two of them never got along."

"Why's that?"

"Part of it was just personality. Danny liked opera and art galleries. You've spent time with Borland. He's an unrepentant barbarian. His idea of a good time is sitting around in his underwear drinking beer."

"There has to be more to it than that," I protested.

"There is. You must remember that EEOC suit we had last year."

"I remember. There was a technician in Borland's lab who claimed that he had made unwanted sexual advances. It was settled as I recall."

"Yes, but not before Danny and Borland got into more than one screaming match. From what I gather there was never any question that Borland had behaved improperly—hell, he bragged about it. Borland announced to everyone when he hired her that he was going to have some fun with her. She couldn't have been more than twenty-two or twenty-three—pretty, but not what I'd call spectacular."

"As I recall she initially went to Danny and complained that Borland was making off-color jokes, sexual references, and I believe the odd pat on the fanny."

"Borland's that kind of guy."

"You can be that kind of guy at home, but not at work," I said. "According to Danny, when the woman first came to him she had no intention of filing a lawsuit."

"She just wanted him to stop."

"That's usually all anyone wants."

"Unfortunately, Borland either couldn't or wouldn't. He never understood why what he was doing was wrong. He used to brag that the girl had a secret crush on him and was making it all up."

"And so she sued," I said. "As I recall, we ended up settling for three years' salary. Stephen was furious."

"So was Danny. He thought Borland had behaved badly and it had cost the company a bunch of money, money that should have been spent on science."

"He was right."

"I know. But I'm just telling you. From that point on there was nothing but bad blood between them."

CHAPTER
19

As I left Carl Woodruff's office I decided to make a trip downstairs to have a look at the reagent room where the PAF was stored. I found it without difficulty, a small windowless storage room behind a door marked "Reagent Supply." The room was lined with shelves and crammed with boxes and bottles of all sizes. When I had expressed my surprise that a storeroom that held a substance as lethal as PAF was kept unlocked, Stephen had countered that Azor was a pharmaceutical company, not a kindergarten. Scanning the labels on the various bottles and jars that bulged from the shelves, I suspected almost everything in there could kill you.

As I walked past the modeling room I saw Michael Childress through the plate-glass window. He was sitting on a high stool looking down the double barrel of a large microscope. Through the open door I could hear Mozart playing softly in the background. Childress looked for all the world like he belonged in one of the those sappy pharmaceutical industry ads.

"Excuse me, Dr. Childress," I said, on impulse.

"Don't bother me," he said, without even so much as

looking up to see who was speaking. I stayed where I was.

"What the hell do you want?" he demanded, looking up from what he was doing.

"I wanted to ask you a question."

"I don't have time for your questions."

"This will take only a minute," I replied, his rudeness making me determined.

"I don't have a minute," he snapped, going back to whatever he was looking at under the scope.

"As it happens, this is the only minute I have," I replied icily, "so I'm afraid you're going to have to stop what you're doing."

"Who do you think you are?" He was really angry now, but then again, so was I.

"I'm Kate Millholland," I said. "I'm this company's chief legal counsel and a member of the board of directors. That means I vote to approve your lab budget and decide whether or not to pay you your salary."

"What is your question?" he asked with the same mixture of hubris and hostility that I remembered all too well from my professors in law school.

"I was wondering what you called Danny Wohl about at home the day after he returned from Japan."

"What?" At least I'd finally managed to get his attention.

"You called him on the Sunday he came back from Tokyo," I said. "I was just wondering whether you wouldn't mind telling me what the two of you discussed."

"Nothing. I never called him."

"Are you sure? Perhaps it was a personal call?" I suggested.

"I'm telling you we never spoke."

"That's strange because the police have copies of

Danny's phone records and there was a call made from your number to Danny's apartment the morning of his death."

"There must be some kind of error in the records then."

"Not likely. Perhaps you've just forgotten. . . ."

"I assure you I have an excellent memory," he interjected huffily. "The last time I spoke to Danny was before he left for Japan."

"Do you mind telling me what the two of you talked about?" I knew there was no way he would tell me the truth, but there was something about the arrogance of his manner that made me reluctant to just let it go.

"Certainly," sniffed Childress with apparent satisfaction. "Danny promised me that as soon as he got back he would see to it that I was moved into a larger and more conveniently located office. A promise I have every intention of forcing this company to honor."

"Thank you very much for your time," I said.

"Is there anything else you wanted to know?"

"No. But I'm sure the police will have their own questions."

"The police?"

I did not answer him. Instead I turned on my heel and left his question hanging in the air.

I spent the rest of the day immersed in matters Japanese. My counterparts at Takisawa were clamoring for Azor's unaudited financials and the three-year budget projections I'd promised to send them last Friday. The foot-dragging on our part was deliberate. We wanted to honor their request to receive the information before they departed for the States, but I wanted to do it so close to their departure date that they wouldn't have enough time to come back with another round of requests for information.

I worked straight through the afternoon, interrupted only by a phone call from Elliott.

"We got the fingerprint results back," he reported.

"The ones from the glass we took from the sink in Danny's apartment or the ones from the coffee cup that Tom Galloway drank out of?"

"Both."

"And?"

"They don't match."

"That figures."

"I knew you'd be disappointed."

"Have you talked to Joe recently?"

"Not since the weekend. I called his house last night and his wife said he's down in Georgia interviewing some woman who claims she was raped by Sarrek and managed to escape."

"Is the woman telling the truth?"

"Joe thinks so. The only problem is she doesn't want to talk to the cops. She's afraid of what the media will do when they find out who she is."

"Can't they protect her privacy?"

"You mean like they did with the Central Park jogger?"

"You have a point."

"Believe me, what the press will do to her will make her wish that Sarrek had finished the job."

"I went to see Dr. Gordon at the medical examiner's office this morning. She's come up with something," I said and told him everything I'd learned so far about PAF as well as what Carl Woodruff and Michael Childress had said when I asked them about the phone calls.

"So that explains the syringe cap in his apartment," observed Elliott once I had finished.

"I'd forgotten all about that."

"Whoever gave him the shot must have dropped the cap. He either forgot about it in the excitement or it rolled someplace where he couldn't see it and had to leave it."

"I also think it means that whoever killed Danny either worked at Azor or knew someone who did."

"I thought you said the place where it was stored was kept unlocked."

"Yes. But the building itself is buttoned up tight. Stephen hires his security guards from Paranoids 'R' Us. There's only one way in and out, and every employee's ID is checked."

"At least that narrows it down some."

"Yeah, to one of the three hundred people who work here."

"Do you know whether employees are fingerprinted when they're hired?"

"No. They're not drug tested either. Stephen doesn't believe in Big Brother."

"If he's serious about finding out what happened to Danny he's going to have to let me start conducting interviews of his employees."

"Do you think the fingerprints on that glass belong to whoever killed Danny?"

"I think there's a good chance. But that's not really the question that's got me bugged right now."

"What is it?"

"Aren't you at least a little bit curious about how whoever killed him managed to get him to sit still while they shot him up with the stuff that killed him?"

* * *

When Lou Remminger found me I was standing in front of the vending machine in the lunchroom with a dollar bill in my hand, trying to decide whether to have cheese crackers or a Snickers bar for dinner. I had a terrible headache from peering at columns of numbers for hours and my back ached from hunching motionless over my desk.

"There you are," she drawled, smiling. She was wearing an army surplus jacket with what I recognized as an Oxford University scarf wrapped around her neck. "Get your coat on, girlfriend. It's time for you to further your scientific education."

"What did you have in mind?" I asked, fearing that it was something that involved the cold room and pulverizing body parts.

"Borland's called a mandatory project council meeting," she replied, "and we've got to get a move on because he gets pissed off when people are late."

It turned out that Borland's weekly meetings were held at the bar of the El Torito Mexican restaurant, an establishment located next to the Oak Brook mall, that served an all-you-can-eat taco bar. After-hours drinking had long been a company sport at Azor, but for the life of me I couldn't understand why Remminger had gone out of her way to include me.

"I talked to a friend of mine. A woman I met in graduate school. Her husband works for Mikos," she said as we pulled out of the parking lot. "She says they don't have diffraction-grade crystals yet, but the internal rumor mill is that they're close."

"How close?"

"Close."

"What about us?"

"Michelle says she'll have a new batch of crystals to try on Friday."

"And Childress?"

"Nobody knows. Childress doesn't tell anybody what he's working on."

"Why not?"

"Because he's a paranoid asshole, that's why."

"Do you think Michelle's new crystals will diffract?"

"I hope so, because if they don't the odds are that Mikos will beat us."

"Why's that?" I demanded.

"Because Michelle will lose two days when the power goes out," snapped Remminger, pounding her fist against the steering wheel for emphasis, "and then she'll have to flush the next three or four days sucking up to the Japanese. At this point in the process, in this kind of race, days matter. Fucking hours matter."

"I can't do anything about the electricity," I told her.

"And the Japanese?"

"At this point there's not a damn thing I can do about them either."

In a country where more people consult a psychic hot line than realize that matter is composed of atoms and molecules, the fierce clannishness of scientists is only to be expected. But I hadn't anticipated the way their peculiar insularity mirrored that of the very rich. Having grown up in what was for all intents and purposes a closed society—one in which a person could be immediately excluded on the basis of their shoes—I found observing another strictly delineated group endlessly fascinating.

When Lou and I arrived, we found a dozen or so investigators crowded around a long table being presided over by Borland. El Torito, with its faux south-of-the-border ambiance, struck me as a bizarre setting for what could alternately be described either as a gathering of the world's brightest organic chemists or the revenge of the nerds.

Someone pulled up a couple of chairs and we squeezed in at the far end of the table between Bryan and Bill, twin chemists from Remminger's lab who lifted weights in their spare time and looked for all the world like a set of matching fireplugs.

"I'd keep my distance from Borland if I were you," whispered Remminger, striking a match and lighting a cigarette. "His hands have a tendency to wander after he's had a few." Remminger and I were the only women at the table. I was the only person wearing a suit.

"Ladies! You need a drink!" boomed the protein chemist, from the other end of the table. He poured us both margaritas from the pitcher in front of him and passed them down. "Better enjoy these while you can. I hear that by next week we'll all be drinking sake."

"Only if we're lucky," grumbled someone I didn't recognize. "I hear that Mikos is close to having diffraction-grade crystals."

"And Elvis has just been recruited by Glaxo. I believe only what I read in *Nature*. Besides, once our sushi buddies ante up we'll have the money to cook up all kinds of new drugs. That is, for those of you who care about making drugs."

"What does he mean by that?" I asked Remminger.

"It's a dig against academics. You see, where we come from making new drugs isn't exactly considered that big a deal. I mean, hey, I wouldn't mind finding a cure for cancer, but scientifically speaking the big prize in all of this is solving the structure of the receptor molecule and synthesizing the new compound."

"The Japanese don't give a damn whether we turn ZK-501 into a drug," complained someone named Kurt, who worked in the protein lab.

"And it's a good thing," a man with a wild black beard who was sitting next to him interjected, "because at the rate we're going we have about as much chance of making a drug as Kurt here has of getting lucky with lovely Kasandra behind the bar." This remark was met with a chorus of hoots.

"Would you just shut up and let me finish," shouted the unfortunate Kurt above the din. "The reason the Japanese don't care whether we make a new drug is that's not what they're really interested in. They could care less if we make money with ZK-501. Don't you see? They already have plenty of money. What they really want is to see how we do it." It occurred to me that Kurt was probably right. "You mark my words. It's all part of their master plan. Ten years from now we're all going to be taking Japanese pills the way we watch Japanese TVs and drive Japanese cars. These guys don't want one new drug, they want the know-how to make lots of new drugs, and if you ask me, whatever they're gonna end up paying us for it, we're selling it to them too cheap."

The next morning I woke up feeling exhausted and vaguely hungover. I dragged myself miserably out of bed and reflected that if there was one thing the scientists of the ZK-501 project excelled at it was putting away tequila. With Danny's funeral set for ten I was grateful that it didn't make sense to even try to get out to Oak Brook.

With my lawyer's wardrobe of dark suits I could have dressed for an infinite number of funerals, but I made a special effort for Danny's sake, selecting a black Armani suit he had often complimented me on.

When I got to my office even Cheryl voiced her approval. "You look very nice," she said.

"Thank you, I'm going to a funeral."

"I've got everything set for your trip to New York. I called and spoke to Mr. Hiroshi Toyoda's private secretary. They will be expecting you at four o'clock. Here are your tickets and your itinerary. Of course Bud Hellman called and said he'd love to take you to lunch or dinner if you have time, but I explained that you were hoping to just get in and out. He also said to be sure and let him know and that they'd make an office available to you if you needed it, etc. . . ."

Hellman was the managing partner of the firm's New York office and within the last year he'd traded in a perfectly good wife for a social-climbing Texas beauty half his age named Babs. Babs made no secret of her social aspirations and practically panted to be in the same room with my mother. The fact that the last time they actually spoke my mother accidentally called her "Boobs" pretty much summed up the matter. Nevertheless, Hellman, with the optimism of a man of sixty who thinks he's going to bed at night with his second youth, always fell all over himself whenever I came to New York.

"What else is new?"

"Not much. The draft-offering documents on Nuland Petroleum were finally messengered over yesterday afternoon. I've given them to Sherman to look over, but there's another set on your desk in case you wanted to read through them on the plane."

"Where's the mail?"

"On your desk. Also your messages. Can I get you some coffee?"

"I would love some," I replied.

It felt wonderful to be back in my own office, behind my own desk, surrounded by my own things. I flipped through the mail, stopping to read items that seemed timely or important. I dictated a few notes and replies.

As Cheryl appeared with my coffee a thought suddenly occurred to me. I quickly picked up the phone and dialed Tom Galloway's number.

"I was wondering if you were planning on going to the funeral this morning," I said, once I'd gotten him on the line.

"Yes. I'm going," he said in a voice so guarded I found it almost impossible to read.

"With John Guttman out of town I thought maybe we could represent the firm together."

"Fine."

"And if you wanted we could probably go early. . . ."

"I'd like that," he said, this time more softly.

"Fine. I'll meet you in reception in twenty minutes. In the meantime I'll give the funeral director a call and let him know to expect us." I assumed there would be no difficulty in arranging what I wanted—a private moment of farewell from a friend who did not wish to draw attention to himself.

CHAPTER
20

When we arrived at the funeral home Mr. McNamara was waiting for us at the door, ready to conduct Tom Galloway into the nether regions of the mortuary. I waited for them in the back of the chapel and tried to drive back the tide of memory that always threatened to overwhelm me on these occasions. I became a widow when I was twenty-five years old and everyone—from people I barely knew to those who stood with me as my husband's body was lowered into the ground—insisted that time would heal me. Now that time has passed I have come to understand that healing is a painful and uncertain process. In five years I have laid down many layers of scar tissue. Waiting for Danny's funeral to begin I was confronted by the fact that it wasn't enough.

A door to the outside creaked open. Through it slipped a sliver of gray winter light and Elliott Abelman. He was dressed for the occasion in a black suit, blue shirt, and wing tips polished to a Marine Corps shine.

"You're early," I said.

"I love funerals," said Elliott, with a grin that drove the darkness from the room. "You never know who's going to turn up. I called the funeral director yesterday. He's going to try to make sure that everyone signs the guest book. I also have a photographer with a telephoto lens on the roof of the building across the street so that he can catch people coming out of the building."

"Did you talk to Stephen about coming out to Azor to question people?"

"He says no. Scientists are apparently very temperamental. He doesn't want their delicate psyches disturbed." I could tell by his tone what he thought of the scientists and their psyches. "I did talk to Joe though. As soon as he gets back he's going to give the Wohl file to his lieutenant."

"Any chance they'll reopen the investigation?"

"That's hard to say. The wheels of justice always grind pretty slowly in this town, but even more so these days."

"Then I want you to be sure to go ahead and check out Michael Childress."

"Is he the crystallographer you were telling me about?"

"Yes. I've been asking around. Supposedly Danny hated his guts, but Childress was always in Danny's office for one thing or other."

"So you think it might have been window dressing?"

"That's what I want you to find out. The other guy is a protein chemist by the name of Dave Borland. There was a lot of animosity between the two men on account of an EEOC suit against Borland."

"Don't worry. I'll turn their lives inside out for you."

"Did you ever find out anything about Hiroshi Toyoda?"

"Yes. He's in the country right now, by the way."

"I know. I'm flying to New York to meet him this afternoon."

Elliott reached into his inside pocket and came out with a small spiral notebook, which he flipped open and consulted before speaking. "Hiroshi Toyoda, age thirty-four, born in Santiago, Chile."

"Chile?"

"His father was attached to the consulate. He lived in Latin America until he was eleven, then his father was assigned back to Tokyo for two years. When he was thirteen, Hiroshi's dad began a six-year stint in Washington, D.C. By all accounts our friend is a pretty cosmopolitan fellow, fluent in Spanish, Portuguese, English, and naturally Japanese. Smart, too—Georgetown, Harvard Law, M.B.A. from Wharton. Comfortably well-off until he married his wife, Fumiko, who is Takisawa's only daughter. Now he's rich, big-time rich. The couple live in Tokyo. They have a country house outside of Nagasaki and a place in Hawaii where they get away a couple times a year to play golf."

"Children?"

"One. A son. His wife is ten years older than he is, by the way."

"Was he in the country when Danny died?" I asked, though with what I now knew about PAF I was even less inclined to suspect Hiroshi of any involvement.

"We're still working on that. But he travels to the U.S. a couple times a month, usually to New York, and always with his private secretary."

"Really? Has she been with him for a long time?"

"You mean him. The secretary is a man. I called the house detective at the St. Regis, which is where he always stays when he's in New York. It seems he always travels with a personal secretary, always a young man in his twenties, but . . ."

"But what?"

"But never the same one twice."

The minister who officiated at Danny's funeral was a downy-faced probationer who offered up a generic service filled with platitudes about eternity and redemption while a plump woman in a green dress played the piano and exuded the humid scent of alcohol.

There were perhaps two dozen people. Stephen and I sat alone together in the front row, and when I turned around, I saw mostly familiar faces. Tom Galloway sat between a representative of Azor's bank and its firm of accountants. Carl Woodruff came, as did Lou Remminger, who, dressed entirely in black, actually managed to pass for just another mourner.

Stephen's assistant, Rachel, looked terribly smart in a black suit from Ann Taylor. I was surprised to see her sitting in the last row beside Elliott Abelman, their heads close together in whispered conversation. Other than that there were perhaps five or six other people, all men, all young, none of whom I recognized. Later Elliott told me that one of them was Danny's neighbor from across the hall. These were the people whom Elliott had come for, hoping one of them would lead him into Danny's other, private life.

The lawyer in me still waited for some long-lost relative to come forward and make a claim on Danny's estate, but so far none had materialized. Apparently Danny's grandmother had been his only relative. The casket was a handsome one of burnished copper—the most expensive one they had.

Stephen delivered the eulogy. He talked feelingly

about his long friendship with Danny and their early struggles. He recalled Danny's judgment and his wit, but it was his obvious grief at his friend's passing that provided the most eloquent tribute.

When he sat down, a young man with auburn hair rose and took his place beside the coffin. He was a soloist from the Chicago Gay Men's Chorus. He stood for a moment, silent and perfectly still. Then simply, without accompaniment, he sang the old ballad "Danny Boy." His voice was a gorgeous, lyrical tenor that rolled out of him effortlessly and filled the dim chapel like a warm light. Until I heard it, I had not realized that it was possible for music to actually pierce the heart.

I did not go to the cemetery. I told myself that Danny would understand. Instead I took a cab straight from the funeral home to the airport for my flight to New York. Because Azor was paying for my ticket I'd had Cheryl book me to New York in coach. When I got on the plane I was rewarded for my virtue with half a soggy turkey sandwich in a Styrofoam container and a seat beside a three-hundred-pound man.

However, once I arrived at LaGuardia I found that Bud Hellman had arranged the full visiting-partner treatment. A driver met me at the gate holding a sign with my name on it—correctly spelled. He relieved me of my briefcase, inquired whether I'd had a pleasant flight, and ushered me to the black limousine that was waiting at the curb.

There was a time, in law school, when I had just assumed I would live and work in Manhattan. New York, after all, is where the big leagues of corporate law are played. Indeed, I spent the summer after my first year of law school clerking at Cravath Swain. Besides the obvious attraction of being asked to be a summer associate at one of the most prestigious law firms in the country, there was also the undeniable charm of living in a different time zone than my parents.

But while I'd found the work at Cravath intermittently interesting I'd ended the summer with a renewed appreciation of the Second City. Arriving in New York in June, I'd been thrilled by the hustle of the city that never sleeps, the sea of taxicabs rushing up Sixth Avenue like the tide. But by July Manhattan seemed hot and dirty, filled with people who, from the senior partners at Cravath to the addled beggars on the street, seemed to feel it was okay to yell at people without reason or explanation.

We fought traffic all the way into midtown. Finally, the driver delivered me to the St. Regis, left me with his beeper number, and went off to wherever it is that limo drivers disappear to. I crossed the sumptuous lobby and found the house phone. I had begun the day at Danny's funeral and then flown a thousand miles to bring the news that he was dead. The fact that I also meant to try to persuade Hiroshi to use his influence with his father-in-law did nothing to lighten the burdens of the day.

I dialed Hiroshi's suite and was instructed by the voice that answered to come directly upstairs. In the elevator I stared at my reflection in the polished brass of the doors. A grim and prim corporate attorney bearing a black briefcase and bad news stared back. As clearly as if she were with me I heard my mother's voice. It said, "I don't understand why you choose to do this." As the elevator doors parted and I stepped out into the long hall that would take me to meet Hiroshi, I had to confess that at that moment I didn't understand either.

I pressed the bell beside the double door to the suite and listened as the four notes chimed sweetly on the other side. A few seconds later the door was opened by a slim young Japanese in an expensively tailored double-breasted suit. I assumed he was the secretary. Indeed, in the manner of a good underling he made no attempt to introduce himself but instead stepped back to let me pass, announcing, "This way, please." I suspected the phrase was the total extent of his English.

I followed him into the living room, which was enormous for New York, not to mention Tokyo. We stood smiling idiotically at each other for a few minutes amid the striped Regency chairs and tasseled curtains. He couldn't have been much over twenty-two or twenty-three and I wondered what kind of services, secretarial or otherwise, he had come to New York to provide.

An inner door opened and another man emerged from the bedroom, hand extended, apologizing profusely for keeping me waiting. From the neck up Hiroshi Toyoda was pure Japanese, but everything else about him was disconcertingly American: his jaunty manner, his mid-Atlantic accent, even his pink Ralph Lauren button-down shirt and his crisply ironed khakis. We shook hands, and he waved me into a seat, dismissing his secretary with a few words of Japanese.

"Thank you for making the time to see me," I said, feeling terrible about what I was about to do.

"My pleasure, my pleasure," replied Hiroshi, "though I must confess I am surprised that Dr. Azorini didn't send Danny to discuss whatever it is you have come to talk to me about."

"I've come to discuss Danny."

"Oh?"

I took a breath. There are no words that can soften the impact of what I had to say. No right way to catapult a person into grief. So I just came out with it. "Danny died a few days ago," I said. "He had a perforated ulcer and he bled to death. It was very unexpected."

For a moment I almost thought Hiroshi hadn't heard me. His face was frozen, impassive, his body completely still. I waited awkwardly, reminding myself that the Japanese disdain the American need to talk all the time and instead value the ability to accept silence.

"I think I should go," I said quietly, after several minutes had passed. "I do not wish to intrude on your sorrow."

"No, no. You have come all this way just to bring me this sad news. You must at least stay and have tea with me."

"I would like that. Thank you."

"If you would be so good as to excuse me for a few minutes, I will make the necessary arrangements."

He rose and retreated into the bedroom. I got up and walked over to the window and looked down at the city traffic. Either Hiroshi was a tremendous actor or his surprise at learning of Danny's death was genuine. I was glad. The negotiations with Takisawa were going to be hairy enough without suspecting our future partners of murder.

Hiroshi returned a few minutes later looking composed and serious. He had changed into a business suit and tie. His demeanor had changed as well. Somehow with the news of Danny's death the Western-style openness he'd displayed when I first arrived was gone, replaced if not by an Eastern reserve, then by a greater formality. While he no longer seemed precisely grief stricken, he did somehow seem more Japanese.

The doorbell rang and a room service waiter appeared with our tea. I stood near the window as Hiroshi fussed over the tray making sure everything was exactly as it should be. When he was finished and the check signed, I took a seat opposite him.

"You know how strongly Danny believed in a strategic alliance between the Takisawa Corporation and Azor Pharmaceuticals," I said, once the tea had been poured. "He believed it presented a unique opportunity to not only make a lifesaving drug, but to put our efforts at the forefront of pharmaceutical research for many, many years. Danny's death has not changed that.

"I have not yet had the honor of meeting your father-in-law, but I have read much of what has been written about him. Everyone speaks of his wisdom and his vision. But I know how difficult it is for American and Japanese companies to establish a relationship of trust. From what Dr. Azorini tells me Danny and your father-in-law had mutual respect for each other based on the value of your long friendship with him. I have come to ask for your help and support in continuing the friendship between our companies even though our friend Danny is no longer with us."

Hiroshi sipped his tea thoughtfully before responding. "In some ways we are not so different in Japan as you in America may think," he said. "Fathers are still fathers, and sons-in-law unfortunately are still the ones who have stolen the affections of their beloved daughters. My father-in-law has achieved much in his long life, but the men of his generation are deeply suspicious of dealing with the West. I would be lying to you if I told you that my father-in-law has no reservations about Dr. Azorini. That he is a doctor, a chemist, and a businessman is something my father-in-law finds difficult to understand. He wonders why Dr. Azorini has not chosen one path as opposed to trying to walk many."

"Dr. Azorini's background has prepared him well for the path he walks as president of a pharmaceutical company," I replied.

Hiroshi nodded, but I could not tell whether he was agreeing with me or merely indicating that I had his attention. "I think it is also a concern that Azor Pharmaceuticals seems to be one man's company."

"Unlike Takisawa?" I countered quickly.

"Ah, but the Takisawa Corporation is more than forty years old, and it will live on long after my father-in-law has gone."

"Then there was a time your father-in-law well remembers when his company was six years old."

"But never a time when it was the product of such a dynamic personality as Stephen Azorini. You must understand, Miss Millholland, I am only playing the devil's advocate. I believe as Danny did that through our investment in Azor Pharmaceuticals our company would be making an investment in the future. But if I am to help you as you ask, I must tell you what concerns you will face from my father-in-law.

"Tatsuro Takisawa lost half his family in the bombing in Nagasaki. You can understand that experience has made him deeply suspicious of the intentions of the West. That Stephen is so unusual, in his background as well as his demeanor, makes my father-in-law very nervous.

Danny's death is most unfortunate in that it is unexpected. Tatsuro does not like anything that rocks the boat. He does not like change and he does not like surprises."

"You have my word," I assured him gravely. "From here on in, I promise, there will be no surprises."

CHAPTER
21

When I arrived at LaGuardia, it was in its usual end-of-the-day nightmare state. Beleaguered businessmen in crumpled suits wearily humped their briefcases and laptops down crowded concourses that reeked of popcorn and seemed to go on forever while babies cried and electric carts beeped. I got to the gate only to learn to my disgust that my plane would be delayed for some unspecified amount of time by fog in Boston. After twenty minutes or so of serious jockeying at the ticket counter I anted up my gold card and snagged the last first-class seat on a flight that left in twenty minutes. Sprinting to the farthest gate on the most distant concourse I managed to make it on board just as they were closing the doors.

As we were about to pull away from the gate the flight attendant announced that there was something wrong with the locking mechanism to the jetway. We sat on the ground for another hour and a half until they were finally able to fix it. By the time I finally arrived at O'Hare, it was after ten o'clock. All I wanted to do was get into my car, go home, and crawl into a tall scotch before doing the same to my own bed. Nevertheless I still had to stop at Azor. With four days to go before the delegation from Takisawa arrived I knew I would never be able to sleep without reading through the day's faxes.

Pulling into the parking lot at Azor I was dismayed to see Stephen's BMW still in the lot. I'm sure his employees just assumed that he never left. His car was there when they arrived for work in the morning and it was still there at night when they left. As eager as I was to tell him about my meeting with Hiroshi, I had been hoping to just run in and out tonight.

"You're pulling night duty," observed Paramilitary Bill, looking up from whatever he was reading at the security desk.

I mumbled my assent and rummaged through my purse for my ID card. I couldn't help stealing a surreptitious look at the magazine Bill was reading. Expecting *Soldier of Fortune* or at least *White Supremacist Weekly*, I was disappointed to see that it was nothing more unusual than a body-building magazine.

I slid my card through the reader and made my way to Stephen's office. I found him at his desk, hunched over his keyboard. He was pecking away furiously using the peculiar, two-fingered technique he had long ago perfected for himself. He was actually very fast, but there was something about all that energy channeled from his huge frame into the tips of just two fingers that always struck me as comical.

"Hi," I said.

"Where've you been?" he demanded, looking up from his keyboard. "I thought your flight was supposed to get in at seven."

"My plane was delayed so I caught a later flight," I

replied, knowing instantly that there was something wrong. It wasn't like him to be rude.

"You should have called. I've had the whole world out looking for you."

"Why? What's happened?"

In lieu of an explanation, he handed me a two-page fax. I immediately recognized from the letterhead that it had come from Takisawa. As I read it I felt as though all the air had been sucked out of the room.

The fax, dated that morning, was as explicit as the dozens before it had been vague. The $40 million deal that Stephen and Danny had originally proposed, the one that had been on the table since the two of them had returned from Japan, had now been deemed by Takisawa's chairman to be too rich. They were now countering by halving their offer.

I looked up from the page at Stephen. I couldn't tell whether he was furious or desperate or perhaps a little bit of both. Having spent the past few days reviewing the ZK-501 project's financial projections, I knew his back was against the wall. If he didn't get Takisawa's money, and get it soon, he was going to have no choice but to pull the plug on ZK-501, take as a loss the $26 million he'd already invested in the drug, and sit back helplessly as he watched the company he'd started begin its sickening spiral into the red.

"This is just high-stakes bluff poker, Stephen. We've got to figure out our next move."

"Maybe. Or maybe we just played hardball too hard."

"I think you're wrong," I said, hoping I sounded more confident than I actually felt. "When I talked to Hiroshi today in New York he really made it sound as though they're going for the deal."

"Maybe they really can't handle the money," countered Stephen morosely, "in which case we are well and truly fucked."

"They have the money," I assured him. "This is too good a deal for them to pass up. You've said it yourself a hundred times. Takisawa is a second-level pharmaceutical company with global ambitions. Their growth strategy is to buy heavily into U.S. companies whose products they license. They're not just determined to barter their way into U.S. market; now they want to gain access to its newest technology, and they're paying big bucks for it. Remember Genlife? Takisawa paid $100 million for them last fall."

"Yeah, but look what happened to Genlife stock. It's dropped twelve points in the last two quarters. Maybe Takisawa feels like they've been burned and now they're having second thoughts."

"No. They're just playing us. Old man Takisawa didn't get where he is by paying retail. This is a classic Japanese negotiating tactic," I said, silently reassuring myself that the books I'd read on doing business with the Japanese couldn't all be wrong. "They always beat you up at the end over price. The important thing is not to give in to it."

"And what do you propose we do?"

"I'm not sure. But at least give me a chance to come up with a counterproposal."

"Fine," said Stephen, grimly looking at his watch. "Have it on my desk at nine o'clock tomorrow morning."

Setting aside my fatigue I spent the rest of the night tearing our original proposal apart, trying to come up with a way to craft a counterproposal that reduced Azor's asking price without affecting the dollar amount that Azor would get up front if the deal were signed. My central dilemma was far from unique, but rather one faced by all small pharmaceutical firms—how to avoid giving up, as the price for developing a new drug, all but a shred of its value. Somewhere around three o'clock in the morning I came up with what I hoped was a workable plan.

The original proposal divided future royalties for the new drug by carving up the world into geographical regions. By taking back Europe, Azor could potentially decide to sell the drug there itself, or it could license it to another partner, perhaps netting another $50 million in a few years. If I could make the numbers work out the way I wanted I figured Azor could now capture—for the reduced price of something less than $30 million—half the world market for a molecule it was nowhere near producing.

I knew Stephen would see it as a reckless proposal, but if my interpretation of Takisawa's pullback was correct—that it merely represented a bargaining position—then I thought there was a good chance they would go for it.

Satisfied that I had finally come up with at the least the skeleton of a workable plan, I pushed my chair back from my desk and went off in search of sustenance from the vending machines. Walking down the silent hallway I was feeling just ragged enough to begin imagining things. Largely deserted, the building almost seemed to have taken on a life of its own, filled with breathy sounds of machinery. Through the ventilation ducts I could hear the nocturnal scratching of the doomed lab animals incarcerated in the basement. Somehow the thought of Paramilitary Bill pacing the lobby with his well-oiled pistol did little to reassure me.

Expecting to have the place to myself, I was surprised to see Michelle Goodwin sitting at a table in the corner of the lunchroom, headphones clamped over her ears, eating a container of yogurt and reading a scientific journal. Of all the ZK-501 scientists she was the one who most preferred to work at night when there was a scarcity of human interference and an abundance of cpu time. Several times I had seen her leaving the building to begin her daily workout as I was just arriving.

Tonight Michelle seemed totally wrapped up in her own thoughts, cut off from the rest of the world by whatever music was coming out of her headphones and the submicroscopic universe that occupied her. There was an intensity about her, even in eating, a singularity of focus. It was a trait I had recognized in all sorts of people who were driven to excel.

Watching her I felt a strange kinship. I suspected that at this point in time Michelle felt she carried the entire burden of the ZK-501 project on her shoulders. Childress she viewed as window dressing, always heading to some conference or other while she concentrated on getting the work done. Like a runner in a relay race, until the structure of ZKBP was solved, she carried the baton alone. Seeing her there, in the middle of the night, I felt fiercely protective. I wanted to make the deal that would let her see the race through to its completion.

I hated to disturb her, but it seemed strange for us to be together in the middle of the night without acknowledging each other. Besides, I was afraid if she caught sight of me unexpectedly I might startle her. Slowly, I moved into her field of vision and stayed there, until she finally looked up.

"What are you doing here?" she demanded. Despite my best intentions I had clearly startled her.

"Stephen needs something on his desk by nine o'clock tomorrow morning," I replied. The emptiness of the building seemed to weigh on our conversation, making small talk seem stilted and our voices seem unnaturally loud.

"It never occurred to me that lawyers had to work through the night." It was obvious that Michelle knew as little about the practice of corporate law as I did about crystallography. All-nighters were so common in the deal-driven areas of law that some firms employed three shifts of support staff to provide coverage around the clock.

A friend of mine from law school liked to tell a story about clerking for a firm in New York that specialized in mergers and acquisitions. One night her husband had woken up at four o'clock in the morning alarmed to find her not there. Worried, he called her office only to have the receptionist inform him politely that his wife would have to call him back because she was in a meeting.

"The Japanese faxed us a proposal today and Stephen wants us to have our reply ready by tomorrow morning," I explained.

"You be careful with the Japanese," warned Michelle.

"Why's that?"

"They have a way of kidnapping people."

"Kidnapping?" I demanded. "I've heard them accused of a lot of things, but never kidnapping."

"Not literally," Michelle replied seriously, "but what they do is every bit as dangerous."

"And what is it that they do, exactly?"

"They dangle their money in front of you and ask you to do backflips for it. But what happens is that in the end you spend so much time working on your backflip that you lose sight of the fact that you're a scientist and not an acrobat."

"I guess it was hard when Okuda walked away from the deal for the integrase project."

Michelle shrugged, noncommittally. "Fool me once, shame on you, but fool me twice, shame on me," she said.

I had the first draft of the proposal on Stephen's desk at precisely four minutes to nine. While he read it I paced the floor nervously. I'd gotten my second wind somewhere around sunrise and I wasn't tired. From experience I knew this second wave of energy would carry me for most of the day, right up until the time when accumulated fatigue hit me like a ten-pound sledgehammer in the late afternoon.

Stephen immediately lit upon two potential problems in the royalty structure—hidden grenades, he called them. We spent half an hour brainstorming a way to defuse them. By the time we had worked out the details it was time for Stephen to head to that morning's project council meeting for the Hemasyn group. Even more important, it was time for Neiman Marcus to open.

At ten o'clock on the dot, I consulted my address book and phoned the manager of Neiman Marcus's downtown store. His name was Mr. Riccardi and he was only one of the legion of Chicago retailers willing to fall on their swords at the merest mention of my mother's name. Like everyone whose job it is to cater to the well-to-do, when I told him what I needed he asked no questions and assured me it would be done.

That accomplished, I spent the next couple hours drafting Azor's final counterproposal. I knew any one of the secretaries would have been happy to do it for me, but I feared a fresh typist would only make fresh mistakes and besides, having gotten it to this point alone, I almost preferred to do it myself.

Once I was finished I took the elevator to the ninth floor and hand-carried the document to Stephen personally for his signature. Having never had occasion to go beyond the first floor, I was mildly surprised to find myself in a parallel universe—labs, lunchrooms, all laid out the same way as for the ZK-501 project, except devoted to different problems.

Once Stephen signed the proposal and the cover letter, I took them back downstairs to my office and, with a sense of occasion, loaded the pages into the fax. My packages were delivered just as I finished. I accepted the two maroon-and-gold shopping bags, thanked the messenger, and shut the door behind him. Then I carefully closed the blinds and emptied the contents of the two bags onto the desk. Enshrouded in tissue was a slate blue Dana Buchman jacket with a black wool skirt. There were also a cream-colored silk blouse, two pairs of DKNY pantyhose—size tall—and an assortment of Hanro cotton underwear.

Some kind soul had tucked in a cosmetics bag crammed with sample sizes of all kinds of makeup and perfume, which, according to the embossed notecard I found inside, the manager of the Oak Brook store urged me to accept with his greatest compliments. I picked up the pocket tape recorder from my desk and dictated a quick thank-you note for Cheryl to type before throwing the manager's notecard into the trash.

I stripped out of yesterday's clothes gratefully and told myself that at this point clean underwear was actually better than sleep. Thinking about the day ahead I was glad I had a meeting with Tom Galloway later that morning. We were set to go over the interrogatories on the new Serezine suit—a task I hoped would be consuming enough that I wouldn't be able to worry too much about how our counterproposal was being received.

With the fifteen-hour time difference between Tokyo and Chicago, it was unlikely we would hear back from Takisawa that day. I was convinced a quick response was more likely to be negative and so I found myself actually hoping for a delay. Still, with so much on the line, I was grateful to have something else to occupy my mind— even if it was a wrongful-death suit.

When Tom arrived, I ushered him into the small conference room adjacent to Stephen's office. Somehow it seemed unfair to ask him to work in Danny's old office with all its painful associations. I expected, with the funeral behind us, that Tom would have seemed easier in my company. But as we settled into our chairs he seemed if anything even more ill at ease. I hoped he wasn't about to unload some new bombshell about the Serezine suits. With our counterproposal in Takisawa's court and without sleep, my nerves were already singing like high-voltage wire.

"I think I owe you an apology," he said, like a little boy coming clean in the principal's office. I couldn't help but wonder whether he was speaking out of genuine contrition or trying to salvage his chances with the partnership committee. "When I stormed into your office the other morning I acted like a real jerk. I realized that at the funeral yesterday. You were only doing what any friend would do and I was so paranoid that I was making it into something else."

"Apology accepted," I said, though nothing had changed in terms of my opinion of him.

"Can I ask you a favor?" he ventured uncertainly.

"That depends on what it is."

"Will you tell me if you find out anything more about how Danny died?"

"Why?" I countered, sensing that Tom Galloway had something he clearly wanted to get off his chest.

"I've heard some things."

"What things?"

"I ran into a guy at the funeral who I recognized from Danny's building. We started talking and he said the building manager told him Danny'd been stabbed. She said there was blood all over his apartment. . . ."

"There was a lot of blood," I replied, "but Danny wasn't stabbed. Though it was the appearance of the apartment that got everyone started asking questions in the first place. I told you in my office how he died. He had a perforated ulcer."

"Does that mean foul play isn't suspected anymore?" asked Tom, sounding relieved.

"No. Just the opposite. The medical examiner has just uncovered evidence that very definitely points to murder."

"I don't get it."

"I'm sorry, for the time being I can't tell you any more. All I can say is we're looking very hard for the person who was with him in his apartment at the time he died."

"Why?" asked Galloway, his composure falling from him like a mask. "What does it matter who was with him in the apartment?"

"Was it you?" I demanded. "Were you the one with him?"

"No," said Tom, "but I kind of know who was." His shoulders sagged miserably and he looked up at me with puppy eyes of remorse. It was no wonder he got away with what he did. I didn't know whether to reach over and pat his head or strangle him.

"What exactly is it that you kind of know?" I demanded.

"I should have told you sooner."

"Told me what?"

"What I told you the other day was true. When I left Danny on Sunday morning he really was fine. But he was also waiting for someone."

"Who was he waiting for?"

"I don't know who."

"That's awfully convenient."

"What I mean is I don't know the person's name. Danny was always careful not to tell me. He didn't want to get them into trouble. But I do know it was someone who worked here."

"Here? At Azor? Do you know what the person's job was, at least?"

"A chemist I think."

I groaned inwardly. "Do you know what kind of chemist?" I prodded.

"I don't know exactly, but it was someone doing research."

Great, I thought to myself, now we're really narrowing it down. Out loud I said, "Was this a friend of Danny's? Someone he was involved with in some way? Why were they coming to his apartment, do you know?"

"We never really talked about the person," explained

Galloway apologetically, "only what they promised they could do for him."

"And what was that?" I demanded.

"Give him an experimental new drug for AIDS."

"What?"

"This researcher knew someone who was working on a very hush-hush new AIDS drug, something like a vaccine, only you took it after you'd been infected and it actually blocked the action of the virus."

"Danny was doing so well on the medication he was taking. He was symptom free. Why would he take a risk on an experimental drug?"

"All Danny did was take medicine," replied Galloway. "He didn't want that to be what his life was about—watching the clock to make sure he didn't eat for an hour before his medication, being careful not to eat for two hours after. The side effects were so terrible there were times he told me that AIDS couldn't be worse. He had days that he felt so weak he couldn't get out of bed, days when his muscles hurt so much he could hardly walk to the elevator, days when he couldn't bear to be touched. When he came back from Japan, he decided he'd had enough. He wanted to give the new drug a try. Danny and I stayed up that whole night Saturday night, talking through his decision."

"How was this new drug given?" I asked, knowing full well what the answer would be. "Was it a pill?"

"No," answered Tom. "It was an injection. It was a series of injections."

CHAPTER
22

Danny's ulcer must have been quite a nasty surprise for the killer. Without it the murder would have been not just an easy but an elegant one. If everything had gone according to plan, the killer would have been long gone by the time Danny had died quietly of an internal hemorrhage. I'm sure he never planned on getting his hands dirty much less on the bloody struggle that had taken place in that apartment.

Of course, the story Galloway told about Danny and the experimental AIDS drug could have been just that—a story, a clever fabrication designed to deflect suspicion from himself. But if what he had to say was true, then someone at Azor was a cold and calculating killer.

Whoever had killed Danny had planned it carefully, laying the groundwork well before Danny's trip to Japan. Assuming it was a researcher at Azor, then the killer was someone of obvious intelligence, someone likely to do a good job anticipating an investigator's questions and able to make sure the answers didn't lead back to himself. Even when things had gone spectacularly wrong and Danny had started bleeding he'd kept his head.

Not only had the killer managed to keep Danny away

from both the phone and the door, but he'd had the presence of mind to clean up the apartment, remove the cassette tape from the answering machine, and get out of the building undetected. The needle cover had been an oversight. A mistake. The question, then, of course, was were there any others?

If there were I was too sleep deprived to grasp them. Besides, there were still the Serezine interrogatories to get through, page after page of formal inquiries that began, "To the best of your knowledge and belief . . ." Tom and I plodded through them, flagging specific questions for Stephen, for the lead investigator on the Serezine project who had long since returned to UCLA, and for those who just required a search of company records for an answer.

During bathroom breaks I stopped back at Danny's office to stare balefully at the empty tray of the fax machine. I also tried to reach Elliott Abelman but succeeded only in leaving messages. Needless to say, I was eager to share Tom Galloway's story with him.

We called it quits at five o'clock. My eyelids felt like lead and every movement was as exhausting as a walk through tall grass. I had reached the point where my lack of sleep posed a very real danger that something would be overlooked or omitted. It was time for me to call it a night.

Driving home I called my mother. Not only was conversation with her guaranteed to keep me awake, but I hadn't spoken to her in a few days and wanted to make sure we were still on track with preparations for the Japanese visit. I managed to catch her just as she was dressing for a trustees dinner at Rush-Pres-St. Luke's, but she was eager, almost excited, to share the details of what she was doing. As we chatted I saw no point in telling her that, depending on Takisawa's response, there was at least a fifty-fifty chance that the deal was dead and all the orchids and the seating charts would have been for nothing.

"Before I forget, you have to call Mimi," declared Mother. "She phoned this morning to say she received an oral report from the structural engineers who came out to look at the apartment."

"What did they say?" I asked.

"They said it will cost somewhere in the neighborhood of forty thousand dollars to remove the soil from the top of the building and repair the damage to the roof."

"Forty thousand dollars? How long will it take?" I demanded, no doubt suffering from the lawyer's predisposition to measure everything in hours billed.

"I have no idea, but they say work can't begin until after the ground thaws in the spring. They also say they can't guarantee it won't cost more if we have a lot of snow this winter, because in that case it's likely there will be even more damage to the roof and they'll have trouble using their heavy equipment."

"There is no way I am going to write a check for forty thousand dollars," I announced.

"Naturally dear. It's Paul Riskoff who's going to have to pick up the tab."

She was right, of course. But Mother didn't know Riskoff like I did. He was one of the most litigious businessmen in the city. It would definitely take a lawsuit to pry that kind of money from him—a prospect that I, in my current state of mind, did not relish.

What next? I thought to myself, hanging up with my mother. Boils? Frogs? Running sores? Clearly I was being punished for something I had done in my past life.

As I turned onto Hyde Park Boulevard I half expected to see flames leaping out of the windows of my apartment.

Instead I saw Elliott's Jeep parked in front of the building. I parked in the alley out back and walked around to the front of the building and tapped on his window. I waited while he rolled it down.

"Are you staking me out?" I demanded, resting my elbows on the door.

"By the time I got your messages and called you back, they said you'd already left to go home. Cheryl gave me your car phone number, but your line was busy so I figured I'd take a chance and catch up with you here."

"I was up all night working on something," I said. "Do you want to come inside and talk?"

"Sure. Have you eaten anything today?"

"Today? I'm not sure. I don't think so."

"Do you have any food in your refrigerator?"

"Maybe I have some eggs or something . . ." I replied, but it was the lack of sleep talking. Not only did I have no recollection of ever seeing any eggs in my refrigerator, but when it came to food preparation my experience was severely limited and did not actually extend to poultry products.

"I'll tell you what," Elliott said. "I'm starved. Let me run out and pick something up. I'll be back in a minute."

I went inside and checked the answering machine. No messages. I took a deep breath and told myself that the longer we didn't hear from the Japanese the better. While Elliott was off rustling up dinner I took a shower. It didn't wake me up, but at least I felt clean. I put on a pair of old jeans and an old U of C sweatshirt. I was just hunting through drawers for a rubber band for my hair when the buzzer rang.

Elliott had gone to Picolo Mondo and picked up Italian food which he insisted on serving on real dishes—dishes he quickly washed and dried before setting out onto the table. After what he'd seen of my housekeeping, he explained, a person couldn't be too careful.

Over creamy risotto with grilled chicken and crisp pinot grigio I told him Tom Galloway's story about Danny and the experimental AIDS drug.

"Is there any chance there really is a new drug like that out there?"

"Of course it's possible," I replied. "That's why Danny bought it. But I don't think it was an AIDS drug in that syringe. Stephen seemed pretty sure from the photos of the liver tissue that it was PAF."

"I'm surprised Danny talked through his decision to try the new drug with Tom Galloway. You'd think Stephen would be the logical choice."

"He didn't talk to Stephen because he knew Stephen would be against it. It would be acting ahead of the facts, something Stephen would never approve of."

"So who at Azor could plausibly come to Danny with the offer of the drug?"

"Plausibly? It could be anyone. These guys move around so much—from drug company to drug company, from university to university. Anyone could make up a story about an old colleague in another lab who'd struck pharmaceutical gold. But the first question ought not to be who could have plausibly approached Danny with the possibility of the drug, but who knew he had AIDS?"

"Who knew?"

"Stephen. Me. Other than that, it wasn't common knowledge, though anyone who watched his habits or perhaps saw him take his medication would have been able to guess. I'll try to ask around at Azor."

"Speaking of asking around, you've got to convince Stephen to let me come out and question the employees."

"There are over two hundred of them. Where would you start? Besides, they're shutting the company down over the weekend. The whole building will be closed so they can put in new electrical transformers. After that, the Japanese will be here. . . ."

"That may be," replied Elliott, getting up to clear the table, "but you said it yourself, these guys move around all the time from project to project and company to company."

"Meaning?"

"Meaning that the longer you wait the bigger the chance that whoever we're looking for isn't going to be there anymore."

I woke up at four o'clock in the morning surprised to find myself on the living room couch. The last thing I remembered was lying down to shut my eyes for a minute while Elliott finished doing the dishes. I told him to leave them until the morning, but he'd seemed almost offended by the idea. Somewhere between dinner and dessert I must have fallen asleep. I sat up and looked around.

The apartment was dark and empty. The comforter from my bed lay on top of me. Elliott must have covered me up before he left. I shuddered at the thought of him seeing my bedroom. It had been so long since I'd picked up in there I didn't think I could remember the color of the carpet.

I got up feeling stiff. I knew that if I went back to sleep

I'd either wake up feeling even worse than I did now or sleep until noon. Neither was a particularly attractive possibility. Instead, I picked up the comforter from the floor and wrapped it around my shoulders, telling myself a shower would do me good. As I passed the telephone I noticed that the answering machine light was blinking. I must have been sleeping so soundly that I didn't hear the phone.

Yawning, I pushed the button that rewound the tape. As the tape rewound, my heart began beating wildly, even though more likely than not it was someone selling long distance service, spared from a tongue-lashing by the fact that I was an especially sound sleeper.

The tape clicked.

"Hi, Kate. It's me, Stephen. I don't know if you're asleep or not, but I thought you'd want to know. I just got a fax from Takisawa. It's too long for me to read the whole thing over the phone, but basically it says they're willing to go along with our counterproposal in principle—whatever that means. I'll leave a copy on your desk. I guess we're not dead yet."

For a minute I just stood there, wrapped in the blanket, and stared at the phone. I pushed the rewind button and listened to the message again. Then I did a little dance around the living room before I went to get dressed.

Friday was marked by a sense of urgency that infected every person at Azor Pharmaceuticals from the secretaries to the scientists. With the power shutdown set for five o'clock, many investigators had spent the night working in their labs, finishing up experiments, while others had arrived before dawn. Things were even more frantic in the ZK-501 labs, because the scientists were working feverishly not just to complete their work but to get their labs ready for Takisawa.

By the time I arrived Carl Woodruff was already pacing the halls, clipboard in hand, looking as edgy as an expectant father in a film from the fifties. His goal, he announced to whoever would listen, was to have everyone out of their labs by four o'clock in order to give the cleaning crew an hour to go through before the lights went out and the building was sealed.

By lunchtime tempers were flaring and emotions running high. Even behind the closed doors of my office I could hear Borland cursing as Carl explained that he would not only have to wear a lab coat during the Takisawa visit, but his girlie calendars would have to come down.

I spent much of the day boxing up the various papers in Danny's office that I would need to work on over the weekend. Unlike at Callahan Ross, where I was not expected to even slit open my own envelopes, at Azor I had to carry the boxes to the car myself. When I was finished I made the rounds of the ZK-501 labs, handing out maps and directions to the party at my mother's Sunday night. When I stopped by Lou Remminger's lab the thought of Lou and my mother in the same room gave me pause. I considered bringing up the subject of appropriate attire but could not think of a graceful way to approach the subject. What was I going to say, "I'm planning on wearing a black Chanel suit. Were you thinking of wearing your nose ring?"

"Do you have a minute?" asked Remminger in conspiratorial tones, as she dropped the invitation absentmindedly onto the chaos of papers on her desk.

"Sure. Why?"

She looked at her watch. "Come sneak down to crystallography with me. Michelle says she's going to try to diffract a new batch of crystals."

"And?"

"And I just have a feeling, that's all."

I followed Remminger down the service stairs past the animal labs where movers were busy loading some of the smaller, more temperature-sensitive animals into transport carriers. When we got to the aquarium window, there were a half-dozen other people milling about, waiting to see what, if anything, was going to happen. To my surprise Stephen arrived shortly after we did. He came up behind us and put his hand on my shoulder.

He bent down and whispered in my ear, "Keep your fingers crossed."

Collectively we held our breaths as we watched Michelle go through it all again. Her face was ashen, and she looked so tired under her dark cap of curls that I wondered how long it had been since she last slept. Michael Childress hovered behind her, hands clasped behind his back like a mad scientist in a cartoon.

Once the crystals were loaded in the generator, Michelle typed in the commands that set the X rays in motion. For several minutes nothing happened. People shifted restlessly from one foot to another and craned their necks for a better view. As the numbers began appearing on the computer monitor, silence passed over the ranks of watchers like darkness in an eclipse. I didn't know whether it was good or bad until Stephen, who could see clearly above everyone else, started cheering.

Suddenly everybody was hugging, laughing. To my enduring astonishment one of the muscle-bound twins from Remminger's lab grabbed me and gave me a big kiss on the lips. As Stephen made his way through the crowd to congratulate her I caught a glimpse of Michelle Goodwin standing mutely in her triumph, her eyes glistening with tears. My heart leapt for her.

Childress, on the other hand, was as animated as a lottery winner, shaking hands and accepting congratulations that no doubt really belonged to Michelle. For now at least, there seemed enough good will—and credit—to go around.

From somewhere Dave Borland appeared, a champagne bottle in each hand, which he swung like a pair of Indian clubs. Stephen's assistant, Rachel, produced a pocket-instamatic and the two crystallographers stood in front of the computer console self-consciously shaking hands for the camera.

Champagne corks popped and Borland doused Michelle and Childress with champagne as if they were baseball players who'd brought home the championship. Michelle's friend from the animal lab managed to scrounge up some gerbil-size paper cups and we all raised our tiny glasses and drank to toast the crystallographers' accomplishment.

Someone facetiously called out: "Speech! Speech!"

Childress needed no further encouragement. He immediately stepped in front of Michelle and began explaining the importance of the discovery. Remminger hissed something under her breath. It sounded suspiciously like "Pig."

From Stephen's point of view the solution of the receptor's structure could not have come at a better time. Twenty-four hours ago the deal with Takisawa had seemed all but dead. Now he not only had an agreement in principle with the Japanese, but a certifiable breakthrough in the form of the first diffractable crystals of ZKBP.

But from the crystallographers' perspective it couldn't have come at a worse time. In a few minutes Michael Childress had a plane to catch and in three hours the power company would shut off electricity to the labs in order to install the new transformers. Michelle would have no choice but to surrender her precious crystals to the safekeeping of a rented freezer. Indeed, even before Childress had finished speaking, the other investigators had begun to slip away, leaving Michelle with her loquacious colleague and a floor full of crushed paper cups to be picked up.

Suddenly Carl Woodruff appeared and grabbed me by the arm. "I need you," he said. "It's an emergency."

"What is it?"

"I need a lawyer."

"What for?"

"To threaten people, what else do you need a lawyer for?"

I followed him at a trot down the hall toward the elevator. On our way up the fire stairs he explained that the company that had promised to rent us the diesel refrigeration unit had just called to say they had made a mistake and it was no longer available.

"Just point me to a telephone and give me their number," I announced. I was not about to have Michelle Goodwin's triumph with the crystals undone by nondelivery of a large appliance.

By three o'clock I was on the loading dock watching the truck back up in order to unload the promised freezer. I'd only had to threaten the dispatcher at the rental company with a lawsuit and dismemberment in order to get him to see things my way. The five hundred dollars extra I offered him helped, too.

"Let's just hope the damn thing works," muttered Borland as we watched them load it on a dolly and push it down the hall. Borland and Michelle had both come to supervise the packing of the freezer and the preparation of the cold rooms.

Borland had already turned the temperature way down in the cold room that had been filled with items that needed to be kept cold but were not considered temperature sensitive. The contents of the remaining cold room would then be shifted into the diesel unit, where the temperature could be maintained to within a tenth of a degree throughout the duration of the blackout. It took us close to an hour, scurrying back and forth between cold rooms, to accomplish the job. We all cursed Childress, who was no doubt savoring the day's success over drinks in first class on his way to Boston while we humped Styrofoam boxes and bottles of reagents up and down the hall.

When we were finally finished, Carl Woodruff produced two rolls of silver duct tape. "It's that time," he announced, handing one roll to Dave Borland and the other to Michelle Goodwin. Working quickly the two scientists sealed the door to the first cold room.

"Are you sure it's going to stay cold?" Michelle asked Borland when they were done.

"Don't worry," he assured her kindly. "We lost power once at Baxter after a big electrical storm. All we did was tape the cold rooms shut and they only lost a degree a day, and it was summertime, too."

Woodruff looked at his watch. "Right on schedule," he chirped. "Now let's get the labs buttoned up so that we can blow this pop stand."

*　*　*

Stephen and I were the last ones to leave the building, but before leaving we took one long last walk through the ZK-501 labs to make sure they had been left in parade condition. The investigators had been instructed to be in the building by seven A.M. on Monday in order to switch on all their equipment. If it had a display and could be turned on, Stephen wanted it on. His goal was to show off labs that glittered like Las Vegas to the Japanese.

As we neared five o'clock a tremendous silence settled over the building. Most of the animals had been moved to other quarters for the weekend. The computers, the ventilation hoods, the special air handling systems had all been switched off. I sensed in Stephen a reluctance to leave, as if he was afraid that somehow he might not be coming back. I put it down to not wanting to give up control, especially on the eve of such an important site visit. He kept finding all sorts of reasons to linger: an oscillator that looked dusty, a piece of tape coming loose off the side of the X-ray generator, a garbage can that needed emptying.

When we came to the diesel-powered refrigeration unit that we'd rented, I let him take his time. It was a walk-in freezer the size of a small shed, powered by a throaty motor that rumbled like a truck. Inside sat Azor's precious ZKBP crystals. Stephen checked the padlock twice to confirm that it was secure and watched the gauges to make sure not only that the temperature was correct, but that there was enough fuel in the tank to keep it running through the weekend. In the end I had to literally take him by the hand and lead him out of the building.

Standing in the parking lot, I realized the temperature had dropped sharply since morning and it had started to snow. The sun had already been down for an hour. A grizzled man wearing a hard hat and an enormous down-filled parka that made him look like the Pillsbury Doughboy came and introduced himself as the job foreman from Commonwealth Edison.

"Security says they've got everybody out of the building, so I think we're ready to rock and roll," he told Stephen.

"Just promise me you'll be finished on Monday morning," said Stephen.

"No problem. We'll have this baby up and running, all juiced up by six A.M."

The foreman raised his hand and gave the signal. Stephen looked like he was going to be sick. Then without a sound or any other kind of warning, the lights went out.

CHAPTER
23

Mother spent most of Saturday driving me crazy. Actually it was Cheryl who bore the brunt of it. I was busy running a different part of the circus. For the past couple of days I'd been trying to convince Stephen that even if we didn't need more lawyers, we needed more bodies. Takisawa, I pointed out, was bringing seventeen people to Chicago. For the purposes of "face" I contended that we needed to have at least that number on our side of the table. Whether he was swayed by my arguments or succumbing to last-minute anxiety, Saturday morning he finally agreed to let me pad the numbers for our side.

Unfortunately that meant that I had to quickly come up with some new faces which I managed to scrape together from Callahan Ross. Included in the group was an associate who'd had some experience dealing with the Japanese. But everyone else was recruited just to fill chairs. Facetiously, Stephen inquired whether we might be better off hiring models in the interest of keeping the billing down.

I spent the morning briefing the Callahan Ross contingent. It seemed only fair that they have some understanding of what was going on in order to help keep them awake. But my main message to them was that their job was to show up and shut up. What I was looking for was dark suits and closed mouths—something Callahan Ross had been serving up faithfully for over a hundred years.

Through it all Cheryl kept sidling in with phone messages from Mother. There was some crisis with the flowers, the wine store had delivered the wrong vintage, the pianist who'd originally been hired had sprained a finger shoveling snow, and had I ever heard anything about the one they were sending in his place. . . . It was not that I did not appreciate these little missives from my mother, but at this point there was nothing I could do about it, and she was making everybody nuts.

We broke for lunch at twelve-thirty and attacked a deli tray from Jacobs Brothers. I was just raising a pastrami sandwich to my lips when I heard myself being paged. I picked up the conference room phone and was surprised to find Elliott on the other end of the line. There were loud noises in the background like someone was sawing wood or running a vacuum.

"What's going on?" I bellowed, once he had identified himself.

"I'm at Danny's apartment. The biohazard people are here cleaning up," he said, shouting over the noise. I put my finger in my free ear in the hopes that it would help. "I need to talk to you."

"What about?"

"Childress."

"Can't you go to a quieter phone?"

"This was the quietest place I could find. I can't leave. Can you come here?"

It made sense that Elliott had to stay. Many of the companies that dispose of biologically active waste recruit their workforce from the ranks of the homeless and the otherwise unemployable. Knowing Elliott, he'd want to make absolutely sure that nothing of value walked out during the cleaning. Still, I didn't really have time for this today.

"When will they be done?" I asked.

"What?"

"When will they be finished?"

"They said they'd be here all day."

I looked at my watch and decided to just get it over with. "I'll be there in fifteen minutes."

Before I left I wrapped my sandwich in a napkin so that I could eat it in the car, but it had started snowing so badly that I didn't want to take my eyes off the road. I switched on the radio to see if I could catch the weather and was dismayed to learn another six inches were predicted.

"Please God," I prayed, "just as long as they don't close the airport."

When I arrived at Danny's apartment, Elliott met me at the door. It seemed as though the biohazard crew had taken over the entire floor. Elliott reported that between the noise and the scary biohazard apparatus the neighbors had for the most part cleared out.

Inside the apartment the bloodstained furniture had been wrapped in heavy black plastic and was being carried out one piece at a time. The carpet was being ripped out in sections and put into an enormous orange dumpster with a large biohazard warning symbol on all four sides. Warnings in Spanish and English declared the contents to be extremely hazardous. No wonder the neighbors had fled. Other workers were busy scrubbing the walls with some kind of high-pressure solvent. They were dressed in bulky biohazard suits like astronauts.

Elliott and I, in search of a quiet place to talk, found a seat on the deep sill of the window at the far end of the corridor adjacent to the elevators.

"So what did you find out about Childress?" I asked.

"Very interesting man, our friend Dr. Childress."

"Why's that?"

"He's a bit of a Jekyll and Hyde."

"Meaning?"

"While his professional life is stellar, his personal life is a mess."

"What kind of a mess?"

"Well, for one thing, he has a criminal record."

"You're kidding! Dr. Michael Childress?"

"The very one. We did some checking and he has a sheet in Boston."

"That's where he lived while he worked for Baxter. What did he get busted for?"

"Two counts of assault and battery, both of which looked like they were a result of bar fights. One DWI and, get this, an arrest for having sex with a minor. Charges for that last one were later dropped."

"Why?"

"Hard to tell. Lots of times those cases are. The kid gets cold feet about testifying in court, some kind of out-of-court settlement is reached, the D.A. decides he doesn't have enough evidence to make a case. Lots of reasons. Unfortunately there's no way to find out because when a case involves a minor the court records are sealed."

"Was it a boy or a girl?" I asked, in a flash of inspired thinking.

"The arrest docket doesn't say. But take a look at his mug shots." Elliott handed me copies of Childress's arrest record. Clipped to the first page were several photographs, all mug shots. In the pictures he looked younger—and drunk—but there was no denying it was Childress. In one of the pictures he had a black eye and a split lip. I flipped to the next one.

"What's he wearing in this?" I demanded.

"I was sort of wondering about that myself," replied Elliott. "It looks like it could be the top of a dress, doesn't it?"

I stared at it for a few minutes. "I don't know," I said finally. "This copy is kind of dark, so it's hard to say. It could just be a T-shirt that somehow got ripped in the scuffle. Do you think he could be some kind of cross-dresser?"

"We haven't turned up anything like that yet, but believe me we're still digging."

"Does he know you're checking him out?"

"No. I've got one operative working in the guise of a freelance journalist preparing a story on him. He actually had lunch with her Thursday and he gave her an interview."

"What did she say he was like?"

"The word she used most often was *asshole*."

"I'm not surprised. You hear that said a lot about Childress."

"As far as the former colleagues she's talked to, it's pretty clear he was not what you'd call well-liked."

"Why?" I asked, wondering whether their reasons might differ from the ones currently in vogue at Azor.

"Well, it seems like he's a pretty hateful guy," replied Elliott, consulting what looked like a typed report. "The consensus seems to be that he likes to take credit for the work of others. There's been a lot of bitterness about that almost everywhere he's been since graduate school. He's also got a reputation for being a busybody—you know, always complaining about his coworkers' conduct. I guess when he left Baxter for Azor there were a lot of people who were happy to say good riddance."

"Can anybody link him with Danny outside of the office?"

"Not so far, but like I said, we're still checking. But while we're on the subject, I remember you mentioning before that Childress used to work for Baxter. Do they do AIDS research there?"

"I don't know, but Baxter is an enormous pharmaceutical house, and not only that, but Childress is well connected, if not well liked, throughout the scientific community. If he came to Danny and said he could get his hands on a new AIDS drug, then it's more than likely that Danny would believe him."

"Interesting."

"Have you compared the fingerprints from his rap sheet against the ones that were found on the glass in the apartment?" I asked.

"I woke up the guy from the forensics lab this morning and made him come in to run the comparison."

"And?"

"They don't match."

"You're kidding," I said, disappointed.

"Don't take it too hard, Kate," said Elliott, putting his arm around me and giving me a friendly squeeze. "After all, it was only a hunch."

"I know," I replied in my best spoiled-little-rich-girl voice. "But it was my hunch and I liked it."

The next morning Stephen and I arrived at O'Hare almost an hour early. Stephen had woken in a nearly manic state, panicked that the roads would be bad and terrified of being late. Fortunately, the snowplows had been out all night and the roads were clear and nearly deserted because it was Sunday. With time to kill before the JAL flight came in, Stephen paced up and down the curb in front of the international arrivals terminal, frantic that the limo drivers wouldn't show up.

After my years with Guttman I recognized these symptoms of type A overload. I left him to make a spectacle of himself in front of the skycaps and went into the terminal in search of a cup of coffee. By the time I located the closest Starbucks and came back outside, the cars had arrived, and Stephen, in his relief, was shaking hands with all the drivers, assuring them how much he appreciated their efforts. We left them shaking their heads behind his back and headed for international arrivals.

The JAL flight landed precisely on time, which struck me as incredible considering the distance it had flown. While we waited for the passengers to clear customs Stephen arranged for four porters with their big carts to help with the luggage. Most of the other people who were meeting the flight were Asian, no doubt waiting for relatives or friends. Standing among them Stephen looked like a big, nervous giant. I found myself wishing I had one of those tranquilizer guns they use on large animals.

After all the frenzied preparations I must confess the actual arrival of the Takisawa delegation was something of an anticlimax—seventeen tired Japanese businessmen in identical black suits that looked like they'd been slept in. They all came up to right around Stephen's waist. Old man Takisawa was the last one past the barrier. He was older than I expected—stooped, graying, and almost frail after the long flight.

After an orgy of bowing we got their luggage loaded into the cars with a minimum of fuss. Stephen rode with the chairman in the first car. I went in the second limo and sat up front with the driver. Traffic was picking up, but it was still not bad. The snow was over, and the sun had come out. When we got close enough to catch our first glimpse of the downtown skyline, I turned around to tell the Japanese and found them already leaning out the windows taking snapshots of the view.

When we arrived at the Nikko, the general manager of the hotel, three of his assistants, and the entire bell staff were lined up outside the front door awaiting our arrival. Old man Takisawa seemed pleased by his reception. Stephen and I stayed long enough to make sure everyone was comfortably settled into their rooms and that there were no complaints.

As we walked back out through the lobby I had to concede that, so far, Mother had done quite a job.

My parents' house is one of the most beautiful on the North Shore. A gem of Georgian architecture designed by Louis B. Sullivan, it sits, surrounded by majestic elms, on a deep lawn of verdant green atop a dramatic bluff overlooking Lake Michigan. I had spent the afternoon at my mother's hairdresser's, albeit against my will, and arrived at my childhood home as coiffed and manicured as I had been on my wedding day.

I got there early not only because I knew that Mother expected it, but in order to be able to enjoy the grand spectacle of her inevitable preparty hysteria. In certain circles Mother was as famous for her temper as for her sense of style, and it was the rare person who got a chance to see her lose it more than once.

By the time I crossed the threshold I knew she had already cranked it up to high gear. Not only could I hear her in the kitchen chewing out one of the caterers for some imagined oversight, but the door to my father's study was firmly shut. Father, of course, never actually studied anything in his life, but this was the one room in the house where he was permitted to smoke cigars and watch what he wanted on TV. From beyond the closed door of this sanctuary I could hear that he had already turned the volume up to drown out the shouting.

By the time Stephen arrived all was serene. The house was filled with the eloquent calm that is so famous for always following the storm. One of the maids had tearfully given notice, and the catering manager, mistaking me for one of the staff, had confided that the way you could tell God had a sense of humor was by whom he had given money to. As usual my mother was completely unrepentant. In her mind, her outbursts were not just par for the course, but the price you had to pay to make a party perfect.

While she would never admit to it, Mother loves to show off her house. It is, after all, a tribute to her taste, not to mention my father's pocketbook. The rooms are grand but beautifully proportioned. Precious objects draw the eye. Some of the antiques have been passed down through generations of Prescotts and Millhollands, while others were specially chosen for a particular spot on shopping trips to France and England. There were just enough China trade heirlooms, masses of blue-and-white porcelain, and old paintings of sailing ships to demonstrate our Yankee lineage. The fresh flowers had been flown in the day before from Hawaii and sumptuously arranged.

Stephen arrived looking like the god of Armani, perfect from the bottom of his hand-sewn Italian shoes to the top of his freshly barbered head. Mother beamed at him as she offered her cheek to be kissed. It struck me, watching from the top of the stairs, that the two of them looked like they belonged together. I, on the other hand, looked like a refugee from a fire sale at Chanel. My mother, who invariably had her dressmaker remove the trademark buttons from her Chanel jackets because she thought them tacky (and besides, anybody who mattered would recognize the designer without having to resort to anything so crass as checking the buttons. . . .), had insisted that I be outfitted in head-to-toe Chanel, buttons and all, in order to impress the Japanese. For herself, she had chosen an elegant Issey Miyake dress in deference to our foreign visitors.

Needless to say, our Azor guests were as oblivious to all of this as I was to particle physics. They started trickling in, in dribs and drabs, unfashionably early and in obvious awe at where they found themselves. In addition to the ZK-501 scientists, Stephen had invited the members of Azor's scientific advisory board. The SAB scientists advised the company in their area of expertise, but more important lent the weight of their credentials to the upstart company. It was interesting to watch my mother size them up, dismissing with a brief lowering of her lids a Nobel prize-winner because he was wearing polyester pants.

The five limousines bearing our Japanese guests pulled into the circular drive at the stroke of seven. Mother, who had entertained three presidents and several foreign heads of state under her roof, afforded them the same treatment. Cocktails were served in the northeast parlor, a heartbreakingly pretty room with enormous mullioned windows that looked out over the lake. In the distance, the lights of the city seemed to glimmer expressly for our pleasure.

This was really my first chance to observe Chairman Takisawa, and I confess my eyes followed him with the concentration of an assassin. If the negotiation with Takisawa could be likened to a high-stakes game of chess, then old man Takisawa was my opponent and whatever impressions I could glean from him before the games began had the potential for being enormously valuable.

That he would prove a daunting adversary I had no doubt. That afternoon I'd finally had a chance to read through the sheaf of articles Cheryl had dug up about him. More than one alluded to the fact that as a young man he'd spent much of World War II interrogating American prisoners of war. Several authors in the business press also pointed out that while Takisawa was fluent in English, he often feigned ignorance of the language in order to maneuver for advantage.

Like most of his countrymen he was diminutive in stature, yet there was definitely nothing small about him. A tough nut was my first impression—a very tough nut. The level of deference he commanded from his subordinates was remarkable, even for a Japanese. Maybe it was my imagination, but it seemed to me as if his subordinates almost feared him. When he left the room to accompany my mother on a tour of the house, the rest of the Takisawa group relaxed palpably.

Mother and the chairman returned from their tour almost forty-five minutes later. I don't know what went on, but they were both beaming. She introduced Takisawa to Herbert Magnuson, the former Japanese ambassador, and his wife, who were happy for a chance to practice their Japanese. Hiroshi, who had arrived that afternoon from New York sans secretary, chatted amiably with Stephen in front of the fire.

The lawyers from Callahan Ross who'd been brought to flesh out our numbers tried hard to pretend they were not impressed, but they all seemed to be busy figuring out what things were worth. I knew they would never be able to look at me the same way again. The ZK-501 scientists were huddled on the periphery and looked completely blown away by it all, like paupers who suddenly find themselves at the palace. I made my way across the room to them.

"Wow, I can't believe this is where you grew up," drawled Lou Remminger, beefing up her Appalachian accent for effect. I was relieved to see she had at least rinsed the purple out of her hair and pulled her jagged bangs back into a rhinestone clip. She wore a simple long-sleeved shift dress and a pair of patent leather Maryjanes. By her usual standards her makeup was practically understated.

Michelle, on the other hand, looked radiant in a simple brown dress in some kind of clingy fabric that showed off her perfect body. Borland, in a tweed jacket and some sort of bizarre nautical-motif tie, managed to look even more disreputable than he did at work. I suspected that it was his one semirespectable outfit, reserved for conferences and presentations, and that I would be seeing it again and again over the course of the next few days.

"Has anybody heard anything about the electric company?" asked Borland. "Will they be done or are we going to be leading these guys around by candlelight on Monday?"

"I called Carl this afternoon," replied Michelle. "He went over to check up on them today. They say they're right on schedule."

"Did I hear my name mentioned?" asked Carl, coming up behind me. It looked as though he'd just arrived, because his face was flushed red as if from the cold.

"Well, well, well. The gang's all here," he said, accepting a drink from a waiter and joining the group.

"Everybody but Childress," observed Remminger.

"He's not here yet?" I demanded, feeling the first stirrings of alarm.

"I haven't seen him," replied Remminger.

"Do you think maybe he got lost?" suggested Michelle.

"Don't worry," said Borland, swinging his arm around as if taking in the entire room. "Michael Childress wouldn't miss all this for the world."

The butler sounded the chimes for dinner and Mother asked Chairman Takisawa if he would be so kind as to escort her into the dining room. He sat at my mother's right at the head of the long table. Stephen sat on his other side while Hiroshi sat at the other end between my father and the former ambassador to Japan. From where I was sitting (between the head of Takisawa's fabrication labs who spoke little English and the head of their pharmaceutical marketing division who, if possible, spoke less) it looked like Stephen and Hiroshi were discussing, of all things, golf.

The table was set with the antique silver and a gorgeous china pattern of rosebuds and ivy that Tiffany doesn't make anymore. In front of each plate was a place card in a tiny silver holder with each name in English and Japanese characters. After the soup course was served I asked in a whisper to have one of the waiters take Michael Childress's place away.

We had agreed on the most traditional American dinner we could think of—roast turkey with corn-bread-and-sage stuffing and all the trimmings. Mother had arranged personally for a gargantuan bird to be delivered from a poultry farm downstate. It was so big that the kitchen staff had laughingly speculated that it must have been fed steroids. Mother's cook, Mrs. Mason, had risen at dawn and spent the entire day dressing, stuffing, and basting the bird, which was now roasted to succulent perfection. She and the head caterer planned to carry it out on a tremendous pewter tray where it would be carved at table side with great ceremony.

When Mother rang the bell signaling that the great moment had arrived, two white-gloved waiters swung open the French doors for the arrival of the turkey. I had never seen anything that large. Mrs. Mason, her ample bosom encased in a crisply starched uniform, looked triumphant. The caterer beamed from beneath the tower of his white toque.

Whether it was because he was nervous, or merely unfamiliar with the house, as they were passing through the doorway he tripped. For a moment I thought he'd recovered himself, but the big bird was too unwieldy. In

one terrible moment it all came tumbling to the ground—
the caterer, his starched hat, and the steaming roast bird.

My first reaction was to burst out laughing, but the
horror of our Japanese guests at this terrible turn of events
was so apparent that the temptation quickly passed. Instead I found myself turning instinctively to Mother.
Without missing a beat she turned to the cook with a reassuring smile.

"Mrs. Mason, once you've cleaned up that mess why
don't you just go right back into the kitchen and bring
out that second turkey." She said it so calmly and with
such confidence, she almost had *me* believing there was
another one.

CHAPTER
24

As soon as I got home I called Elliott Abelman. I didn't care that it was after midnight. After we'd filled the limousines with tipsy Japanese I'd spent the ride back from Lake Forest reassuring Stephen about Childress's absence, murmuring about missed planes and bad weather in Boston. What made it worse was that I hadn't told him Tom's story about Danny trying a bootleg experimental AIDS drug or what Elliott had learned about Childress's seamy past. Now I felt consumed with guilt, terrified that in trying to shield Stephen from the anxiety during the Takisawa visit, I had actually set him up for an infinitely bigger shock.

Elliott picked up the phone on the third ring. His voice was thick from sleep.

"Are you okay?" he demanded immediately after I'd identified myself.

"Michael Childress didn't show up at the dinner tonight," I reported miserably.

"I thought he was supposed to be out of town this weekend. At least, that's what he told my operative when he called her on Friday."

"He called her Friday?"

"Yeah. He wanted to tell her about some big discovery he was on the verge of making. He told her she might want to hold off finishing the article for a couple of days so that she could take advantage of all the interest his work was going to generate."

I remembered what everyone had told me about Childress's appetite for self-aggrandizement and was not surprised. "He was in Boston for some kind of conference, but he was supposed to be back in time for the dinner tonight," I said.

"Have you tried calling his house?"

"No," I replied, wondering if the pressure of the Takisawa visit was making me stupid.

"Let me put you on hold for a minute and I'll try calling him on my other line."

I waited through the dead air on the line, shifting the phone from one ear to the other in order to take off the Chanel earrings that I would never wear again.

"No answer," reported Elliott, coming back on the line. "Do you want me to send somebody over there?"

"To do what?"

"To check if his car is there, if the lights are on."

"No," I replied, feeling ashamed for having jumped to conclusions. "For all we know he just missed his flight from Boston and is planning on catching an early plane to O'Hare in the morning."

"Do you know what flight he was supposed to take?"

"No."

"Or where he was staying in Boston?"

"No. I was just worried that one of your operatives might have done something or said something that spooked him."

"Listen, Kate. There's no way he could have known we pulled his sheet. Besides, the woman who interviewed him really is a freelance journalist. The fact that he called her right before he left town only confirms that he believes she is what she says she is."

"Do you think there's a chance he might have been arrested?" I asked. "Boston is his old stomping ground, after all. It would certainly explain why he might have missed his plane."

"As soon as we get off the phone I'll see what I can find out from the Boston PD. While I'm at it, do you want me to check the hospitals?"

"If you don't mind."

"I'll get right on it. I'll call you if I find out anything. In the meantime you'd better get to bed. It's late and I know you have a big day tomorrow."

"You're right," I sighed, and wished him good night. Then I hung up the phone and made my way to my bedroom. Elliott was right, I did have a big day tomorrow, but I still didn't have any illusions about being able to sleep.

I drove out to Oak Brook through the darkness, arriving with sunrise still more than an hour away. Commonwealth Edison had promised us electricity by six o'clock and I was there to make sure they delivered. Even more than we needed Michael Childress, we needed electricity. As a precaution I'd reserved a meeting room at the Nikko, and Stephen and I had packed up everything he needed to make his presentation in case there was a problem that prevented us from getting into the building. But I couldn't imagine a worse way to impress a group of businessmen who came from a culture that prized organization and planning above almost everything else.

When I pulled into the parking lot Stephen's car was already there. I wondered whether he'd been there all night. He was pacing anxiously in front of the building wearing a parka over his business suit. The thermometer on the bank at the mall across the street said it was only two degrees.

"Are they going to be ready in time?" I asked, once I'd gotten out of the car and crossed the parking lot. I was happy to see that the snowplow company had already been out. At least the lot was clean and freshly salted, and the sidewalk to the front door shoveled.

"They keep telling me yes," replied Stephen miserably. His stress level was clearly stratospheric. Suddenly I wished I'd stayed at home a little longer. "But they also said it looks like some of the water pipes might have burst in the basement, because it's been so cold."

"I thought the main was turned off for just that reason."

"I know. But there's an auxiliary line that goes into the animal labs that we couldn't find a shutoff for. Carl said that when he called the water company about it, they told him it would be all right."

"How do you know it's burst? Have you been inside the building?"

"No. They won't let anyone in until the power is back up. But come here and I'll show you."

I followed Stephen around the side of the building, holding onto his arm so that I didn't fall on the ice in the dark. My feet were freezing through the flimsy soles of my pumps and by the time we got to the loading dock, my ankles were numb from the cold. I wondered how long it would take once they turned the furnace back on before the building would be warm. The thought of Stephen being able to see his breath during his presentation filled me with dread.

"Look at this," said Stephen, pointing to an enormous puddle that came from underneath the door of the loading dock.

"Whatever it is, we're going to have to get in and clean it up. How much longer until we have lights?"

Stephen looked at his watch. "They say forty minutes."

"Any chance we could wait in the car?" I ventured.

I took it as a good omen when the power came back on ten minutes early. Even though we still had to wait outside in the cold for the security system to reboot and the key card system that regulated entry to become operational, I didn't mind. At least we had light. Next we'd have heat. And finally, God willing, we'd have Michael Childress.

By the time we were able to get inside the building, quite a crowd had gathered: maintenance people who Stephen had ordered to report early to make sure the building was ready for the Japanese, investigators from the various labs throughout the building anxious to see how their experiments had fared through the blackout, and the scientists of the ZK-501 project steeling themselves for their ordeal with Takisawa.

There was a long line and not a little jostling as people had to swipe their ID cards through the reader one by one. Once we were inside, Stephen, Carl, and I made a beeline for the basement. Sure enough, there was water everywhere. With an eye on the clock, Stephen rolled up his sleeves and supervised the cleanup personally. In the meantime, the rest of us followed Carl's orders, scurrying around switching on lights and flipping on equipment.

At some point Lou Remminger appeared, though seeing her in a pressed white lab coat and understated makeup, I confess I barely recognized her.

"I just came down to check to make sure everything was okay. I heard some pipes broke," she explained. With all the rest of us running around like marines getting ready for an inspection drill, there was something almost Zen-like in the chemist's calm.

"There's just a mess in the animal labs," said Woodruff.

"Did the modeling room stay dry?" Remminger asked.

"Yes. None of the cables or the computer equipment got wet. Is everything all set to go in your lab?" inquired Woodruff.

"Do you want to come up and check, Mom?"

"No thank you," he replied. "I'll take your word for it."

Michelle emerged from the crystallography lab and joined us. I understood why Stephen had insisted on lab coats. Not only did they cover the worst of the scientists' crimes against fashion, but they made everybody look like a grown-up.

"Has anybody seen Childress?" Michelle asked anxiously. "He's supposed to be making the crystallography presentation this morning. His slides are here, but I haven't seen him."

"Has anybody tried calling his house?" Remminger inquired.

"I think Carl said he tried him early this morning and all he got was the answering machine," reported the crystallographer.

"You don't think this is all some kind of prima donna

shit?" said Remminger. "It would be just like him to do something crazy like this just to draw attention to himself."

"Do you really think so?" inquired Michelle uncertainly, just as Dave Borland came barreling down the hall, long strips of silver duct tape trailing from his hands.

"What is it?" I asked.

Borland paused for a minute, as if struggling to catch his breath.

"Michael Childress just turned up," he announced finally.

"Thank god," I exclaimed.

"Turned up?" asked Michelle Goodwin nervously. "What do you mean turned up?"

"Turned up where?" demanded Remminger.

"Come with me," replied Borland.

CHAPTER
25

Michael Childress lay on the floor of the cold room. His arms were folded peacefully across his chest. He was stark naked. He was also very definitely dead.

"Somebody go get Stephen," I commanded in the sharp voice of emergency. I whirled around to face Borland. "Did you touch anything?" I demanded.

"I . . . oh . . . I don't know. . . . I don't think so. . . ." stammered the protein chemist. His gruesome discovery had stripped him of all his usual bravura. "I must have, but only to make sure he was really dead."

"What else would he be, for Christ's sake?" drawled Remminger, who seemed if not amused, then downright unaffected.

"Why isn't he wearing any clothes?" asked Michelle Goodwin in startled tones as she peered over my shoulder to get a better look at him.

"What do you think those marks are on the floor?" inquired Remminger, ever the scientist.

I hadn't noticed them before. My eyes had been drawn to the bruising on his knees and his fingers. The digits were so bloody and raw, they looked like they'd been chewed by some kind of animal. But once she'd pointed them out I saw quite clearly what she was talking about. In the thin layer of frost that covered the metal floor of the cold room, on either side of the crystallographer's body, were arcing marks—the kind we used to make as kids when we made angels in the snow.

"Maybe he killed himself," Michelle ventured uncertainly.

It was as if we were all having separate conversations, everyone just saying the first thing that came to his mind, no one taking anything in or, for that matter, taking his eyes from Michael Childress's naked corpse.

"Are those his clothes there next to him?" I asked, looking at the disorderly pile of dark clothing.

"What the hell is going on?" barked Stephen as he made his way down the hall toward us, with Carl Woodruff trailing close behind. "Everyone is supposed to be up in the lunchroom."

"It's Childress," I said, breaking away from the group and walking toward him. "It looks like he got locked in the freezer over the weekend."

"What? Is he okay?"

"He's dead," I said.

"He's better than dead," blurted Remminger. "He's frozen like a Thanksgiving turkey."

The rest of us were momentarily struck mute by her inappropriate outburst. For a minute Michelle looked as if she was about to say something, but instead, she heaved a great sob and broke into tears. Borland put his arm around her shoulder to comfort her, but she shrugged it off and made a dash for the ladies' room.

When Stephen got there, we all stepped away from the cold room door so he could get a good look.

"What are we going to do?" demanded Carl, looking like a man who's just dropped a winning lottery ticket through a subway grating. "We've got the Takisawa people due to arrive any minute."

"Lou, go make sure Michelle is okay," ordered Stephen, as if waking from a dream. "Tell her she'll have to make the crystallography presentation. Let's just hope he left the slides he was going to use somewhere where we can find them."

"Michelle knows where the slides are," I said, not believing the conversation was actually happening. "Somehow I don't think that's what Carl is worried about."

Stephen raised his hand to silence me. Then he turned to address the others.

"You all go back upstairs to the conference room and don't say a word about this to anybody. Kate and I will figure out the best way to handle this. I'll be upstairs in a minute."

The scientists left reluctantly, still stunned by what had happened. I thought the chances of them keeping what they'd seen to themselves were somewhere between zero and none. I lost no time in sharing my assessment with Stephen.

"I don't think you appreciate the delicacy of the situation, Kate," he snapped. "The whole company is hanging by a thread, and now . . . this!"

" 'This,' as you so aptly put it, is a matter for the police. There is no way around it."

"There has to be some other way to handle it," protested Stephen.

"There is no way to 'handle' it at all. This is one of those unambiguous situations. All we can do is call the police. I'll try to explain the situation to them and see if I can get them to be discreet. . . ."

"I don't think that calling the police is necessarily in our best interests under the circumstances," said Stephen calmly, pushing the cold-room door shut and adding his fingerprints to whatever else the crime lab was going to find there.

I knew what he was thinking and I couldn't believe it. How could anyone so intelligent even contemplate something so stupid? Suddenly my stomach felt exactly the same way it did when as a kid I'd crest the top of the first big hill on the roller coaster.

"We have to call the police and we have to call them now," I said reasonably.

Stephen stepped into the modeling room, picked up the telephone that hung on the wall, and punched in a number.

"Hello, security? This is Dr. Azorini. I want you to station someone at the elevator and the stairs to the basement. We have to make sure no one comes down here. We've had an equipment problem over the weekend and I don't want anyone coming down until we're sure there hasn't been a radiation leak." He hung up the receiver and turned to me. "See? That wasn't so hard, was it?"

"Stephen Anthony Azorini," I said sternly. "This is not some situation you can finesse your way around. There is a dead man lying on the floor of this freezer and if we don't call the police, we will be committing a felony."

"Do you really want the Takisawa people to pull into the parking lot and have the first thing they see be a half-dozen squad cars parked out front with their lights flashing? Do you have any idea what is riding on this visit? Do you?"

"What you're proposing to do could land you in jail," I countered. "If you're so afraid of what the Japanese will think, then call them in their limos right now and tell them you're still having trouble with the electricity out here and have the scientists make their presentations downtown."

"That's not acceptable."

"Neither is failure to report a death to the proper authorities."

"I didn't say we weren't going to report it. I'm just asking what it would hurt if we waited?"

"It would be wrong," I said, frustrated that he would let his desperation to make a deal with Takisawa cloud his judgment, "and it will hurt you. Cover this up now and I guarantee it'll come back and bite you. You don't think the cops will be able to tell that the door to the cold room has already been opened? Or that Borland touched the body, for Christ's sake? Do you think it's all right for you to ask all of us to lie to the police? Even if we were all willing, how do you think you, Dave, Carl, Michelle, Lou, and I will keep our stories straight? The only way is to do the right thing and tell the truth."

"What difference will it make if we call the police now or if we call them at five o'clock?"

"I'm not even going to dignify that with an answer," I snapped, suddenly losing patience. "I am an officer of the court and I won't be a party to any deception. I'm willing to do everything in my power to see if we can't get this handled as quietly as possible. If we can get the local cops to play ball, there's a chance we can keep it from Takisawa. But the only way you're going to keep me from calling the police is to lock me up with Childress right now."

Stephen fixed me with such a murderous look that for a moment I honestly thought I was going to be spending the day with a dead man.

"Just handle it," he said finally. Then he turned and walked away, leaving me alone in the basement with the body.

I called 911 from the phone in the crystallography lab and told the dispatcher to direct the police to the back of the building by the loading dock. Then I called Elliott Abelman and told him what had happened. He said he was on his way. That done, I went outside and waited for the police.

As I shivered on the loading dock I found myself wondering, not for the first time, whether it was Elliott's inquiries into Childress's past that had frightened him into suicide. Coming on the morning of the Takisawa visit, it might have been just the kind of dramatic "fuck you" to Stephen I imagined Childress to be capable of.

Unburdened by serial killers and afflicted with no crime more serious than shoplifting, the Oak Brook police responded quickly to my report of a dead man in the freezer. Two incredibly clean-cut officers who looked like they'd just graduated from bible college arrived within five minutes of my call.

As succinctly as I could I told them what had happened. I also explained that the building had been closed over the weekend with the power shut down for the new transformers. I described how the temperature had been turned down in the cold room and about its being taped shut in order to help keep cold air from escaping.

"Did anybody check to make sure there was nobody inside before it was taped shut?" the older officer asked.

"I don't know if they checked," I replied, "but I was there while it was being taped. Believe me, if there was somebody inside who wanted to get out, we would have heard them."

"And nobody missed this guy Childress over the weekend? Not even his wife?"

"He wasn't married. Besides, we all thought he was in Boston attending a conference."

"What kind of work did he do here?" the younger of the two officers asked while the older one pulled on some sort of plastic gloves that looked like baggies with fingers.

"Dr. Childress was a chemist," I replied, balking at the prospect of trying to explain X-ray crystallography under these circumstances.

"You want to show us where the body is, ma'am?" the one with the gloves asked with a nod.

I led them to the cold room. They opened the door and stepped inside. Through the open door I watched as they squatted down beside the body. The younger officer pulled a set of plastic gloves from his pocket as the other uniform briskly touched Childress's neck, no doubt making sure he was dead.

"You'd better get on the radio and call it in as an accidental death slash possible homicide," he said to his partner. "Then you better page Jerry and tell ID to get the hell out here. Tell them we're going to be needing the morgue wagon."

As he talked I took another look at the dead crystallographer. I'm not sure that even in life Childress had been much to look at naked, but the cold certainly hadn't helped. He was a skinny little man with pale skin and pubic hair that had begun to turn gray. The skin on his face was a dusky shade of red, and even though his arms were folded over his chest, I could tell that, like his knees, they were badly bruised.

"What's all this in here with him?" asked the younger officer, pointing to the bulky Styrofoam containers that lined the shelves and were stacked up on the floor.

"They're research supplies," I replied.

"No food? Nothing to eat or drink?"

"I don't think so."

He got up and examined the inside of the door carefully without touching it.

"That's funny. It looks like the emergency release handle is broken. Do you have any idea how long it's been that way?"

"I have no idea," I replied, seeing my suicide theory evaporating before my eyes.

"You mind telling me who actually found the body?" asked the second officer, pulling a notebook from his pocket and starting to write.

"Dr. Dave Borland."

"Is he a medical doctor, ma'am?"

"No. He's a chemist."

"Just like the dead guy?"

"Yes. This is a pharmaceutical company. They're all chemists here."

"Where is this Dr. Borland, ma'am?"

"He's upstairs."

"We're going to need to speak to him and get his statement."

"I'll be happy to go get him for you if you like."

On my way up to the first floor I took the stairs two at a time. If things were proceeding on schedule Stephen should have just finished his presentation. I opened the door of the first-floor lunchroom. Partitions had been erected to block the refrigerator and sink from view. A podium had been brought in and a large screen for slides set up in the front of the room. Chairs, which Stephen had personally selected so that he could be sure they were comfortable, had been rented and arranged in rows.

Lou Remminger was at the podium speaking with great authority about her theory that ZK-501 consisted of two distinct regions—binding and affector. The Japanese scientists were taking notes so furiously that the tables in front of them shook. I slipped into an empty chair beside Borland.

"The police are here," I whispered. "They want to talk to you." From across the room Stephen shot me an inquiring glance, which I chose to ignore. Borland rose to his feet with a little grunt and together we slipped out of the room.

"Do you know if anybody checked to make sure the room was empty before they taped it shut?" I asked once we were out in the hall.

"What kind of idiot do you take me for?" he answered. "Michelle and I both looked. Believe me, there was nobody in there when we closed it up. Besides, if he somehow got shut in there by accident all he'd have had to do was use the emergency release to open the door. It wouldn't be hard to push through the duct tape, even for a wimp like Childress."

"The cops say the emergency release was broken."

"Broken? Since when?"

"I don't know," I replied as we arrived in the basement. During the short time I was upstairs more police had arrived. The team from the county crime lab was there in their Day-Glo jumpsuits with their tackle boxes full of equipment. While Borland gave his statement to the two uniformed officers I lingered in the hallway and watched the forensics team go about their business. No one objected to my presence. Indeed, they all seemed happy to accept my being head of the company's legal department as a valid reason for staying.

The plainclothes detectives arrived just as two jump-suited attendants wheeled a stretcher into the cold room. I couldn't help but notice that on top of the sheets was a neatly folded body bag. The two detectives were as clean-cut as the uniformed officers, though older and not as good-looking. They ambled down the corridor, each carrying a steaming Styrofoam cup of 7-Eleven coffee. From where I was standing it sounded like they were talking about last night's Bulls game.

While television may have given us the myth of the raging pursuit and the high-speed chase, I knew that the real business of solving murders was much more leisurely. After all, by the time the homicide cops show up, the bad guys are long gone. Not only that, but the victim sure as hell isn't going anywhere.

The two detectives' names were Rankin and Masterson. Rankin was the taller of the two, with a whippet build and a buzz haircut. He seemed to be acting as the primary investigator. They ignored me and immediately made a beeline for the uniformed officers who were busy questioning Borland. From what I could see, the protein chemist did not appear to be enjoying himself at all.

Elliott, having no doubt hit the worst of the rush-hour traffic, arrived a few minutes later. I was ridiculously glad to see him. He came up and put his arm around me, and I must admit, I clung to him.

"You've got to stop killing people, Kate," he whispered into my hair. "I think the cops are beginning to catch on." I made a face and pulled away from him. "So Michael Childress turned up dead. No wonder he missed his plane. Any chance of it being suicide?"

"If it is, he hid in the cold room before it was taped shut on Friday afternoon, broke the emergency release handle, took off all his clothes, and then lay down to make snow angels before he died."

"You didn't tell me he was naked."

"I was saving the best for last."

"Any chance he got locked in there by accident?"

"I guess it's possible. No one would think to look for him because we all assumed he was on his way to Boston, but two different people checked the room before it was sealed up."

"How do they keep track of people?"

"It's a swipe-card system. You have to run your ID card through a magnetic card reader when you enter or exit the building. The information is automatically logged into the computer. Friday afternoon before they locked down the building, the security guards were supposed to make sure that every person who had entered the building that day had also exited."

"Maybe they made a mistake."

"Maybe they did," I said. "Do you think there's some connection with Danny Wohl's death? I mean, you start poking around Michael Childress's past, and two days later he turns up dead. That would be quite a coincidence."

"You realize this means giving up Galloway to the cops."

"I can't."

"Then I'm going to have to do it."

"Blades is going to be pissed at me, isn't he?"

"I'm assuming that right now Blades is the least of your worries. Why don't you tell me what it is you want me to do?"

For the rest of the day Elliott ran interference with the police. Stephen's assistant Rachel acted as his handmaiden, spending the day slipping discreetly in and out of the presentation room delivering whispered summonses. By this method the detectives were able to interview everyone who'd been involved in finding the body or who'd worked with Childress without attracting the attention of the Japanese.

I ended up spending almost two hours with the detectives, telling them not only what I knew about the discovery of the body, but about Azor in general and the rough outline of the deal with Takisawa. Throughout it all, they were not only courteous and professional but, I came to realize, very sharp. While their questioning of me was painless, it was so thorough that I felt physically drained when it was over.

I went upstairs to rejoin the group in the conference room and sent Stephen downstairs to take my place. He spent most of Michelle Goodwin's presentation being questioned, which was not an entirely bad thing. I doubted that even under the best of circumstances Michelle was particularly good at the lectern, but today, struggling with Childress's slides, she seemed painfully bad.

Things seemed to pick up somewhat after lunch, with Stephen moderating a question-and-answer session between Takisawa's scientists and his own. I took the opportunity to slip away to look for Elliott. I found him alone in the modeling room, poring over a computer printout of Friday's card swipes.

"Where are the cops?" I asked from the doorway.

"Gone for now," he replied, looking up with a smile. "You look tired."

"I feel dead. Speaking of dead, where's Childress?"

"They took him away hours ago. I spoke to Joe. He's going to see what he can do about getting Julia Gordon to do the post. He says he figures she owes him after how Danny Wohl's autopsy was handled."

"What do the cops think?"

"They're pros, which means they're not saying. But I think it's pretty obvious they've ruled out suicide. The emergency escape handle looks like it was deliberately tampered with. The cuts and bruises on his fingers and hands correspond to bloody fingerprints on the inside of the door where it looks like he tried to claw his way out."

"Any chance he died someplace else and his body was dumped in the freezer in order to astonish us when we opened the door?"

"It seems unlikely."

"I don't know," I mused. "The whole thing is just too bizarre."

"You know what puzzles me is this computer log. Granted, it's difficult to decipher because there are so many different individual entries. With three-hundred-plus people working in this building, it's amazing the number of times people come in and out. Still, I've gone through it item by item twice now and everybody's accounted for. Childress arrived at eight fifty-six in the morning, and he swiped out at three thirty-two in the afternoon."

"Does anybody remember seeing him leave?"

"No. But the guard who was doing duty at the security desk said that wasn't necessarily unusual, especially if he didn't have a briefcase or any other kind of bag that needed to be checked out."

"What time was his flight to Boston supposed to leave?"

"Five-ten."

"That's cutting it close. I would have guessed he was the kind of guy who liked to get to the airport early. I know things were sort of crazy with the big breakthrough in the crystallography lab, but everyone was pretty well out of there by quarter to two. So I guess the question is, what was he doing between one forty-five and three thirty-two?"

"Well, for one thing he called my operative and told her all about his big discovery."

"What time?"

"She doesn't remember exactly, but she says she thinks somewhere around two."

"Maybe there were other people he called as well."

"The cops'll subpoena the company's phone records if they think it's important."

"Do you?"

"Maybe. Maybe not. But I'll tell you a couple of things they're definitely going to want to know."

"What?"

He ticked them off on his fingers. "They're going to want to know what happened to his car. It's not in the lot and it's not at his house. They found his plane ticket to Boston in the pocket of his pants, but so far his keys haven't turned up. They're also going to want to know what happened to his ID card. They looked everywhere for it, and it didn't turn up."

"Anything else?"

"Yeah. They're going to want to know why he was naked."

CHAPTER
26

Mother was unable to join us at the Everest Room for dinner that night. The Art Institute was having their quarterly trustees meeting. It had been scheduled months ago, and Mother had no choice—they were voting on the budget, and she had to go. As I drove downtown to the restaurant I could not remember a time, not even when I was a little girl, when I felt like I needed her more.

I told myself it was just lack of sleep. After all, I'd worked on cases, some of which had dragged on for months, that were so emotionally difficult they made finding a dead body in the freezer look like a harmless April Fools' joke. Staying unruffled was what I got paid the big bucks for.

There was no denying I was irritated with myself. I'd had clients throw furniture, break down in tears, and start throwing punches—and I'd never taken any of it personally. After all, when you came right down to it, it was always the client's ass that was on the line—not mine. But as much as I'd believed I would be able to keep our business and professional lives separate, I had to confess I was feeling not only furious with Stephen, but hurt as well.

Stephen hadn't spoken to me since our argument that morning outside the cold room. Not one single word. At lunch he'd taken pains to ignore me and when I'd come to his office after we'd shoveled the Japanese into their limos and sent them on their way, he'd actually gotten up and closed the door in my face. This was petty, junior-high-school stuff, but after what I'd done for him— coming to work on the Takisawa deal full time, trying to squeeze in work for my clients at night and on the weekend, putting myself into my mother's debt in order to enlist her help on his behalf—I felt I deserved better.

On the passenger seat beside me was the folder with Mother's explicit instructions regarding the night's arrangements, including a copy of the contract with the restaurant spelling out the menu, and a seating chart she'd faxed over to Cheryl, who'd in turn faxed it out to Oak Brook for me. I was hoping the arrangements had all been carried out according to plan. Otherwise I was going to have to give Mother's recipe for catharsis— chewing out the catering staff—a try.

I pulled up to One Financial Plaza, the gleaming home of the Mid-America Commodity Exchange, behind the Board of Trade Building on LaSalle Street. Ignoring the bemused expression of the valet at the sight of my car— this was Bentley and Testa Rosa territory—I handed over my keys and took the exterior escalator to the entrance of the building. Walking through the lobby to the bank of express elevators that would whisk me to the fortieth floor, I could not fault my mother's judgment for choosing the Everest for dinner. Perched atop the city's financial center, it not only commanded one of the most spectacular city views to be found outside a tourist observation deck, but the entire restaurant had been conceived of to please the palates—and egos—of powerful men.

The manager met me as I stepped off the elevator. One tuxedoed waiter took my coat while another offered me a glass of champagne from a silver tray with the chef's compliments. The restaurant was elegant and masculine without being clubby. Crystal chandeliers, white damask tablecloths, and the stiff formality of the waiters were offset by the whimsical faux leopard-skin carpeting. The food, I knew from experience, was uniformly excellent— adventurous but seldom daring—like the financial high rollers who were the mainstay of their clientele.

Mother's instructions had been carried out to the letter. A long table had been set up along the west side of the lower dining room commanding a prime view of the city lights spread out like a jeweled blanket beneath us. The table had been decorated with the orchids that had caused Cheryl so much grief, arranged in very tall bud vases so that they would seem to bloom above the heads of seated diners.

From my folder I pulled the stack of place cards the calligrapher had prepared and consulted the seating chart Mother had prepared for me. At first I thought she was playing some kind of elaborate joke—either that or she'd been drinking. According to her diagram, she had old man Takisawa sitting between Lou Remminger and Dave Borland. Hiroshi was at the far end of the table between Stephen and Childress. I quickly pulled the crystallographer's place card and tore it up. Hiroshi would have to make do with Michelle instead.

I looked at my watch. The busboys were busy filling the water glasses from silver pitchers. If everything was going according to schedule, Stephen and the contingent from

Azor were already waiting in the lobby for the arrival of the limousines bringing the Takisawa people from the Nikko. There was no time to fiddle with the seating, so I decided to trust my mother's judgment. I had just laid down the last place card when the maître d' appeared at my elbow and discreetly whispered my mother's favorite words: "Your guests have arrived, Madame."

If Stephen thought the seating arrangements were peculiar, he said nothing to me; indeed, he said nothing at all to me that night. But by the time the salad course was served, all my reservations about Mother's plan had been completely erased. Every time I glanced in his direction, the chairman of the Takisawa corporation was smiling. From time to time he even laughed out loud.

Things were rockier at my end of the table where Mother had relegated the bulk of the non-English speakers. All they could manage was a few polite inquiries about Dr. Childress's health. After some discreet probing, it became obvious that Stephen had told them the crystallographer had suffered from acute appendicitis while attending a conference in Boston. In reply to their inquiries I said that the last I heard, the world-famous crystallographer was resting comfortably.

The waiter had just served the cheese course—accompanied by a truly wonderful twenty-year-old port—when the maître d' discreetly slipped me a note. It was a message from Elliott saying he would be waiting to pick me up downstairs at ten-fifteen.

I checked my watch, made my excuses to my dinner companions, and left my port with great regret. I thought about letting Stephen know I was leaving but thought better of it. After all, he wasn't the only one who'd gone to junior high.

* * *

Elliott was already waiting for me when I got downstairs, sitting in his Jeep with the motor running. The exhaust from his engine made great billowing clouds of white smoke in the cold night air. The streets of the Loop were deserted. Stepping into the private detective's car in my low-cut dress and high heels, I felt, for just a moment, like a character in a movie.

"Where are we going?" I asked.

"The morgue," he replied with a sly smile.

"Why the morgue?"

"Joe called me about an hour ago. Julia Gordon is giving your friend Dr. Childress his last physical. Blades thought you might like to see what develops firsthand."

"Are you sure this is okay with Dr. Gordon?" I demanded, praying fervently that it was not. I'd already had enough dead bodies for one day. Besides, I'd never seen an autopsy and I wasn't sure that I wanted to, especially not so soon after dinner.

"Dr. Gordon says come on down. The more the merrier. I think she figures this is a good way to keep your boyfriend and his well-connected friends off her back."

"Great," I replied miserably, huddling down into the folds of my cashmere wrap.

Unfortunately we didn't have far to go, and soon we were pulling into the parking lot behind the Robert J. Stein Institute for Forensic Medicine. A ten-foot chain-link fence topped with barbed wire had been erected around Sarrek's trailer, and the entire area was lit up like a prison yard. Elliott explained that double-deck tourist buses had taken to stopping there, and they'd erected the fence to keep out souvenir hunters.

We parked the car and I followed him into the

building, feeling ridiculous in my evening clothes. The attendant at the desk told us that Dr. Gordon was in autopsy suite three and that she was expecting us. With a growing sense of dread I followed Elliott down the hall.

"Are you okay with this?" he asked with an inquiring look as we approached the door.

"I can hardly wait," I replied, determined not to disgrace myself. Elliott smiled and took my hand. I was so nervous about where I was going that I did not protest.

"It's about time you two showed up," said Joe Blades by way of greeting from the far side of the room. He looked like he'd put on weight since I'd seen him last and his skin, always pale, had taken on a pasty fluorescent-induced pallor that I suspected was from too much time at his desk doing paperwork on the Sarrek victims and not enough time on the basketball court.

"Dr. Gordon," said Elliott. "Thanks for the invite."

"Are you kidding? The mayor himself called me this morning and told me to give you every cooperation." While Stephen may not have been talking to me, I reflected that he'd certainly wasted no time in getting on the phone to everybody else. "Besides, you know I always do my best work with an audience," she continued, turning back to her work. On the metal table in front of her lay the now thawed body of Michael Childress. His major organs had been removed and his empty center yawned at us grotesquely.

On the ceiling above the body was an overhead camera mounted on tracks so that it could be moved and focused over different regions of the corpse. A microphone dangled somewhere above Childress's chest with a foot pedal to turn it on and off as the pathologist dictated her findings. On a clipboard beside Childress's head I could see a predrawn diagram of a generic body on which Dr. Gordon had already begun scribbling notes.

To the pathologist every body tells a story and as queasy as I felt in my high heels and evening dress, I intended to stick around to hear how this particular one turned out.

"Where are Rankin and Masterson?" asked Elliott, casually taking a seat beside his friend. "I can't believe they're so busy they can't show up for their own case."

"They just ran across the street to grab dinner. They'll be back in a couple minutes. Why don't you tell them what you've told me so far, Doc?" suggested Blades.

"As long as you understand that all of this is preliminary and so far off the record that it doesn't even exist," she warned us.

Elliott and I chorused our agreement.

"Do you know how he died yet?" I asked.

"So far all the evidence points to hypothermia, most likely some time during the day on Sunday. I can't pin the time down any better until I get the rest of the lab results back."

"Can you tell whether he was alive when he went into the freezer?" inquired Elliott.

"Most definitely," replied Gordon, setting the lungs on an electronic scale and making a note of their weight. "I've noted swelling in the extremities—ears, nose, etc.—also, focal ulcers of the gastric mucosa and evidence of pancreatic hemorrhage, all of which are consistent with death caused by hypothermia."

"But if he was freezing to death, why was he naked?" I asked. "His clothes were right there beside him. . . ."

"I'd say it was a textbook case of paradoxical undressing," replied the medical examiner matter-of-factly as she

made an incision at the back of Childress's head and began
to pull his scalp down over his face.

"What is paradoxical undressing?" I asked, studying
my shoes.

"It is a relatively common phenomenon seen to some
degree in close to seventy percent of deaths due to exposure to the cold. It can vary from the stage when the
person is just beginning to undress to total nudity. The act
of disrobing is thought to occur just before unconscious-
ness sets in. The reason, in theory, being that with sufficient lowering of the body temperature the blood vessels
in the extremities dilate, giving a false feeling of warmth
and causing the victim to undress. The fact that Dr. Childress took his clothes off and then apparently lay down
and tried to make snow angels in the layer of frost on the
cold-room floor is completely consistent with the kind of
disorientation that he would experience prior to death
from hypothermia. The injuries to his hands and feet and
the bruising on his knees most likely occurred earlier."

"You mean before he went into the freezer?" asked
Elliott.

"No. When he was trying to claw his way out. The
bruising on the heels of his hands and the underside of
his wrists were probably made when he tried to summon
help by pounding against the inside of the cold-room
door, while the trauma to his fingers makes it look like he
made repeated attempts to pry the door open."

I looked at Dr. Gordon and said nothing. I could not
help but think these were things no one should ever have
to know.

"So then how did he get into the cold room in the first
place?" asked Elliott finally. "Did he walk in on his
own?"

"Interesting you should ask. There are no signs of any other kind of trauma besides the ones we've just discussed, that is, there were no marks that would indicate he'd been knocked unconscious or in any way bound. However, if you look at the side of his upper thigh, you'll notice something a little unusual."

Elliott walked over to the body and took a good look. I stayed where I was, willing to get the news secondhand.

"It looks like a needle mark," he observed.

"Yes. It does."

"Funny place for one, though."

"I agree. What makes it even more interesting is that we've got the preliminary results back on the first round of our toxicology screen."

"Already?" demanded Elliott.

"Believe me, strings have not only been pulled," replied Dr. Gordon, "but they've been pulled hard. What's interesting is that we've gotten a positive reading for opiates."

"So he was drugged before he was put in the freezer," observed Elliott.

"Tell them the best part, Doc," urged Blades with something akin to glee.

"Our toxicologist has identified the opiate as phenokynamine."

"I've never heard of it," said Elliott.

"That's because it's a veterinary tranquilizer," replied Dr. Gordon. "It's used only for animals."

CHAPTER
27

By the time I got up the next morning I was ready to do something I was actually good at. I was tired of all my fruitless speculation about who had killed Michael Childress and Danny Wohl. I was sick of wondering about what had become of Childress's car and worrying about the impact on Tom Galloway's career once the press got wind of his relationship with Danny Wohl. "Oh, it won't be so bad," Elliott had quipped. "It'll be just like coming out on *Oprah*."

I never thought it would come to this, but after trying to find some kind of solution in the ever shifting investigation into what Joe Blades had come to refer to as the Azor murders, I was actually looking forward to sitting down and negotiating with Takisawa. When I arrived at Azor, the first thing I did was go to Stephen's office. His greeting was so chilly that I decided not to mention my trip to the medical examiner's office the night before. I figured he could wait and get the news from the Oak Brook police.

In contrast, the Japanese appeared in exceptionally good spirits. I learned from Lou Remminger that after dinner Dave Borland had led a group of Takisawa scientists on an impromptu tour of Rush Street, during which he'd learned a thing or two about the Oriental appetite for debauchery. More important, he reported that the Japanese scientists were practically salivating at the prospect of the proposed joint venture.

The exception appeared to be Chairman Takisawa. He remained silent and aloof during morning coffee and the level of nervous attentiveness on display from those around him seemed to bode no good. The day's agenda called for another elaborately staged show-and-tell for the scientists, while the business people for both sides were set to huddle in Azor's conference room and attempt to craft a deal.

From the beginning things went badly.

The deal on the table called for the Japanese company to provide support for thirty researchers at $200,000 per scientist per year for five years—a rule of thumb that included compensation, equipment, and supplies—totaling $30 million. If Azor succeeded in producing a drug, Stephen proposed splitting the revenues in half. In addition there were several provisions regarding patents and licensing, the distribution of worldwide rights, and the training and education issues that the Japanese had up until now held so dear.

But obviously Chairman Takisawa had other ideas. He began by explaining with great deference that despite Azor's recent success with isolating diffractable crystals of ZKBP, he doubted our scientists would be able to develop a drug. The most he could hope for was that they would be able to help Takisawa scientists find their own. Knowing what I did about the level of expertise of Takisawa's scientists, much less their chairman, I recognized this statement as ridiculous on its face.

Stephen could barely contain himself, but I knew it was important that we hear Takisawa out. I put my hand on his leg under the table and pinched him—hard—as a signal to say nothing. I felt sick but also struggled to remain impassive. Even though I tell myself I didn't inherit my mother's temper, as I sat there listening to all of Takisawa's well-thought-out reasons for trying to screw us I wanted to climb over the table and throttle him with his skinny little tie.

Thirty minutes later, it was clear that what Takisawa was proposing was much less than we'd hoped—namely $25 million for worldwide rights to any new anti-inflammatory drug that Azor produced. Before Stephen had a chance to speak, I thanked Chairman Takisawa profusely for sharing his thoughts with us and suggested we adjourn for our mid-morning break. Then I whispered to Stephen that I needed to talk to him.

Trying to remain calm, I followed him into his office.

"You never even gave me a chance to ask him how much they're willing to give us up front," complained Stephen angrily, once he'd shut the door.

"You shouldn't ask them," I replied.

"What do you mean I shouldn't ask them?" he exploded, clearly at the end of his rope. What he had intended as a coup had now suddenly turned into, at best, a scraping negotiation with Takisawa setting performance milestones and royalty schedules. "That's the absolute first thing you'd want to know when you start talking about this kind of deal."

"Listen to me, Stephen," I said, looking him steadily in the eye. "You shouldn't ask them, because this isn't the kind of deal you ever want to get involved in. You say yes to this, I don't care under what terms, and old man

Takisawa will have you tied up with strings and have you dancing like a marionette."

"Unfortunately we don't have any other choice," replied Stephen, running his fingers through the thick waves of his hair. "If we don't get the money soon, not only will we lose any chance at being first with the drug, but the board will have my resignation, and I'll be working in some clinic somewhere looking into babies' ears and telling fat people to give up smoking."

"Get a grip on yourself, Stephen," I advised him. "You're forgetting Millholland's first law of negotiation."

"What is that?"

"When the opposition starts fucking with you, you fuck them back. Borland told me this morning that their people are hot for our science. I'm telling you, they want this deal."

"They're sure as hell not acting like it."

"Come on. Old man Takisawa is an arrogant son of a bitch, not to mention one shrewd negotiator. How else do you think he got where he is?"

"What's your point?"

"My point is that arrogant men understand arrogance. You of all people should know this."

"So what do you propose we do?" Stephen answered, ignoring the dig.

"Go back down the hall and tell old man Takisawa that you have sent for their cars and that Rachel will be happy to help with the arrangements for their return flight to Tokyo."

"You can't be serious."

"Yes, I am. Tell them to get lost."

"After everything we've already sunk into this deal? You must think I'm out of my mind."

"Do you remember what you said to me that day in the car?"

"What day?"

"The day you got me into all this. The day you talked me into taking over the negotiations with Takisawa. You told me you trusted my judgment. Well now I'm telling you the time has come to put up or shut up. Trust me. Takisawa is just playing games. You've got to either fold or call their bluff. But if you don't, it's the first step down a very bad road. Say yes to them now and Takisawa will have a leash around your neck so fast that before you know it you'll be barking like a dog."

Stephen stood behind his desk and considered what I had said. I could not read his expression, but the pounding of my heart filled my ears and sweat trickled down the inside of my silk blouse like a cold river of fear. I tried hard not to think about what a large piece of my life I was gambling on this one moment. I tried not to second-guess myself. When it came right down to it, my judgment was the only thing that separated me from a thousand other lawyers in this town. When I stopped trusting it, it would be time to quit and hit the cocktail-party circuit full time.

"Okay," he said, getting slowly to his feet. "We'll try testing your level of arrogance against theirs. You'd just better hope you're right about this."

Old man Takisawa's shock at what Stephen had to say was so convincing that if I hadn't known better, I might have thought it was genuine. Oh no, he assured us, there had obviously been some sort of miscommunication. With his poor command of English he had obviously misstated his company's position.

From there it was all downhill. By the end of the day we had hammered out an agreement in principle that was everything Stephen had wanted. Once it was signed, Azor Pharmaceuticals would gain a powerful ally, someone who could take ZK-501 to market and yet would leave him in charge of his own company. Better still, he would have money enough to see the project through to completion, to have a chance to meet his most ambitious goals.

We sent the Takisawa people back to the Nikko in a celebratory mood. Once we closed the doors on their limos, Stephen and I sat down to go over the terms of the deal one last time. After I was sure nothing had been overlooked, I could begin drafting the text of the final, binding agreement that would be signed by Stephen and Takisawa before the Takisawa delegation returned to Japan—the one I looked forward to jamming down Jim Cassidy's and the other board members' throats.

Once we had finished, Stephen was expansive, practically euphoric. His earlier displeasure with me was completely forgotten, erased by delight in having gotten what he'd wanted. While there was no denying that I, too, was pleased about the deal, I found myself wishing I could let my irritation with Stephen go so easily.

When everyone else left for dinner, I began work on the agreement. Frankly, I was grateful for the chance to miss yet another business dinner, especially this one. Mother had arranged for a night out at Al Capone's Steak House, an infinitely tacky beef-and-brew place on Kinzie that featured an animatronic show about Chicago's gangster past, complete with a reenactment of the St. Valentine's Day Massacre.

Considering Stephen's family connections, I told my mother
that I thought the outing was in exceptionally bad taste.

"Of course," she'd replied cattily, "that's why the
Japanese will absolutely adore it."

I worked happily for hours, culling the relevant language from the various drafts of the proposal and the
notes I had made during the course of the day. I hoped to
have a solid draft before I left, which I planned on dropping at Stephen's apartment on my way home. Judging
from his mood I was pretty sure he'd try to get me to
stay. I figured I'd cross that bridge when I came to it.

I worked steadily, completely absorbed by the task at
hand and oblivious to everything around me. When I
finally looked up I was surprised to see it was nearly ten
o'clock. I decided to stretch my legs and get a Diet Coke.
It felt good to get up, but it felt even better to make
progress. With all the ups and downs of the past few
weeks it was hard to believe we could have a signed
agreement in less than twenty-four hours. As I made my
way to the lunchroom I told myself that Danny would
have been proud.

Standing in the neon glow of the coke machine I fished
quarters from my pocket. A crashing noise and the sound
of a pair of male voices startled me. The labs in this part
of the building were dedicated to the ZK-501 project and
all of those investigators were supposed to be enjoying
their scenic trip into Chicago's past. I stooped to retrieve
my can of soda from the chute at the bottom of the
machine and looked out into the hall. I hadn't slept
decently in days and I was nervous as a cat.

I stepped out into the hall, but there was no one there,
only a big hazardous-waste container, a dumpster on
wheels, all by itself in the middle of the corridor. It was just

the men from the biohazard company making their rounds, emptying the hundreds of biohazard containers, large and small, that were scattered throughout the building.

As I popped open the top of my can two men emerged from Lou Remminger's lab wheeling another, albeit slightly smaller container. Watching them in their orange coveralls reminded me of Danny's apartment.

For a moment no bells went off, no blinking lights, no loud cries of "Eureka!", no shouts of "Kate is a genius!" But suddenly I knew what I should have known all along, what should have been obvious from the first day I'd come to work at Azor. If my mind hadn't been so cluttered with thoughts about deals and drugs and dinner plans, it would have been glaringly, blindingly obvious.

Quite simply, I looked at the hazardous-waste containers that could be found in practically every room of the building, and I knew exactly what Danny's killer had done with the cassette tape and the bloodstained clothes that had been removed from his apartment.

CHAPTER
28

No doubt the men from the disposal company thought I was crazy when I started grilling them about their handling of the containers. I especially wanted to know how often the dumpsters were emptied and where the stuff that came out of them was taken. When I asked them if they ever looked to see what was inside the bins, they were certain I was out of my mind. They assured me there was no telling what was inside the containers—anything from radioactive materials to dog cadavers. Of course, I thought to myself, that was the inherent beauty of the thing.

Mentally kicking myself for not having figured it out sooner, I went back to my office and immediately called Elliott Abelman. While he wasn't prepared to start handing out hosannahs quite yet, he did agree that the idea made sense. He promised he'd try to get in touch with the biohazard company first thing in the morning.

He also told me he'd just gotten off the phone with Joe Blades. Apparently Michael Childress's car had turned up in a satellite lot at O'Hare airport. Whoever had left it there had taken the ticket from the lot with them so that there was no way of knowing when it had been parked there. Also, he assured me, I would be happy to know that in light of Michael Childress's death the Chicago PD had agreed to reopen the investigation into the death of Danny Wohl.

I hung up the phone and tried to force myself to get back to work. Even if my theory about the bloody clothes was correct, it was likely to remain just that—a theory. I had no idea how many different companies, hospitals, and universities this particular biohazard company was contracted to, how many hundreds or thousands of dumpsters were emptied who knows where every week. The chances of being able to find the missing cassette among all that hazardous waste, even if we could find somebody willing to look, had to be close to zero.

Somebody had been very clever. Somebody, even when he was improvising, had been able to cover his tracks very well. I felt discouraged and outwitted, and I didn't much like it.

And then it occurred to me. If Danny was killed by someone at Azor then whoever had used the biohazard disposal containers to dump the bloody evidence would have had to come back to the labs to do it. He'd be anxious to get rid of the evidence as soon as possible, which meant he'd most likely have come out to Azor on the Sunday that Danny had died. Why not? People came and went at all hours and the killer wouldn't want to risk keeping the incriminating evidence any longer than was necessary. Besides, if he waited to bring it to work on Monday, there would only be more people around. All I had to do was look at the videotape from the security cameras in the lobby from that Sunday.

I was so excited about this plan that I immediately

went upstairs to talk to the security guard. To my dismay I found Paramilitary Bill on duty. He was sitting at the security console, frowning with great concentration at something he was reading. When I got closer, I saw that it was a computer printout of some kind.

"How long do you keep the tapes from the security cameras?" I asked, pointing to the lenses mounted high up in the corners just below the ceiling.

"That's classified," he replied promptly. I examined his face for some indication that he was kidding and found none.

"I need to see the tape from two Sundays ago," I continued, in no mood to put up with any psycho bullshit. "Where are they kept?"

"I can't show them to you without a direct order from my supervisor."

"And who is that?"

"Mr. Goodnall."

"Is he working tonight?"

"No ma'am. He's on days."

"Then who is his boss?"

"Excuse me, ma'am, but I don't rightly understand the question." Apparently Bill was easily stumped.

"Do you think it might be safe to say Dr. Azorini is Mr. Goodnall's boss?" I continued, trying very hard not to lose my temper. Bill might be a borderline moron, but he was a card-carrying–militia-member kind of moron—not to mention armed.

"Dr. Azorini is the president of the company," replied Paramilitary Bill uncertainly.

"Now, Bill, I don't know if you listen to office gossip, but you've seen Dr. Azorini and me leaving together enough nights to have formed your own opinion about whether the stories that we are sleeping together are true. Dr. Azorini is downtown right now at a very important dinner for our Japanese guests. I have no problem calling him at the restaurant and having him get on the phone to give you permission to show me those tapes. But I'd think it would probably be safer in terms of career advancement if you just told me where the tapes are kept."

"In a closet in the back of the guards' room," he replied, apparently convinced.

"Do you have a key?" I asked.

"Right here," he said, opening the cabinet underneath the desk to display a peg board hung with rows of keys, all neatly labeled.

"Could you please see if you could find the tape from two Sundays ago for me?"

"I'm not allowed to leave my post," he ventured. Oh shit, I thought, here we go again.

"What if I stay here while you go and look?" I offered sweetly. Bill thought that one over for a while and finally agreed.

While I waited for Paramilitary Bill to fetch the tape, I watched the bank of video screens mounted in the console in front of me. Every thirty seconds the images changed, flicking from one set of empty corridors to another, covering the entire building every four minutes or so. I remembered what Elliott had once told me about the limits of video surveillance. While the presence of cameras may act as a deterrent and the tapes themselves provide evidence, their effectiveness in stopping crimes in progress is very limited. The simple truth is that no one can stand to watch nothing for very long. They'd done studies where they'd sent naked women running in front of the camera. The women had gone completely unnoticed by the guards whose brains had been blitzed out by the sheer boredom of monitoring the screens.

"Did you say last Sunday or the Sunday before last?" Bill asked, reappearing a few minutes later.

"The Sunday before," I replied.

"That's what I thought you said."

"Did you find it?"

"No, ma'am," he said, scratching his skinhead haircut. "The box is right there on the shelf where it belongs, but it's empty."

"Are you sure?"

"Yes ma'am. I looked real good." Now that I'd gone through the trouble of exerting my authority he seemed afraid that he was in some kind of trouble.

"Not to worry, Bill," I reassured him. "It's no big deal. If it's not there, it's not there."

"I think it's a conspiracy," confided Bill seriously.

"What do you mean?" I asked.

"Someone's been messing with the security data."

"Messing with it how?"

"I've just finished printing up the swipe-card log for the day so it's up-to-date for Harry, who's scheduled to relieve me at midnight. But there's something wrong with it."

"What's that?" I asked.

"You know how you have to use your swipe card to sign in and out of the building?"

"Yes."

"Well, everybody's swipe card has a number assigned to it. Dr. Azorini, his number is 001, I guess because he's the company's number-one guy." At this Bill laughed, amused by his own joke. "Then take me, my number is 214."

"Does that mean that every time you swipe your card

the computer prints your number next to the time?" I offered.

"That's right. That's right."

"So what's been going on?"

"Well, I think somebody's been fiddling with the numbers."

"Fiddling how?" I demanded.

"You know how Dr. Childress got found in the freezer yesterday. Well, his number was 321. I remember that because the cops wanted to see the whole log for last Friday—you know, the day they shut the building down—and they were looking for the time that number 321 swiped out, on account of it being Childress."

"Yes. That might turn out to be very important," I said, realizing for the first time just how important. Whoever had killed Childress had had to make sure it looked like he had left the building, otherwise there would have been people looking high and low for him. I couldn't believe I hadn't thought of this before.

"But that's why I think there's somebody playing tricks on me," continued Bill doggedly. "See here on the sheet for today, clear as day, ID number 321 logged in at seven-sixteen."

I looked at the sheet. Bill was right. It was there just as plain as day, ID number 321.

"There must be some mistake," I said.

"That's just what I was sitting here thinking when you came. But I'll be darned if I can think of how they did it."

"Did number 321 log out yet today?" I asked, as a terrifying idea occurred to me.

"No. I checked. That's why I think it's some kind of trick. There aren't more than a dozen people left in the building this time of night, counting you and me, and most all of them's up in the virology labs."

"And the building's locked down for the night?" I asked him, trying to keep the urgency out of my voice. "The front door is the only way in or out?"

"There's the emergency exits in the basement, but there's an alarm that goes off when you open one of them."

"Listen, Bill," I said. "This could be serious. I want you to do something."

"What's that?"

"I want you to be sure to not let anybody leave the building until I tell you."

"I don't think I get you. . . ."

"I'm going to go back to my office and make a phone call. In the meantime, I want you to make sure no one leaves the building."

"What am I supposed to tell them?" he protested.

"Tell them it's Dr. Azorini's orders. It shouldn't be for very long. Just until the police come."

"The police?" Bill demanded, alarm creeping into his voice. I was secretly amused to see his tough-guy act begin to evaporate at the merest hint of actual trouble.

"It's just a precaution. But first we've got to find out who's been playing these tricks with Dr. Childress's ID."

Quickly I made my way back to my office and rooted in the drawer for Detective Rankin's card, the one he'd given me with his number on it. Whoever answered the phone informed me that Detective Rankin was unavailable. When I asked about Detective Masterson he told me that he was out on a call. Then I called Elliott and left a message with his answering service. I thought about what I had said to Paramilitary Bill about summoning the police, but now with the phone in my hand I found I had no one else to call. While I thought I had a good chance of being able to explain to one of the detectives assigned to investigate Childress's murder my fears about his killer being in the building, the prospect of making the same point to the police dispatcher seemed hideously impractical.

And yet there was someone in the building who had used Michael Childress's ID to get into the building that morning. The only trouble was that I had no way of knowing who that person might be. Briefly, I considered setting off the fire alarm just to see who left the building, but I knew it was hooked up to a halon system that automatically dumped fire-retardant gas throughout the building. Halon puts out fires much more quickly than water does, but it is also much more expensive. Stephen complained that every false alarm cost him fifteen thousand dollars, but with so many valuable experiments underway in the building the halon system was essential.

I figured it couldn't hurt to take a walk through the building. Even though I had no way of knowing whether my suspicions were correct, my curiosity would not allow me to sit still.

I took the service stairs to the basement and found myself wondering whether it was really true that the only way out of the building was through the front door even at this time of night. What about the men from the biohazard company? Surely they came in and out through the loading dock with their containers. How did they get in and out? And what about on Friday when everyone was frantically working to get the building ready for the electricity to be cut off? The door to the loading dock had

been open most of the afternoon as trucks had come to
pick up animals and the freezer unit was delivered. No
doubt there would have been ample opportunity for
someone to have slipped in or out unobserved. That, of
course, was the trouble.

The trouble also was that everyone who worked in this
building was so wrapped up in his own little world, in
his own submicroscopic sliver of the universe, that he
was completely oblivious to what was actually going on
around him.

I took the shortcut past the mechanical room and the
machine shop and turned the corner behind the animal
labs. The animals, now all returned to their proper envi-
ronment, scratched and snuffled in their darkened cages.
As I passed by the cold rooms I couldn't help but suppress
a shudder. Both were now padlocked from the outside—a
compromise Elliott had worked out with the police rather
than sealing them off with crime-scene tape.

Glancing down the hall I was surprised to see a pool of
light spilling out of the aquarium window of the crystallography lab. I told myself not to be alarmed. No doubt
Michelle had left the light on by mistake—either that or
one of the cleaning people who'd gone through earlier
had forgotten to turn it off. I'd seen Michelle talking to
Stephen earlier as they'd waited for Borland and the
others to join them for dinner.

I peered cautiously through the window and immediately felt ridiculous. The room was empty. Nothing sin-
ister was afoot, just a light carelessly left on, nothing
more. I stepped inside and looked along the wall for a
switch. That's when I saw it.

Draped on the back of a chair behind the computer
console was a white lab coat. It wasn't the lab coat that

held my attention, but what was clipped to the front of it. Michelle had not only left the light on in her hurry, but had left her ID card behind as well.

Slowly, I crossed the room to look at the ID. The picture was the usual unrecognizable blur, and all but the first five letters of the name were obscured by the bulky rectangular radiation tag, but instinctively I knew there was something wrong. I read the letters out loud: M, I, C, H, A—Michael, not Michelle. With my heart beating faster I knelt down to be sure. I squinted at the picture. The ID belonged to Michael Childress, not Michelle Goodwin.

I rocked back onto my heels as the various pieces of the puzzle clicked noiselessly into place. Not some man who'd been having an affair with Danny, not someone intent on bringing down the company, but quiet, shy, fiercely obsessed Michelle. Michelle, the woman whose dreams of the future hinged on her solving the structure of ZKBP and getting the credit for it.

I never saw what hit me. Something heavy swung with terrific force. I don't remember the moment of impact or the moment when I first realized I was hurt. The only sensations were the warmth of my own blood oozing through my hair, and watching the world spin around me. My reactions no doubt slowed by concussion, I fell to the ground and looked up just in time to see Michelle Goodwin getting ready to take another swing at me. In her hand was a metal instrument that looked like a small baseball bat. Borland had one just like it in the protein lab. It was a special heavy-duty pestle used to pound spleen tissue into a bloody pulp.

Instinctively I curled up into a ball to ward off the impact of the next blow and, without consciously deciding to do so, rolled under the desk. The pestle hit the edge of the desk with a terrific impact as I scrambled to my hands and knees, trapped like an animal. Michelle had all the advantages. Not only did she have a weapon, but she was in tremendous shape physically. Mentally, she had already shown herself capable of killing two men.

Terrified, I realized my best chance was to try to get away from her even if only out into the hallway, where there was some chance Paramilitary Bill would catch sight of me on the video monitors. I wondered if, in his effort to follow my instructions and make sure that no one left the building, he would even bother to look at them.

"Fight back," I told myself. I had read somewhere that people who had survived deadly attacks all had one thing in common—they all reported that they'd made the decision, consciously and early in the attack, to fight back. They had been willing to trade injury, even grievous injury, in exchange for survival.

Above me Michelle was hissing and muttering, spewing forth a steady stream of profanities and demanding that I come out. I took a deep breath and propelled myself with all my strength against her legs, throwing her off balance so that she fell forward with her entire weight on top of me. After that I did everything I could think of. I clawed, I scratched, I bit into her leg so hard that I tasted her blood even as she kicked me in the face to be free of me.

The instant her weight was off of me I scrambled to my feet and headed for the door. My odds did not seem particularly promising. Not only was she a trained athlete, but she was dressed for the lab in tennis shoes, while I was hampered by a tight skirt and a pair of three-hundred-dollar Italian high heels.

I realized I would never make it to the elevator or even

the stairs without her overtaking me. Instead I darted into
the darkened animal lab and crouched, panting and terrified, behind a row of caged monkeys that had been selec-
tively raised to have a predisposition to high blood
pressure.

I looked around in the dark for the nearest phone and
saw to my dismay that it was at the opposite end of the
room. I thought about making a run for it but decided I
needed to find some sort of weapon first. It was only a
matter of time, possibly seconds, before Michelle Goodwin came through the door swinging her deadly pestle.
I had chosen my spot badly. There was nothing within
reach that could be used as a weapon except twenty-
pound bags of dog chow that were piled in a corner and a
case of paper towels.

I saw her in the doorway framed against the light of
the hall. She wasn't even breathing hard but was staring
into the darkness with the calm intensity of a predator.
Instinctively I wanted to talk to her, to try to reason with
her. Then I thought about Childress's fingers, bloodied
from trying to claw his way out of his icy prison, and
decided I would only be digging my own grave.

When she switched on the light, I was ready for her.
Holding a bulky bag of dog food across my chest, I used
it like a battering ram as I charged, knocking her off her
feet and back out into the hall. I barreled into her,
shoving her against the wall, and grabbed for her neck
with all my strength.

I knew that while I must be screaming, I was probably
also crying. All I remember was holding on to her neck
with all my might while she landed blow after blow.

In the end it was Paramilitary Bill who saved her life.
Two minutes more and I would have choked her dead.

Oddly, it wasn't the sight of us trying to kill each other on the video monitor, but the howling of the terrified animals from the animal labs that had drawn him from his post. Still, it took all his strength to pull us apart, and even then she did not stop. Indeed the worst blows came while he watched, almost as if she drew strength from having an audience. I'll never forget the look on Bill's face when he heard the sound my forearm made as it was shattered by the flailing pestle.

Everything that came later had the flavor of an anticlimax, though by the time the police came, I had at least managed to compose myself. Looking back, the strangest thing was that it never even occurred to me to call Stephen. Indeed, when he showed up later, no doubt tracked down by Paramilitary Bill, I was actually surprised to see him. We never even really talked. I was busy giving my statement to Detective Rankin when Stephen arrived.

Elliott had shown up much earlier, at almost the same time as the police. Once he'd received my message, he'd called back immediately. When I didn't answer, he called the police and then got into his car and broke the speed record out to Oak Brook. He found me sitting in the hall—someone must have dragged a chair out of one of the labs—I don't remember. I was holding a chemical cold pack to a bleeding gash in my face with my good arm while paramedics fitted the broken one with a splint.

Before I would let him drive me to the emergency room, I insisted we go back upstairs to my office so that I could put the draft of the agreement on Stephen's desk where I could be sure he'd see it in the morning. I tried not to get too much blood on it. Then I paged Claudia to have her meet us in the emergency room. I insisted we drive to Hyde Park instead of going to some doc-in-the-box suburban hospital. On the way I explained to him about Michelle.

"You see, Michelle has only ever wanted one thing and that is to be famous in her field, which is X-ray crystallography. And I've got to hand it to whoever steered her into crystallography in the first place—they knew what they were doing. It was just perfect for someone like her. Obsessed, driven, single-minded, a highly intelligent loner. The problem is that success in crystallography is as much about luck as it is about science. A good crystallographer can go his or her entire career without solving the structure of a really important molecule. So far, Michelle had had her chance at solving three of them, and every time, circumstances kept her from her prize. Straight out of graduate school she'd worked in a lab that was destroyed by a fire set by a disgruntled employee, and two years' work was lost. After that she went to work on one of a pair of enzymes related to the function of aspirin, and while she did get some attention for successfully solving the structure, it turns out the other enzyme is the one that mattered.

"Based on her success with that, Stephen hired her to work on the company's integrase project—that was an experimental AIDS drug they were working on—but they spent so much time trying to sell a deal to fund the project to a Japanese company called Okuda that another pharmaceutical company beat them to the structure."

"Is that why she killed Danny? Because she didn't want this deal you're working on with the Japanese to go through?"

"Yes. You see, she didn't care if Azor ever turned

ZK-501 into a drug. She didn't care if the company went bankrupt. Her interest has always been in purely academic research. All she wanted was to solve the structure of ZKBP so that she could return to academia wrapped in glory. She was afraid the company would get involved in another lengthy negotiation. She was desperate to prevent what had happened with Okuda from happening to her again."

"Desperate enough to kill someone?"

"They all told me, every one of them, Borland, Remminger, even Stephen. I just wouldn't listen."

"What did they tell you?"

"In science no one cares how you get there, only that you get there first. Besides, killing Danny was so easy. He had come to her to ask about new AIDS drugs—she was the logical person to confide in. Not only did she have the expertise, but they were natural allies against Childress. All she had to do when he came home euphoric about the Japanese was to convince him to try some new treatment and inject him with PAF. I'm sure that when he started vomiting up blood it gave her a nasty surprise. It was obviously a struggle, but she had the strength and the presence of mind to keep him from getting help.

"I should have realized it was a woman from the way she managed to clean up the kitchen. I'm sure it never occurred to her that they'd look inside the drain for traces of blood. Other than that, she handled herself perfectly, even going so far as to steal the key to the guards' room from the security desk at Azor and dispose of the videotape showing her coming into the building with the athletic bag containing the hypodermic, the syringe, and her bloody clothes."

"Do you think they're her fingerprints on the glass that was on the sink in Danny's apartment?"

"Yes, I do. I think that was her one mistake, at least with Danny's murder. She made a couple more with Childress."

"Such as?"

"Such as mixing her ID card up with his. She had to have it in order to make it look like he'd left the building, but obviously, in her hurry to get rid of the evidence, she switched the two. The names are so similar, and both of them are all covered up with radiation tags, you can see how it would be easy to do."

"I thought Borland said he checked the inside of the cold room before he taped it shut."

"He did. But he had Michelle check it after him. All she had to do was ask Childress to come into the cold room with her to check something and then stab him with the hypodermic full of animal tranquilizer. I'm sure that when Dr. Gordon gets her final test results back, she'll discover he was given enough to stun an elephant. Once Childress was out, all Michelle had to do was drag him off behind one of the piles of boxes. Nobody would see him unless they actually walked into the cold room, looking for something on one of the shelves.

"Then all she had to do was slip out of the building at some point and move his car. She didn't have to take it to the airport then, only somewhere out of sight. With any luck maybe someone will remember seeing her. I guess what really bothers me most about all of this is how clever she was. When you think about it, there really isn't that much evidence . . . " I said.

As we approached Hyde Park I realized the shock was

finally wearing off and I was starting to hurt in all sorts of places.

"Don't worry," Elliott assured me as we pulled up to the emergency room entrance. "Now that the cops know where to look, they'll get enough to bring a case against her. Joe'll see to it. Besides, look at the bright side," he said, as Claudia rushed through the double doors and pulled open the passenger door to shovel me into a waiting wheelchair. "There's no way she'll be able to beat the rap for assault."

CHAPTER
29

Elliott stayed with me while I waited to be X-rayed, and watched as Claudia stitched me up. He fetched me water and held my head so that I could sip it through a straw. As Claudia sewed, Elliott told her the story of what had happened, which she listened to without comment, frowning intently over her work. The only really bad part was when they set my arm. It hurt so much that I screamed, but in the end I got to choose the color of the cast which was some small consolation. I picked black because it goes with everything—I am my mother's daughter, after all.

The sun was starting to come up on another day when Elliott finally took me home. By then I was so full of pain medication and limp with fatigue that simple things, like the stairs and finding my keys in the bottom of my purse, seemed impossibly hard and beyond my grasp.

In the end I allowed myself to be undressed like a child. Elliott winced at the sight of the bruises on my shoulders and back and proclaimed himself amazed that I hadn't broken any ribs. While he went off in search of ice packs, I slid gratefully between the sheets.

351

"You should go to bed," he said, helping me pull the few remaining hairpins from what remained of my French twist.

"I am in bed," I replied groggily.

"I meant with me," he said, kissing me chastely on the forehead.

"That's very smooth," I replied dreamily. "Do you always proposition women who've been beaten up? I'm sure you get lots of girls that way."

"I don't want lots of girls. I want you."

"All I want right now is to go to sleep," I murmured.

"I don't mean right now."

"I don't know how I feel about that," I said finally.

"Perhaps you won't know until you try," he replied, kissing me one last time before standing up to go. "I think sometimes you just have to do the experiment."

If you liked Fatal Reaction,
don't miss the other Kate Millholland novels:

PRINCIPAL
DEFENSE

Kate Millholland may be an heiress, but she works hard for her money as a mergers-and-acquisitions lawyer in Chicago's most aggressive firm. When Azor, the high-tech, high-profit pharmaceutical company founded by her sometime lover, Stephen Azorini, faces a takeover, Kate will do anything to stop it from happening.

But the stakes rise even higher when Stephen's teenage niece, Gretchen, is killed. Everyone knows that if Gretchen's shares go to the corporate raider, Stephen will lose everything—so Kate plunges into an investigation of murder.

by GINI HARTZMARK

Published by Ivy Books.
Available at your local bookstore.

FINAL OPTION

When lawyer Kate Millholland arrives at the home of Bart Hexter, one of Chicago's most powerful players in the futures market, she finds him behind the wheel of his Rolls-Royce, clad only in a pair of red silk pajamas, with two bullets in his head.

Topping the list of suspects—including his wife, his mistress, his personal assistant, and his children—is Kate, whose scheduled meeting with the dead man makes her the prime candidate for murder.

by GINI HARTZMARK

Published by Ivy Books.
Available at your local bookstore.

BITTER BUSINESS

At the request of a colleague, Chicago attorney Kate Millholland agrees to represent the Cavanaugh family's company, Superior Plating & Specialty Chemicals—and discovers that the family is as corrosive as the chemicals it produces.

She never expects to uncover the sordid, fatal secrets that bind the Cavanaughs together—the least of which is murder.

by GINI HARTZMARK

Published by Ivy Books.
Available at your local bookstore.

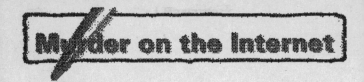

Murder on the Internet

Ballantine mysteries are on the Web!

Read about your favorite Ballantine authors and upcoming books in our monthly electronic newsletter MURDER ON THE INTERNET, at
www.randomhouse.com/BB/MOTI

Including:
- What's new in the stores
- Previews of upcoming books for the next four months
- In-depth interviews with mystery authors and publishing insiders
- Calendars of signings and readings for Ballantine mystery authors
- Bibliographies of mystery authors
- Excerpts from new mysteries

To subscribe to MURDER ON THE INTERNET, please send an e-mail to
moti-dist@cruises.randomhouse.com,
with "subscribe" as the body of the message. (Don't use the quotes.) You will receive the next issue as soon as it's available.

Find out more about whodunit! For sample chapters from current and upcoming Ballantine mysteries, visit us at
www.randomhouse.com/BB/mystery